SAVAGE BLOOD

HEATHER ATKINSON

First published in Great Britain in 2025 by Boldwood Books Ltd.

Cover Design by Judge By My Covers

Cover Images: Depositphotos and iStock

A CIP catalogue record for this book is available from the British Library.

Paperback ISBN 978-1-80415-222-5

Large Print ISBN 978-1-80415-221-8

Hardback ISBN 978-1-80415-220-1

Ebook ISBN 978-1-80415-224-9

Kindle ISBN 978-1-80415-223-2

Audio CD ISBN 978-1-80415-215-7

MP3 CD ISBN 978-1-80415-216-4

Digital audio download ISBN 978-1-80415-217-1

This book is printed on certified sustainable paper. Boldwood Books is dedicated to putting sustainability at the heart of our business. For more information please visit https://www.boldwoodbooks.com/about-us/sustainability/

Boldwood Books Ltd, 23 Bowerdean Street, London, SW6 3TN

www.boldwoodbooks.com

1

Carly Savage's eyes filled with tears as she saw the belly of her lover, Jack, being ripped open by a brutal knife thrust, blood spilling out onto the floor, innards poking through the vicious wound...

'Carly,' called a voice. 'Can you hear me?'

She jumped, the present crashing over the past like a tidal wave, and suddenly that horrible scene was replaced by the bar where she worked. Carly turned to see a perfect lookalike for Lydia Deetz from *Beetlejuice* staring back at her.

'Sorry, Briony, I was miles away,' said Carly, shaking herself out of the traumatic memory.

It was a policy of the owner of Death Loves Company, the gothic-themed bar she managed, that when working, all staff referred to each other by the name of the character they were dressed up as, but she didn't have the energy for it. Her hand had automatically gone to the gold heart pendant around her neck, which Jack had given her, that she never took off. Also on the chain was the diamond ring he had intended to propose to her with but had never got the chance.

'That's okay,' replied Briony with a gentle smile. 'We're out of fivers again.'

'I'll go and get some,' said Carly with a weary sigh.

Eric Draven from *The Crow* moved to stand beside Briony as they watched Carly, who was dressed up as Morticia Addams, totter on her high heels through a door that led to the office.

'She's getting worse,' commented Eric, whose real name was Ollie, his tone bitchy. 'You should be running this place instead. She's no' up to it any more.'

'How can you be so cruel?' retorted Briony, who was very fond of Carly. 'Her boyfriend was murdered.'

'Three months ago. You'd think she'd start to get over it by now.'

'How do you get over something like that?'

'I'm not completely unsympathetic,' he replied with a black-lipped pout. 'But this is a business and she keeps messing up. She's always giving people the wrong change and mixing up orders from the brewery. It's thanks to her that we've no white wine.'

'Because she's got bigger things on her mind than some cheap plonk. How would you feel in her place?'

'If I was in her place, I'd have pulled myself together by now.'

Briony narrowed her eyes. 'You're after her job.'

'I am not. I just want this place to be run efficiently again. I mean, it's getting really embarrassing.'

'There's a customer waiting to be served,' Briony told him coldly.

Ollie gave her one of his annoying smirks before putting on his best smile for a customer he knew tipped well.

Carly returned to the bar a couple of minutes later and restocked both tills with five-pound notes.

'Why don't you take a break?' Briony asked her kindly. 'You look really tired.'

'How can you tell with all this make-up?' Carly replied with a weak smile.

'We're no' busy. Me and Ollie can hold the fort.'

'Aye, all right then. These heels are killing me.'

Briony wasn't fooled. Carly had gone from happy and energetic to bad-tempered and lacklustre. It was as though her boyfriend's death had sucked all the strength from her limbs. Even now, she stood with her shoulders slumped, arms hanging limply by her sides. The only time she was animated was when her temper, which was always close to the surface these days, was roused.

Before Carly could head into the office to take a break, an argument erupted between two male customers. Briony was dismayed by the darkness that filled her manager's eyes, as though Carly was glad about the prospect of violence. When the row quickly descended into a fist fight, Carly stomped out from behind the bar, her energy suddenly returning.

'Oy, you two, break it up,' she yelled.

'Fuck off, ya silly bitch,' spat one of the men before driving his fist into his opponent's stomach, knocking him off his feet.

Carly's response was to knee the man in the crotch before punching him full in the face. The other customers were astonished when this slim young woman sent him crashing backwards into a table.

When two of his friends leapt to their feet, intent on defending him, Carly snatched up a pint glass, smashed it on the edge of a table and brandished it threateningly.

'Come on then,' she yelled.

The two men stopped and glanced at each other before holding up their hands and retreating. Briony, who had remained safely behind the bar, noted Carly looked disappointed that they had decided not to fight.

'Ollie,' barked Carly, making him jump.

'Yes, boss?' he said, wide-eyed.

'Clean this mess up, and you two piss off before I call the polis,' she told the two fallen men.

Sheepishly they picked themselves up off the floor and left, all antagonism between them seemingly forgotten.

Briony watched Carly dump the broken end of the pint glass in the bottle bin before storming into the office.

'Now I know why you want her gone,' Briony told Ollie as he collected the brush and dustpan. 'You're scared of her.'

'I am not,' he retorted, tilting back his head proudly.

'Aye, ya are,' she smirked.

Ollie glared at her indignantly before heading out from behind the bar to clean up the mess. Briony's smirk fell. She couldn't really blame him for being afraid of Carly. Her boyfriend's murder had changed her. These days, most people were afraid of Carly Savage.

* * *

Carly entered her small flat. Once she'd shared this place with her father and two sisters. It had been crowded but it had been home. Now her father was dead and Jane spent the majority of her time with her girlfriend, Jennifer. Their younger sister, Rose, was usually either with her boyfriend Noah or her best friend Tamara. Carly was glad they were both so happy living their own lives and she was relieved when she had the place to herself as she found people, even those she loved dearly, got on her nerves very easily. Since Jack's death, Jane and Rose alternated sleeping at the flat so Carly was never alone at night when solitude was exactly what she wanted. So it was a relief to return now and find no one was home.

She'd changed into her own clothes at work and taken off the long black wig, but she hadn't yet removed the Morticia Addams make-up, which she did before pulling on her pyjamas. She then padded into the kitchen and poured herself a large glass of white wine before curling up in front of the telly. A Sylvester Stallone action film was playing, one of Jack's favourites, so she elected to watch it. Carly smiled as she recalled how he would cheer along the protagonist. She'd really enjoyed his enthusiasm and the pleasant memory warmed her, but not for long. Inevitably, as it always did, the horror of his death eradicated all that positive emotion, leaving her feeling cold and sick inside. The world thought Jack had died alone in an alley in Glasgow city centre after being stabbed by a mugger. Very few people knew that Carly had actually witnessed his murder and that he'd been killed by her own cousin, Dean, who had been revealed to be an obsessive psycho. She'd thought Dean was one of her best friends, a man she could always rely on, when in fact he'd been her biggest enemy. He'd taken from her the man she'd loved and who she'd intended to spend the rest of her life with.

Carly drained the glass of wine, wanting the alcohol to blot out the horror of Jack's murder, but it continued to replay before her eyes – the way his jaw had gone slack and his eyes had widened with shock, the horrific ripping sound as Dean had dragged the blade sideways causing Jack's insides to bulge out.

'Christ,' she breathed, a prayer as well as a curse as tears spilled down her cheeks. She fought the impulse to refill her wine glass. She'd been drinking a lot more than was good for her, but the pain was too much.

Retrieving the bottle of wine from the fridge, she refilled her glass and gulped down that too, feeling slightly better when the comforting haze started to surround her. Screwing her eyes shut, she concentrated on all the good times she and Jack had shared. Their relationship had lasted just a few months but it had been intense. Images of him smiling down at her filled her head, obliterating the horror of his last moments. She'd been one of the very few people who'd been able to make him smile and who he'd bestowed smiles upon. He'd had a reputation for toughness and violence but he'd never been that way with her. She'd only ever had the best of him.

Thankfully the city had finally forgotten about his murder. For weeks she'd had to endure people online saying he'd got what he'd deserved. Stupid, ignorant people who'd never met Jack but thought themselves qualified to judge him. All they'd known was that he was an ex-convict who'd been put in prison for attempted murder, even though it had been self-defence. His so-called victim had then gone on to murder an innocent woman yet still all those fucking idiots had thought he'd deserved to die in such a terrible way. They'd never laughed along with him, loved him or been loved by him.

For a while, Carly had been caught up in obsessive thoughts of vengeance, not only against Dean but against every single one of the ignorant pricks who'd derided him online. She'd fantasised about tracking them down and beating the living shit out of them. She'd even gone as far as to speak to a local hacker to see if they could trace the arseholes through their IP addresses. Thankfully her family had talked her out of it. Now she only blamed two people – Cole Alexander, her ex-boyfriend who had plotted with Dean against Jack, and Dean himself. She still dreamed of finding Dean and killing him but her uncle had hidden him too well. All she could be certain of was that he wasn't in the country any more. Beyond that, who knew? Toni McVay, known as the Queen of Glasgow, the most feared and respected crime boss in the whole of Scotland, had covered up the truth of Jack's murder well. Jack had worked directly for her and, as Carly's family had worked under Jack, they were also under her control too. Carly and Rose were the only Savages who weren't involved in the Glaswegian underworld, although Carly had once been deep in it until she'd left to live the legitimate life.

She polished off the bottle of wine, disgusted with herself, but the alcohol numbed the worst of her pain. She drifted off on the couch, the empty glass slipping from her hand.

2

'Just me,' called Jane as she entered the flat at eight o'clock the following morning. She frowned when there was no response. It had been Rose's turn to stay over last night and she should be up by now, getting ready to go to college. Carly was no doubt still asleep after working late at the bar.

Jane opened Rose's bedroom door. She wasn't there and her bed didn't look like it had been slept in. Fear immediately gripped her, her mind rocketing back to the time when Rose had been kidnapped.

'Please, not again,' she whispered.

The front door opened, and she whipped round, hands curling into fists. She sighed with relief when Rose entered.

'Morning,' she beamed. 'You just up?'

'No, I've just got back. Where have you been?'

'Noah's.'

'You were supposed to be here last night.'

'No, it was your turn.'

'It was yours. You asked me to swap so you could go to Noah's cousin's wedding at that posh hotel on Saturday.'

Rose's eyes widened. 'Oh, crap, I forgot.'

'That means Carly's been on her own all night.'

'Oh, shite, I'm sorry,' Rose said, looking stricken.

Jane frowned at her before flinging open the door to Carly's room, which used to be clean and neat but was now a chaotic mess, clothes all over the floor, bed perpetually unmade. 'She's not here.'

'God, this is all my fault,' breathed Rose.

Jane hurried into the kitchen that also acted as a living room and sighed with relief for the second time when she saw Carly sprawled on her front on the couch, one arm hanging off it, an empty wine glass on the floor.

'She's here, thank Christ,' said Rose.

Jane picked up the wine bottle off the coffee table. 'It's empty,' she whispered so as not to disturb Carly.

'Her drinking's getting worse,' said Rose sadly.

Sensing someone standing over her, Carly jumped awake. She immediately groaned and put a hand to her head.

'Another hangover?' demanded Jane, folding her arms across her chest.

'No, I'm just tired,' muttered Carly. 'It was a busy night at work.'

'That bottle was full yesterday and now it's empty.'

'What bottle?' she replied as she slowly sat upright.

Jane shoved it under her nose. 'This one. You're going through a bottle a day and that's only the ones we know about.'

'You're exaggerating. Have we got any paracetamol?'

'I'll get you some,' said Rose, eager to help.

'She can get it herself,' retorted Jane. 'You gave yourself the hangover, Carly, you can deal with it.'

'It's no trouble,' said Rose, producing the pack of paracetamol from a cupboard and pouring a glass of water before handing both to Carly.

'Thanks,' she replied, taking them from her. 'You're an angel.'

'No problem.' Rose smiled sweetly.

'This is getting out of control, Carly,' said Jane. 'You've got to cut back on your drinking.'

'I will from today,' she replied.

'You said that a week ago and you still haven't done it.'

Carly swallowed a couple of tablets and gulped down the water before responding. 'What's the big deal? You drink too.'

'Nowhere near the amount you do. You're in serious danger of becoming an alcoholic.'

'Can we leave the lecture to another time?' She grimaced, rubbing a hand across her aching forehead.

'No. Someone's got to talk some sense into you before you throw your life away.'

'For God's sake,' grunted Carly. She shot to her feet and screwed her eyes shut when her head pounded. Once the thumping had stopped, she strode out of the room with her chin tilted indignantly.

'Don't,' said Rose, grabbing Jane's arm when she moved to follow.

'We can't keep sitting back and doing nothing,' Jane exclaimed.

'I know but she's in no mood to hear it. She'll only think you're nagging and that will push her even further away from us.'

'You're right,' she muttered. 'I'm just scared for her.'

'Me too.'

There was the slam of the bathroom door followed by the sound of the shower running.

'Let's speak to Uncle Eddie and Harry,' said Jane. 'We need to stage an intervention.'

* * *

Carly took a long, leisurely shower, which went some way to easing her hangover. After blow-drying her hair and throwing on jeans and a jumper, she returned to the kitchen and was relieved to see her sisters had gone. Guilt crept over her. She could see what her behaviour was doing to them and she hated herself for it. She loved them both dearly; they'd been close their entire lives, but she wanted no one's company but her own. That was when Jack felt closest to her.

The day stretched out before her, long and empty, until four o'clock that afternoon when she had to go into work to set up for the night. First, she would make her daily pilgrimage to Jack's grave and beyond that she had no idea.

Her thoughts were interrupted by her phone ringing, the sound grating on her nerves.

'What?' she said impatiently as she snatched it up. Carly rolled her eyes at the sound of her boss's stammering voice on the other end. 'Now?' she retorted when he said he needed her to come into work as there was something important they had to discuss. 'Fine. I'll be there in an hour,' she added before hanging up.

Carly had a lot of contempt for the owner of Death Loves Company. He called himself a reality TV star but, in her opinion, he was nothing but an attention-seeking loser. Personally, she found him ridiculous, but he was her employer, so she had no choice but to obey his summons.

Conscious of the fact that she was way over the legal limit to drive, Carly had to take the bus to Death Loves Company, which took almost an hour, not helping her mood or her hangover any.

By the time she arrived, her temper was close to the surface. She entered the bar to find the owner, Ricky, was already there.

He was accompanied by a tall, bald, muscular man she'd never seen before.

'What's this about?' she demanded the moment she was through the door.

Ricky gave her his best smile, his teeth ridiculously white, his skin a hideous orange and black hair badly dyed. 'Carly, thanks so much for coming at such short notice.' He gestured to one of the bar stools. 'Take a seat.'

Ricky looked to his companion sheepishly when she remained standing, staring at him with contempt.

'Why don't you take a seat like Mr Allan suggests?' said the bald man in a very deep voice.

Carly gave him the same scornful stare before looking back at her employer.

'Right, well,' began Ricky awkwardly. 'I'm afraid I've had a complaint about your behaviour...'

'It's that wee worm Ollie, isn't it?' she spat. 'He's after my job.'

'It's nothing to do with him. It was from a customer who claims that you punched him last night.'

'Aye, so?'

'Carly, you can't punch customers.'

'I was breaking up a fight. He hit another customer first, so I did what I had to do.'

'He says you also threatened his friends with a broken glass.'

'I'm entitled to protect myself.'

'I spoke to a couple of other witnesses who said the danger was over by that point. There was no need for you to threaten them with a piece of jaggy glass. I've looked at the CCTV footage,' he said, hastily speaking over her when she opened her mouth to reply. 'I've seen what happened and I agree, you went too far.'

'Fine. I'll tell you what – the next time a fight breaks out, I won't lift a finger. I'll call you instead and you can come down here and sort it out.'

'I... I don't think that's the solution,' he stammered.

'This is a bar,' she told him as though he were five years old. 'People can get violent when they drink. I'm the only one here capable of splitting up a fight. No one else can do it, especially not that weak wee coward, Ollie. It's always left to me, so instead of pulling me up about doing my job, you should be saying thank you.'

'Believe me, I appreciate all your hard work and you've done a sterling job since Diana left, but what you don't know is that the man you punched is the son of a local MP.'

'So?'

'So this man is very influential and he's upset about what happened to his son.'

'Then he should tell his son no' to drink more than he can handle and start fights in bars.'

'He's insisting you're sacked.'

Carly arched an eyebrow. 'Excuse me?'

Ricky looked at his companion for assistance. He'd liked Carly at first but since her boyfriend's death she'd become scary, hence the back-up he'd brought with him.

'Mr Allan is saying that you're fired,' the bald man told her politely but firmly.

'I'm fired because I stopped your precious MP's son from beating the shite out of another customer, is that what you're saying?' she yelled at Ricky.

'This isn't me, Carly,' he replied placatingly. 'He's threatening all sorts of trouble for my bar. If it was my choice, of course I'd keep you on.'

Her lip curled with disgust. 'You're so weak.'

Her words filled him with shame. 'I really don't want to fight this man, he's pretty powerful...'

'No, he's not,' she snapped back. 'I've seen true power and the sort politicians have isn't real because it's easily taken away from them. You can bow down to the authorities but I'm not afraid,' she yelled, jabbing a finger in her own chest.

'I really am terribly sorry about this,' Ricky said, taking a step back towards his friend. 'I'll pay you a month's wages on top of what I already owe you.'

'I want three months,' she barked.

'Aye, okay, three months. I'll pay you right now,' he said, producing a wad of notes from his pocket and counting out the money. Rather than hand it to her, he placed it on the bar and took another step back, as though expecting some sort of explosion.

With a scowl, Carly snatched up the money and stuffed it into her jacket pocket. 'Give Briony my job,' she told Ricky. 'She's smart and great with the customers. Ollie's a lazy arsehole who will stick his tongue right up your hole in order to get it.'

'Thanks for the advice.'

'I'll go and grab my stuff,' she snapped, a challenge in her eyes.

Ricky held up his hands. 'No one will stop you.'

Carly stomped into the staff room and emptied her locker, which contained a make-up bag, a spare pair of shoes and a chocolate bar. She stuffed the lot inside a carrier bag she found under the sink before heading into the office. The bald man lurked in what he thought was an intimidating manner in the corridor but which just made Carly roll her eyes. On the desk was a framed photo of Jack, which she carefully placed in the bag so it wouldn't get damaged. There was a small bottle of vodka in one of the drawers, but she decided to leave it where it was. It was nearly empty anyway.

Carly left the office, the bald man following her back into the bar where Ricky waited.

'Did you manage to get everything?' he asked her, putting on a chirpy front.

'Aye, I think so,' she replied, taking one last look around to ensure she hadn't forgotten anything.

'Mr Allan has treated you very generously,' said his bald friend. 'I suggest you leave. Now.'

Carly's smile was mocking. 'You don't scare me. I've seen much worse than you in my time. Goodbye, pricks,' she said, giving them both the finger before striding out, slamming the door shut behind her as hard as she could.

Only once she was heading down the street did Carly let her emotions show. Losing her job was more devastating than she'd let either of those idiots know. It was the last thing she'd had left and now it was gone. She's already lost Jack and the life they'd planned together, her father was dead, Dean and the relationship she'd thought they'd had had been an illusion and her sisters were moving on with their own lives. She hadn't needed the job – Jack had left her a big chunk of money – but it had been a reason for her to get out of bed in the morning and she'd had responsibilities, people had relied on her. Now she was rudderless. Without any purpose she felt useless, a complete waste of space.

She hopped onto the bus that would take her back to Haghill and gazed out of the window as she pondered the mess her life had become. The worst thing was she could see no way out of the bleakness. Since losing Jack all her get-up-and-go had gone. Without her job, she truly began to fear what would become of her.

On her return to Haghill, Carly walked to the cemetery where Jack had been buried close to her parents. She stared down at his grave, which she kept carefully tended, ensuring it was weed-free and always supplied with fresh flowers. The red roses she'd placed there just the day before were a bright spot in the dull winter grey, reminding her of drops of blood. She recalled Jack's own blood leaking from his terrible wound and shivered.

'Well, I've gone and got sacked now and all because I punched some arsehole who was starting a fight,' she told the grave. 'I cannae get anything right any more. My sisters are always going on about my drinking. I'm causing them so much worry but I don't have the energy to care about anyone else's feelings. Just getting through each day without you takes me everything I have.'

Carly knelt down and pressed a hand to the grave. Already the grass was growing over it and she let her fingers trail through the green blades, which were coated in an icy dew. Immediately the cold began to seep through her jeans to her knees. It was a particularly chilly December and the breeze sliced through everything like a knife.

There was the sound of footsteps behind her and she shot to her feet. Jessica Alexander was approaching Carly's parents' graves holding a bunch of flowers.

'What are you doing here?' said Jessica with surprise.

'That's a stupid fucking question,' retorted Carly.

Jessica's eyes widened when Carly stormed up to her, hands bunched into fists.

'Where the hell are you going to put those?' she demanded, pointing to the lilies Jessica held.

'I just wanted to pay my respects to your father,' she replied reasonably.

Carly snatched the flowers from her hands. 'Do you think I'd let his grave be tainted by anything from you, you old bitch?'

Ricky Allan wasn't the only one who was intimidated by the person Carly Savage had become. Everyone knew how much angrier and more violent she was now and Carly hadn't exactly been a girl guide to begin with.

'They're for your mother's grave too,' said Jessica placatingly. 'I regret what I did and I'm trying to make amends.'

Carly thrust her face into hers. 'You'll stay away from them, do you hear me? If I catch you up here again then the next grave being dug will be yours.'

Jessica Alexander, matriarch of the Savage family's biggest rivals, had once been the most arrogant woman in Haghill. Although not a fighter herself, she had always been confident in the abilities of her three sons to protect her. Plus, her good looks and brilliant green cats' eyes had attracted the attention of more than one powerful man. Now those men had deserted her. Cole, the youngest of her sons and the most intelligent by far, had fled after he'd plotted with Dean to kill Jack and take over his position. Her two older sons had moved out of the area, wanting to distance themselves from the dangerous scheming of their mother and younger brother. Now she was alone in Haghill, reviled by the majority of the residents. It had been a dramatic wake-up call for her.

'Okay, I'm going,' said Jessica. 'But you should know that I'm not the woman I was.'

'I couldn't give a shite. Now piss off before I break your fucking jaw.'

Jessica sighed sadly before walking away, Carly glaring after her. When she'd gone, Carly decided to put the lilies on a grave that always seemed to be neglected.

'There you go, Elizabeth Brannigan,' she said as she placed the flowers before the fading headstone.

Carly straightened up, breathing hard with anger. Jessica had had an affair with her father Alec when her mother had been dying of cancer. Carly was the only member of her family who knew this and she'd promised her dad she'd keep quiet about it. He'd bitterly regretted the affair, which had been brief and hadn't involved any emotions on his part. Jessica had wanted him for years and had caught him at his most vulnerable. She was a twisted, manipulative bitch and Carly hated her. Jessica and her sons had taken potshots at her family for years, trying to topple them from the prominent position they now held in the local area, but they had failed each time. Carly's thoughts moved from the matriarch to her youngest son, Cole. He'd been Carly's first love, until he'd been sent to prison and had come out a cold, pitiless monster with big ambitions. She'd badly injured Cole when he and Dean had attacked her and Jack. She'd smashed a vase into his face and the last time she'd seen him he'd been slumped on his knees, screaming while blood poured from his many wounds. He'd escaped before Toni McVay could get hold of him and nothing had been heard of him since. Carly knew he wasn't done with her and the Savages. He would pop up again one day and she had the feeling he'd be even more of a monster when he did.

The icy wind blew, making her shiver again, and she glanced around the empty graveyard. After saying goodbye to Jack and her parents' graves, she left hastily, the whispering of the wind accompanying her the entire way.

3

'We have to do something,' announced Jane. 'Carly's on a downward spiral. If she carries on this way, she's gonnae end up an alcoholic.'

She sat on a couch in her uncle's living room, Rose beside her. Their uncle, Eddie, and his son Harry sat opposite the sisters. Recent events hadn't just changed Carly, they'd affected them all, especially Harry. The betrayal of his younger brother had hurt him badly and his personality had also turned darker and more bitter. He wasn't as happy-go-lucky as he'd used to be. Although he still retained his sense of humour, he was a lot quicker to violence. Eddie seemed more world-weary, the absence of one of his sons a constant niggling pain, although this unceasing ache was tempered by the knowledge that Dean was alive and safe, well out of reach of any vengeance Toni McVay or Carly might inflict on him.

'Jane's right, we have to do something,' announced Rose. The news of Dean's betrayal had changed her too. She'd lost a lot of the sweet innocence she'd once possessed. Her love of mayhem and a good scrap had only increased. She'd just turned eighteen but already she seemed a fully-fledged adult. 'She's so sad all the time.'

'That's understandable after what she went through,' said Eddie. 'I cannae imagine what it was like having Jack die in her arms with his insides hanging out.'

'I know but it's getting worse when she should be getting better. We've asked her to see a therapist loads of times, but she refuses. She's so stubborn.'

'She's an adult. We cannae force her. What that lassie needs is a wake-up call, something to snap her out of it.'

'Such as?' said Jane.

'Nae idea,' he sighed helplessly. 'It's breaking my heart seeing her go down this path but I don't know how to stop it. The more we nag her, the more she'll push back.'

'The immediate issue we need to tackle is her drinking.'

'But how?' said Rose. 'We know she hides bottles.'

'We need to stage an intervention,' replied Jane. 'We need to tackle her as a family. Having a word with her individually isn't having enough of an impact. Together, we might finally get through to her.'

'It's worth a try,' said Eddie. 'What do you think?' he asked Harry.

'I think we should leave her alone to come out of it in her own time,' he replied.

'It's no' worked so far,' Jane told him.

'She's got enough on her plate without us having a go at her.'

'Rose?' said Eddie, turning his attention to his youngest niece.

'We have to do something,' she said determinedly. 'If it was any of us in her position, she wouldn't stop until she'd got through to us.'

'You're right, doll. Right, let's do it.' Eddie got to his feet. 'No time like the present. I'm guessing she'll be in.'

'Probably,' said Jane. 'The only places she goes are the pub, work and the cemetery.'

Carly sat slumped at the kitchen table nursing a glass of wine when there was the sound of the front door opening. Before she could hide the wine glass, her sisters had entered with her uncle and cousin. They looked so grim her heart leapt with fear.

'What's happened?' she demanded.

'Nothing,' replied Jane, taking the seat to her left while Rose took the one on her right. Eddie and Harry occupied the chairs at the opposite end of the table.

'We just felt it was time for an intervention,' added Jane.

Carly's eyes narrowed. 'I thought people only held those for drug addicts.'

Jane pointed to her glass of wine. 'And alcoholics.'

'I am no' an alcoholic,' Carly exclaimed.

'It's one o'clock in the afternoon.'

'So? It's just one glass.'

Sadness filled Jane's eyes. 'That's the problem, Carly. It's no' just the one.'

'We're no' here to argue,' said Eddie when Carly opened her mouth to yell back at her older sister. 'We're just worried about you.'

'There's no need,' she scowled. 'I'm fine.' When she reached out to pick up the wine glass, she saw Jane's raised eyebrow and retracted her hand.

'No, you're no', doll,' continued Eddie. 'And who can blame

you after what you went through? Any one of us would be the same. The grief's tearing you apart. You need professional help.'

'Like a psychiatrist?' she spat. 'I'm no' mad.'

'None of us think you are and I don't mean a psychiatrist. I mean a grief counsellor.'

'I don't want to see anyone. I don't want to talk about it.'

Tears filled Rose's eyes when Carly anxiously wrung her hands together and she shifted uncomfortably in her seat, as though fighting the urge to run. She placed a gentle hand on Carly's arm. 'We hate seeing you suffer like this.'

'I'll be fine, I just need more time,' she replied, eyes tick-tocking from side to side while continuing to grind her palms together.

'It's been three months,' said Jane. 'And it doesn't seem to be getting any easier for you.'

'I didn't realise there was a time limit on grief,' snapped back Carly.

'We're not saying there is but you're struggling. Please, let us help.'

Carly swallowed down hot tears. 'You can't help me. No one can.' They were all startled by the way her eyes narrowed, pain becoming predatory, that unnerving gaze fixing on Eddie. 'Unless you're finally gonnae tell me where Dean's hiding?'

'You know I cannae do that, doll,' he replied.

'Getting my hands on that twat is the only thing that'll cheer me up.'

'Revenge is no' the way to recover.'

Carly shot to her feet, the legs of her chair scraping noisily across the floor. 'It's not revenge, it's justice,' she yelled. 'A life for a life.'

'Killing Dean won't make you feel better,' he told her calmly. 'It will only make you hate yourself.'

'If you believe that, then you don't know me at all.' She slammed her fist down on the table. 'This intervention is over.'

'No, Carly, wait,' called Jane, shooting to her feet as her sister yanked open the back door and stormed out.

'Let me talk to her,' said Harry.

Jane sighed and nodded before slumping back into her seat.

Harry exited the flat just in time to see Carly vault the back wall and drop down on the other side. He did the same and jogged after her, catching her up at the end of the back street.

'Go away,' she told him. 'I'm no' in the mood for company.'

'Well, fucking tough because you've got it.'

Carly stopped and turned to face him.

Harry smiled at the surprise in her eyes. 'You're no' the only one recent events have changed.'

'Oh, aye? And what do you think of Dean?'

'I fucking hate him,' he rasped, throat choked with emotion.

'Really?' she said guardedly.

'Aye, really. I never thought I'd say that about my own brother, especially when we've been so close, but I cannae get over his betrayal. It's eating me alive.'

Carly recognised some of her own pain in her cousin when he ran an agitated hand through his thick light brown hair.

'What would you do if you saw him again?' she asked him.

'Well, I wouldnae be able to kill him like you want to but I'd beat the living shite out of him. I'd want him to hurt like he's hurt us.'

Carly studied him closely before linking her arm through his. 'Fancy going for a drink?'

'How no?' He smiled.

* * *

Derek, landlord of The Horseshoe Bar, watched Carly and Harry down more drinks. It was a relief to see her actually smiling for once, but it wasn't a good smile. The pair looked to be plotting together. They were well on their way to being drunk and it wasn't even one o'clock in the afternoon.

Taking out his phone, he headed into the back room to make a call.

'Jane, hen,' he said when she answered. 'I'm worried about Carly and Harry. They're here in the pub and they're pretty pished. No, there's no trouble so far but I get the feeling there will be.' At the sound of a crash from the direction of the bar, he peered out to see Harry and Carly launch themselves at three men. 'Oh, Christ, they're in a fight. Get over here quickly.'

Derek hung up and charged into the fray but he was too late. While Harry felled one man with a roundhouse kick to the face and the second with a powerful uppercut, Carly kneed the third man in the crotch and headbutted him. It was over before anyone could register what was happening.

'What did you do that for?' Derek demanded of the Savage cousins.

'They came in here to cause trouble,' Harry told him.

'They must have only just walked through the door,' he exclaimed.

'It's true, Derek,' said Carly. 'The pricks marched in and said they were gonnae smash up the place.'

'Why would they do that? I've never even seen them before.'

'Whatever the reason, that's what they intended to do,' said John, one of the regulars. 'They told us all to clear out or we'd have our cunts kicked in.'

'Dirty bastards,' growled Derek.

'You ought to be saying thank you to Carly and Harry.'

'Aye, I'm grateful,' he replied. 'But why would they want to smash up my place? I've done nothing to them, that I know of anyway.'

'Let's find out,' said Harry.

He studied the fallen trio, deciding who was the most conscious after being hit. He grabbed his chosen victim by the arm and dragged him towards the back room. Carly and Derek followed, the latter closing the door behind them.

Harry shoved the man into the only chair in the room where they could study him properly. He appeared to be in his mid-twenties. He had a shaved head, his nose was long and narrow and cheeks sunken, or rather one was. The other was rapidly swelling from where Harry's foot had struck it.

'Who are you working for?' was Harry's first question.

The man's response was to spit at him. He was knocked sideways off his chair by Carly's fist in his face.

'You broke his nose,' grinned Harry. 'Nice one.'

'Thanks,' smiled Carly.

Derek did not like the pleasure in Carly's eyes whenever she inflicted pain on someone. 'Perhaps you should let Eddie deal with this?' he told them.

'We can handle it, can't we, Carly?' said Harry.

'Absolutely,' she replied.

Harry dragged the man back into his chair and pinned him there with one hand. 'Every time you refuse to answer a question, we'll break something. Next time it will be your elbow. Do you understand?'

He spoke so coldly the hairs on the back of Derek's neck rose. Their prisoner nodded once, although he still appeared defiant.

'Good. Now, why were you going to smash up Derek's nice pub?'

'We were paid to.'

'By who?'

'Dunno.'

Harry grabbed his left arm and twisted. There was a crack and the man screamed.

'Oh dear, it looks like he's gonnae pass out,' said Carly before backhanding the man across the face, silencing his screams.

'Jesus Christ, will you two calm down?' exclaimed Derek.

'If we don't find out what's going on then they'll return with reinforcements,' Harry told him.

'I don't care, I will not allow someone to be tortured in my back room.'

'Let's at least find out who he is,' said Carly, patting down the man's jacket. She located his wallet and flipped it open. 'His name's Owen Auchter. Twenty-five years old. Lives in Wellhouse. Who are those two idiots you came in with, Owen? Relatives of yours or just friends?'

'I think he's gonnae be sick,' said Harry.

Derek snatched up the bin and shoved it under Owen's face just as he vomited.

'What a lightweight,' grinned Harry.

'Lightweight?' cried Derek. 'He's just had his elbow and nose broken, he's entitled to throw up.' He whirled round when the door burst open. 'Thank Christ you're here. This situation has got well out of control.'

Jane and Eddie frowned at the scene.

'What the bloody hell is all this?' spluttered the latter.

'This idiot and two of his friends came to smash up the place. Luckily Harry and Carly were here to stop them, but they decided to drag this one in here and start torturing him. Harry broke his elbow.'

'What do you think you're playing at, son?' said Eddie, who looked more sad than angry.

'Getting us the answers we need,' replied Harry rebelliously. 'And ensuring these pricks never come into Haghill again.'

'Derek's right, you've gone too far. Both of you wait out there and keep an eye on the other two while me and Jane question him. Don't fucking argue,' he snarled when it appeared they were going to answer back.

Carly and Harry both gave him a hard look before exiting the room. Eddie sighed heavily as he wondered for how much longer he'd be able to control them.

'This is bollocks,' said Carly when she and Harry entered the bar area to find the two men attempting to push themselves upright.

'I know,' replied Harry, planting his foot in the middle of one of the men's backs, pushing him back down. 'But we have to do as my da' says.'

Carly kicked the second man in the ribs, causing him to squeak and curl up into a ball. 'Why?'

'Because he's head of the family. And he's also one of David and Elijah's lieutenants.'

'So are you and Jane.'

'But he's their first lieutenant. Me and Jane are the seconds. He's higher up the chain.'

'I suppose. I just hate being told what to do.'

'You're out of this life anyway. I should never have dragged you into it. You've got your nice legit job at Death Loves Company.' He spotted the way Carly's eyes flickered. 'Don't you?'

'I was sacked this morning for punching a customer but I only did it to break up a fight.'

'That's no' fair. Shall we go and give that arsehole Ricky a good kicking?'

'The wee shite's no' worth the effort. Besides, I got three months' wages out of him. I just don't know what to do with myself now. I was wondering about getting back into the family business.'

'But you wanted out. No way would they let you go a second time if you changed your mind.'

'I wouldn't change my mind. I've nothing else left.'

Harry gave her hand a gentle squeeze, moved by the sadness in her tone. 'That's bollocks, Carly. You've got us.' He rolled his eyes when the man pinned beneath his foot began to struggle feebly. 'You're a slow learner,' he told him before giving him a swift boot in the side, making him yelp.

'I've made my mind up,' said Carly. 'I need a reason to get out of bed in the morning otherwise I won't bother.'

'My da' might veto you getting back in until you've got over what happened to Jack.'

'Then I'll go over his heid. I've always got on well with David. He'll let me back in.'

'Doubtful. He knows how upset you've been. You're better going to Elijah.'

'You think?'

'Aye. I'll take you to see him once we're done here.'

'Brilliant, thanks. But why are you helping me when you know the rest of the family would be against it?'

'Because, if I was in your position, I'd want someone to give me a reason to keep going.'

Carly gave his arm a gentle squeeze. 'I'm glad that at least one person understands.'

'Aye, well, Dean did a number on us both,' he growled, expression darkening as he kicked the fallen man again just because it made him feel a little better.

Eddie, Jane and Derek came out of the back room with Owen, who was a startling shade of grey, sweat beading on his forehead with pain. He cradled his injured arm tenderly to his chest.

'We got what we needed without any more violence,' Eddie told Carly and Harry.

'Only because we'd already done the hard work for you,' Harry retorted.

'Don't gi'e me any fucking lip,' he told his son, pointing a warning finger at him. 'We're gonnae drop him off at hospital. You can let his pals go.'

'What if he blabs to the hospital staff?'

'He's no' that stupid. Now then, I've told Derek no' to serve you any more drinks. You've done enough damage for one day.'

Eddie and Jane gave them a hard look before leaving with Owen.

'That's charming,' scowled Carly. 'We stop Derek's pub getting smashed up and we're the bad guys.'

'You still up for talking to Elijah?' asked Harry, who was equally pissed off.

'Too right I am. Let's go.'

'Carly, hen, can I have a word?' Derek called after her as she stalked to the door with her cousin.

'Later,' she snapped back before leaving.

Derek's eyes filled with hurt and he hung his head.

'Don't look so down,' John told him. 'She'll snap out of it one day. She's just in a lot of pain.'

'Aye, I know, but I'm worried she'll self-destruct before she gets the chance to recover. Jack's murder has set that lassie on a very dark path.'

4

Elijah Samson smiled, creasing his thin weasel face unpleasantly. He lolled back in the chair that Jack had once occupied in the office at the rear of the café where he and David conducted business.

'So, you want back in, do you, Carly?' he said.

'Aye,' she replied. Before coming here, she and Harry had gone to a café and drunk several cups of coffee, sobering them both up.

'Why, when you were so desperate to get out?'

'Because I've realised this is what I'm meant to do.'

'What brought about this flash of inspiration?'

Carly's muscles clenched with tension at his patronising tone. She'd always considered Elijah rather an unpleasant character, but Jack had thought very highly of him and that was good enough for her. Elijah had also remained loyal to him, for which she would be forever grateful.

'I lost my job at Death Loves Company for punching a customer. I see you already know,' she added when he appeared unsurprised.

'I did hear a wee whisper.'

'That made me realise I can never have a legitimate job. Violence is in my blood, so I may as well use that fact to my advantage and make more money than I ever could working behind a bar.'

Elijah's patronising smile vanished and he nodded thoughtfully. 'All right, that makes sense. Harry,' he said, sharp gaze turning to her cousin standing beside her. 'What do you think of this?'

'It's a good idea,' he replied. 'Carly was born for this life.'

'I want to talk to her in private.'

Harry glanced at Carly, who nodded, and he left.

'Take a seat,' said Elijah, indicating the chair opposite his desk.

She obeyed and regarded him expectantly, surprised when his expression softened.

'Jack meant a hell of a lot to me,' began Elijah. 'He was one of the very few true friends I've ever had. I also know how much he loved you, so I'd be failing him if I let you back in when your heid's all over the place. You were there when that cunt killed him; he died in your arms. That's enough to fuck up the strongest of us. The last thing I want is you charging headfirst into a dangerous situation because you're knotted up with grief and getting yourself killed.'

Carly paused to gather her thoughts before replying. She hadn't expected such concern from this man who was known for being cold and ruthless. 'I get where you're coming from, but I've felt totally lost since Jack died. The only thing I had was my job at the bar and then I lost that too. I need something to keep me going, keep me alive. I cannae tell you how many times I've considered lying down beside his grave and never getting up again.' Carly was surprised that she'd opened up to this man. A single tear escaped the corner of her eye and slid down her cheek. Hastily, she wiped it away, embarrassed about showing such weakness.

'Don't be ashamed of your tears,' he told her. 'They show what Jack meant to you. You should be fucking proud of them. I'd love to gi'e you a job, I know what you can do, but I'm still worried that it's too soon.'

'Then let me prove to you that it's not.'

'No, I'm sorry. I don't think you're ready. Come and see me in a couple of months and we'll talk again.'

Carly shot to her feet and glared down at Elijah, hands bunching into fists.

The sardonic smile returned to Elijah's lips. 'The violence in your eyes convinces me I've made the right decision. Go ahead, smash up my office if it'll make you feel better. I'm no' caring but it'll destroy your chances of working for me again for good.'

It was with an enormous effort of will that Carly spun on her heel and stormed out, fighting the urge to slam the door shut behind her.

'Well?' said Harry, who was waiting for her in the corridor.

'He said I'm no' ready. I've to come back in a couple of months.'

'Really?'

'He said Jack was his friend and he'd be doing him a disservice taking me on when I'm still grieving.'

'I see his point, even though I don't agree with it. Sorry, Carly. I got your hopes up for nothing.'

'It's no' your fault. I appreciate you trying to help. You're the only one who has any faith left in me.'

He slung an arm around her shoulders. 'Let's go and grab something to eat, I'm starving. It's on me.'

'Sounds good,' she replied with a weak smile. 'I could use a big glass of wine.'

'And I could use a pint.'

'Even though your da' told us no' to drink?'

'I'm twenty-five years old. If I want to drink I bloody well will.'

* * *

'It's ten o'clock, where are they?' exclaimed Jane, dragging her fingers through her short brown hair.

'I'm sure they're okay,' replied her girlfriend, Jennifer. 'They're both adults and very capable of taking care of themselves.'

'But they havenae been themselves lately. Neither of them are thinking straight. What if they've got into another fight?'

'Then I feel sorry for whoever's stupid enough to take them on.'

'Jane's right,' said a wide-eyed Rose. 'They've both been so reckless lately. It would be easy for them to get into big trouble.'

The three women were at the Savage Sisters' flat. They'd spent the last two hours repeatedly calling Carly and Harry but neither of them had picked up. Jane had sent The Unbeatable Bitches – the fierce girl gang she led – out searching the scheme and surrounding areas for them but neither had been spotted.

'And they know the rules,' continued Jane. 'No one stays out of contact for this long. It keeps us all safe.'

'I'm sure they'll turn up soon,' said Jennifer, more for Rose's sake than anything. As the baby of the family, they went out of their way to shield her even though she was as much of a demon as her older sisters when riled and was perfectly capable of holding her own in a fight.

'Where's Uncle Eddie?' said Jane. 'He should have been here by now. Finally,' she added when there was the slam of the front door. 'Anything?' she asked the moment he entered the kitchen.

'Nope,' he replied, sinking into a chair looking weary. 'I've visited everyone I can think of. Elijah told me something very interesting though – he said Carly came to him asking for a job.'

'What did she do that for?' groaned Jane. 'She's got a great job at the bar.'

'She was sacked yesterday for punching a customer.'

'I suppose it was only a matter of time,' said Jennifer.

'That job was the only thing keeping her going and now it's gone,' said Rose.

'Please tell me he turned her down,' Jane asked her uncle.

'Aye, he did. He didnae deny that he'd love to employ her, but he said she's no' in the right heidspace for it. He said she wasnae happy and she and Harry left together. That was at two o'clock this afternoon and no one's seen them since.'

'They must have gone straight there after leaving The Horseshoe Bar.'

'That's what I'm thinking, and I bet they went to a pub so Carly could drown her sorrows, even though I told them no' to go drinking.'

'No offence, Uncle Eddie, but we know what they've been like recently. They just do what they want now and they egg each other on too. They're a lot more reckless when they're together.'

'Because they understand how each other feels,' said Rose. 'Carly lost Jack and Harry lost his brother.'

'I lost one of my sons too but you don't see me going off the rails,' replied Eddie.

'Because you're older and wiser and you've experienced betrayal before,' she said, thinking of his ex-wife who'd run off with another man when their boys were just children. 'This is the first time Harry's really felt it deeply, no' even his maw hurt him like Dean did and he's struggling to handle it. Carly's the only one who understands and it's bonded them.'

'Do you know something, doll,' said Eddie with a gentle smile. 'You're very wise. Sometimes you seem a lot older than your years. I wish Carly had your sense because she and Harry need their bloody heids banging together. Christ only knows what they're up to right now.'

* * *

Carly and Harry were laughing as they left the pub in Glasgow city centre, the angry shouts of the landlord following them as they drunkenly weaved their way down the darkened street.

'What a walloper,' chuckled Harry. 'Did you see how upset he got just because I won on his puggie?'

'To be fair, you didn't win,' replied Carly. 'You kicked the machine until it started spitting out coins all over the floor.'

Harry produced two handfuls of ten pence pieces from his jacket pockets. 'Look at that lot.'

'Aye, there must be about four quid there,' she grinned, shaking her head.

'That's four quid more than I had before, which in my book is a win. Let's find another pub with a landlord who has a sense of humour.'

'Good idea.' Carly took out her phone to check it. 'Oh, shite.'

'What?'

'Seventeen missed calls from Jane, eight from Rose and six from your da'.'

'Have they nothing better to do?'

'You should check yours.'

Harry tugged his phone free of his jeans pocket and squinted at the screen. 'Eighteen calls from my da', twelve from Jane and five from Rose.'

'Maybe something's happened?' said Carly anxiously.

'Like shite it has. They're just checking up on us.'

'Still, I'd better call them just in case. Jane,' added Carly when her sister answered. 'Is everything okay?' She huffed and rolled her eyes when Jane launched into a lecture.

'Told you so,' smiled Harry.

'I'm a grown woman, for God's sake,' snapped Carly when she eventually managed to get a word in edgeways. 'If I want to go to the pub I can. I'm no' slurring. I've had a couple of shandies, that's all. See, smell my breath,' she said before breathing all over the phone.

'That's so funny,' chuckled Harry.

'We're no' ready to come back yet. Because we're having fun, or have you forgotten what that is?' Carly barked before hanging up.

'She is so gonnae make you pay for that,' Harry told Carly.

'She can try,' she muttered, stuffing the phone back into her pocket.

'Maybe we should head back? It's cold.'

'Lightweight.'

'I'm no' a lightweight.'

'Prove it then.'

'Fine, I will. Let's go in there,' he said, taking her hand and leading her into another pub just down the road.

They had one drink each before catching a taxi back to Haghill. Carly would have liked to remain out longer in defiance of her older sister but the calls from Rose were making her feel guilty.

Harry and Carly got out of the taxi at the top of the street and walked the rest of the way to the flat, hoping the cold air would sober them up.

'Ready for a lecture?' said Harry.

'As ready as I can be,' she replied.

'Remember, we're adults, we can do what we like.'

Carly nodded. 'You're right.'

He smiled and gave her hand an encouraging squeeze before they entered the flat.

'Finally,' they heard Jane and Eddie yell in unison.

Carly and Harry looked at each other and rolled their eyes while removing their coats and damp shoes. They wandered into the kitchen to find Jane and Eddie standing, arms folded across their chests. Jennifer was leaning against the kitchen counter cradling a mug of tea. She gave them a sympathetic smile. Rose sat at the table, looking both upset and relieved.

'Just what the hell do you think you're playing at?' exploded Jane, relief that they were both safe morphing into anger. 'Have you any idea how worried we've been?'

'We only went into the city centre, for God's sake,' said Carly.

'I knew it, you were slurring on the phone. You're both drunk.'

'We are not,' replied an indignant Harry.

'Aye, ya are. You're swaying on your feet. Sit down before you fall down.'

'I'm fine standing,' said Carly.

'Me too,' added Harry.

'God, you're stubborn,' sighed Jane.

'I'll make you both a coffee,' said Jennifer, switching on the kettle.

'Thanks,' Carly told her before scowling at her sister. 'At least someone's welcoming.'

'I told you both no' to drink,' said Eddie. 'So why did you?'

'Because we're adults, Da',' replied Harry. 'You cannae order us about.'

'Oh, yes, I can. I'm head of this family.'

'That doesnae mean you can control every aspect of our lives. When we're working, aye, you're in charge. You don't get a say outside of that.'

'What's happening to you two? Can't you see where you're gonnae end up if you keep going on like this?'

'Blame Dean for that,' replied Carly coldly. 'Everything was great until he turned traitor and ripped Jack's guts out.'

'Carly, please,' said Jane, not unkindly, nodding at Rose.

'She's an adult now and she can handle it. Stop babying her all the time. She's more of a terror than the pair of us put together.'

'I'm fine, honestly, Jane,' assured Rose. 'But Carly, please, you need to listen to us. Your drinking is out of control. I understand it's the only thing that helps your pain but it's no' the way to deal with it. We've seen drink destroy so many people and I'm terrified you're going the same way.'

'And you're no' helping,' Eddie told Harry. 'You should be encouraging her to stop, no' taking her to pubs.'

'For Christ's sake, will you stop nagging?' exclaimed Harry. 'I'm bloody sick of it.'

'Me too,' said Carly. 'If you want me to start getting over Jack's death then back off.'

Eddie held up his hands. 'Fine, we'll back off, but answer me this – if Dean had been obsessed with Jane rather than you and he'd killed Jennifer, what would you say to your sister if you had to watch her drinking herself into an early grave?'

Hot emotion welled up inside Carly's chest. She wanted to say that wouldn't have happened because Jane wouldn't have been stupid enough to give Dean her location like she had. It was her fault Jack was dead. He'd told her to tell no one where she'd been staying and she'd broken her word because she'd thought she could trust Dean. Now Jack was dead and her life was in tatters. It wasn't just grief tearing her apart, it was guilt too.

'I'm going to bed,' she said before hurrying from the room, desperate to escape.

'See what you've done now,' Harry told his father.

'I'm trying to talk some sense into her. I'm no' exacerbating her drinking problem by taking her out to get pished.'

'Aye, we had a few drinks, but do you know what else she did? She smiled and she laughed. When was the last time you made her smile?'

Eddie was lost for words, not something that occurred often.

'Where do you think you're going?' Eddie called after him as he left the room.

'Home. I'm tired.'

'This conversation isnae over.'

'Aye, it is,' Harry called back.

Eddie grunted with frustration when the slam of the front door echoed through the flat. 'I don't know what to do,' he said, sinking into a chair at the table, shaking his head. 'I really don't know what to do.'

'Maybe Harry's right and Carly will snap out of it in her own time?' offered Jennifer. 'And when she does, he will too because they're fuelling each other.'

'But what will Carly do now she has no job and Elijah won't employ her?' said Rose quietly, conscious of Carly just down the hall.

They all looked at each other helplessly, not a clue how to help those they loved.

5

Carly woke to another stinking hangover. She staggered out of bed and swallowed a couple of paracetamol. The thought that she had to go into work briefly occurred to her, until she recalled that she'd been sacked, so she returned to bed and attempted to drift back off, but the memories kept sleep at bay. Jack had shared this bed with her so many times. Closing her eyes, she recalled the feel of his arms around her, his lips on her skin, the murmur of his voice in her ear. She had thought the memories would start to fade, that his face would begin to blur, but everything remained in stark clarity. This was a blessing but it was also a curse because the memories only exacerbated her pain.

Realising sleep wouldn't come, she got out of bed and decided to enjoy a long, luxurious soak in the bath. She ran the water as hot as she could bear it and filled it with sweet orange and cinnamon bubble bath. Carly climbed in and sank back into the water, enjoying the warmth. It was another very cold day outside.

She must have drifted off because the next thing she knew there was the slam of a door that made her jump awake.

'Carly?' called a voice.

She sighed. It was Jane, no doubt back for round two. Carly didn't respond, hoping her sister would think she was out and leave. This thought saddened her. She'd never wanted her older sister to go away before. Some of the bubbles tickled her nose and she sneezed. The door opened and Jane came in.

'Do you mind?' snapped Carly.

'What's the problem? There are so many bubbles in there the only thing I can see is your face. And don't worry, I'm no' here to have a go at you.' Jane perched on the edge of the bath. 'I feel really bad about that rammy yesterday. I just got so scared when I couldn't get hold of you. I couldn't stop thinking about the time the Alexanders kidnapped you.'

More guilt joined the burden Carly was already carrying. 'I'm sorry too but you know I've never been able to handle being lectured.'

'I wasnae trying to lecture you, I was only trying to help. I know you got sacked from Death Loves Company. Why didn't you say anything?'

'Because it's too depressing. I really have nothing now.'

'You still have your family. You're no' alone, Carly.'

'I know but it feels like I am. It's like I'm stuck in this bubble of grief that keeps me separate from everyone else and I don't know how to break out of it, and don't tell me I need a counsellor.'

Jane, who had been about to say that very thing, decided on a change of tack. 'Well, get dressed because I'm taking you out.'

'I don't want to go out.'

'Tough. I thought we could go shopping and have some lunch. I'm buying.'

Carly forced a smile. 'I appreciate the offer, but I cannae stand the thought of shops and people.'

'The only time you leave Haghill is to go to work and you cannae do that any more. You need to get away for a bit.'

'I don't want to go anywhere.'

'But—'

'No, Jane,' she barked. When her sister's eyes flickered, she took a deep, calming breath. 'I just want to stay here.'

'Well, if you're sure?'

'I am. Now, if you don't mind, I need some privacy.'

'Oh, right,' Jane mumbled, getting to her feet. 'Let me know if you change your mind.'

Jane hesitated at the door and looked back at Carly, hoping she'd say she would come after all, but she'd already closed her eyes in dismissal.

* * *

Outside on the pavement, Jane took out her phone and called her uncle. 'She wouldn't come,' she told him when he answered.

'Bugger,' he replied. 'I had hoped that would work but perhaps it's for the best. Elijah's summoned us, there's been some trouble. We'll pick you up on the way.'

Jane hung up and waited on the pavement. A few minutes later her uncle's Vauxhall Astra appeared around the corner, Eddie and Harry in the front seats. Jane got into the back, her spirits low.

'You okay, doll?' her uncle asked her as they set off.

'Aye. I'd just hoped Carly would come out and we could have some fun together, like in the old days. Anyway, what's this trouble?'

'I don't know, Elijah wouldnae go into details over the phone.'

Jane looked to Harry. 'How's your hangover?'

'I don't have a hangover,' he retorted.

'Aye, ya do. You're as white as a sheet.'

'Okay, maybe I have a wee bit of a headache but that's all.'

'Yeah, right,' she said cynically.

'I hope you're no' gonnae start last night's argument up again?' he retorted bad-temperedly.

'I wouldn't dream of it,' she smiled, holding up her hands.

They completed the rest of the journey in silence, Eddie wondering how his family had come to this. Just a few months ago they were on top of the world. Now his brother and the sisters' father were dead, Carly was going off the rails, Harry not far behind her, and his younger son was in exile. It boggled his mind how quickly things had changed. He had no idea how to fix them when it was his responsibility as head of the family.

* * *

'God, you three are depressing to look at,' commented Elijah when they entered his office.

'You're no' wrong,' said David, his co-boss, who stood by the window. 'I take it Carly's no better?'

Eddie and Jane shook their heads.

'She was pissed off I wouldnae gi'e her a job?' said Elijah.

Jane glanced at David, wondering what he knew. Judging by the fact that he didn't react to that news, Elijah had already told him. 'Just a bit,' she replied.

Elijah chuckled. 'She's a fiery one. I did think for a moment she was gonnae punch me.'

'She's no' stupid.'

'No, but she is very angry. One day she will take all that rage out on someone and I feel sorry for whoever she chooses because she might just kill them.'

'Carly's no' a murderer.'

'Of course she is and so are you. Everyone in this room is capable of it. Do you think Toni would employ any of us if we weren't?' He grinned when the Savages all appeared uncomfortable. 'Look at them,' he told David. 'They'd never even thought of that before.'

'You said there was some trouble,' replied Eddie, keen to move the conversation on.

'We've had word of that wee fanny, Cole Alexander. He was recently seen in East Kilbride.'

'The twat,' growled Harry. 'Let's get over there and grab him.'

'Just hold your horses there, pal,' Elijah told him. 'I said he was seen there recently, meaning he's no' there now.'

'Bollocks,' Harry said, hands curling into fists.

'Why is he anywhere near Glasgow?' said Eddie. 'He must know Toni's after him, he's no' stupid.'

'No, he's not,' said Elijah. 'He was visiting someone called Willy Brown who used to work for Toni's brother, Frankie, years ago, until he got shot during a robbery. He recovered physically but he completely lost his bottle, so Frankie dropped him. I want you three to go and speak to Willy personally and then I want you to speak to Cole's brothers, Ross and Dominic. See if they've ever heard of Willy.'

'Will do,' replied Eddie.

'The fact that Cole's still in the area indicates the sod's up to something.'

'We wondered with your insight into the Alexander family if you had any ideas what that could be?' said David.

'Nae idea,' replied Eddie. 'I thought he would have been far away by now, probably in another country. That would be the sensible thing to do.'

'But Cole's got ambition,' said Jane. 'He once told Carly he wasn't content living what he called an ordinary life. He wants money and power. Perhaps failure hasn't put him off trying to get it.'

'I'm sure that bastard twisted Dean's mind,' said Harry, his expression dark and angry. 'If it hadnae been for him, my brother might no' have turned traitor.'

'It's possible,' said David reasonably. 'Or maybe it would have still happened. We'll never know. Do you think Carly could give us her insights into what his next move might be? She knows him well.'

'You mean she knows the man he used to be, before he was sent to Barlinnie,' replied Jane. 'She doesnae know the Cole who attacked her and Jack that terrible night.'

'Or it could have given her a deeper understanding of his character. Please ask her, but only if you think she's up to it.'

Jane just nodded, trying to decide whether it would be wise to drag Carly into this.

'Well, don't just stand there,' Elijah told the Savages. 'Get your arses over to Willy's hoose asap. The longer Cole's left at large, the stronger he gets. David has his address.'

David handed Eddie a slip of paper.

'Is he likely to gi'e us any trouble?' Eddie asked them.

'Doubtful but stay on your guard anyway,' replied David. 'He might be expecting someone to come calling after Cole paid him a visit. Willy was a terror back in the day but no' so much now. He lives alone, so you won't have any family to worry about.'

'Ever heard of Willy Brown?' Jane asked her uncle once they were back in the car and on their way to East Kilbride, a town in Lanarkshire, south of Glasgow.

'Nope. You?'

'No. There must be some connection to the Alexanders though if Cole felt he could visit him.'

Half an hour later they were pulling up outside a beige

pebble-dashed semi-detached house with a monoblock drive. There was a cluster of overgrown bushes at the foot of the drive obscuring the house from the road. While the other houses on the road were neat and freshly painted, this one was sad and neglected, a blue wheelie bin overturned on its side at the foot of the drive, scattering cardboard and paper across it.

'At least all the overgrown shrubbery will give us some privacy if things get rough,' commented Harry.

The three of them got out of the car and walked up the driveway. Eddie rang the bell but when it appeared it wasn't working, he knocked instead. Just as they were beginning to think no one was home, the door was pulled open by a man in his sixties who propped himself up with a walking stick.

'What ya wantin'?' he scowled.

'Willy Brown?' replied Eddie.

'Aye, what of it?'

'My name's Eddie Savage. Can I have a word?'

Willy's frown fell and he nodded resignedly. 'Aye, he said you'd come.'

'Who?'

'Cole. Come away in then.'

Willy turned and led them into a rather pleasant lounge. The furniture and décor looked dated but it was clean. An aged Yorkshire Terrier lay on the rug before the electric fire, fast asleep.

'You wantin' some tea or something?' said Willy.

Eddie took in the way the man struggled to shuffle along and shook his head. 'No, thanks, we're good. How do you know Cole?'

'His granda' used to be a friend of mine. Me and Ted Alexander got up to a few shenanigans together. Poor Ted passed away ten years ago. We were terrors when we were together,' he added with a fond smile. 'Cole thought I could help him.'

'Help him how?'

'He wants to take this city from Toni McVay.'

'He must be mad,' commented Harry.

'Aye, I think he is. He's no' the nice boy I remember. No' surprising really. If I looked like that, I'd be pissed off too.'

'What do you mean?' said Eddie.

'His face is covered in scars. He said someone smashed him in the face with a vase. They did a real number on him. Shredded him to shite, they did. Because he's in hiding he couldnae go to a proper surgeon to have the damage fixed. Some dodgy backstreet sod who'd been struck off for malpractice fixed him up, or rather, made it worse.'

'And that's why he wants to take over the city?'

'No. He wants the city because he's a greedy wee sod. I tried to persuade him no' to do it, to just cut his losses and run. I'd hate to hear that the eyes of Ted's youngest grandson ended up in one of Toni McVay's glasses cases but he wouldnae listen.'

'And yet you still grassed him up to Toni's people?' said Jane.

'Aye, course I did. My first loyalty is to the McVays. When I got shot in the leg on that job, Frankie pensioned me off very nicely. He paid off my hoose and gave me a huge chunk of money so big I've still got some of it left all these years later. Frankie might have been psychotic but he could be generous too. Anyway, Cole kept going on about someone he'd made a deal with who would support him.'

'Who?'

'He wouldnae say.'

'Why bring us here for this?' demanded Harry. 'You could have just told Elijah this over the phone.'

'Because I've something to show you.'

He pointed to a sideboard at the back of the room with his walking stick. 'In there.'

They all looked to the squat teak piece of furniture uncertainly.

'On you go, son,' said Eddie.

'For God's sake,' Harry sighed before walking over to the sideboard. He hesitated before pulling it open. Inside was a large wooden box and nothing else.

'Aren't you gonnae take it?' demanded Willy. 'It's no' gonnae bite you, ya big jessie.'

Harry took the box out of the cabinet and placed it on the coffee table.

'Someone bloody open it then,' said an exasperated Willy.

'I'll do it,' said Jane when Eddie and Harry stared at the box mistrustfully.

She opened the lid to reveal a stack of letters and photographs.

'What you have there is a timeline of the history of the Alexander family,' said Willy. 'Starting when me and Ted first met in 1975 before Cole or his brothers were even born, right the way up to Ted's death in 2015.'

'How can this help?' frowned Harry.

'It details all the family connections going back decades. There might be some names in that lot who Cole would go to for help. You see, me and Ted were pals but I wouldnae trust him as far as I could throw him. I never trusted anyone I worked with. I kept records, lots and lots of records so if they did set me up, I'd have something to retaliate with. Thankfully that never happened. Maybe I was a bit paranoid, but I felt a lot safer having all that information.'

'Nae offence,' said Eddie, 'but all this info could be out of date by now if it ends nearly ten years ago.'

'That's just the information about the Alexanders. I have stuff about people up to the present day, any one of whom could be helping Cole. Take it, it might help.'

'Okay,' said Eddie slowly. 'Thanks.'

Willy waved a dismissive hand. 'I'm tired now. You can see yourselves out.'

Ten seconds later, Willy seemed to be asleep.

'What a mad old bastard,' commented Harry.

'I'm old, no deif,' said Willy without opening his eyes. 'And if you're no' out of here in ten seconds flat, you'll get my stick shoved right up your arse and I'm no' referring to my walking stick.'

'Out,' Eddie told his son, jabbing a finger at the door.

'I don't need to be told twice,' said Harry, snatching up the box and hurrying outside.

'I wasn't expecting to come away from that meeting with homework,' said Jane once they were back in the car.

'There's a ton of photos in here,' said Harry, lifting the lid and peering inside. 'It'll take forever to go through.'

'Maybe Carly could work on it?' said Jane. 'It'll give her something to occupy her mind. Hopefully it might even keep her off the booze.'

6

They returned to the flat to find Carly curled up on the couch staring blankly at the television. Jane was relieved to see that she wasn't holding a glass of wine.

'Hi, Carly,' she said cheerfully.

'All right,' her sister mumbled back without looking their way.

On the screen there was a loud explosion, a car bursting into a flaming fireball. The sweaty, muscular hero looked on from a distance, holding the grenade launcher he'd just used to blow up the baddie's car, a cigar clamped between his teeth and a smug look in his eyes.

'We need your help with something,' continued Jane.

'I am no' dressing up as a tart to act as a decoy on a collection again.'

'It's no' that.' Jane picked up the remote control that sat on the couch beside her sister and paused the film.

'Hey, I was watching that,' frowned Carly.

'Finally, I've got your attention.' Jane sat beside her and held her hands out for the box, which Harry passed to her. 'We've had word about Cole,' she began.

Carly sat up straighter, her eyes narrowing. 'Where is he?'

'He was at a house in East Kilbride but he's gone now. He was visiting an old friend of the Alexander family's, someone called Willy Brown. Did Cole ever mention him? He was a good friend of his granda's.'

'No, I've never heard of him.'

'Cole told him that he wants to take down Toni McVay.'

'That proves it. He is mad.'

'Probably. He's trying to round up supporters. Willy's first loyalty is to the McVay family. He used to work for Frankie McVay, so he grassed on Cole to Elijah.'

'Cole's no' stupid. He must have known Willy would tell.'

'Maybe not.'

'Course he did. He wanted someone to go to this Willy's house, probably you lot.'

'You really think so?' said Eddie.

'Aye, course.' Carly pointed to the box Jane held. 'What's that?'

'All the information Willy's gathered over the years against everyone he worked with,' replied her sister. 'It was his insurance policy in case anyone dobbed him in to the polis. There's letters and photos going back decades. We wondered if you'd take a look through it all, see if there's anything that could help us?'

'Help you do what exactly?'

'Find Cole.'

'This lot won't help you. Cole went there because he wanted you to know he was there. Simple as. Maybe you should check the box? There could be more in it than photos and letters.'

With that, she picked up the remote control and pressed play, the sound of gunfire and explosions filling the air once more.

'Christ, get it out of here,' exclaimed Eddie, snatching the box from Jane's hands and charging towards the back door. Harry rushed to open the door for him and he and his father ran outside with Jane following.

Eddie dumped the box in the middle of the garden and they all took several steps back.

'I don't know what we're expecting,' said Jane. 'An explosion or a poisonous snake maybe.'

'It could be anything knowing Cole bloody Alexander,' said Eddie. 'Carly made a bloody good point. Why else would Cole visit some old has-been with a stick?'

'Please don't talk about his stick,' replied Harry with a shudder.

'What do we do?' said Jane. 'We cannae tip the contents out onto the grass because it's wet. Everything will get ruined.'

'I've got an idea,' said Eddie before charging across the lawn, trainers squelching in the soggy grass. He flung open the door of the communal shed, rushed inside and came out pushing a wheelbarrow, the wheels of which left gouges in the grass.

'This is dry,' he told Jane. 'Tip the lot in here.'

She nodded and did as he'd suggested. Eddie snatched up a stick and stirred the letters and photos around with it, searching for anything that shouldn't be there while Jane and Harry studied the box.

'Well,' said Jane. 'There's certainly no hidden explosives.'

'No tracking devices either,' said Eddie.

'Why would Cole put a tracking device in the box?' said Harry. 'He knows where we all live.'

'You never know,' sniffed Eddie.

'Maybe there's some information he wants us to find,' said Jane, pointing to the heap of letters.

'It's the only explanation. All right, you two get that lot put back in the box and put the wheelbarrow away while I go and check on Carly.'

'He's no' going to check on Carly,' muttered Harry as he watched his father head back inside the flat. 'He just wants to get warm again, it's baltic out here.'

'Probably but let's no' argue,' replied Jane. 'The sooner we're finished the sooner we can get back inside.'

They hastily returned the items to their box and Harry manoeuvred the wheelbarrow into the shed before they went back to the flat, where they found Eddie sitting on the couch beside Carly, both of them staring at the television screen.

'You look nice and warm,' Harry snapped at his father.

'Aye, I'm good, thanks,' Eddie grinned back.

'Now we know the box is safe,' said Jane, 'do you think you could look through this lot for us, Carly?'

Her sister sighed heavily and paused the film, stopping a car as it spun through the air. 'Why me?'

'Because you know the Alexander family better than us. You might notice something we'd miss.'

'I doubt it,' Carly replied sullenly.

'Hey, you,' Harry told her. 'Some old git threatened to shove something frightening up my arse and then I got half-frozen out there looking for something that didnae exist, so the least you can do is sift through a few old letters in warmth and comfort.'

Jane threw him a warning look, which he dismissed with a wave of the hand.

Carly turned to look at her cousin over her shoulder, her scowl smoothing out. 'Fine, I'll take a look if you're gonnae be a big girl about it.'

'Put it this way – I won't stop whingeing until you do.'

Jane was delighted when her sister's lips actually twitched with amusement, and she bestowed upon Harry a grateful smile.

'Give me the box then,' said Carly.

Jane placed it on her knee and Carly opened the lid. She picked up the top letter. 'This one's dated 1984. This job will take forever.'

'On the bright side,' said Eddie, 'you'll probably read about a lot of juicy secrets no one else knows.'

'I need a cuppa to help me warm up,' said Jane. 'Anyone else want one?'

They all said yes, even Carly, so Jane rushed to put the kettle on before her sister changed her mind and asked for a glass of wine instead. She opened the fridge door and froze. Inside were three more bottles of white wine that hadn't been there yesterday. Obviously, her sister had paid a visit to the corner shop while they'd been out. When she turned around, she was startled to see Carly staring back at her, daring her to say something. Not wanting to start an argument, Jane just grabbed the milk and closed the fridge door and Carly returned to her perusal of the letters with a satisfied look.

When Carly appeared to be absorbed in her work, Jane, Eddie and Harry left to talk to Ross and Dominic Alexander, Cole's older brothers.

As soon as the front door had closed behind them, Carly sighed and tossed the letter she was holding onto the coffee table. She'd wanted something to occupy her time but the sheer volume of letters was overwhelming.

She glanced at the fridge, the urge for a glass of wine rising inside her. Maybe her family was right and she did have a problem? But the thought of coping without alcohol was daunting. It was the only thing that could get her through each day. But her drinking was also hurting the people she loved. No, she must resist.

Carly's gaze flicked back to the box sitting on the coffee table.

Her family needed her help and it wasn't like she had anything else to do.

'Stop being useless,' she told herself. 'You wanted something to do and you've got it.'

With a sigh, she picked up a handful of letters. The first one she came to was to the mysterious Willy Brown from someone called Dexy Mathers.

'What a stupid name,' she muttered.

She couldn't see why this letter had been kept as all Dexy did was witter on about going to some dodgy disco and brag about how many women he'd got off with, which was clearly an exaggeration. Unless Dexy was married at the time? That was the only reason Carly could come up with for why Willy would keep this letter.

She scanned a few more letters, all of which were equally uninteresting. There was no mention of any crimes because no one was stupid enough to write them down. Some were postcards of holidays ranging from the Norfolk Broads to Spain and Greece. She was starting to wonder if Willy had been having her family on. That was until she came to a letter that mentioned the Alexander family, the name leaping off the page at her. It was dated 1994 from Cole's grandfather, Ted. It spoke about Oscar Alexander, who she knew had been Jack's father. Ted was telling Willy about Oscar getting sent to prison for being a paedophile. Jack would have been about five years old at the time.

Frantically, Carly shuffled through the rest of the letters, looking for the same spidery handwriting belonging to Ted. She found a whole sheaf of letters and she hastily scanned through them. The majority were just more irrelevant boasts about Ted's sexual conquests, despite being married to Jessica's mother. Finally she found another letter that mentioned Oscar and Jack. It was dated ten years later when Jack would have been fifteen.

Oscar was being released from prison and was joining his wife and son in Yorkshire where they'd moved after he'd got sent down to escape the scandal. It boggled Carly's mind that Jack's mother would allow Oscar anywhere near her son after he'd been done for assaulting young boys. Her hands shook when she read how it was suspected Oscar had abused Jack too. Ted wrote that the boy was tough and fiery but he turned quiet and insular around his father. He was worried about his grandson and had told his daughter and Jack's mother, Sadie, that the boy could stay with him in Glasgow but she'd turned him down, saying she wanted them to be one happy family again in Castleford. Ted was worried about Jack's safety with Oscar in the house.

When the letter ended with no further information, Carly tossed it aside and hastily looked for the next. There was just one more that mentioned Jack. Ted had paid a visit to Yorkshire three months after Oscar had been released. He said the paedo bastard was even fatter and more repulsive than ever. He didn't know what Sadie saw in him, especially as she was so pretty. Jack was once again the quiet, reserved boy he'd been before Oscar had been sent down. Worried about him, Ted had taken Jack aside and had been furious to see bruises on the boy's wrists, as though he'd been restrained. He'd given Oscar a good kicking and pushed Sadie up against the wall by the throat. It hadn't mattered that she was his daughter; she was failing her son. Ted told them both that if either of them laid a finger on Jack again he'd put them both in the ground personally. He wanted to hear from Jack every week and he'd pay them a visit every month to make sure the boy was safe, and if he suspected otherwise then they were both dead. He had asked Jack to come back to Glasgow with him, but the boy was so afraid of his father he'd refused. Ted said both Oscar and Sadie were so scared of the warning they'd been given he anticipated Jack would be safe from now on, but he would always worry for the boy. The very last sentence caused Carly to gasp with shock.

The letter fluttered from her hand as tears filled her eyes. Jack had told her about his father being a paedophile. He'd hated him with a passion and had been glad when he'd died of natural causes. He'd hinted to her that his father had been violent to him but he'd never mentioned the abuse had been sexual.

Carly stared down at the letter, that horrible last sentence standing out in stark relief, a cruel taunt.

I think Jack was his father's first victim.

Desperately, she sifted through the remaining letters, casting aside the ones that weren't covered in that now-familiar spidery scrawl, but the remaining letters just said Oscar was behaving himself. The last mention of Jack was the day of Oscar's funeral. Ted had gone to make sure the bastard was really dead, and to the prison to visit Jack, who hadn't bothered to ask the governor for permission to attend the service. He'd just been glad his father was gone.

By the time she'd finished, the living-room floor was littered with discarded letters.

Carly bit her lower lip as she tried to fight the impulse to drink, fresh tears spilling down her face.

'Fuck it,' she muttered before stomping over to the fridge and flinging open the door.

She removed a bottle of wine, opened it and poured herself a glass, which she downed in a few gulps. The rising frenzy inside her was dampened by the alcohol but the pain at what that little boy had suffered overwhelmed her. She refilled the glass and drank that down too before taking the bottle back to the couch where she swigged directly from it, tears continuing to stream down her face unchecked.

'Why didn't you tell me, babe?' she rasped.

She already knew why – because he couldn't bear to. Like all victims, he'd partly blamed himself, been overwhelmed with shame, but he'd done nothing wrong. The full weight of responsibility lay on the shoulders of his bastard of a father. If she ever found herself in Yorkshire, she'd piss all over Oscar Alexander's grave.

* * *

The first thing Rose smelled on entering the flat was alcohol, even stronger than usual.

'Oh no,' she said, rushing into the kitchen.

She came to a halt in the doorway at the sight of Carly sprawled on the couch, an empty wine bottle in her hand. The reason the smell was stronger was because she appeared to have fallen asleep before finishing it and some of the contents had spilled onto her, staining her pyjamas.

'Carly,' Rose sobbed, a tear sliding down her face.

Dozens of papers were strewn across the floor. Rose picked up the one that lay closest to Carly, the paper covered in a narrow scrawl. As she read the contents, she grew increasingly appalled.

'Bloody hell,' she breathed before tearing her phone from her coat pocket and calling Jane.

7

'For Christ's sake,' sighed Jane. 'Can't you just answer a simple question?'

She stood in the kitchen of the flat Ross and Dominic Alexander shared in Bishopbriggs, becoming increasingly exasperated by the way the brothers evaded every question they were asked.

'What do you want to know?' said Ross smugly.

'You know already,' she yelled. 'Don't make me fucking repeat it.'

'Something about our granda', wasn't it? I don't quite remember. Do you, Dom?' he smirked, turning to his brother.

Dominic, who recalled the torture he'd endured at the hands of Jane and her girlfriend, Jennifer, wasn't being so arrogant. 'Maybe we should tell them...'

'No' without something in return,' Ross snarled back. He looked at Eddie. 'Me and Dom need to fund our new life in Dundee. We'll tell you what you want, for a price.'

'How much?' he sighed.

'Three grand.'

'Piss off,' retorted Harry. 'We're paying you nothing. All this trouble is down to your prick of a brother.'

'No' just him,' replied Ross, green eyes hard and cold. 'If I remember correctly, your brother was the one who ripped Jack's insides out.'

'Fuck this,' growled Harry. 'It's time to do things my way.'

He'd bounced Ross's forehead off the kitchen table before the other man could even react. Ross's eyes widened and he attempted to speak before collapsing forward, spark out.

Dominic jumped when Harry pointed a digit at him.

'Start fucking talking before Jane fries your pubes off again.'

'All right,' he said, holding up his hands. 'I'll tell you what you want to know. Granda' was way more successful than any of us and he made a big amount of cash. I think Cole went to Willy because Granda' stashed a lot of his earnings, and I don't mean in a bank. He hid it somewhere. Back in the mid-nineties it totalled about half a million.'

'And Cole definitely knows about this money?' Harry asked Dominic.

'Aye. Maw and Da' talked about it for years. They tried to find it but never could. If you ask me, that's what he's after now.'

'Word is he's trying to build an army to take down Toni McVay,' said Eddie.

'It wouldnae surprise me. My wee brother's turned into a monster,' he said sadly.

'Have you seen him since Jack's death?'

'Naw, he wouldnae come near us. Toni's people have been hanging around hoping he'll show up. If you think Ross is ambitious and greedy that's nothing compared to Cole. Ross has the good sense to know when he's beaten. It's why we're moving to Dundee. Unfortunately, Cole thinks he's smarter than everyone else.'

'Smarter even than Toni herself?'

'Aye.'

'Then he's an idiot.'

'Probably.'

'And you really havenae seen him?'

'No.'

'Have you spoken to him?'

'He called us a couple of weeks after Jack died asking if we knew where Granda' had stashed his money. Of course we'd no idea.'

'I suppose if you knew, Ross would be in the Bahamas by now.'

'Exactly, and he would have ditched me as well.'

'Who else might know where the money is?'

'Nae idea. I didnae really know Granda'. I found him a bit scary, to be honest. He was a big, violent bastard. Even Ross was wary of him.'

'Did Cole get on with him?'

'He didnae really know him either. We all tried to stay out of his way.'

'What about your maw? Would she know anything?'

'If she does, she's never told us.'

'And like Ross, she'd have ditched you all and gone abroad if she'd found the money.'

'Exactly, although she's changed lately. She's no' cold and ruthless like she used to be. She wants to build bridges with us again.'

'And are you?'

'God, no. We're moving to Dundee and we never want to see her again. She told us everything. She said she was in on Cole's plan to take over from Jack but she didnae know about Dean. She'd no idea they'd teamed up.'

'Did she know they were gonnae kill Jack?' demanded Jane.

'Aye. Cole knew he had to get rid of him permanently if he was gonnae take over.'

'The stupid bastards,' Jane yelled, slamming her fist down on the table. 'Jack wanted out, he wanted to leave with Carly. There was no need to kill him.'

Jane shot to her feet and turned her back on them all, thinking how her sister would still be happy and whole if Cole hadn't been such a greedy bastard and Dean an obsessive loon.

'Does Jessica know what Cole will do now?' said Eddie.

'No,' replied Dominic. 'She's no' seen him since the night Jack died.'

Jane's phone rang. 'Rose, now's no' a good time... Oh, God, really? We're on our way. Stay with her.' She hung up and looked to her uncle and cousin. 'We've got to get back to Haghill. It's Carly.'

Unwilling to say any more in front of Dominic, the three of them hurried outside.

'What's wrong with Carly?' said Harry as they rushed to the car.

'Rose found her spark out on the couch after downing a bottle of wine.'

'Christ, no' again,' said Eddie.

'It's not just that. Rose said she was surrounded by a load of old letters and one of them mentioned something that happened to Jack when he was younger.'

'What?' replied Harry.

'I don't know, Rose didnae want to say over the phone.'

Ten minutes later they were pulling up outside the flat and they burst inside, rushing straight through to the kitchen where Rose anxiously paced, Carly still out cold. Rose had taken the bottle from her hand and attempted to clean up the spilt wine, but the smell of alcohol still hung heavy in the air.

'Thank God you're here,' breathed Rose. 'I don't know what to do.'

'You kept an eye on her,' replied Jane. 'Which is the only thing you can do. Has she woken up?'

'No. She's sparko. This was the letter,' Rose added, holding it out to her sister.

Jane took it from her and read it, her eyes widening. 'Jesus, we should not have given her that box.'

'Why not?' said Eddie. 'What's wrong?'

'This letter is from Ted to Willy. You remember how Jack's da' Oscar was a convicted paedo?'

Eddie and Harry nodded.

'Ted reckoned Jack was his first victim.'

'Oh my God,' groaned Eddie, dragging his hands down his face. 'That's the last thing that lassie needed to find out.'

'No wonder she felt the need to drink herself into oblivion. That news on top of everything else she's dealing with must have been too much.'

'Carly said Cole wanted us to get hold of those letters,' said Harry. 'Is that why, so he could torture her some more? Hasn't the bastard done enough to her?'

Carly jumped awake at the sound of his voice and regarded them all with bleary, bloodshot eyes.

'Stick the kettle on, Rose,' said Jane. 'Make her a strong coffee.'

Rose, glad to be given something to do, nodded and rushed to obey.

'Are you okay?' Jane asked her sister gently, taking a seat beside her as she pulled herself up to a sitting position.

'My heid,' Carly groaned. Her eyes widened. 'I'm gonnae throw up.'

She shot up off the couch and raced into the bathroom with Jane following.

There was a small sob and Eddie saw Rose had her back turned to them, her shoulders shaking.

'Oh, hen,' he said gently.

He went to her and wrapped his arms around her. Rose buried her face in his big chest to stifle the sound of her tears, not wanting Carly to hear.

'It's okay, she'll get through this,' he told her, hugging her tightly.

'I'm so scared she won't, that it's too much for her,' she rasped.

'Nothing is too much for a Savage, okay? Things look bleak now, but she will get through all this and one day everything will be easier.'

'What if she becomes an alcoholic? What if it only gets worse?'

'It won't, I swear to God,' he said, hoping he could keep that particular promise. 'Carly's one of the strongest people I've ever met. She will beat this.'

'I don't feel like I'm doing enough to help her.' Rose looked up at him with her big soft eyes. 'What else can I do?'

'Nothing, hen. You're doing all you can. Just keep loving her. Now dry those tears and make that coffee. Carly's gonnae need it.'

She wiped her eyes on the backs of her hands and nodded determinedly. 'Yes, Uncle Eddie.'

'Good girl.'

Carly returned to the room a few minutes later with Jane and she slowly sank onto the couch, looking pale and unwell. Rose handed her a mug of strong coffee and she accepted it but made no move to drink it.

'Better?' Eddie asked her.

'No' really,' she mumbled.

'We've seen the letter,' he told her, deciding dancing around the issue wouldn't help. 'We're so sorry, if we'd known that was in there...'

'At least we know now what Cole was up to,' she replied.

'He thinks you're a threat to him. He's trying to break you, doll. Do not gi'e the bastard the satisfaction.'

'It's more than that,' said Harry. 'It's revenge. Willy told us Cole's face is fucked up really badly. He couldnae go to hospital for treatment, so some dodgy doctor patched him up and now he looks like Frankenstein's monster. These letters are payback.'

'You're probably right, son. Cole's a diabolical wee cunt.'

'I'm gonnae kill him,' said Carly.

She spoke softly but with such purpose they all turned to look at her.

'No, you won't, hen,' said Eddie gently. Eddie noted his niece's hazy eyes and slightly slurred speech. Carly was still pissed but he wasn't sure her words were just down to the drink alone.

'Yes, I will,' she replied with that same steady resolution. 'I cannae get hold of Dean so he's the next best thing.'

'You loved him once.'

'That was ages ago and he was a different person back then. Like you said, he's a monster now. He needs putting down and I'm the one to do it.'

'Nae offence,' said Harry, 'but what makes you think you'll get to him before Toni's people?'

'Maybe I won't but if I see him, he's fucking deid.'

'Don't talk like this,' Jane told her, covering her hand with her own and nodding in Rose's direction.

'Oh, sorry,' Carly told her younger sister. 'Don't mind me, I'm just mouthing off.'

'No need to apologise,' she replied. 'I hope you do kill him.'

'Rose, don't talk like that,' said Jane.

'Why not? We all want him gone. What's the point in pretending?'

'But we don't want Carly to be the one to do it.'

'This sort of talk is getting us nowhere,' said Eddie. 'We need to speak to Jessica Alexander.'

'I'm coming with you,' announced Carly.

'No, you're no'.'

'Why not?' she demanded.

'Because you're in your pyjamas, you stink of booze and you're pished. We can handle it.'

'But—'

'I said no,' he retorted, deciding a firm hand was in order.

'Fine,' she muttered, folding her arms across her chest.

'Sorry, hen, but that's just the way it is. Rose, stay with her.'

'Rose has to get back to college,' Carly told him.

'Err, it's Saturday,' mumbled her younger sister.

'Is it?' said Carly, looking startled by that fact.

'Aye,' said Rose, embarrassed for her.

'Oh. Well, it's easy to lose track of time when you're no' working.'

'You only lost your job two days ago,' replied Eddie. 'No more drink, okay? It's addling your brain.'

'If you had stuck in your heid what's stuck in mine then you'd want your brain to be addled too,' she yelled back.

'What you don't realise is that the alcohol makes it all worse, no' better. I'm no' getting into a row about it now,' he continued when it looked like she was going to continue arguing. 'We have to get to Jessica before her sons can warn her. I'll let you know how we get on.'

Rose was a little alarmed by the way Carly glared at their uncle's retreating back. It was as though she was contemplating inflicting bloody violence on him.

'So, what now?' said Rose with forced cheer. 'Do you want to watch a film?'

'I need to get out of these pyjamas,' muttered Carly. 'They stink. I'll take a shower.'

'I don't think that's a good idea,' Rose replied, noting the way Carly swayed as she stood up. 'How about I run you a nice hot bath instead? I'll wash your jammies too.'

'Aye, all right. Thanks, Rose.'

'You're welcome. I just want to help you.'

Carly's expression turned gentle and she patted her sister's hand. 'You already do, sweetheart, more than you know.'

8

To Rose's surprise, Carly didn't spend long in the bath. Twenty minutes later she was out again and getting dressed. She entered the kitchen looking a lot more alert and purposeful, although the haziness of her eyes said she was still a little drunk. Thank God she hadn't downed the entire bottle of wine and had spilled quite a bit of it instead.

'I'm off out,' Carly announced.

'But I was about to make us some dinner,' replied Rose. 'Where are you going?'

'Jessica bloody Alexander's.'

'Why would you want to visit that nasty old bitch?'

'I want to ask her about what Jack's da' did. I have to know for sure if Oscar abused Jack.'

'Why? It'll only cause you more pain.'

'I won't be able to relax until I know for sure. It was all supposition on Ted's part in those letters.'

'Leave it until another time when you're feeling stronger. Besides, Jane and the others are there.'

'Then I'll wait outside until they're gone. Now, I'm going, so you can either stay here or you can come with me.'

'I'll come,' said Rose.

Carly smiled at the way her sister's eyes lit up with the excitement of an adventure. 'Nice one. We'll have to walk because I'm way over the limit to drive.'

'That's fine, it's no' far.'

They pulled on their shoes and coats and stepped out into the dreich weather.

'So how are you going to handle it?' Rose asked Carly as they strode down the street together.

'I'll ask Jessica nicely,' replied Carly. 'And if she doesnae tell me what I want to know, then I'll hit her until she does.'

Despite how terrible she felt inside, physically as well as emotionally, Carly smiled and in turn that smile delighted Rose. Her older sister had a mission again and some of her old self had returned.

They waited around the corner at the bottom of the street until Eddie's car had passed them by. After they'd gone, Carly rang Jessica's doorbell politely but no one answered.

'There she is,' said Rose when she spotted Jessica peering out of the window to the left of the door.

Realising she'd been spotted, Jessica's eyes widened and she let the curtain fall back.

'I bet she's going to run,' said Rose.

Carly tried the door and it opened so she stormed inside, followed by Rose. They encountered Jessica in the hallway.

'Carly, I've just spoken to your family,' said Jessica, holding up her hands and retreating. She grimaced when she backed up against the wall.

'Aye, well, I've got some different questions. Just one, actually. I want to know about Jack's da', Oscar. Did he abuse Jack?'

Clearly, Carly's family hadn't broached the subject with

Jessica on their visit because she appeared astonished by the query. 'Why do you want to know?'

'Just answer the fucking question.'

'I don't really know very much, my da' never talked to me about it.'

'But I bet you overheard something.'

'All right, I did hear my parents discussing it once after my da' got back from Yorkshire.'

'I knew it. You probably had your ear pressed to the door. Well, what did you hear?'

'I'm willing to tell you but it won't make you feel any better. No good comes from dredging up the past.'

'Spit it out, unless you want your face smashing in.'

'Fine, have it your own way but don't say I didn't warn you. Do you want to sit down?' Jessica said, gesturing to the living room.

'No, this isnae a social call. Get the fuck on with it.'

'My da' said he spoke to Jack. He was only about fourteen or fifteen at the time. Jack, I mean. No' my da'.'

'Stop stalling,' hissed Carly.

'Jack said Oscar would sneak into his room and touch him. The first time it happened he was four years old.'

Carly's face crumpled and she turned so the Alexander matriarch wouldn't see her pain. She took a deep breath to ensure her voice was steady before saying, 'Keep talking.'

'Jack wouldn't give him any more details than that. He was scared and ashamed. It only stopped when Jack got bigger and stronger. That's all I know, I swear.'

'So there's no doubt it happened then?' rasped Carly.

'No doubt. I'm sorry.'

'No, you're no'.'

'I am. I know you don't believe me, but I really have changed.

You can come and talk to me any time about Jack, if you like. I have lots of stories.'

Carly whipped round to face her, shaking with indignation. 'As if I'd let you tarnish his memory with your viciousness. He meant nothing to you, he told me often enough. You couldn't even be arsed to go to his funeral.'

'I didn't go because I knew you wouldn't want me there. I didn't want to make that day even harder for you.'

'Oh, aye, because you're a regular saint, aren't you? I don't buy this new you for a moment. It's just another of your sneaky tricks.'

'It's no trick,' replied Jessica without a flicker of her usual arrogance. 'I've lost everything – my husband left me, Dominic and Ross are moving to Dundee and I don't know if I'll ever see Cole again. The friends I thought I had were only using me for what they could get out of me and they've deserted me too now my family has no power around here any more. I'm struggling for money and for the first time in my life I'm having to work.'

'Aye, I heard. Part time in the corner shop. Big deal.'

'I know I might sound pathetic but it's all new to me and I'm struggling.'

'Like I care. You're finally getting what you deserve after being a narcissistic parasite your entire life. Where's Cole?'

'I really don't know. Your uncle just asked me the same thing.'

'You must have some idea.'

'I don't, I swear.'

'Have you seen him since the night Jack died?'

'Just once. He contacted me and asked me to meet him at the house of an old friend in Greenock. He wanted to say goodbye because he had to leave the country to avoid Toni McVay.'

'I didn't think he was the sentimental type.'

'He's not, at least, no' any more. He was when he was a wee boy,' she said sadly.

Jessica squealed when Carly shoved her back against the wall by her neck.

'Until the day you grassed him up to the polis and got him thrown into Barlinnie,' yelled Carly. 'That was what changed him. I might have given him the scars but you'd already turned him into a monster.'

'I know and I'm suffering for it now.'

'And so you should because everything that's happened started with that moment. Even Jack's death.'

'No, don't, please,' cried Jessica, eyes widening when Carly's hand formed into a fist.

'You know what, you're too pathetic even to hit. I don't know why you insist on hanging around Haghill. No one wants you.'

Carly released her and Jessica put a shaky hand to her throat.

'Because I want to make things right,' said the older woman. 'There was a time when you really were the daughter I never had, before I realised how much Cole loved you. I became spiteful and jealous because I was afraid of you taking my baby from me. He was the only one of my sons who still loved me.'

'And you voluntarily destroyed that love. God, you're a fucking idiot.'

'Wait, don't go,' called Jessica when Carly headed to the door, Rose following. 'We should talk some more.'

'I've got better things to do with my time. Get out of Haghill, Jess. Staying won't be good for your health.'

With that the sisters departed, leaving Jessica with tears rolling down her face.

'Is that it?' Rose asked Carly, having to rush to keep up as her sister stormed along the pavement.

'I got what I wanted,' she replied. 'Why, what you were expecting?'

'I thought you'd give the silly cow a good slap for a start.'

'I wouldn't waste my time.'

'Do you believe she's a changed woman?'

'Not for a second. She's a manipulative bitch just trying to get some sympathy.'

'So what are we doing now?'

'I don't know about you but I'm going to the cemetery.'

'But it's really cold and it looks like it could start raining,' said Rose, looking up at the threatening sky, heavy grey clouds rolling in.

'I don't care, I have to go. Why didn't he tell me about what his da' did?'

'I'm sure he meant to, he just didn't get the chance, and he was a tough man. It would have been so difficult for him to talk about it. I bet he didn't even know how to start that conversation.'

'Probably. Christ, it breaks my heart,' Carly said, blinking away tears.

'Carly,' called a voice. 'Wait.'

The sisters stopped and turned. Four of The Unbeatable Bitches, members of Jane's girl gang, were hurrying up to them.

'What's wrong?' Carly asked them.

'We've had word someone's smashing up the nail bar,' replied Leonie, one of Jane's lieutenants. 'We're on our way there. We've tried calling Jane but she's no' picking up.'

'Why would anyone smash up a nail bar?' frowned Rose.

'No idea but let's get over there,' said Carly before breaking into a sprint, delighted at the prospect of violence.

Rose and The Bitches raced after her. The heavens chose that moment to open, drenching the women in icy rain, but Carly's blood was up and her eagerness for battle infected the other women, the adrenaline pounding through their veins negating the effects of the cold.

As they turned onto the street the nail bar was on, they were greeted by the sounds of smashing glass and yelling. Carly didn't stop to assess the situation as she knew she should, she just raced up to the three men who'd just thrown a wheelie bin through the shop window.

'Look at this lot,' laughed one of the men, pointing at the advancing women. 'Come on then, sweetheart,' he told Carly, who was at the head of the pack. 'If you think you're hard enough.'

'Oh, she is that,' said one of the old ladies standing across the street, watching the scene. 'You're in for a shock, ya tadger.'

'Shut it, ya mad auld bat,' he told her. He looked back at Carly, fully expecting some sort of parley before violence ensued.

She snatched up an aerosol that had fallen out of the wheelie bin and threw it at his head. However, her aim was off and it completely missed the three men and landed with a harmless clank in the middle of the road.

Rose was shocked to realise that Carly was in fact still drunk. She'd seemed stone-cold sober when tackling Jessica and it had been easy to forget that only recently she'd downed almost a full bottle of wine.

'Look at her, she's pissed,' laughed the man, his friends joining in, braying like donkeys.

This only inflamed Carly's temper more and she charged at them. Her aim with her fist was true and she punched the lead man in the face, sending him stumbling backwards.

'Don't laugh at my sister,' yelled Rose before springing onto the man, knocking him onto his back and twisting his crotch. 'That's right, baby,' she said with relish when he shrieked. 'Scream for me.'

Leonie and the other three Bitches made short work of the remaining two men.

'All right, Rose, that's enough,' Carly told her. 'He needs to answer a few questions.'

'Fine,' her sister sighed before getting to her feet.

'Why did you throw a wheelie bin through that window?' Carly asked Rose's victim.

When he failed to reply, having curled up into a ball, fighting back tears of pain, Carly kicked him in the ribs.

'Answer the fucking question,' she yelled. 'Or my sister will rip your tiny meat and two veg right off.'

'We... we were paid to,' he said, shaking with agony.

'By who?'

'I don't know.'

'I bet Owen Auchter's a friend of yours, isn't he? Didn't his broken elbow teach you a lesson, you fucking idiot?'

She kicked him again, eliciting another yelp. There was so much anger inside Carly that was bursting to escape and violence was a good way to exorcise some of it. She looked to the other two men, thinking it would be easier for them to talk as they weren't in intense pain. The Bitches stood aside as she stormed up to the men.

'Who paid you to do this?' Carly demanded of them. 'Start talking before you end up with twisted baws like your wee pal over there.'

'Cole Alexander,' one of them hastily replied.

'Don't tell them anything, ya fanny,' his friend told him.

'Shut that prick up,' Carly told The Bitches.

The man was kicked and punched until he went quiet. Carly turned her attention back to the man who'd given her Cole's name. 'Where is he?'

'Dunno,' he replied. 'He wouldnae tell us that.'

'You must have met up with him somewhere?'

'Aye, we did, at my pal Freddy Cunningham's house in Cranhill.'

'Do you know Cole personally?'

'Naw, just through Freddy.'

'I want Freddy's address.'

He reeled off an address in a resigned voice, realising resistance was useless.

'How does Freddy know Cole?' said Carly.

'They've been pals for years.'

'Why is Cole doing this?'

'Don't know. He's keeping his plan close to his chest.'

'How much did he pay you?'

'Five hundred quid each.'

'Keep an eye on them while I try and get hold of my uncle,' Carly told The Bitches.

Eddie answered after just a couple of rings. She told him to get his arse round to the nail bar ASAP.

Ten minutes later, Eddie arrived with his friend, Peanut, a huge black man with cauliflower ears from his time as a feared boxer. Peanut was named after his allergy, his only weakness.

'What have you lassies been up to now?' said Peanut, accompanying this statement with one of his big grins.

'These numpties put a wheelie bin through the nail bar's window on Cole's say-so,' replied Carly.

'Why does Cole want to smash up a nail bar?' replied Peanut. 'Did he no' like the manicure they gave him?'

The Bitches and Rose tittered. They all found Peanut charming and he was disappointed when Carly didn't laugh. He missed the sound.

'He's attacking local businesses to make us look bad,' replied Carly. 'He paid these pricks five hundred quid each.'

'Where's he getting the cash from?' said Rose.

'We'll discuss that later,' replied her uncle.

'Do you want to ask them any questions?' said Carly, gesturing to the men.

'Naw, I reckon you've got anything useful out of them. Ladies, you may deal with them in your usual inimitable way,' Eddie told The Bitches.

'Can I help them?' Rose eagerly asked.

'Knock yourself out, doll.'

'Yes,' she exclaimed before assisting Leonie and the others to strip the protesting men naked.

'I love this bit,' grinned Peanut as he watched the women slap and kick the yelping men down the street, the bystanders cheering them on.

'You okay, hen?' Eddie asked Carly.

'Fine. I went to speak to Jessica,' she quietly told him. 'She confirmed what it said in those letters about Jack and his da'.'

'Christ, I'm sorry,' he said, patting her shoulder.

'I wish Jack had told me. It must have been so difficult carrying around a secret like that.'

'Aye. I'm sure he would have told you, given more time. It would have been hard for a man of his reputation admitting he was a victim.'

'That's what Rose said.'

'That lassie is wise beyond her years. Let's go to Elijah with what we've found out about Cole.'

'You're taking me with you?'

'Aye. You've earned that right.'

'Thanks.'

'Nae bother, doll,' he replied, delighted to see some of the old Carly was back.

'Where are Jane and Harry?'

'On another job.'

'That explains why Leonie couldnae get hold of Jane. What did Jessica tell you about Cole?'

'That she's seen him once and she's no idea what he's up to. We asked her about that money her da' hid and she said she's heard about it but she's nae idea where it is.'

'That must be true. If the greedy cow did know she would have taken it and jetted off abroad by now.'

The Bitches and Rose decided to go for a drink at the pub to celebrate their victory, leaving Carly, Eddie and Peanut free to go to the office behind the café where Elijah and David awaited them. Eddie and Carly related what they'd learnt.

'I don't know why the stupid bastard's still in Glasgow,' said David. 'It's only a matter of time before Toni gets hold of him and gouges out his eyes.'

'The sooner that happens the better if you ask me,' said Elijah. 'I don't like it. The slippery git's up to something. We need to find out what and quickly. Carly, doll, I reckon you could be at the centre of his plan. I want you in on this.'

'Yes,' she smiled.

'I doesnae mean you're back working for us full time but we will pay you for your trouble.'

'I won't let you down,' she said seriously.

'You do realise you're gonnae be the bait?'

'I do and I'm fine with it.'

'Good.'

'I know Freddy Cunningham,' said David. 'I'll come with you to talk to him, he might open up more with me there.'

9

David drove Carly, Eddie and Peanut in his silver BMW into Cranhill. Freddy's home was a tiny modern semi-detached with off-street parking. A dinky Citroën sat on the drive.

'Freddy lives with his girlfriend,' explained David as they pulled up outside. 'She's a proper fucking banshee. I hope she's no' in because she'll give us more trouble than Freddy himself.'

They got out of the car and walked up to the door, which opened before they could even knock.

'David,' said the tall, nervous man with spiky dark hair. 'I had the feeling you'd come calling.'

'I bet you did,' David said, striding inside without waiting to be invited, Carly, Peanut and Eddie following. The front door led directly into the small lounge.

'Do you want a brew?' Freddy asked them. 'I've got some snowballs in too.'

'No thanks, this isnae a social call. Is anyone else here?'

'Naw, Monica's at work.'

'Good. Why the hell are you working with Cole Alexander?'

'He didnae gi'e me any choice. He's a fucking loon and said

he'd burn down my hoose if I didnae help him. I only gave him the names of a few pals who would be willing to cause a bit of mayhem for a few quid. I swear to God that's all I did.'

'How do you know him?'

'I used to do some business with his brother, Ross, but I've no' seen him in months. Cole wanted someone outside Haghill to help him.'

'Help him do what exactly? What's his end game?'

'Something to do with some bird called Carly who fucked up his face.'

'That's me,' said Carly.

'Oh, right. Well, you really did a number on him, doll. He won't need a Halloween mask this year. He looks like Freddy Krueger had a go at him.'

'Serves him fucking right,' she glowered. 'He's stupid if he's risking Toni McVay getting hold of him just to get back at me.'

'I don't think it's just that. He wants to take over around here.'

'And he thinks he can do that by paying idiots to throw wheelie bins through nail bars' windows? Well, your pals have been battered, stripped naked and thrown out of Haghill. I hope their poxy five hundred quid is enough compensation for that.'

'They have, have they?' smiled Freddy, looking amused at what had happened to his unfortunate friends.

'We need to find Cole asap,' David told Freddy.

'I wish I could help but no way would he share that information with me.'

'You're lying,' Carly told him.

'No, I'm no'. Honest,' he said, addressing this comment to David.

'You suspect where he is though,' replied Carly.

'I really don't know anything.'

Carly snatched up a vase sitting on the windowsill, tipped the water and flowers onto the floor and smashed it against the wall, pointing at him with the jagged end.

'Oh, Christ, that's Monica's lead crystal vase,' he exclaimed. 'It belonged to her gran. She's gonnae go mental.'

'That's your problem and if you don't want to end up looking like one of Freddy Krueger's victims too, then you'll tell us what you know right now.'

'All right, all right,' Freddy cried, holding up his hands. 'Cole did mention the doctor who patched him up lived near Stobhill Hospital in Springburn. He said it was lucky as it meant he didnae have far to go to get back to the safe house.'

'You're saying he's hiding out in Springburn?'

'I'm saying it's a possibility. This was a few weeks ago, so even if he was staying in that area, he might no' be now. If he's any sense, he'll keep moving around.'

'It's worth a try,' said David. 'Let's go.'

Carly let the piece of vase she held drop, which shattered when it hit the floor, and they all left.

'Nice one, Carly,' said David. 'You got him to open up.'

'He might no' have done if he hadn't already seen what I did to Cole.'

'I've got a contact in Springburn we can visit,' said David.

'No,' replied Carly.

'Excuse me?' he frowned.

'Cole isnae there, he's in Haghill.'

'How do you know?'

'I just do. We're here and Jane and Harry are working. Who's keeping an eye on the scheme?'

'The Bitches are there,' replied Peanut.

'Some of them are, the rest are at work. Cole sent those three idiots to send us out of Haghill on a wild goose chase. They were just a distraction.'

'Or he could be hiding out in Springburn,' said David.

'We can look there but I bet it's a waste of time.'

'What do you think?' David asked Eddie.

'Out of us all, Carly knows Cole the best,' he replied.

'All right, we'll head to Haghill.'

David drove them back and they parked outside The Horseshoe Bar. Carly rushed inside, the others following, to find Rose safe and rather merry, sitting with Leonie and the other three Bitches.

'Has everything been okay since we left?' Carly asked her sister.

'Aye, fine.'

'I hope you've no' had many of those?' demanded Carly, pointing to the vodka and Coke in Rose's glass.

Rose thought her sister was being an enormous hypocrite but decided not to comment. 'It's my first one and there's only a wee bit of vodka in it. Besides, I'm eighteen now, so I can drink if I want.'

'No' when we're expecting more trouble.'

'Really?' Rose said with delight, leaping to her feet, finding violence more intoxicating than alcohol. 'Where?'

'We don't know yet but we have to keep an eye out.' Carly looked to the four Bitches. 'Look around the scheme, let us know if there's any trouble. See if you can get hold of any more of The Bitches and get them to help.'

'Yes, Carly,' replied Leonie. Even though Carly wasn't one of The Bitches, her authority was such they felt they had no choice but to obey.

The four of them got up and headed to the door.

'No' you,' Carly told Rose when she moved to follow.

'Why not?' she replied. 'I can help.'

'I want you where I can keep an eye on you.'

Rose pouted and folded her arms across her chest.

Carly turned to the three men. 'What now?'

Eddie smiled. 'I was gonnae ask you that. You've done well so far.'

'You know how Cole thinks,' David told her. 'Where would he hide?'

'I don't know why you keep saying that,' she replied. 'I've no idea how he thinks.'

'Your gut must be telling you something.'

Carly sighed as she pondered this question. What David didn't realise was that thinking was an enormous effort for her in her present state. It was like wading through treacle and it sapped what little strength she had. Still, this was her chance to get rid of one of the bastards who'd killed Jack. Cole might not have wielded the knife but he was the puppet master who'd brought about the entire situation. He'd spotted Dean's weakness and used it as a weapon and he would pay for his manipulation.

'He'll be somewhere connected to our family, so he can feel superior.'

'The flat?' said Rose.

'No, too obvious. It'll be somewhere important to us, somewhere that means a lot.'

'What is it?' said Rose anxiously when Carly gasped.

'The graveyard,' she replied before charging out of the pub.

They all piled into David's BMW and he gunned the engine before setting off at speed. A couple of minutes later they were pulling up outside the cemetery, Carly flinging open the door before the car had even stopped properly.

'Carly, wait,' called Eddie, throwing off his seatbelt.

Rose was the fastest, racing after her sister on the wet ground. Her foot skidded on some damp grass and she went down, twisting her ankle.

'Bollocks,' she yelled with annoyance. 'Don't bother about me, go after Carly,' she told David, who was right behind her.

He nodded and sprinted into the graveyard.

'Peanut, wait with Rose,' said Eddie, who puffed and panted after them.

Carly passed her parents' graves first but saw they were just as they'd been the last time she'd been here. She hurried past them to Jack's, immediately noticing something was wrong.

'No,' she breathed, coming to a startled halt before the grave.

The marble headstone had been smashed to pieces, the surface of the grave torn up, as though someone had attacked it with a spade, the roses she'd placed there ripped to pieces, the red petals looking like a stream of blood across the grave. Memories of the blood pouring from Jack's stomach hit Carly with such force she sank to her knees, a keening wail emanating from the back of her throat.

'Oh, Christ, I'll kill the bastard,' yelled Eddie. He knelt by his niece's side and wrapped an arm around her. 'It's okay, hen. We'll fix it.'

'Why did he do this?' she cried. 'Jack's dead. Isn't that enough for him?'

'What's this?' said David, pulling a clear plastic bag free of the shard of marble that still stuck out of the ground. The bag had been attached to it with tape. He opened it and pulled out a folded piece of paper. 'It's addressed to you, Carly.'

She wiped away her tears and held out her hand for it. David passed it to her and she unfolded the letter.

'It's Cole's writing,' she told them. 'He says he's leaving the country but one day he will come back and when he does, he'll take everything from us just as we took it from him.'

'Why bother sending people to throw wheelie bins through windows?' said Eddie. 'And why vandalise Jack's grave?'

'He did the first one to show us that there are people still willing to defy our family and Toni McVay too, and that working for her doesnae make us invulnerable. He did this to Jack's grave to hurt me. He says he's no' finished with me. One day I will have to pay in blood for what I did to his face.'

'The petty wee shite's gonnae come back and get himself killed,' said David.

'And I'll be the one to do it,' said Carly, dragging herself to her feet and screwing up the paper in her hand.

'No, you won't,' David told her. 'We've got people who can deal with him. Forget about the walloper.'

Carly looked to her uncle. 'I'll forget about Cole if you tell me where Dean's hiding, so I can kill that twat instead.'

'You know I cannae dae that, doll,' he said gently. 'Besides, I don't know where he is now. He went abroad and he never gives me his location.'

'Then how can you be certain he won't come back?'

'He might be a loon but he's no' stupid.'

'You don't get it. Cole's leaving to regather his strength and he might just contact his old partner.'

'Dean won't do that. He knows he cannae win against Toni. He'll never come back to Scotland and he'll make sure no one can ever find him.'

'Then Cole will have to pay the price alone for what happened to Jack.' The sight of her dead lover's disturbed resting place was tearing up Carly's soul even more and the urge for a drink rose inside her, desperate for something to take the edge off the worst of the pain.

'Why don't you go home?' David told her gently. 'We'll sort this out. By the time we're done, you won't even be able to tell it was disturbed. I'll even pay for a new headstone.'

'No, I want to pay for his new stone.'

'Okay, if you like. Take her home, Eddie.' He held out his car keys. 'Then come back for me and we can sort this out.'

'Aye, okay,' Eddie replied, slowly clambering to his feet, grimacing at the pain and cold in his knees before taking David's keys from him. 'Come on, doll. Let's go and sort out Jack's new headstone.'

Carly nodded and got to her feet, taking one last look at the grave before leaving with her uncle. Peanut had assisted Rose to limp back to the car.

'Was Cole there?' Rose asked them.

'No,' replied Eddie. 'He left a note saying he's leaving for a while. The sick sod had vandalised Jack's grave.'

'That's disgusting.'

'I'm taking you two home. Peanut, can you stay with the girls in case Cole hasnae left?'

'Aye, nae bother,' he replied. 'Whatever you need.'

'Thanks, pal.'

Eddie dropped the three of them off at the flat before heading back to the cemetery. Peanut followed the sisters inside. Carly sank onto the couch in the kitchen shivering with cold, shock and rage. Rose wrapped a blanket around her while Peanut switched on the central heating and put the kettle on.

'Carly?' said Rose, sitting beside her. 'Are you okay?'

Carly was in fact in a world of pain, but she forced a smile for her little sister's sake. 'I'm fine,' she said. 'I have to call the undertaker and order Jack another headstone.'

'You need to stop shivering first.'

'Here you go,' said Peanut, handing Carly a mug of tea. 'That'll help.'

'Thanks,' she smiled, taking it from him, wondering if they'd protest if she stuck some brandy in it. Deciding she didn't have the stamina for an argument, she sipped her tea, the warmth making her feel a little better, but it did nothing to ease the ache inside her.

Ten minutes later, Harry and Jane burst into the flat.

'Uncle Eddie called and told us what happened,' said Jane, rushing to her sister's side, Rose giving up her seat for her. 'We're so sorry we weren't here for you.'

'It's no' your fault,' replied Carly. 'You didn't know what was going to happen.'

'Did you see Cole?' demanded Harry.

'No.' Carly produced the note from her pocket and held it out to him. 'He left this at Jack's grave.'

Harry read it out loud for Jane's benefit. 'The dirty bastard,' he growled, scrunching up the paper in his hand. 'How dare he blame you for what happened? It's his own fault his face got fucked up.'

'I bet he doesn't come back,' said Jane. 'He's just trying to scare you, Carly. Don't let him.'

'I'm not scared of Cole,' she replied. 'And I hope he does come back because I'm gonnae kill him.'

'You're no' a killer, Carly.'

'Yes, I am. I felt it when I saw Jack being murdered. I would have killed Dean if you lot hadn't turned up.' She spoke quietly and with purpose, making it impossible for anyone to contradict her.

'Well, I think we've seen the last of Cole Alexander,' said Jane. 'Forget about him.'

'Never. I will get revenge for Jack. He wouldn't have stopped until both Dean and Cole were dead if I'd been the one murdered.'

'Don't talk like that,' said Rose, stifling a shiver.

Carly didn't reply but neither did she try to reassure her sister, sinking back into the couch with her mug of tea.

'If you two are staying here,' Peanut told Jane and Harry, 'I'll head back to the graveyard and see if Eddie and David need a hand.'

'Thank you,' Carly told him sincerely.

'You're welcome, doll,' he replied, patting her shoulder before leaving.

After she'd finished her tea, Carly phoned to order a fresh headstone for Jack. Feeling better once that was done, she wanted to be alone with her thoughts, but her family were reluctant to leave her in case Cole was still about or she turned to the drink again. At five o'clock, Jane had to leave to meet Jennifer, and Rose had arranged to go over to Noah's.

'Don't worry, I'll stay with her,' Harry told the sisters while nodding at Carly, who was sitting on the couch watching another of Jack's favourite action films.

'Thanks, and please don't let her get drunk,' Jane told him.

'I won't.'

The sisters left, anxiously glancing back over their shoulders at Carly, who waved goodbye but didn't speak.

'So,' said Harry when they'd gone. 'I don't know about you, but I fancy a drink.'

Carly turned to him with a frown. 'Jane said no' to let me get drunk.'

'Aye but she didnae say you couldn't have a drink, did she?'

'True,' she replied with a small smile.

Harry wandered over to the fridge. 'Have you only got wine in?'

'Aye.'

'I suppose it'll have to do,' he sighed, taking a bottle out of the fridge. He returned to the couch with the bottle and two glasses. 'So, what are we watching?'

'Some Bruce Willis film,' she replied, attention already back on the screen.

'I think I've seen this one. It's good.'

'Jack was fond of the older films from the eighties and nineties. He said they weren't as smug as modern films.'

'He got that right. Films today are so up their own arses.'

They watched the rest of the film in companionable silence and when it had finished, they started to chat, Harry telling her about his various nightmare dates and being chased by angry boyfriends, pleased when Carly laughed.

'Why is it only you can make me laugh any more?' she said.

'Because I'm a clown. That's what my da' would say if he was here.'

'You're no' a clown, Harry. You're a good man,' she said, patting his hand. 'Right now, you're the only person I can really communicate with.'

'We're pretty similar. We have more in common than you ever did with...' He stopped himself before he said his brother's name. 'That arsehole,' he added instead.

'You're probably right,' she replied, topping up both their glasses with more wine. Already they were on to the second bottle.

'Jane's gonnae kill me,' he said. 'You're starting to look pished.'

'If I'm pished then so are you.'

'No, I'm no',' he retorted. 'Aye, well, maybe a bit,' he relented when she raised an eyebrow. 'I can drink lager all day and be fine but wine goes straight to my heid.'

'Because you're a big lassie,' she chuckled before draining her glass.

'You know, I had a thought.'

She placed her glass on the coffee table and turned to look at him. 'The way you said that sounded like I might no' like your idea.'

'You might not. In fact, I'm risking getting punched just for saying it, but I have to. Since Dean left, I've been dreaming of ways to get some revenge on the prick. Da' refuses to say where he is, so there's only one thing I can think of – doing with you what he never got to do.'

'What the hell are you saying?'

'I know you never slept with Dean. I want what he never got.'

'You're right, I should punch you.'

He shrugged. 'Sorry, I didnae mean to offend you, but you have to admit it would feel like we were getting our own back on him.'

Carly's eyes tick-tocked from side to side before she grabbed Harry's face in both hands and pressed her lips to his. Harry slammed his glass on the table before pulling her to him and kissing her hard. They both went rigid at the same time and released each other with a grimace.

'Urgh, that just felt weird,' said Carly, wiping her lips on the back of her hand.

'You're right,' he replied. 'I mean, you're gorgeous but it felt like I was kissing my sister.'

'That really was like incest,' she shuddered.

'Then I guess we should just stick to being cousins,' he said.

'And friends.'

Harry smiled. 'Good friends.'

Carly smiled back and nodded.

'Well, I don't know about you, pal,' he said, 'but I'm starving. Do you fancy pizza? It's on me.'

10

By the time Eddie and Peanut returned to the flat, Carly and Harry had polished off the pizza, the food absorbing the alcohol and sobering them both up. The empty wine bottles and glasses had been cleared away and they were sipping tea instead, so Eddie assumed neither of them had been drinking, to his infinite relief. Carly certainly looked better than she had earlier, and he had to admit that his son did have a good effect on her.

'Jack's grave is back to normal now,' Eddie told them. 'Apart from the headstone.'

'I've already ordered a new one,' replied Carly.

'Excellent. Anyone who didnae know what had happened wouldnae be able to tell.'

'Thank you, I really appreciate it, especially as it's so cold out there.'

'Nae bother,' he replied, blowing on his hands.

'I'll make you a brew, Da',' said Harry, taking the hint.

'Cheers, son.'

Harry got up to switch on the kettle and Eddie took his place beside his niece.

'How are you holding up, doll?' Eddie asked her.

'No' so bad,' replied Carly. 'I'm over the shock of seeing Jack's grave like that.'

'David told Toni what happened. She was raging and has got her people looking for Cole even harder. She told them to particularly concentrate on known smugglers who'll ferry people in and out of the country for a price but it's possible he's already escaped.'

'He will have. Cole is frighteningly smart.'

'To be on the safe side, I don't think you should stay here on your own tonight. Why don't you come back to ours? We've got a spare bedroom.'

'I'm sure I'll be fine.'

'I've got the *Lethal Weapon* boxset. I know that was a favourite of Jack's. We can have a cosy film night together, the three of us.'

'Well, okay,' she replied, once again lacking the stamina for an argument. 'I'll go and pack an overnight bag.'

'I thought she'd put up more of a fight,' Harry quietly told his father once Carly had left the room.

'Aye, me too. Maybe she's been enjoying your company and doesn't want to give it up?'

'No one ever has before.'

Eddie's phone rang and he pulled it out of his pocket.

'Hello?'

From the way Eddie shot to his feet and immediately headed for the back door, Harry knew Dean was on the other end of the line. He remained where he was while his father went out into the garden, not wanting anything to do with his younger brother, pain etched into his handsome face.

Carly returned carrying an overnight bag. 'Where's Uncle Eddie gone?' she asked Harry.

'He's taking a phone call in the garden.'

'Why? It's freezing out there.' Her eyes narrowed. 'He's talking to Dean, isn't he?'

'I don't know for sure, but I reckon so.'

Carly dumped the bag on the floor and stormed outside, Harry doing nothing to stop her. As her uncle had his back turned and was absorbed in the conversation, he didn't notice her approach.

'Hey,' he said when the phone was snatched from his hand.

He turned to see Carly sprinting back to the flat clutching his phone.

'Carly, doll,' he called, making chase.

She ran inside, slammed the door shut and locked it.

'Open up,' yelled Eddie, banging on the back door. When he got no response, he rushed to the window. 'Harry, open the door right now.'

'Don't you dare,' Carly told her cousin.

'Sorry, Da',' Harry called to his father through the glass. 'She's scarier than you.'

'Ya wee sod, I'm gonnae kick you up the arse for this,' Eddie yelled at his son, who grinned back at him.

Carly put the phone to her ear. 'Dean,' she said.

There was a pause before his voice replied, 'Carly, is that you?'

'Aye, it's me, ya murdering shite.'

'God, it's good to hear your voice. I've missed you so much. I think about you all the time.'

'Do you think about Jack too?' she rasped.

'Look, I didnae want it to come to that, but he left me no choice. He wouldn't let you go.'

'I didn't want him to let me go, I loved him,' she cried.

'No, you didnae. You love me really, I know it, and I still love you, Carly.'

'You want me?' she said, voice low and dangerous.

'More than anything.'

'Then tell me where you are and I'll come to you.'

There was another pause as he'd already noted the threat in her tone. 'What will you do when you get here?'

'Kill you,' she hissed.

'You don't mean that.'

'I swear to God I do.'

'You had feelings for me once.'

'I still do, only those feelings are now hate. You took Jack from me, you took my future from me and I'll take your life from you. So tell me, Dean – where the fuck are you?'

Harry watched quietly, noting the way she gripped the phone so tightly he thought it might break and the fact that she didn't blink as she spoke. He found it both freaky and intimidating and it was a reminder of what this woman was capable of.

'Where are you, Dean?' she pressed when he remained silent, willing him with every fibre of her being to give her a location.

There was a bang as the front door was flung open. Alarmed by the noise, Harry rushed into the hall to find it was just his father.

'Tell me,' Carly spat into the phone, knowing she had just seconds left.

'I can't,' replied Dean.

'You fucking coward.'

Eddie tore the phone from Carly's hand. 'Son, are you there? Hello? He's hung up,' he added with a regretful sigh. 'What did he tell you?' he demanded of Carly.

'Nothing, except that he loved and missed me. He wouldnae tell me where he was because I said I would kill him. Did he tell you where he is?'

'No, he never does and even if he did, I wouldnae gi'e you his location.'

'When are you going to stop protecting your murdering bastard of a son?' she yelled.

'I'm no' protecting him, I'm protecting you. You'd never forgive yourself for killing your own cousin.'

'I wouldn't have a problem with it.'

'Of course you would. You'd never be able to look at me or Harry ever again. This family's been torn up enough and I won't let us be damaged any more. By shielding him I'm protecting us all. Don't you get that?' he exclaimed.

'Then you should have turned him over to Toni to sort out.'

'How could I? Even after everything he's done, he's still my boy. If you ever become a parent, then you'll understand. I cannae hand over my own son to be murdered.'

Carly snatched up a pan sitting on the draining board after being washed and slammed it down on the counter with a bang. 'He doesn't deserve to live after what he did.'

'Dean's death won't bring Jack back. Nothing can do that.'

Carly released a wild scream filled with pure rage and raised the pan again. For a moment, Eddie thought she was going to bring it down on his head, until she struck the counter with it again. On the third blow the handle snapped and the pan bounced off the counter and hit the floor, leaving a gouge in the lino.

'Jeezo, hen, you've got to calm down,' Eddie told her. 'Harry, talk to her,' he pleaded with his son, hoping he could get through to her.

'Leave me alone,' Carly cried before running to the front door. After stuffing her feet into her trainers and yanking her coat off the hook, she raced outside, slamming the door shut behind her.

'Don't just stand there, go after her,' Eddie told Harry.

'What's the point?' he replied. 'She won't listen. You're best letting her calm down first.'

'Cole could still be out there.'

'God help him if he encounters her when she's in that state, she'd rip him apart.'

'We cannae just let her wander the streets alone, it's nearly dark. Come on.'

'Fine,' he sighed.

After pulling on their coats, the two men hurried outside but the street was quiet, no sign of Carly.

'God, what the hell is she going to do now?' said Eddie anxiously. 'This would happen just when she was starting to seem more like her old self.'

* * *

Carly paced the streets, muttering to herself as she repeatedly went over her conversation with Dean. She'd failed to get a single clue as to his location. He could be anywhere from Dublin to Dubai. Worst of all, she had no way of finding out. Vengeance seemed out of reach and she was tormented by the thought that if it had been Jack on the hunt, Dean would already be dead.

'I'm sorry, babe,' she whispered. 'I've failed you.'

Carly shivered and stuffed her hands into her pockets. The temperature was rapidly dropping. Already ice was forming on the windscreens of the cars parked at the kerb. It was going to be a very cold night and her trainers weren't doing much to keep out the chill. But she couldn't go back to the flat and face a lecture from her uncle.

Deciding she needed something to warm her up, she headed in the direction of the pub, not really seeing her surroundings as she once again analysed her conversation with Dean, wondering what she could have said differently to make him give up his location. Sucking up to him with words of love would have probably done it. He was just mad enough to believe that she still cared about him. Telling him she wanted to kill him hadn't been the smartest move. Perhaps she would get another chance to speak to him and she could tell him her feelings had changed, that she would come to him so they could be together and then she would finally get true justice for Jack.

These thoughts so consumed Carly that she failed to notice two people were following her.

'Oy, Savage,' called a voice.

Carly stopped and turned to see it was Karen McLaren. She was a crony of Emma Wilkinson who had taken over leadership of The Bitches when Jane had left to look after their sick father. Jane had brutally taken the leadership back and Karen had never forgiven the Savage family for the downfall of her beloved leader. Whereas Emma had been cowed and subdued and never set foot in Haghill, Karen still lived here and was as gobby as ever. She was accompanied by a friend of hers called Nicole. Even though it was freezing cold, Karen wore her usual blue jeans and a lumberjack shirt left open to reveal a white crop top and plenty of bare midriff.

'Don't start, Karen,' Carly told her. 'I'm no' in the mood for your shite.'

'I bet you're still mourning Jack, aren't you?' said Karen, zero sympathy in her eyes. 'Everyone's saying it's turned you into an alky who cannae get through the day without a drink.'

Carly sighed. Karen sounded so stupid and childish with no idea what real suffering was. She looked down the street; the pub was in sight. The cold was really seeping into her feet now. She could just keep walking and soon be in the cosy, friendly atmosphere of The Horseshoe Bar. She wouldn't have a white wine, it was too cold; maybe something warming like a whisky or a vodka. The thought generated an ache of longing inside her.

'Oy, Savage, are you listening to me?' snapped Karen.

Carly rolled her eyes and turned back to face her. 'What?'

'I said everyone's saying you're an alky.'

'Aye, I heard you. Is that it, only I'm cold?' she snapped before walking away, wishing the stupid cow would shut up so she could continue to mull over her conversation with Dean.

'Looks like you're a coward as well as an alky,' called Karen as she and her grinning friend hastened to follow. 'You're weak, Savage. You're a disgrace to your family name.'

'Whatever,' Carly retorted over her shoulder.

'You were only tough when Jack was around because you knew he'd protect you. Well, that twat's gone. Tell me, did they stick his insides back in before they buried him or did they chuck them away and leave him empty?'

Carly came to an abrupt halt, clutching at her hair as the horrifying memories played in her head. Karen and Nicole took this to mean weakness when in fact it meant overwhelming rage. It poured through Carly's veins like molten lava as all the emotion that had been building up inside her over the last three months burst its banks again.

Karen strutted arrogantly up to Carly and shoved her in the back, knocking her forward a few paces. 'Jack and your family are no' here to protect you now.'

Carly whipped round to face the two women, whose smirks fell at the fury in her eyes.

'What makes you think I need protecting?'

It was Nicole who made the first move, attempting to back-hand Carly across the face. Carly dodged and kicked her in the stomach before punching her in the face. Nicole staggered backwards and fell off the kerb, landing in the road.

Karen was a tougher prospect. She managed to get in a couple of hits to Carly's face but, to her horror, her opponent barely seemed to feel them. With a cry of rage, Carly leapt at her, knocking her onto her back. Carly landed on top of Karen and began pummelling her with her fists.

'I'll fucking kill you for what you said about Jack,' she screamed while punching Karen repeatedly in the face.

Karen held up her hands to shield herself but Carly tore through her defences.

'Stop it,' cried Nicole, attempting to drag Carly off her friend.

Carly drove her elbow into Nicole's stomach before delivering an uppercut to her jaw that put her on her back. Now she was down, Carly resumed pounding Karen, who could only lie there defenceless, head snapping from side to side as she was repeatedly hit with Carly's left fist then her right. Blood poured from her nose and mouth. Carly grimaced when she felt a tooth cut into her left knuckle, but this didn't encourage her to stop.

'Stop, Carly, you're gonnae kill her,' cried a voice.

She ignored it, intent on taking out all her rage and pain on this woman who had interfered in her life once too often.

Then arms wrapped around Carly and dragged her backwards. She fought to get back at Karen, she wasn't done yet, but she was pulled away from her prey.

When she was released, Carly drew back her fist, striking as she turned. The blow connected with a man's stomach, and he dropped to his knees, coughing.

'Oh my God, Derek,' she cried when she realised she'd punched the man who'd been like a second dad to her, who had done nothing but help her, her entire life.

He tried to respond but couldn't as the wind had been knocked out of him.

'I'm so sorry,' she babbled, desperate to make it up to him. 'I didn't realise it was you.'

Carly looked round at the faces of the regulars in the pub, people she'd known since she was a small child and who were now regarding her with fear. She glanced down at her hands, which were cut and bruised and stained with blood.

'Someone call an ambulance,' exclaimed one woman, rushing to Karen's side. She was coughing on the blood that had filled her mouth, her pretty face an unrecognisable mask of damage and swelling.

Carly, horrified by what she'd done, ran off into the night.

'Wait, Carly,' gasped Derek as he attempted to get to his feet.

'Take it easy,' replied John, placing a hand on his shoulder. 'You'll never catch up with her anyway.'

'Someone needs to find her,' breathed Derek. 'She's no' herself.'

'I'll call Eddie,' said Brenda, another pub regular, who held her mobile phone in her hand. 'If we go after her, we'll just get what Derek got.'

* * *

Carly ran home, praying no one was there. To her relief, the flat was in darkness. She rushed into the bathroom and frantically washed her hands, dismayed by the amount of blood that swirled down the plughole. There was a cut to her left knuckle from Karen's tooth but she didn't bother to treat it. What was the point? If Karen died, then she would be arrested for murder and no way was she going to spend decades in prison. It would be better to die of an infection.

'God, what have you done?' she demanded of herself, staring at her pale, haggard reflection in the bathroom mirror. Karen was a stupid, mouthy cow but she hadn't deserved that. Carly knew she'd completely lost control. What if next time she hurt someone she loved?

Tears spilled down her cheeks as she gripped onto the edge of the sink, wrestling with herself. She thought she'd felt despair before but that had been nothing compared to the feelings that overwhelmed her now. The pressure of living suddenly seemed far too heavy; she couldn't bear the burden any longer. There was only one place she wanted to be, only one person she wanted to be with.

Carly left the flat and ran down the street to the corner shop. She burst inside, startling the assistant, who sat behind the till reading a magazine.

'Evening, Carly,' said the cheerful Asian man.

She ignored him, causing his smile to fall as she was normally so polite.

Carly snatched up two bottles of vodka from the shelves and stormed over to the counter, slamming them down in front of him.

'You having a party?' he said, smile faltering when he saw the state her hands were in. It was clear she'd just given someone a beating.

'No,' was her curt reply.

Realising she wasn't in the mood for a chat, he rang through her purchases. She paid for them before snatching up the bottles and running out of the shop, leaving him staring after her, bemused.

Carly clutched the bottles to her tightly as she hurried in the direction of the cemetery. It was even colder now, a sparkling frost coating the pavement. The skies were clear, the moon and a few stars shining brightly, hinting that the temperature would drop even more.

So familiar was Carly with the route through the cemetery to Jack's grave she could manage it in the dark, the only light coming from the gibbous moon. She fell onto her knees at his resting place, clearly marked by the shattered shard of marble sticking up out of the ground, its silhouette at odds with the rest of the smooth rounded headstones.

Carly unscrewed the lid of one of the vodka bottles and took a few gulps. It was cheap stuff and it went down her throat like fire, warming her from the inside. A few more glugs and a third of the bottle was gone. Finally, that warm haziness began to envelop her, numbing some of the horror of what she'd just done. The alcohol even helped banish the cold from her bones, which seeped through her jeans as she was slumped on the icy ground. Carly continued to drink but she took her time, not wanting to throw it all back up again. By the time the first bottle was half-empty, her head was spinning but it created a welcome sense of unreality, making her problems feel as though they were far away. She placed a hand on Jack's grave, clutching at the freshly turned dirt.

'Take me away, babe,' she whispered. 'I hate it here without you.'

She drained the first bottle of vodka and fell forward, landing on top of the grave. Despite the frost pressing against her cheek, she smiled, certain she felt movement around her. He was here.

'Take me with you,' she whispered. 'Please.'

11

Jane, Eddie, Harry and the rest of the assembled crowd watched Karen being loaded into the back of a waiting ambulance. The area where the attack had occurred was outside a few businesses which had closed for the night, all except for the pub and the takeaway up the street. The police were in attendance and everyone denied seeing anything. The bystanders said they'd been alerted by the sound of screams and by the time they'd got outside the perpetrator had fled, leaving just Karen and Nicole. No one was going to tell the police anything, not even the victims. Everyone knew the Savage family worked for Toni McVay, and dragging her into a police investigation was a certain way to get your eyes scooped out of your head. The two uniformed officers knew the witnesses were lying but could do nothing to encourage any of them to talk. Both Derek and the owner of the takeaway had already ensured the footage had been erased from their CCTV systems, which were the only two cameras on the street.

'We have to find Carly,' Eddie told Jane and Harry as they

drove away from the scene, leaving behind the flashing lights of the emergency vehicles.

'Let's try the flat first,' replied Jane.

They rushed back to the flat and although Carly wasn't there, they found damp trainer prints leading down the hall into the bathroom, the white porcelain sink stained pink.

'I bet she went to buy more alcohol,' said Jane, who was starting to panic. 'She'll want to drink herself into oblivion after what she's done.'

They were alarmed by the vivid description the shopkeeper gave them of Carly's angry, dishevelled appearance and the fact that she'd just purchased two bottles of vodka.

'She cannae be on her way back to the flat or we would have passed her,' said Eddie once they'd left the shop.

'And we know she won't go anywhere near the pub,' replied Harry.

'What about Jack's old flat?'

'She won't be there,' replied Jane. 'He was renting that and it was let out to someone else last month.'

'What about her friends?'

'She won't go to them, there's no one she's close enough to. She'll be upset, hurting, so she'll go somewhere that will give her comfort.' Jane's eyes widened. 'Jack's grave.'

The three of them jumped back in the car and Eddie set off at speed.

'Take it easy, Da',' said Harry. 'The polis are about.'

He eased off the accelerator but only slightly.

A few minutes later, they pulled up at the cemetery and the three of them hopped out.

'Jeezo, it's pitch black in there,' commented Harry.

'You scared, son?' replied Eddie.

'Naw, course not. I just don't want to fall over,' he said, taking out his phone and switching on the torch.

Eddie and Jane did the same with their own phones and the three of them picked their way along the path that wound through the graves.

'We must have gone past it,' panted Eddie, out of breath as the path sloped slightly upwards. 'It wasnae this far.'

'It only feels further because it's dark,' replied Jane.

'There,' said Harry. 'I can see the outline of Jack's broken headstone.' He cast the light of his torch sideways, illuminating the figure sprawled on top of the grave like a sacrifice to a dark god. 'Jeezo, it's Carly,' he exclaimed.

They rushed forwards, Eddie slipping on the frosty ground and almost falling.

'Carly,' said Jane, throwing herself down by her sister's side. 'Carly?' she cried louder when she didn't respond. 'She's unconscious.'

'I'm no' surprised,' replied Harry. 'She's polished off a full bottle of vodka.'

'Look at her lips, they're blue,' said Jane, shining the torch on her sister's face. The bright light in such a dark place should have been enough to rouse anyone, but Carly didn't react.

'We need to get her to hospital,' said Eddie.

'I'll carry her to the car,' replied Harry, shoving his phone into his coat pocket and scooping his cousin up in his arms.

Still Carly didn't respond, her head falling back, arms hanging down limply. It was only then they noticed the second bottle of vodka, which fell from her hand. Eddie picked it up.

'Thank Christ this one hasnae been opened,' he said.

They hurried back to the car and Harry placed Carly in the back seat. As they set off, Jane did her best to wake Carly, calling her name and tapping her face.

'She's not responding,' said Jane, tears filling her eyes. 'And she's so cold.'

'She'll be fine,' replied Eddie with more certainty than he felt. 'The lassie's strong.'

'The heater's on full blast,' said Harry.

'Carly, can you hear me? Carly?' cried Jane.

Fortunately, Glasgow Royal Infirmary was only a mile and a half away. As it was so late, the roads were quiet, so they were pulling up outside the A&E Department just a few minutes later.

Harry leapt out of the car, flung open the back door and picked up Carly, Jane closely following as he hurried inside the hospital, leaving Eddie to park the car.

'Help, she's unconscious,' cried Harry, rushing up to the reception desk.

The receptionist, alarmed by how blue Carly looked, immediately called through for assistance. Carly was placed on a stretcher and she was rushed into the depths of the hospital while Harry and Jane were told to take a seat in the waiting area.

They both sank into a chair, Jane burying her face in her hands while she got her emotions under control, aware of the eyes of the other people in the waiting room on them both, wondering what had happened.

'She's in the best place,' said Harry, placing a hand on Jane's arm. 'She'll be fine.'

Jane raised her head to look at him. 'We found her lying on a grave. What does that tell you?'

'It tells me she got pissed and fell asleep.'

'I think she went there to join Jack.'

'You mean she was trying to kill herself?'

Jane nodded.

'No fucking way. That's no' our Carly.'

'Everyone has their limit and what happened earlier with Karen might have been the straw that broke the camel's back.'

'Well, we won't know until she wakes up.'

'If she does wake up. She drank a full bottle of neat vodka.'

'A pal of mine drank a full bottle of tequila and he was fine, apart from a killer hangover.'

'Did he do it in a graveyard in freezing temperatures?'

'Well, no, but Carly's a fighter.'

'That's the problem. She's lost her fight.'

Harry didn't know what to say to that, so he wrapped an arm around Jane and she rested her head on his shoulder, fighting back tears.

* * *

Carly was confused. Something was covering her mouth and she didn't like it. She tried to push it away, but it refused to move.

'You need to leave it there, sweetheart,' said a voice. 'It's helping you breathe.'

'Jane?' she murmured, just pronouncing this one word draining her strength.

'It's me. You need to rest.'

Carly forced her eyelids open. Rather than the usual hangover, she felt even worse, as though her bones had been replaced with lead. She smiled weakly when she saw Jane and Rose sitting together by her side.

'What... is this?' she said, indicating whatever was covering her face.

'It's an oxygen mask,' replied Jane. 'We found you at the graveyard. You've got alcohol poisoning and hypothermia, which affected your breathing, so you need to leave the mask on. There's an IV in your left arm because you were dehydrated.'

'How do you feel?' Rose asked her anxiously.

'Shite,' said Carly. 'How long have I been here?'

'It's one o'clock in the afternoon,' replied Jane. 'We found you at eight o'clock last night. The doctor said you're gonnae be okay, you just need to rest. They want to keep you in for observation. Your temperature was dangerously low, a combination of the weather and the alcohol. I didnae know booze lowered your body temperature.'

'Karen... how is she?'

Jane glanced around before replying. They were on a ward with three other patients but no one was listening. 'Fine. Fractured cheekbone, concussion and a few broken teeth but nothing life-threatening.'

'Thank God,' breathed Carly. 'I was so worried I'd... you know.'

'Well, you didn't, so it's all good. She'll get over it.'

'And Derek too. I didnae mean to hit him.'

'He knows and he's fine about it. He's been so worried about you.'

'I have to apologise to him.'

'He already knows it was an accident.'

Carly's hand automatically went to the necklace Jack had given her, eyes flaring with panic when she found it wasn't there.

'Don't worry, it's here,' said Jane, producing the necklace with the ring attached from her pocket. 'The hospital removed it for safekeeping.'

She placed it around Carly's neck and she settled back into the bed, instantly calmer.

'Everything's okay, so try no' to worry,' Jane told her.

Carly turned her head away from her sisters when tears prickled her eyes.

'Rose, why don't you get Carly something from the shop?' said Jane. 'A book or a few magazines? She'll need something to occupy her while she's stuck in here.'

'You're trying to get rid of me, aren't you?' scowled Rose.

'Fine, I am. I want to talk to Carly in private.'

'Why didn't you just say so?' Rose replied, getting to her feet. 'But I will get you something to read, Carly.'

'Thanks, sweetheart,' Carly replied weakly.

Jane didn't speak until Rose had left the ward.

'What the hell did you think you were doing?' she hissed at Carly. 'The doctor said if we hadnae found you so quickly you could have died in that graveyard.'

Carly pulled the oxygen mask aside. 'Everything got on top of me. Hitting Karen and then Derek broke me. Especially Karen. I thought I'd killed her,' she whispered.

'Well, you didnae and the mouthy cow's had that beating coming for a long time.'

'Do the polis know it was me?'

'No. No one talked, no' even Karen and Nicole. Don't worry about it.'

'Aren't the hospital staff suspicious? They must have seen the state of my hands.'

'I said you fell over in the graveyard and banged them. I don't know if they believed me, but they've no' asked any awkward questions.'

'So I'm not going to be arrested?'

'No.'

'Thank Christ.'

'What were you trying to do up there?'

'I just wanted to be with Jack again.'

Jane's eyes filled with tears. 'You were trying to kill yourself?'

'I really don't know. I was just so messed up. I felt him around me. I'm sure he was there.'

'Perhaps he was,' replied Jane, swallowing down her tears. If that thought made her sister feel better, then she wasn't about to take it away from her.

'There's something else, something that's been weighing me down since Jack died.'

'Go on.'

'It's my fault he was murdered.'

'How do you work that one out?'

'He told me no' to tell anyone where I was and I told Dean. If I hadnae done that Jack would still be alive now.'

'Oh, sweetheart. This has been eating you up, hasn't it?'

Carly nodded, lower lip trembling as tears spilled down her cheeks.

'I'm glad you finally told me but nothing that happened that night is your fault. Dean and Cole are the ones to blame.'

'How could we not spot what Dean was?'

'I don't know. He fooled us all, including his own father and brother who've known him his entire life. Jack's murder wasn't just about his relationship with you. It was about his position too. Dean and Cole would have still killed him because of that alone. At the end of the day, you were the only person who ever gave Jack any happiness and you showed him the loyalty none of his own family ever did. That meant the world to him. You've got to let go of all the bad stuff before it overwhelms your good memories of him. Look at what it's doing to you.'

'I know and I'm trying.'

'And please, I'm begging you, never pull a stunt like this again.'

'I won't.'

'You swear on Maw and Da's graves?'

'I swear and I will figure out a way to get over this,' said Carly, feeling strength and resolve fill her for the first time in months. If she ever had a wobble again, all she had to do was think about the anguish in her sister's eyes.

12

Carly returned home two days later, still a little weak but otherwise okay. The bad weather had moved in with plummeting temperatures and even some snow. Carly remained in the flat resting and drinking tea. She didn't touch any alcohol, not that there was any. Jane had disposed of all the drink in the house, even the small bottle of Advocaat that had sat there for years. The urge to drink had finally loosened its hold on Carly, not just because of how awful the alcohol poisoning had left her feeling but because she was terrified of losing control again. Even though she hadn't been drunk when she'd beaten Karen and punched Derek, she feared that getting drunk again might lead her back down that same dark path. Karen had been released from hospital with no lasting damage. Derek had visited Carly at the hospital and assured her that his chunky gut had absorbed most of the impact anyway. It was a comfort to Carly knowing their close relationship hadn't been affected.

All the rest she was getting plus quitting the drink made Carly feel a little better physically, but no amount of rest could help her deal with the emotional pain. Two weeks after her release from hospital, she came to a decision and made her announcement when her sisters, Jennifer, Harry, Eddie and Peanut had come to the flat to eat pizza together for tea one evening.

'I've got something to tell you,' began Carly when they were all gathered around the kitchen table. 'I've decided to go travelling.'

'You mean you're hiring a campervan and going up to the Highlands?' replied Eddie.

'No, I mean I'm going abroad. I've never left Scotland before and I want to see the world. Thanks to the money Jack left me, I can afford to do it.'

'That's a good idea,' said Jane. 'You could use a change of scenery. You'll come back in a couple of weeks and feel much better.'

'I'm no' talking about going for a couple of weeks. I'm thinking months.'

'Months?' said Rose, face falling.

'Everything here reminds me of Jack. I cannae breathe in Haghill. I have to get away.'

'But that doesn't mean you have to go for so long. Like Jane said, a couple of weeks—'

'A couple of weeks won't do it. I need a good long time to think about my future and what I'm gonnae do now.'

'You're no' coming back, are you?' demanded Rose, eyes filling with tears.

'Of course I will. I'll always come back because you're all here.'

'You just don't know when?'

'No. I want to see so many places – Italy, Greece, Croatia, France. Now's the ideal time to go while I don't have a job to worry about and I've got the money.'

'I agree you need to get away,' said Eddie. 'But I'm worried about you travelling around the world on your own, doll.'

'I can take care of myself.'

'Aye but you've been through a lot, you're still fragile.'

'I'll be fine. I'm actually really excited about this idea and to be honest, the thought of staying here being tortured by all the memories is so depressing. It's no' that I want to go, I *have* to go.'

'Have a good time,' grinned Harry, raising the slice of pizza he held in a toast.

'Thank you,' she replied with a fond smile.

'How can you say that, Harry?' demanded Rose. 'We've already lost Maw, Da' and Dean and now Carly's going. It's nearly Christmas too, our first without Da'.'

'I won't go until the New Year,' replied Carly.

'And you'll be back for next Christmas? Promise, Carly, or I swear to God I'll stop you from leaving.'

'I promise I'll be back for next Christmas. Hand on heart,' Carly said seriously.

'Well, okay, but I'll miss you.'

'I'll miss you too, sweetheart.'

'You'll have to send us a postcard from everywhere you visit,' Jennifer told her.

'I will.'

'Take my advice and go to Sorrento,' said Peanut. 'I met the most amazing woman ever in the Piazza Tasso,' he added with a whimsical smile. 'Giovanna, her name was. Beautiful, funny, clever and very bendy too. Apart from Scotland, Italy has the best women in the world.'

'Carly's no' going away to meet women,' Rose told him.

'Aye, I know, but I grab any chance to brag about my conquests and I planted my flag in Giovanna more than once.'

'Classy,' replied Jane flatly.

Peanut grinned, shrugged and bit into a slice of pizza.

'I'll miss you all like crazy,' Carly told them. 'But this is the right thing for me and I promise I'll stay in touch. You'll always know where I am.'

'Well,' replied Harry. 'I hope you have a great time. I'm a wee bit jealous, if I'm honest.'

Carly smiled back. For the first time since Jack had died, she felt like she had a future again.

After they'd finished eating, Eddie took Carly aside.

'I hope you're no' going abroad to look for Dean?' he began.

'What? No, course not. That would be like looking for a needle in a haystack anyway. This isnae about revenge, I promise. It's about me finally healing.'

'You swear?'

'On Jack's grave.'

Eddie nodded, knowing she wouldn't make an oath like that without meaning it. 'Very well. What can I say then except happy travels?'

13

TWELVE MONTHS LATER

'Jane,' called Rose from her bedroom. 'Can I borrow your black pencil skirt?'

'Do I own a black pencil skirt?' her sister called back from the kitchen.

'Aye, you know, the one that makes my arse look great.'

'What is she talking about?' Jane asked Jennifer, who was sitting at the kitchen table flicking through a bridal magazine.

'No idea,' she replied. 'What's taking her so long? We're only going to the pub.'

'Fergus Saunders is gonnae be there and she's trying to impress him. He's the first boy she's fancied since she broke up with Noah, so she wants to make a good impression.'

Due to Jennifer's flat having a bad damp problem, she and Jane were now living together at the Savages' flat. It was 15th December and Carly had been away for almost a year.

'I see,' replied Jennifer. 'Hey, what do you think of these floral centrepieces?' she added, holding the magazine out to Jane.

Jane took it from her, the engagement ring glinting on her

finger. Jennifer had proposed to her six months ago and their wedding was in four days. Carly had promised to be back in time to be a bridesmaid.

'They look more appropriate for a funeral,' commented Jane.

'I think they're classy.'

'I'd rather have sunflowers.'

'It's December. They're no' appropriate.'

'I want something with some colour. I don't like the all-white, it's too depressing.'

'How about red roses?'

'I thought we'd already got our centrepieces. Aren't we having anemones?'

'Dunno, I've lost track. We'll have to ask our wedding planner. Rose,' called Jennifer. 'Have we got our floral centrepieces for the wedding ready?'

'Aye,' she called back from her bedroom. 'Anemones and roses.'

'There you go,' Jane told Jennifer. 'We don't even need to think about it. Thank God she's organised because we don't have a clue what's going on.'

Rose entered the kitchen wearing a tight black skirt and an equally tight light blue top. 'There's only four days to go,' she told them. 'Why wouldn't the floral centrepieces be sorted? Honestly, I don't know what you two would do without me. All you have to do is put on your dresses and turn up on time. Do you think you can manage that?'

'Wow,' said Jennifer. 'You should be on that programme about those bridezillas. You'd soon whip them into shape.'

'I've so enjoyed organising this wedding I'm thinking of becoming a wedding planner,' Rose smiled.

The front door opened and Eddie, Harry and Peanut entered.

'You ready to go?' said Eddie.

'Aye, we are,' replied Jane. She nodded at Rose. 'Now Cinderella's finally decided what she's wearing.'

'Well, you'd better get changed then, doll,' Eddie told Rose. 'Chop chop.'

'But I am changed,' she exclaimed.

'Oh. You look very nice.'

Rose looked down at herself before sighing. 'I need to change.'

'No, you don't, you're fine as you are.'

'You said I look nice,' she called back as she stomped towards her bedroom.

'What's wrong with that?'

'You know nothing about women, do you?' Rose retorted before slamming her bedroom door shut.

'Never say a woman looks nice,' Peanut told him. 'It'll only give you a world of pain.'

'I hope she hurries up. Me and Brenda have been getting close and I agreed to meet her for a drink tonight.'

'Why don't you go on to the pub then?' replied Jane. 'We can follow when Rose is ready, or are you afraid of Brenda?' she added with a mischievous smile.

They heard the front door opening again.

'Did someone just walk in?' frowned Jane.

'Just me,' called a voice.

They all looked at each other in surprise.

'Is that...' began Harry.

'Carly,' they heard Rose screech.

Everyone rushed into the hallway to see Rose embracing her older sister.

'You came back early,' said Jane as she raced to Carly, Rose stepping aside so she could hug her. 'We were supposed to pick you up at the airport on Tuesday.'

'I got an earlier flight. I wanted to come home.' Carly's hair was much shorter, just brushing her shoulders, and it had been lightly curled. She was tanned and her eyes were bright.

'So you're staying?'

Carly smiled and nodded. 'Aye, I am.'

'Yay,' cheered Rose, flinging her arms around her again.

The rest of the extended family greeted Carly with more hugs before they all headed into the kitchen together.

They were relieved that Carly looked so well. She hadn't been back to Haghill since her departure in early January. Although she had kept in regular contact with postcards, emails and phone calls, they'd still worried about her, but she looked so fit and healthy, all their fears that she'd still been drinking heavily immediately evaporated.

'Were you on your way out?' Carly asked them.

'We were going to the pub, but we can stay in,' replied Jane.

'No, I'll come with you. It'll be nice seeing everyone again, especially Derek.'

'He'll be delighted to see you, he's always asking about you.'

'Did he get my postcards?'

'Aye, and he put them all on his fridge, like we did,' said Rose, gesturing to the collection.

'You look fantastic, doll,' Eddie told her. 'Obviously travel agrees with you.'

'It does,' she replied. 'I had a brilliant time.'

'How are you feeling?'

'Much better. I think I managed to get over what happened. It'll always hurt but it doesnae overwhelm me any more.'

'And you're okay being back in Haghill?'

'I am so far.'

'Aren't you tired?' said Jennifer. 'Do you need to rest first?'

'Naw, I only flew from Paris. It's no' a long flight.'

'What was Paris like?' she asked eagerly.

'Stunning and the food is amazing.'

'I hope you don't mind but I'm living here now. I had to give up my flat because of some dodgy black mould.'

'Why would I mind? You're family now,' smiled Carly.

'Great,' Jennifer smiled back, relieved. 'We're saving to buy our own place but it'll take some time.'

'That's fine by me. After the people we've lost, it's nice that our family's growing.'

Jennifer beamed and hugged her.

'Are we going to the pub?' said Rose anxiously. 'Fergus is gonnae think I'm no' coming.'

'Fergus?' smiled Carly. 'Who's he, a cat?'

Rose frowned while Harry and Peanut laughed.

'Actually, he's the most gorgeous man who ever walked the earth,' said Rose eagerly. 'He's really funny too.'

'What happened to Noah?'

'We broke up. It wasnae working.'

'You were crazy about him once.'

'He's too immature for me,' Rose shrugged. 'No' Fergus though. He's brave and strong and soooo wise.'

'In that case, we'd better get to the pub before Fergus rides off on his white horse.'

* * *

Carly was a little reticent about going into The Horseshoe Bar. The last time she'd seen everyone her hands had been covered in Karen's blood and they'd all been staring at her in horror.

'We've got a surprise visitor,' announced Harry as they walked through the door.

Carly regarded the room uncertainly when everyone looked her way. She breathed a sigh of relief when a cheer went up and the regulars rushed to greet her. Brenda was the first to reach her and pulled her into a tight hug.

'It's so good to see you again,' said Brenda. 'The place hasnae been the same without you.'

'Thanks,' replied a delighted Carly. 'It's good to see you too.'

'I love your hair, you look even prettier.'

'There she is,' exclaimed Derek, gently sweeping Brenda aside so he could pull Carly into a bear hug. 'Bloody hell, I've missed you so much.'

'Missed you too,' she smiled, hanging on to him.

'This calls for champagne,' he announced, making the room cheer. 'I didnae mean for all of you, just the Savages,' he added, eliciting a few boos. Derek scowled. 'Stick your boos up your arses.'

The Savages and their friends seated themselves at a large table while Derek fetched the champagne and the barman arranged the glasses.

'How are you feeling being back here?' Jane quietly asked Carly.

'Good,' she replied. 'I missed you all so much. I remember the time I spent here with Jack, but the memories are nice now. They don't hurt so much.'

'That's good,' said Jane, patting her hand.

Jane, Rose and Eddie anxiously watched how much Carly had to drink. They all noted that she switched to orange juice after just one glass of champagne. Eddie relaxed and started chatting up Brenda, who had joined their table, as had Derek. Rose also felt this was her cue to go over and join Fergus, who was a tall, strong-looking boy with gelled dark hair.

'So,' said Carly. 'What have I missed?'

'Derek had piles,' called John, who was propping up the bar as usual.

'You big-mouthed git,' Derek snapped back. 'I told you that in confidence.'

'Oh, sorry,' John smiled before taking a swig of lager.

'Your life's no' your own around here,' muttered Derek.

'Did the piles clear up?' Brenda asked him.

'No' that it's any business of yours but aye, they did.'

'So things have been pretty quiet then?' smiled Carly.

'Aye,' said Derek. 'The big news is Jane and Jen's upcoming wedding.'

'I can't wait,' enthused Brenda. 'I've never been to a gay wedding before. How woke am I? Eddie, you're still taking me, aren't you?'

'Course I am, doll. I'll be proud to have you on my arm.'

'So, which was your favourite place out of everywhere you visited?' Jennifer asked Carly.

'Dubrovnik in Croatia. It's so beautiful. The Old Town's amazing and I've never seen such turquoise water anywhere.'

'Sounds lovely,' smiled Brenda. 'The most exotic place I've been to is Cirencester,' she added miserably.

'Don't worry, doll,' Eddie told her. 'I'll take you to exotic places with turquoise water and white sandy beaches.'

'Where are you thinking of? The Shetland Isles?' grinned Peanut.

'I meant Hawaii or Bali,' said Eddie.

'Oh yes, take me to Bali,' cried Brenda, throwing her arms around Eddie's neck.

'I think you'd better go easy on that, hen,' Derek told her, taking away her glass of champagne.

The evening erupted into a celebration, but Carly stuck to soft drinks for the rest of the night while everyone around her got drunk. She had feared that coming home would reignite all the old pain but it didn't. Carly found she could now enjoy her memories of Jack and the love they'd shared. She could still see him as clear as day holding court in the pub, those dangerous dark eyes of his finding her even though the room was busy, the smile that curled his lips when their gazes connected causing a thrill to run through her. The sadness hadn't gone though, as well as the gnawing thought of the future she'd lost. If he hadn't been killed, she would now be the one looking forward to her wedding day. Her hand, as it always did when thinking of Jack, drifted to the necklace he'd given her.

Carly shook herself out of her reverie. These thoughts were depressing and dangerous. They would only take her back down that dark path she'd struggled to get herself off. What her family didn't know was that rather than head to a foreign country while she was still so fragile, she'd flown to Leeds Bradford Airport from Glasgow and then travelled to Castleford, wanting to see where Jack had grown up. She'd even kept her promise to herself and pissed all over his father's overgrown, untended grave after sneaking into the cemetery at night. She'd shocked herself but the act had been cathartic and had made her feel a little better. The three weeks she'd spent in Castleford, exploring not just Jack's old stomping ground but Yorkshire itself, had been difficult. As the awful feeling she'd been left with after the alcohol poisoning had receded into memory, the urge for a drink had risen again but she'd fought it. While she was in Yorkshire she'd felt unwell and not herself, but she'd resisted the demon on her back until she'd managed to shake it off altogether.

Once Carly had felt she was ready, she returned to Leeds Bradford Airport with the intention of taking the first flight available, which had been to Zakynthos, a Greek island. That had been the start of her adventure. Now she only had one drink at a time, constantly conscious that her old nemesis could return and sink its claws into her once more.

Carly smiled as she regarded her family and friends, some of whom were the worse for wear. Here was where she belonged and it was time to begin the next phase of her life.

14

Jane shuffled into the kitchen, short hair stuck up in patches, wincing against the daylight streaming through the kitchen window. It was a cold December day but clear and sunny.

'Jeezo, my heid,' she groaned, sinking into a chair at the kitchen table.

How awful she felt was offset by how radiant Carly looked. Her sister was brewing a pot of coffee, appearing fresh and well-rested.

'Here you go,' said Carly, pouring her a glass of water and handing her a pack of paracetamol.

'Cheers,' said Jane, gratefully tossing two tablets into her mouth and washing them down with the water.

'I went to see Jack's grave. It looked really tidy. Thanks for looking after it.'

'Nae bother.'

'I put some flowers on it and on Maw and Da's too.' Carly regarded her suffering sister with concern. 'Do you have to work today?'

'No, thank God. I wouldnae be fit for it.'

'You still doing the same work for Elijah and David?'

'Aye, although me and Harry have been given more responsibility. We run a crew together now and do all the debt collections.'

'Really? That's great. Is there a spot on that crew for me?'

'You still want back in?'

'Aye. I've done a lot of soul searching and I know it's what I'm meant to do. I'll only fail if I try to go legit again, especially with my entire family working in the business.'

'Rose isnae in it. She's doing really well at college. She even said yesterday she wants to be a wedding planner because she's done such a good job arranging mine and Jen's do.'

'That's fantastic but I'm no' Rose. She'll happily settle down one day with a nice man running her own successful business, but I'm cut from a different cloth. Everything went wrong when I tried to go legit. Ironically, being in the life kept me safe, especially with Cole still wanting his revenge.'

'He won't come back.'

'He will, you can bank on it. I'll have greater protection working for Toni.'

'You know your own mind but it's no' my call. I'm happy to have you on my crew but Elijah and David have the final say.'

'I get it. I'll go and see them. Are they still at the same place?'

'Naw, they moved to a different café. One of us will need to take you over there.'

'I can ask Harry if you're no' up to it.'

'Do you need some cash? I expect you're skint after all that travelling.'

'No, I've got over half of the money Jack gave me left. I took work whenever I could get it, mainly in restaurants and bars, and I lived simply. I need a purpose. Doing nothing is really bad for me.'

'Aye, I remember. Okay, if you think it's right, you have my blessing.'

'Thanks,' Carly smiled, placing a mug of coffee before her older sister.

'You're an angel,' said Jane, picking it up and blowing on it to cool it.

'Morning,' trilled Rose, entering the kitchen, looking just as bright and fresh as Carly. 'You look like shite,' she told Jane.

'Thanks,' her sister replied flatly. 'How are you so chirpy? You were putting it away last night.'

'I switched to orange juice halfway through the night. No way was I gonnae risk getting drunk and making a dick of myself in front of Fergus.'

'How did it go with him?' replied Carly.

'Brilliant,' Rose said, her dreamy expression returning. 'He's such a gentleman, he even asked if he could kiss me. He's taking me out for a meal tonight. You don't mind, do you, Carly? I know you've only just got back but I've been waiting for this date for ages.'

'Course I don't mind. Go and enjoy yourself. Don't you have college this morning?'

'Naw, we've broken up for the Christmas holidays. I'm going shopping for a new outfit for my date tonight. Do you want to come?'

'Why not?' smiled Carly, thinking it would be nice to spend some time with her wee sister.

* * *

Carly enjoyed a pleasant trip out with her little sister, who chose a sexy black dress for her date. After having lunch, Carly drove them back to Haghill, her uncle having taken care of her little car in her absence. After dropping Rose off at Tamara's so she could show her friend her new outfit, Carly returned to the flat to find Jane curled up on the couch in her pyjamas, staring blankly at the television. Harry was there too and he said he'd take Carly to speak to Elijah and David as Jane was still suffering with her hangover.

They left together, Carly driving as Harry thought he might still be over the limit after putting it away last night. Harry directed her to a back street café not far from the one Elijah and David had previously used as their base. Carly found it a little sad that they were no longer using the premises Jack had selected but she understood the importance of not staying in one place for too long.

David greeted her warmly while Elijah was his usual slightly creepy self.

'So, we're told you still want a job?' opened Elijah.

'Aye,' replied Carly. 'I took your advice and went away to get myself together.'

'I must admit you look a lot better than you did the last time we met. What do you think, David?'

'I agree,' he replied. 'She looks back to her old self.'

'My only concern is that you've been out of the game for a while,' Elijah told Carly. 'You might have lost your edge.'

'I wouldnae say that,' she replied confidently. 'I had to batter some creep in Bodrum when he thought he could take advantage of me.'

'Where the hell's Bodrum?'

'Turkey. He wasnae Turkish though, he was a tourist from Inverness.'

'Aye, well, you've got to watch those Teuchters.'

'And there was the tour guide who cornered me in Athens. I

made him regret his bad life choices,' she replied with a wicked smile.

Elijah chuckled. 'You've still got spirit, I'll gi'e you that.'

'I've travelled around the world on my own and into some dodgy places too. I've no' lost my edge. In fact, it's sharper than ever.'

'Well, what can I say to that? Welcome aboard.'

'Thanks,' she smiled.

'You can join Jane and Harry's crew and we'll see how you get on. You know the routine, nothing's changed.'

'Who will I be working with?'

'I'll leave that up to your sister and cousin to decide, they know what they're doing. Actually, I'm glad you came. We need a meeting with you all. We're having some trouble but I cannae gi'e you any more details just yet, no' without Toni's permission.'

'She wants to discuss it with you all personally,' David told the Savages.

'It must be serious then,' said Harry.

'Aye, it is. We'll be in touch soon.'

'I wonder what's happened?' Carly asked Harry after they'd left, heading downstairs from the office to the café below.

'Nae idea, I've no' heard of any trouble,' he replied. 'I'm hungry, do you fancy something to eat?'

They entered the café itself, which was dated and rather depressing, the tables chipped and stained with brown rings. The woman behind the counter coughed into her hands.

'I want a coffee but no' here,' said Carly.

'Fair enough,' he replied, grimacing when the woman coughed again and sneezed.

* * *

Toni McVay's summons arrived later that afternoon via a phone call from Elijah to Eddie telling him and his family – including Carly and Peanut – to go to an address on the Gallowburn scheme.

'I wonder if we'll meet the infamous Blood Brothers again?' said Jane.

'Probably, if we're gonnae be on their turf,' replied Eddie. 'Whatever's going on is serious, so I want you all on your best behaviour, okay?'

'I hope I don't get molested again,' commented Harry.

'What's that?' Peanut asked him.

'Toni felt up mine and Dean's thighs the last time we had a meeting on the Gallowburn,' he replied.

All eyes turned Carly's way. No one had mentioned Dean since her return but the way her eyes narrowed said she hadn't forgiven what he'd done.

At seven o'clock that evening, Eddie's car set off containing his son, two nieces and Peanut. Gallowburn was only four miles away from Haghill. They drove through the darkened streets of the scheme, which was substantially bigger than their own, until they rolled to a halt outside a semi-detached house that occupied a corner plot. There were no signs of life, no cars parked outside or lights on inside.

'Is this the right place?' said Peanut, who was sitting in the front seat.

'Aye,' replied Eddie. 'Seven Dubton Street.'

'Someone's coming from around the back of the house,' said Jane.

Two shadowy figures approached, avoiding the orange glow cast by the streetlight standing on the corner.

'It's two of the Blood Brothers,' said Harry. 'The big one and the fat one.'

'For God's sake, don't go calling them that to their faces,' Eddie told him.

Digger, the taller and more muscular of the two men, knocked on the driver's window, which Eddie wound down.

'You coming in or are you gonnae sit there all night?' said Digger.

'We're coming in,' replied Eddie.

'Well, be quick, it's bloody freezing,' grumbled Gary.

The Savages got out of the car and followed the two men around the back of the house and inside the kitchen where Toni McVay awaited them. She wore black trousers with high-heeled boots and a thick black fur coat, her hands encased in leather gloves. Her curly black hair hung to her shoulders. She looked beautiful but serious. As always, her lieutenant and bodyguard, Caesar, stood by her side, a thick grey wool coat over his suit, the scars curling up from the corners of his mouth showing more prominently than usual as his lips were pressed into a grim line.

On Toni's other side was Logan, leader of the Blood Brothers. Despite their gang's name, the three members weren't related, although they had been best friends since childhood. Logan was a tall, slender, serious-looking man with a mop of dark curls. His handsome, angular face was just as grim as Caesar's.

Toni's sharp eyes assessed them all as they entered. 'Sit down,' she said imperiously, gesturing to the large dining table without a word of apology for dragging them out on a cold, dark night.

They obeyed, gathering around the table while Toni, Caesar and Logan remained standing. Gary and Digger took up position at the back of the room. Eddie didn't like it that his family were the only ones seated, but you didn't argue with Toni McVay.

'We've had a little trouble with some pathetic wee prick called Melvin Bell,' began Toni, who slowly paced back and forth as she spoke. 'He incited a couple of families in Cranhill and Wellhouse against me, namely the Cunningham and Burns families. Melvin has been neutralised. He's been lifted for dealing nitazenes and he's currently looking at some serious prison time. He, however, was just a puppet. The real culprit is Cole Alexander.'

'He's back?' said Carly.

Toni's black eyes were turned her way. 'Aye, but then again, you always knew he would return, didn't you?'

'Aye. When did he come back?'

'I don't know exactly,' said Toni, clearly finding it difficult to make this admission. 'All I know is it wasn't long before you returned.'

'I hope you don't think the two are linked?'

'Carly,' said Eddie, warning in his tone. His niece had spoken to Toni in a challenging manner.

The corner of Toni's mouth lifted. 'I wondered whether you'd be weaker or stronger after your ordeal, Carly. Clearly, you're stronger than ever. Good because you're gonnae need that strength. You'll also be a target of his, which is why I wanted you at this meeting.'

'Excellent. That means I can kill him.'

Toni was quick to spot the glance that passed between Eddie and Jane. 'You thought the desire for revenge would die with her coming to terms with her grief?' she asked them.

'Well, aye,' replied Eddie.

'Take it from someone who knows, there's very little that can kill the need for revenge. It sinks into your bones, becomes a part of you.' Toni looked back at Carly. 'We're going to need that rage too, beautiful.'

'You've got it,' Carly said.

'Good girl. It won't matter to Cole that Melvin's been lifted, his plan's already set in motion. In short, he's started a rebellion against me and he's chosen his targets well. He's selected families in areas dividing Haghill from Gallowburn, two of my strongest territories.'

'Surely that won't matter,' said Harry. 'I mean, you own most of Glasgow.'

'You're right, handsome, I do, but that comes with a price. There are those who resent my reign, who are jealous of my power and wealth and want it for themselves. Their greed is strong enough to overcome their fear, in some of them at least. They want to replace me with someone they think they can control – Cole.'

'No one can control him,' said Carly.

'Precisely, but he's very clever and has made them think they can.'

'But he's just some back street loser,' said Peanut. 'You're the Queen of Glasgow with powerful contacts around the world. He's a nothing compared to you.'

Toni tossed back her mane of hair, eyes flashing with pleasure. 'Of course, you're right, but anyone can be taken down. I'd be stupid to think I was invulnerable. Some of my biggest and most powerful allies come from backgrounds just like Cole's. He is smart, which automatically makes him a threat. Naturally I've got my people out searching for him but so far nothing, just as we couldn't find him the last time we looked, even though I have eyes and ears all over the city. I want you all to think where he could be.'

'I know Cole's da' had a few contacts who could be hiding him,' said Carly. 'Members of the old school.'

'Names?'

Carly reeled off three names that meant nothing to the assembled company.

'I don't think they're involved in the life any more,' continued Carly. 'But they'd probably know how to hide Cole.'

'Interesting,' said Toni thoughtfully. 'I suppose I've been so concerned with those still in the game I forgot about those out of it. Caesar, set our people on with tracking down those men.'

'Yes, Boss Lady,' he replied.

'That's very smart thinking, Carly,' Toni told her. 'Elijah tells me you're on Jane and Harry's crew.'

'I am.'

'Excellent. You'll be an asset to me. Cole's attempting to build a wall between Haghill and Gallowburn. In short, he's trying to isolate your schemes, not only from me but from each other. I want your family to work with the Blood Brothers to target anyone who might come onto your turf, because they will. Cole will need to make me look weak and attacking places under my protection is the ideal way to do that. If he's successful then there will be uprisings in other areas. When you are targeted, I want you to be merciless. Show no quarter.'

'Just how far should we go?' said Eddie.

'I'm no' saying you have to top anyone but make sure they're incapable of causing any trouble for a long time.'

'I don't get why Cole would do this,' said Harry. 'He must be mad.'

'He is,' said Toni. 'Mad with greed and ambition. It's a shame Jack's not here because he was onto his last planned takeover way before anyone else and he ensured Cole failed. But that was just when Cole had ambitions to take over Haghill. Now he wants the entire city. Fucking up his face really brought out the beast in him,' she told Carly with a disturbing smile.

'So, what do we do now?' said Eddie.

'Now you and the Blood Brothers need to bond. There's a very nice pub not far from here called The Bonnie Brae. I suggest you all go there together and talk. And no fighting, okay? This is a team-building exercise. If any punches are thrown, then eyeballs will be scooped out of heids. Do I make myself clear?'

They all nodded.

'Wonderful. Caesar, let's go. I've had to cancel my tickets to the opera tonight to deal with this mess,' she announced, eyes flashing. 'I do hate it when these petty annoyances interfere with my social life.'

With that she stalked to the door, her bodyguard following. Caesar opened the door and peered out, ensuring the coast was clear before stepping outside, hand sliding to his inner jacket pocket. Toni pulled up the collar of her fur coat and followed him out, the door slamming shut behind them.

The Savages and the Blood Brothers looked at each other.

'Well,' said Eddie, deciding to take charge of the situation. 'Where's this pub then?'

15

Eddie and Logan led the way, chatting amiably, and Digger fell into step beside Carly while Gary walked with Jane. Peanut and Harry were left to bring up the rear.

'I like them tall,' Gary grinned at Jane.

'Aye, that's great,' she replied.

'You're a beautiful lady. Proud and strong.'

'You should know that I'm getting married in three days.'

'He's no' good enough for you.'

'To a woman.'

'Oh.'

Jane's lips twitched. 'I bet you're regretting walking with me now.'

'Naw. Toni said we all need to get to know each other,' he said, casting Digger a jealous frown.

'There's no need to look like that,' Jane told him. 'If your pal tries anything, my sister will rip his baws off.'

'Well, that's all right then,' he said, looking more cheerful.

When Digger clamped a large hand down on Carly's backside, she stopped and rounded on him.

'Touch me again and I'll rip off your hand and stick it up your arse.'

'All right, take it easy,' said Digger, holding up his hands.

Logan turned to frown at his friends. 'Behave yourselves.'

The rest of the walk to the pub was made in awkward silence, Eddie and Logan the only ones talking. Their group entered the large warm pub and it immediately became clear how highly the Blood Brothers were regarded by the local community as everyone rushed to greet them and shake their hands.

'Wow, I didnae think Gary and Digger would be so respected,' Carly told her family.

'Remember this is basically a diplomatic mission,' replied Eddie. 'So best behaviour, okay.'

'Tell that to Digger. He grabbed my arse.'

'And you immediately made him regret it, so let it go. Sit down all of you while I get the drinks in.'

Eddie joined the Blood Brothers at the bar and began chatting with the jovial landlord and his scary-looking wife.

'Why is everyone looking at us like we're visitors from outer space?' said Harry quietly, referring to all the customers.

'They're trying to work out if we can be trusted,' replied Peanut. He gave a table of thirty-something women his best smile. 'Evening, ladies.'

Unable to resist that grin, they all returned his smile.

Harry decided to try a similar charm offensive and winked at two younger women sitting at the next table. 'All right, dolls?'

They gave him a haughty look before returning to their conversation.

'Obviously they're lesbians,' he muttered. He caught Jane's look. 'Nae offence.'

She rolled her eyes and shook her head.

The Blood Brothers and Eddie returned with the drinks and

the Blood Brothers sat opposite the Savages. The room had gone eerily quiet as everyone tried to listen in.

'So,' opened Eddie. 'What do you boys like to do?'

'We're no' boys, we're men,' growled Digger.

'Sorry, it was just a figure of speech. When you get to my age anyone under forty seems like a wean. No' that I'm calling you a wean,' he hastened to add when Digger's eyes flashed. 'Christ, I'm making a mess of this. Peanut, you've always got a good story to tell.'

'Do I?' he replied.

'Aye. Go on then. Tell a story,' said Eddie impatiently.

'About what?'

'I don't know, anything.'

'Okay,' said Peanut slowly, placing his pint glass on the table, giving himself time to think. 'Well, there is the one about this contortionist I went out with. We met when she performed at a private party and we did it in a cupboard... Maybe not,' he mumbled when they all stared back at him.

'I really want to hear the rest of that story,' said Digger eagerly.

'You would, ya perv,' Gary told him.

An awkward silence descended on the group again.

'Toni told me you're getting married soon,' Logan said to Jane.

'Aye, in three days,' she smiled back.

'Who's the lucky man?'

'Actually, she's a woman. Jennifer.'

'Oh, sorry for assuming. Toni never mentioned who you were marrying.'

'Don't worry about it. I'd invite you three but it's too late to change the seating plan.'

'No problem, we weren't expecting an invite and we

wouldnae expect you to change anything for us. Where are you going on your honeymoon?'

'We're not. We want to buy a house, so we decided to save the money instead. We're spending the wedding night in a nice hotel though.'

'Good idea. It's really hard getting on the property ladder these days.'

'You've got that right.'

Silence once again descended on the group.

'What's going on here?' said Carly.

'What do you mean, doll?' replied Eddie.

'Why are we so awkward around each other? I mean, we have a lot in common. We're from the same background and we do the same job. Why are we finding it so hard to communicate? I'll tell you why,' she continued when Gary opened his mouth to reply. 'It's because we don't know if we can trust each other yet, so let's get it out in the open. The sooner we're honest about it, the sooner we can deal with it.'

'You're right, we don't trust each other yet,' said Logan. 'That's no' surprising given everything we've all been through.'

'Let's get pished and have a laugh,' said Gary. 'That's the best way to get over it.'

The rest of the men agreed that was a great idea and Digger called to the landlord to bring them another round of drinks.

'I'll just have an orange juice,' chimed in Carly.

'You cannae get pissed on that shite,' Digger told her cheerfully.

'I don't drink. I only ever have one.'

'How?'

'Because I spiralled after Jack was murdered and started drinking really heavily. I nearly died of alcohol poisoning.'

'Oh,' said Digger awkwardly.

'But that's no reason why you lot cannae get pished.'

Her smile brought the grin back to his face. 'Aye, good on ya, doll.'

The men cheered when the landlord and his wife brought over the second round of drinks and they all began to relax in each other's company. Harry even joined Digger and Gary at the fruit machine, the three of them laughing and joking together.

'I'm sorry about Jack,' Logan quietly told Carly, taking the chair beside her that Harry had vacated.

'Thanks,' she replied.

'I met him a few times to discuss business. He was a man to be respected. He certainly didnae deserve that end.'

'You're right and I'm gonnae get revenge for him,' Carly said, gaze darkening. 'And since I cannae get hold of Dean, Cole's the one who'll pay.'

'But Cole didnae kill him.'

'No, but he was the puppet master. He recognised how unstable Dean was way before any of us did. Don't get me wrong, Dean shoulders the majority of the blame for killing Jack, but I don't think it would have gone so far without Cole's manipulation.'

'You used to go out with Cole?'

'Aye. He was a nice man once. Prison turned him into what he is now, as did his narcissistic bitch of a mother.'

'I see. Toni thinks you're the key to finding Cole, that he'll come back to this area for you. He knows you're a danger to him.'

'Fucking right I am.'

Logan watched her take a sip of orange juice, enjoying her strength and the aura of danger that surrounded her. Already he recognised how unique she was.

Jane, noting the way Logan was staring at her sister, engaged Carly in conversation. Logan rose and joined his friends and

Harry at the fruit machine, although he did intermittently glance at Carly, who was oblivious to the attention.

'Penny for them?' Jane asked her sister when she appeared to be lost in thought.

'I'm just thinking about Cole, wondering where he could be,' she replied. 'I don't want Toni to find him, no' before I can kill him.'

'You're still intent on doing that?'

'Of course. Just because I've been able to move through the grief doesnae mean I'm no' still gonnae get justice for Jack.'

'I meant to ask – was there anyone while you were away?'

'God, no. That was the last thing I wanted or needed.'

'And how about now?'

'You mean would I want another relationship? No. I'd feel I was being disloyal to Jack.'

'You're only young, he wouldnae want you to be alone for the rest of your life.'

'I know. Maybe one day but certainly no' right now, and look at my track record – first there was Cole, then Dean and finally Jack. All three men were doomed in different ways. What if I'm a jinx?'

'That's shite, Carly. You've got to stop blaming yourself for the actions of others. Cole got twisted up by prison and it was Jessica's fault he ended up in Barlinnie, no' yours. Jack's death is Dean's fault and as for Dean, well, he was just a loon.'

'Logically I know you're right, but I cannae shake the feeling that I'm somehow to blame.'

'You've got to get rid of that feeling before it destroys you.'

'I'm working on it, believe me.' Carly took a sip of orange juice, sighed and replaced the glass on the table.

'You want something stronger, don't you?'

'Aye but I daren't. I'm never getting addicted to anything ever again. It makes you weak.'

'I'm relieved to hear it.'

Jane glanced Logan's way again and saw he was still watching Carly. Her sister had the knack of fascinating men without even knowing it and the leader of the Blood Brothers was the latest in that line. Jane just hoped it didn't go bad like it had every time before.

* * *

The rest of the Savages were a little worse for wear the next morning, but Carly was bright and fresh.

'You've got the right idea sticking to soft drinks,' mumbled Jane as she shuffled into the kitchen. 'Two mornings in a row I've woken up with a hangover.'

'The Blood Brothers party hard, don't they?' smiled back Carly.

Rose entered the kitchen at that moment. 'Did you say the Blood Brothers?'

'Aye.'

'Why are you talking about them?'

'We had a meeting with them last night.'

'That's awesome. I've heard all about them. Their previous leader was murdered by a hitman and it was such a shame because was as hot AF. I mean, really gorgeous. Such a waste,' she said sadly.

'Because he was hot?'

'Does there need to be another reason? Why were you meeting with them anyway?'

'Toni thinks we should get to know each other so we can work together.'

'We? Are you back in the business?'

'I am.'

'Good.'

'You're pleased?'

'Aye. It makes you happier and let's face it – you were born for it. You'd never go the distance in a boring, legitimate job.'

'I wouldnae say that. I enjoyed working at Death Loves Company.'

'You would have got fed up of it one day. Carnage is in all our blood.'

'I hope you're no' thinking that means you can get into this business too?' said Jane sternly.

'Naw. Don't get me wrong, I love a good fight, but I want to be an entrepreneur. I've already decided I'm going to set up my own business as an event planner. I'll be my own boss. No one will tell me what to do. You'll always be beholden to Toni but that's no' for me. As long as I can have a good scrap now and then I'll be happy and let's face it, being part of this family there'll always be someone to fight.'

'You're gonnae be a powerful businesswoman,' smiled Carly.

'That's the plan,' announced Rose, hand on hip. 'It's lucky I decided to switch my course to a HND in Business. We're studying decision-making and risk-taking, which is right up my street. Anyway, I'm off out. Me and Tamara are going to the cinema. We're watching the new Finn Wolfhard film.'

'What's the film called?'

'Who cares? We get to look at him for two hours, that's all we're bothered about. By the way, the photographer called and said he'd double-booked and wouldn't be able to photograph your wedding, but don't worry. I threatened him with solicitors and all sorts and he quickly backed down. I reckon the git got offered a bigger job and wanted to take that instead, but he'll be there. He knows I'll hunt him down if he's a no-show. If he calls again and tries to get out of it, tell him Uncle Eddie's ready to start a case against him.'

'Uncle Eddie?'

'Aye, I told the photographer he's a shit-hot lawyer who's defended the biggest cases in the city.'

'You'll go far, Rose. Do you know that?'

'I do,' Rose grinned. 'Right, see you later.'

When she'd gone, Jane smiled at Carly. 'Are you as proud of her as I am?'

'Too right I am. I don't think we need to worry about her future.'

'But we do need to worry about our own. I don't like all this latest shite. What if Cole actually manages to topple Toni?'

'Course he won't.'

'But—'

'He won't,' said Carly. 'Because I'm gonnae kill him.'

Jane didn't bother to argue because she knew it would be pointless. 'Did we make any arrangements for today?'

'You mean you don't remember?'

'Remember what?'

Before she could reply, Harry, Eddie and Peanut arrived.

'Are you no' ready?' Eddie asked Jane.

'Ready for what?'

'She's forgotten,' said Carly.

'What have I forgotten?' exclaimed Jane.

'We're showing the Blood Brothers around the scheme. We said it would be a good idea if we familiarised ourselves with each other's territories. We're heading over to the Gallowburn after we've finished here.' The doorbell rang. 'That'll be them.'

'Shit,' said Jane, leaping up and rushing into her bedroom.

'I'll let them in,' said Harry.

He returned with Logan, Gary and Digger in tow, none of whom looked the worse for wear after the previous evening's festivities.

'Morning,' said Digger cheerfully. He smiled and clapped his hands together. 'Everyone ready?'

'We're just waiting for Jane,' replied Eddie.

'Typical woman, always late. Why don't you stick the kettle on while we wait, sweetheart?' he asked Carly. His grin dropped at her stony expression. 'Or I can do it if you show me where everything is.'

She broke into a smile. 'Sit down, I'll make the tea.'

'Cheers, doll,' he said, taking a seat at the table. 'It's no' gonnae be much fun tramping around the streets in this weather. It's bloody freezing.'

'But necessary,' commented Logan, leaning against the kitchen counter not far from Carly and watching her from the corner of his eye.

'Aye, I suppose,' said Digger.

'You got any biscuits?' Gary asked Carly.

'You're supposed to be dieting,' Digger told him.

'I need the calories to protect me from the cold.'

'What a load of shite. You should come to the gym with me. It'll do you the world of good.'

'I hate gyms, they're full of posers.'

'I agree, Gary,' said Eddie. 'I've never been to a gym a day in my life and look at me, the picture of health.' He ended this statement by patting his beer belly, which jiggled.

Gary regarded him with a raised eyebrow before leaning into Digger and whispering, 'I'll come with you tomorrow.'

Jane entered the kitchen, having hurriedly pulled on some clothes and dragged a comb through her hair. The first thing she noticed was Logan leaning against the kitchen counter, watching

Carly make the tea. Carly herself appeared not to have noticed the attention, or if she had she was choosing to ignore it.

'Do you want a hand?' Jane asked her, placing herself between her sister and Logan.

'No, thanks, I've got it,' Carly replied.

They all gathered around the table to chat and drink their tea, the awkwardness of the previous evening now gone. Harry got on particularly well with Digger, the two sharing a similar sense of humour, while Gary and Peanut enjoyed swapping stories. Jane noted that Logan was by far the quietest and most serious of the Blood Brothers. He talked with them all amiably enough but those sharp eyes of his were continually drawn to Carly. She'd elected not to speak, enjoying listening to the conversation rather than joining in.

16

Once they'd all finished their tea, the Savages and Blood Brothers left the flat. Eddie took it upon himself to act as tour guide, all of them following his pre-planned route around Haghill while he gave a running commentary.

'And here's where Harry threw up after downing tequila shots in the pub,' Eddie cheerfully informed them while pointing to the doorway of a hairdressers just a few doors down from The Horseshoe Bar.

'Jeezo, you didnae need to tell them that,' groaned his son.

'I'm just giving them some local colour,' Eddie smiled back.

The group continued on their way. As they rounded the corner, they almost walked into Karen, who was accompanied by two of her cronies. All the blood drained from her face when she spotted Carly. The two groups came to a halt, staring at each other.

'On you go,' Eddie told Karen.

Peanut, Harry and Logan stepped aside so the three women could walk through the middle of their group. Carly was shocked when Karen didn't give them any of her lip. Instead, she passed them by, head bowed.

'What was that about?' said Gary.

'Carly beat the living shite out of her,' replied Harry. 'It served her right too, she was a gobby bitch. But no' any more,' he added with a satisfied smile.

Jane saw that Logan regarded Carly with even keener interest while Carly was busy watching Karen retreat down the street. Karen, for her part, kept glancing back over her shoulder at Carly as though afraid she would attack her again.

Once the tour was completed, Jane was a little dismayed by the men's suggestion that they all go to The Horseshoe Bar for a drink to warm up after tramping about in the cold.

'Don't you think we put enough away last night?' she said.

'You feeling rough, doll?' Gary asked her.

'Just a bit.'

'Don't worry, you can have a lemonade,' he smiled, patting her arm.

'Don't patronise me,' she replied, making his grin drop.

'We need to see the local boozer if we're to learn everything we need to know about this scheme,' said Logan. 'But Jane's right,' he told his friends. 'No alcohol. We've got to show them around the Gallowburn yet.'

'We're gonnae look like a right bunch of jessies if we go in there and order soft drinks,' replied Digger. 'Our reputations will be shot.'

'Good point. Okay, you can have one pint each then we go to the Gallowburn.'

This compromise settled on, they all walked to the pub together, Logan falling into step beside Carly.

'Don't feel bad,' he told her.

'About what?' she replied.

'I saw the guilt in your eyes when that woman went by. She could have caused you and your family a lot of trouble in the future. You just made sure that won't happen.'

'You're right, she would. Thanks,' she said, looking a little brighter. 'I never thought of it like that.'

'You're welcome.'

Carly regarded Logan with more interest. At first, she'd thought he had the same quiet seriousness Dean had possessed, which had worried her, but she saw there was kindness there too. She'd assumed the glint in his eyes had been cunning. Now she realised they sparkled with intelligence. She got the feeling there was more to the leader of the Blood Brothers than met the eye.

'Who's this then?' smiled Derek, who was behind the bar polishing glasses.

'Logan, Digger, Gary,' replied Eddie, making the introductions.

'Nice to meet you, boys. Are you relatives of this lot?'

'Naw,' replied Harry eagerly. 'These are the Blood Brothers from the Gallowburn scheme.'

'Really? I've heard of you. Nice to meet you, lads.'

'You too,' replied Logan. 'You've got a nice place here.'

'Thanks. It's the heart of the community, if I do say so myself.'

Derek served their drinks and then quietly asked Carly if she would watch the bar while he went to the bathroom as he was working on his own. His bladder was notoriously weak and he was always having to nip off to spend a penny.

Derek rushed off in the direction of the toilets while Carly took up position behind the bar.

'You look a natural behind there,' commented Logan, who had elected to sit at the bar.

'I used to work here,' she replied as she pulled a pint for a regular. 'I enjoyed it too.'

Carly began to grow a little uncomfortable as she was reminded of when Dean had sat at the bar to watch her work. Even the look in Logan's eyes was similar.

Seeing her sister was becoming uneasy, Jane sat beside Logan and engaged him in conversation, allowing Carly to breathe easier. The moment Derek returned, Carly shot off to the toilets. Thankfully they were empty, so she gripped onto the sink and fought off the unwanted memories of her murdering bastard of a cousin.

'Carly, are you okay?' said Jane as she entered the toilets.

Her sister straightened up and smiled. 'Aye, why wouldn't I be?'

'I've seen how Logan looks at you. He fancies you.'

'Aye, I just realised.'

'How do you feel about that?'

'I'm no' interested in any man.'

'He's good-looking.'

'I don't care. I lost the love of my life, so there's no point.'

Jane decided not to come out with useless platitudes about her having the rest of her life ahead of her. Clearly Carly wasn't ready for another relationship, and Jane thought that was wise.

'The way he sat at the bar and watched me work freaked me out a bit,' continued Carly. 'It's what Dean used to do. What if he's the same as Dean?' she said, eyes wide.

'I don't think it's fair to brand Logan a psycho because we don't know him, but there's no doubt he's a dangerous man. He wouldn't be leader of the Blood Brothers if he wasn't. Shall I get Uncle Eddie to tell him to back off?'

'No, I don't want to cause any animosity, no' when we're all supposed to be working together. I'll just keep him at arm's length. Hopefully he'll soon get the message.'

'Okay. Ready to go back out there?'

Carly nodded determinedly.

They left the toilets and rather than head back to the bar, Carly took a seat at the table between Harry and Peanut, resolutely refusing to look at Logan, who had remained at the bar.

Jane took the stool beside the leader of the Blood Brothers and asked Derek for a glass of water.

'Is Carly okay?' Logan asked her. 'She looked a little worried about something.'

'Just memories of Jack,' she replied. 'He was the love of her life and she's still getting over his death.'

'I heard he died in her arms.'

'He did and it was a brutal death. Thank God she's so strong because that would have broken a lot of people.' Jane turned to him with a meaningful look. 'I don't know how long it'll take her to recover from the trauma.'

'I understand.'

'Good because we don't want anything getting in the way of the alliance between our two groups.'

'I agree. She's just such a unique woman.'

'She is that. Her grief nearly killed her, but she came through it. Carly doesnae need any complications right now.'

'Don't worry, I'll just admire her from afar.'

'Thank you. Despite your fierce reputation, I get the feeling you're a good man.'

'I try to be. It's like walking a tightrope in this business.'

'That's true. Sometimes it's hard working out what's the right thing to do. The lines become blurred.'

'I always think that as long as you look after those you love, then you're on the right track.'

Jane was a little surprised by this feared gang leader expressing such a sentimental statement and she wondered if he was taking the piss, but he looked entirely serious. Thankfully her uncle announced that it was time to head over to the Gallowburn scheme, so she was saved from replying.

The Savages followed the Blood Brothers in Peanut's car and this time Logan led the tour. Gallowburn was larger than Haghill, so it took them more time to cover it. By the time they'd finished, they were all freezing.

Logan took them to a café for something to eat and Gary and Peanut pulled two tables together so they could sit as a group. They all elected for something light, except Gary and Eddie, who ordered an enormous fry-up each.

'That greasy shite's gonnae kill you,' commented Peanut with distaste as he watched Eddie cut into his fried egg, the runny yolk spilling across the plate.

'Probably, but at least I'll die happy,' he replied.

'So, Jane,' said Digger. 'Tell us about The Unbeatable Bitches.'

'What do you want to know?'

'Well, how many of them are single for a start?'

'Sorry about him,' Logan told Jane. 'He's got a one-track mind.'

'Don't worry about it,' she replied. 'He's no' the first man to be fascinated by The Bitches but I wouldnae recommend pissing them off. Allies or not, they will strip you naked in the middle of the street and beat you if you insult them.'

'I'm even more fascinated now,' grinned Digger.

'Do they help keep watch over the scheme?' Logan asked Jane.

'Aye,' she replied. 'They're my eyes and ears. They always let me know the moment any trouble kicks off.'

'That's good. We've got the same arrangement here, only our crew's mainly male.'

'Tell your people no' to give The Bitches any shite because they will pay for it.'

'I will. Excuse me,' said Logan when his phone rang. He got to his feet and headed outside to take the call.

Carly watched him through the window, which was steamed up thanks to the warmth inside and the cold outside. Logan's expression told her nothing but he paced back and forth as he spoke. The call didn't last long and when he hung up, he remained in thoughtful silence on the pavement for a full thirty seconds before coming back inside.

'I've just had a worrying phone call,' he said as he sat down. 'Craig Lawson's been communicating with Cole Alexander.'

'Are you saying that prick's involved in Cole's shenanigans?' said Digger.

'It's looking that way.'

'Who's Craig Lawson?' said Eddie.

'He's to us what Cole Alexander is to your family. He's serving life in Barlinnie for murder. I suspected he might be involved, so I asked a couple of contacts on the inside to keep an eye on him.'

'Who did he kill?' said Jane.

The Blood Brothers looked at each other.

'Someone called Ben Wilson,' replied Logan. 'He also knew about Allegra Abernethy's murder.'

'The girlfriend of your previous leader?'

Logan nodded.

Allegra's relationship with Jamie Gray was rather a romantic one. She'd been the daughter of one of the richest men in Glasgow. Cameron Abernethy had objected to her dating a scheme rat, as he'd referred to Jamie, who'd come from a struggling single-parent family. When Allegra had rebelled against Cameron, he'd killed her.

'Allegra's da' and Craig tried to kill Jamie,' continued Logan. 'They sent a load of their minions in to distract us so they could take him out. It was such a huge fight the papers even reported on it. They called it the Battle of Gallowburn.'

'We've had a few do's like that ourselves,' said Eddie.

'Craig and Cameron tried to hang Jamie from the hanging tree in the middle of the scheme but Jamie battered the hell out of them.'

'Wait, you have a hanging tree?' said Harry.

'Aye. We call that area The Gallows. It's where they used to hold public executions in the bad old days.'

'I'd like to see that,' said Carly.

'Why?' frowned Eddie.

She shrugged. 'It sounds like interesting history.'

'We can head over there, if you like?' Logan told her. 'We passed the area on the tour but we didnae go near the tree. It's a creepy spot, to be honest. Only drunk teenagers go near it. Anyway, I found out Craig Lawson is related to the Alexander family.'

'Seriously?'

'Aye. Second cousins through Cole's maw, Jessica.'

'That bitch,' glowered Carly.

'The two families fell out about something years ago and don't have much to do with each other but I reckon that's all changed now. My contact thinks Cole's been communicating with Craig through a third party in the prison.'

'Who?'

'He doesnae know but he's trying to find out.'

'I don't like this at all,' said Jane.

'More bloody Alexander cockroaches crawling out of the woodwork,' grumbled Harry.

'I'll let you know as soon as I hear more,' said Logan.

'I've got contacts in Bar-L too,' replied Eddie. 'I'll see what they know.'

'It feels like a web's being woven around us all,' commented Carly.

'That's very poetic, doll,' said Eddie. 'And I fear you're right.'

17

After they'd finished at the café, they headed towards the very heart of Gallowburn, a wide expanse of grass with a huge twisted oak tree sitting in the middle. At the edge of this expanse were houses, their backs turned to the hanging tree, as though they didn't want to look at it. Carly shivered as the icy breeze sliced through them all. Despite the houses and cars around them, the spot felt isolated and eerie.

'Creepy,' commented Harry.

'Aye, it is,' replied Logan. 'Us locals avoid it if we can.'

'Are there any ghost stories?' said Carly.

'A few. The people who live in the surrounding houses have reported weird sightings. Occasionally a body's been seen swinging from the branches. The polis have been called out a few times but when they get here they don't find anything. Some people say they've heard the shouts of the crowd watching someone being executed.'

'Well, that's disturbing,' said Peanut.

They all looked up when soft white flakes began to fall.

'Hey, it's snowing,' said Gary unnecessarily. 'I bloody love snow.'

'We don't get proper snow,' replied Digger. 'Just stuff that turns to brown slush the next day.'

'I don't know, it's getting pretty heavy,' said Eddie when the flakes thickened and came down faster, whirling and eddying through the air. 'We'd better get back to Haghill while we still can.'

The Savages said goodbye to their new allies and hurried back the way they'd come. Carly glanced over her shoulder and saw the Blood Brothers had been reduced to mere shadows in the swirling snow, standing beside the hanging tree watching them go.

'They're gonnae freeze if they stay there,' said Harry, falling into step beside her.

Almost as though they'd heard him, the three men turned and headed in the opposite direction to themselves before being swallowed up by the snow.

'Gary and Digger might like a laugh and a joke,' continued Harry. 'But I reckon they can be seriously scary bastards when they want to be.'

'I agree,' said Carly.

'Logan too. He fancies you, by the way.'

'So Jane's already said.' The way she spoke indicated she wasn't going to discuss it any further.

The roads were already coated in white, and Peanut took his time driving them back to Haghill, visibility seriously reduced.

'I hope it isn't like this on my wedding day,' said Jane.

'At least we're no' going far,' replied Eddie. 'And you're having the ceremony and reception all in one venue.'

'True but I'm thinking of the photos. If it's like this on the big day, it'll look more like a trek through the Arctic than a romantic wedding.'

'This weather's also a good opportunity for someone to cause some chaos,' commented Peanut from the driver's seat.

'Surely anyone who tries to attack us in this weather will be as blind as we are?' said Harry.

'Maybe, maybe not.'

'We need to stay alert tonight,' said Eddie. 'Our enemies might decide to take advantage of this snow.'

* * *

The three Savage Sisters and Jennifer settled down to a cosy night in together. It was still snowing outside but they'd drawn the curtains against it, the kitchen just lit with lamps as they watched a spooky film.

The heroine was making her way down a dark corridor in the creepy mansion, her way lit only by a candle. There was a creak up ahead, beyond the pool of light cast by the flickering flame. The heroine stopped, the light shaking as her hand trembled with fear. She jumped when the door to her left slowly swung open to reveal...

There was a bang at the front door of the flat.

'Jesus,' shrieked Rose, throwing the bowl of popcorn she held into the air. They all attempted to dodge and failed when the popcorn came down on them like sticky rain.

'It seems we've got a visitor,' said Jennifer.

'And I'm gonnae rip off their baws,' scowled Rose, plucking pieces of popcorn from her hair.

'We're no' expecting anyone,' said Jane. 'Get ready.'

The four women hurried into the spare bedroom that had once belonged to the sisters' father, Alec. They grabbed a baseball bat each, the weapons kept propped up against the wall. They also took a Taser each and a cannister of pepper spray.

'I'll open the door,' Jane told them. 'You be ready.'

The women nodded in response.

Jane unlocked the door and gripped the handle. 'One, two, three.'

She yanked open the door, all three drawing back the bats.

'Woah, it's us,' cried Eddie as he, Harry and Peanut held up their hands defensively.

'Jeezo, you had us worried,' breathed Jane, lowering the bat.

The men hurried inside, Peanut closing and locking the front door behind them.

'Is the back door locked?' Eddie asked them.

'Aye,' replied Jane. 'Why, what's happening?'

'Someone was lurking around our hoose. Fortunately, Peanut decided to stay with us in case of any trouble. We went out to look and saw someone jump over the back wall and run off. We thought they might come here.'

'Let them try,' said Rose, brandishing the bat.

'Why have you got popcorn on your heid?' frowned Harry.

'That's your fault. I jumped when you lot banged on the door and threw it all in the air.'

'It's in your hair too, Jen,' Peanut told her.

'You knocked just as the ghost was about to pop out at Marianne,' replied Jennifer.

'Who?'

'The woman in the film.' A scream emanated from the kitchen. 'That'll be her now.'

The men stamped the snow from their boots and followed the women into the kitchen where popcorn was still scattered across the floor. Rose began sweeping it up with the dustpan and brush.

'Any idea who was lurking around your house?' Carly asked her uncle.

'Naw, we just saw a figure.'

'Hopefully they'll have frozen to death by now.'

'The snow's even thicker out there. It provides a good cover but it's hard to see. We might all have to hunker down here for the night.'

'Well, there's the bed in Da's old room. Two of you can share that and one of you can have the couch.'

'I'll take the couch,' Eddie said hastily. 'You two can share the bed,' he told Harry and Peanut.

'Piss off,' retorted the latter, who'd been peering out of the kitchen window, looking for any intruders. 'You're best sharing with your boy. It's just creepy if I do it.'

'Amen to that,' replied Harry.

'Fine. Me and Harry will take the bed, you can have the couch.'

Carly stared out of the window at the swirling mass of snow.

'You okay?' Jane asked her.

'I'm wondering if it's Cole out there.'

'It was probably just someone playing a prank.'

'They'd have to be a moron to play a trick like that in this weather. No, there's more to it. Cole's smart. He'll know something like that wouldn't be enough to scare three men like them. He wants us all here tonight.'

Eddie overheard this and stood on her other side. 'You think so, doll?'

'I know so.'

'What could it achieve?'

'No idea but he must have a plan.'

'I hope he's no' thinking of setting fire to the flat with all of us inside,' whispered Jane so Rose wouldn't overhear.

'I don't think he'd risk that,' replied Eddie. 'No' when we're in a block of flats. It would be a sure-fire way to involve the polis.'

'It won't be anything as obvious as that,' said Carly, keeping her gaze on the window. 'Cole probably has something much more devious in mind.'

Movement caught Jane's eye. 'Is someone out there?'

Carly and Eddie both looked too.

'It's hard to tell with the snow,' replied the latter. 'Harry, turn out the lights.'

Harry obeyed, plunging the room into darkness. They gathered together, gazing into the dizzying white whirl. A figure stepped forward, breaking through the flakes, scattering them momentarily before they resumed their swirling vortex. The figure came right up to the window, staring at them through the glass.

'Cole,' murmured Carly.

His green eyes flicked around the assembled faces until they found her. Snowflakes had settled on his long eyelashes. Although it was dark, the white of the snow cast its own glow, illuminating his face. Carly heard a gasp, she assumed from Rose, and she couldn't blame her. The scars on Cole's face were highlighted in vivid relief. They cut across his chin, cheeks and forehead, twisting and distorting what had once been a handsome visage. The worst of the damage came from a scar that sliced through his left cheek, across the middle of his nose and then the right cheek in an arc from where Carly had slashed him with a shard of the shattered vase. This had misshapen his once aquiline nose, making the end appear bulbous. Each scar was thick, ridged and angry, reflecting the rage that shone in Cole's eyes.

He ignored the others, concentrating the full force of that

disturbing gaze on Carly. Slowly, he raised his hand and dragged his index finger across his throat in a threat.

'Bastard,' yelled Harry. 'I'll kill him.'

'No, Harry,' called Carly. 'Don't go out there. It's a trap.'

Peanut and Eddie between them grabbed Harry and held him fast.

'Are we just gonnae let him get away?' exclaimed Harry, struggling against them.

'If you go out there you won't come back,' Carly told him. 'No' in one piece anyway.'

This finally caused Harry to go still.

Satisfied her cousin couldn't escape, Carly turned back to Cole, whose black hair was now coated white. He pressed his hand to the window right where her face was before sliding it down the glass, making a squeaking sound before turning and walking away, the snow swirling around him like a cloak before he vanished.

'What the hell was that about?' said Jennifer.

Carly yanked the curtains closed. 'He was trying to lure us out there. God only knows what sort of trap he's set.'

'His face,' said Rose. 'It was so bad.'

'That's his own fault,' replied Eddie. 'If he hadnae been a scheming wee shite, he wouldnae have been smashed in the face with a vase. It's no' fair him trying to put the blame on our Carly.'

'I wonder what he was trying to achieve?' said Jennifer.

'We'll check it out in the morning. Hopefully we'll be able to find a clue. That way we might be able to guess how he'll come at us next. Let's get a good night's kip. We're gonnae need it.'

* * *

The Savages, along with Peanut and Jennifer, passed the night undisturbed. The snow had stopped during the night and the dawn had brought a weak sun that managed to break through the cloud. The ground was coated in a thick blanket of virginal snow.

Eddie opened the back door and they all stared out at the rear garden. No trace was left of Cole's visit, the snow having filled in his tracks.

'I hope there's no' any booby traps out there,' commented Rose. 'That's a shared garden.'

'We won't know until the snow starts to melt,' said Eddie. 'Is anyone likely to go out there?'

'I don't think so,' replied Carly. 'It's mostly elderly residents in this block, so they'll all be staying indoors.'

'Still, we cannae take any chances. We need to go around all the residents who have access to that garden and tell them to stay out of it until we give the all-clear but before we can dae that, we need to check the front path.'

They all rushed to the front door, which Eddie pulled open. The path from the door to the street was also carpeted with snow.

'There could be anything under that lot,' commented Peanut.

'Exactly, pal.'

'How do we make sure it's safe?' said Harry.

'Do you fancy a wee stroll?' smiled Eddie, making his son scowl.

'I've got an idea,' said Jane.

She disappeared back into the flat and returned carrying a brush. She leaned out of the door and began to gingerly sweep the path. All that was revealed were the stone flags, so she cautiously crept further along, continuing to sweep away the innocent snow, constantly expecting to reveal a nasty surprise. But there was nothing.

'Stop,' yelled Peanut.

Jane came to a halt, gripping the brush tightly as she glanced back over her shoulder. 'What is it?'

'Take three steps back slowly.'

Jane obeyed, continually looking down at the ground but seeing nothing.

'The danger's no' down there,' he told her. 'It's up there, between the trees.'

There were two small trees outside the flats either side of their path standing just under six feet tall. Squinting, Jane caught a glint of metal in the sunshine. 'Is that a hook?' she said.

'Aye,' replied Peanut. 'A few of them. Fish hooks strung on wire right at face height, for you and your sisters anyway.'

'Son of a bitch,' she hissed.

'I heard of some psycho using that same booby trap to defend their meth lab. Simple but effective and very nasty.'

'Let's take them down before someone gets hurt,' said Eddie.

Jane propped up the brush against the wall and hugged Peanut. 'Thank you. If it hadnae been for you, I would have been badly hurt.'

'Any time, doll,' he smiled, hugging her back.

A shocked Jennifer threw her arms around her fiancée.

Eddie and Harry between them dismantled the booby trap. After checking no more nasty surprises had been left for them at their front door or around their cars, they returned inside.

'It says a lot that Cole chose something that would hurt our faces,' said Carly.

'He wanted to maim someone,' commented Eddie. 'He was hoping one of us would run out there in the dark with all that snow and get a faceful of fish hooks. We'd have had nae chance of spotting them in that blizzard.'

'That's true,' said Peanut. 'I only saw them because the sunlight was hitting the metal.'

'And we've nae idea where Cole is now,' said Harry.

'I take it we can expect more sly attacks like this one?' said Jane.

'Absolutely,' said Eddie. 'So we need to stay on our guard. We also need to check the back garden.'

'Shall I nip out and pick up some brushes?' offered Peanut.

'Aye, please, pal. Jennifer and Harry can go with you. Safety in numbers and all that. While you're out, we'll go round the residents and warn them.'

They all departed on their various errands and met up back at the flat forty minutes later. The back garden was thoroughly checked but no booby traps were found, so they reconvened in the kitchen to warm up with a cup of tea each and to discuss their next move.

'At least the sun's starting to melt the snow,' Rose told Jane and Jennifer. 'So hopefully it'll be fine for your wedding day.'

'Fingers crossed,' replied the latter.

'I hope Cole doesnae decide to pull any of his tricks at your wedding,' said Eddie.

'That's what's worrying me,' replied Jane.

'How would you feel about bringing in the Blood Brothers to help keep an eye on things? They don't have to attend the ceremony, they can just keep watch outside.'

'I can get The Bitches to do that.'

'But they're your pals. Surely you want them inside for the ceremony? And your best women are bridesmaids.'

'Well, I suppose we could. What do you think, Jen?'

'It's a good idea,' she replied. 'Those fish hooks show that we cannae take any chances.'

'Okay, we can ask them. They might no' agree though.'

'I think they will,' said Eddie. 'Now that's the wedding sorted out we need to discuss how we're gonnae get Cole.'

'There's only one way,' said Carly. 'You'll have to use me as bait.'

'No,' said Jane and Rose in unison.

'What do you think, Uncle Eddie?' Carly said.

'If you weren't my niece, I would think it was a good idea but I'm reluctant to do it. This sod is incredibly dangerous. I get the feeling he'd be able to sense any trap a mile off.'

'Maybe but that doesnae mean he won't be able to resist walking into it if it gets him what he wants.'

'It's out of the question,' said Jane when their uncle appeared to be considering it.

'I understand why you're worried, hen,' he replied. 'But it might be the only way to end this.'

'I will not let Carly join our parents and Jack in the cemetery,' she retorted.

'We won't let that happen.'

'I don't care, I'm no' having it. We've already lost enough people. Do you think Da' would want Carly being put at risk?'

The mention of his deceased younger brother decided Eddie. 'You're right, we won't do it.'

'But it's the only way,' said Carly.

'Then we need to figure out a better way,' said her uncle. 'I know you're keen on getting revenge but it's no' worth your life, and Jack wouldnae want you putting at risk either.'

'Do we mention last night to Toni?' said Harry.

'Christ, no. If she found out we let Cole wander off into the snow then she might decide some eyeball gouging is in order.

You're right, Carly, doll, we do need to lure Cole into a trap but with different bait. What else does he want?'

'Toni,' said Peanut. 'He'd come out of hiding to take her down.'

'That's like using a shark to catch a halibut,' commented Harry.

Despite the tension, they all laughed.

'I don't think Toni would agree to be bait,' said Eddie. 'And I'm no' crazy about asking her either. We could use Cole's maw but he wouldnae gi'e a shite.'

'So we're back to square one?' said Harry.

'Maybe we should concentrate on the wedding and think about all this after?' offered Rose.

'If we do there's a chance one of us will be at the wedding with fish hooks sticking out of their face,' said Peanut grimly.

18

The Blood Brothers agreed to hang around outside Jane and Jennifer's wedding and make sure no one tried to interfere.

The day prior to the wedding was quiet enough, apart from for Rose, who spent her time triple checking all the arrangements and making sure everyone was ready to play their part. Carly drove her sisters into the city to collect their dresses from the boutique while Jennifer went to a different boutique with her own bridesmaids to collect their dresses. That evening they went out on their respective hen nights. Jennifer and her hens went to a nightclub in the city, Jane and Jennifer wanting to stick to the rule of not seeing each other until the wedding.

Jane's hens consisted of her sisters, Rose's best friend Tamara, Harry, Eddie, Peanut and half The Bitches, while the other half of the girl gang accompanied Jennifer.

'How does it feel to be honorary women?' Rose grinned at the three men, their party occupying a table in The Horseshoe Bar.

'Fantastic,' grinned back Harry. 'I've always wanted to know what happens on a hen night.'

'Don't get excited,' replied Jane. 'This is gonnae be a few quiet drinks followed by a meal and then an early night. I don't want to be hungover on my wedding day.'

'So no male strippers then?'

'Why don't you take a moment to think about that statement?'

'Oh, aye,' he said when he recalled who Jane was marrying. 'Great, a sexy female stripper then?'

'No strippers. Like I said, I just want a quiet drink.'

'Well, that's disappointing. Shall I ask Derek to fetch us some Bovril and slippers?'

'How no'? It sounds pretty nice.'

'This is gonnae be a fun night,' he murmured to Peanut, making him grin.

A delivery driver entered with a parcel and headed over to Derek.

'All right, pal,' said Derek. 'You're working late.'

'I'm catching up after the snow yesterday,' mumbled the driver. 'Bloody stuff caused chaos with the deliveries yesterday. Anyway, this is for Jane Savage.'

'She's over there,' he said, nodding at her table. 'She's the one wearing the bride badge.'

'Cheers,' the man replied before wandering over to her table. 'Jane Savage?'

'Aye.'

'Delivery for you,' he said, holding the parcel out to her.

'For me? Why are you bringing it here and no' my home?'

'This is the address the sender gave us.'

'Who's the sender?'

'Sorry, pal, I don't have that info. Night.'

'Night,' she murmured back, staring at the box she held in trepidation.

'Are you expecting anything?' Carly asked her.

'Nope.'

'Give it here, doll,' said Eddie, holding his hands out for it. 'I'll open it.'

Jane handed the parcel to her uncle, who placed it on the table.

'Here you go, Da',' said Harry, producing a penknife from his pocket and holding it out to him.

'Thanks, son.'

Eddie took it from him and used it to carefully slit open the tape binding the box shut. He handed the knife back to Harry and glanced around the table before pulling back the flaps of the box.

'There's two dolls inside,' he said.

Gingerly he put a hand in, as though afraid the dolls would bite him. He picked up one and placed it on the table. The doll was made of cloth and was fifteen inches long. It wore a white wedding dress. It had a noose around its neck and there were small stitches across its face that resembled scars. Its light brown hair had been cut short to resemble Jane's.

'God, that's creepy,' said Rose.

Eddie produced the second doll and placed it beside its friend.

'The hair's longer on that one,' said Rose.

'Because they're meant to represent Jane and Jennifer,' replied Carly.

'Want us to go after the delivery driver?' said an outraged Tammy, who was one of The Bitches.

'There's no point, he'll be long gone by now,' replied Jane. 'Derek,' she called across the room.

'Aye?' he called back from behind the bar as he pulled a pint.

'Do you know that delivery driver?'

'Aye, that's Nawaz. He's been doing this round for a couple of years now.'

'Thanks,' she replied. 'I've no doubt these are from Cole,' Jane told the others, gesturing to the dolls.

'Does this mean he's gonnae cause trouble tomorrow at the wedding?' said Rose.

'He's probably just trying to put us on edge.'

'He wants to spoil it but we won't let him.'

'Too right we won't,' said Carly. 'Everything will be fine as long as we stay on our guard. Are you going to tell Jen about this?' she asked Jane.

'I think I should. It's better if she's warned.'

'We won't let anything spoil your big day, doll,' Peanut told her. 'You're gonnae have a great time and make some lovely memories. No vindictive wee shite will get in the way of that.'

'Thank you,' she smiled back. 'Could you throw those away, Uncle Eddie?' she added, gesturing to the dolls with a grimace.

'Course I can,' he replied, putting them back in the box and closing the lid. 'Hey, Derek,' he said, getting to his feet. 'Can I shove this in your outside bin?'

'Aye, go for it,' he called back.

'I'll go with him,' said Peanut.

'Well, that put a dampener on the evening,' sighed Jane as the two men left on their errand.

'We've got the meal yet at the Chinese restaurant,' said Rose. 'We'll have some good food and a laugh and forget about this.'

The hen party and its honorary men enjoyed their meal, which lightened the atmosphere. Jane was almost able to forget about the dolls and concentrate on tomorrow.

Harry, Eddie and Peanut said they would stay over at the flat again that night in case of any trouble. Jennifer was staying at Leonie's flat and would get ready for the wedding there.

The Savages and Peanut had said goodbye to their friends and were talking and laughing together as they walked down the street, Harry and Carly arm in arm. The evening was cold but there'd been no sign of any more snow and the remnants of the last deluge had turned into a dirty slush.

Rose frowned as they approached the flat. 'There's something hanging from the door.'

They all stopped.

'It's another doll,' said Eddie.

'Careful,' said Peanut when his friend took a step forward. 'Don't forget the fish hooks.'

Eddie nodded, took out his phone and switched on the torch. He shone it across the stretch of air between the two trees but could see nothing. He then checked the path.

'It looks clear,' he said.

The others anxiously watched as he tentatively walked up the path, alert for any booby traps. The old, defunct graveyard that sat across the street only added to the menace in the air. When Eddie reached the front door, he tore the doll free of the tape that had been used to stick it there before checking the door.

'It's safe,' he called.

'Who's the doll supposed to be this time?' Jane asked him.

'No one,' he said, hiding it behind his back. 'Get the door open quickly, Cole could be hanging about.'

Jane unlocked the door and they hurried inside. Once they were all in, she closed and locked it.

'Let's have a look at the doll then,' said Rose.

'You don't want to do that. I'll just throw it away.'

'You're hiding something, Uncle Eddie.'

'Show us, Da',' said Harry. 'We can take it.'

Eddie sighed and held it out. The doll was of the same as the previous two, only this one had its hair cut to its shoulders, just like Carly's. Its face also bore the stitched scars, only there was a long gash across the stomach in red to represent blood.

'I'm sorry, hen,' said Eddie sadly. 'I didnae want you to see it.'

Carly took a deep breath before replying. 'It's just a stupid doll. It cannae do any harm.' She forced a smile. 'Who wants a coffee?'

'Sounds lovely,' smiled Eddie, proud of his niece's strength.

Carly headed into the kitchen first while the others stripped off their coats and shoes. Only once she had her back to them all did she allow her smile to drop and the shiver she'd been stifling to ripple down her spine. Did Cole intend to slit her open just as Dean had ripped open Jack? The thought of suffering the same agonising end was very distressing.

No, she would not let Cole get to her. The doll couldn't hurt her, it was just an intimidation tactic. She hoped Cole didn't have anything nasty planned for tomorrow. If he did spoil her sister's big day, she would make him suffer.

* * *

'You look gorgeous,' smiled Rose.

'Are you sure?' replied Jane, looking down at herself.

'Absolutely. Tell her, Carly.'

'She's right,' replied Carly. 'You look stunning.'

'I don't feel right in a dress. I havenae worn one since I was eight years old.'

Jane had no idea how elegant she looked. Rather than a flouncy meringue, she'd opted for something closer fitting, her satin ivory dress plunging to the floor, flattering her tall, lithe figure. The neck was v-shaped, the bodice decorated with tiny fake pearls.

'Jen's gonnae be so proud of you,' smiled Rose. She waved a hand before her face. 'I think I'm gonnae cry.'

'Steady on,' replied Carly. 'We havenae even got to the venue yet.'

Jane peered out of the window. 'At least it's sunny and bright. I don't think we'll get any snow today.'

Eddie knocked on Jane's bedroom door. 'You decent, hen?'

'You can come in, I'm ready,' she called back.

The door opened to reveal Eddie in a smart blue suit. He'd remained behind with the sisters as he was giving Jane away. Peanut and Harry had already gone on to the venue to meet up with the Blood Brothers and make sure everything was safe.

'You look so beautiful,' he said, eyes filling with emotion. 'I wish your parents were here, they'd be so proud of you, doll.'

Jane also turned misty-eyed. 'Thanks.'

'The car's outside. You ready for your big moment?'

She smiled and nodded, Rose handing Jane her bouquet of red roses and anemones. They headed outside to the waiting limousine. The neighbours who hadn't been invited to the wedding had come out onto the street to wave them off. There were a couple of bigots on the scheme who were against a gay wedding but the majority had been very accepting of it.

Before they got in, Eddie asked the chauffeur for the password. The owner of the limo company had been a bit bemused by his customer's insistence that the driver give them a prearranged password, but the extra cash Eddie had bunged him had soon silenced his objections. The last thing Eddie wanted was for them to be hijacked by a scarred loon on Jane's wedding day. The cannister of pepper spray in his suit pocket made him feel only slightly better.

The three women got in the back of the car together, Rose

fussing over the way Jane sat down, ensuring she wouldn't crease her dress.

'I cannae believe you're getting married,' Carly told Jane.

'Me neither,' she smiled.

'It's a good job you're marrying one of The Bitches,' said Rose. 'No other woman could handle you.'

'I'll take that as a compliment,' replied Jane wryly.

19

Fifteen minutes later, they pulled up outside the wedding venue, which was an events centre situated beside the Forth and Clyde Canal. They'd arranged it so Jennifer would be there first and Jane would arrive second. All the guests had already gone inside.

The chauffeur got out to open the doors for them.

Once they were out of the car, Rose smoothed Jane's gown.

Logan, Digger and Gary were hanging around discreetly, keeping an eye out. All three wore smart expensive suits and Logan had even tamed his curls, which were combed back off his face.

'Hello, ladies,' smiled Digger. 'You're all looking gorgeous.'

'Are they the Blood Brothers?' Rose whispered to Carly.

'Aye.'

'Awesome. They're pretty hot, even the tubby one.'

'You think anything in trousers is hot,' Carly whispered back.

'Thanks for coming,' said Eddie, shaking the men's hands in turn.

'No problem,' replied Logan. 'Everything's quiet. We've stationed a few more of our people up and down the street, so they can let us know if anyone approaches. Elijah and David have sent a few men too. They're keeping watch at the back of the building.'

'Good. It sounds like you have it all in hand.' Eddie looked to Jane. 'You ready, doll?' he smiled, holding his arm out to her.

'Aye, I am,' she smiled back, accepting his arm.

Carly and Rose followed them inside where they were led by a member of staff to a big barn door. The large space was lined with chairs, the ceiling strung with fairy lights and on both sides of the room was a row of enormous vases bursting with flowers of all colours and descriptions. Every seat was occupied and Jane coloured when all eyes turned her way. She'd never liked being the centre of attention. Instead, she focused her gaze on Jennifer and her eyes widened. Her betrothed usually dressed casually, so it was a shock to see her done up to the nines. Jennifer had plumped for a very sleek off-the-shoulder mermaid gown that clung to her thighs and flared out at the bottom, pooling slightly at the back. Her long dark hair had been pulled back into a low bun, a thick choker of pearls around her neck. The effect was incredibly elegant and Jane couldn't help but beam. Jennifer, similarly struck by Jane's appearance, smiled right back at her.

The four of them progressed up the aisle that cut through the middle of the rows of seats to UB40's cover of Elvis's 'Can't Help Falling in Love'. Eddie took Jane's hand and placed it in Jennifer's before he took his place off to one side with Rose and Carly. Leonie and Donna, two of the senior Bitches, were acting as Jennifer's bridesmaids.

The ceremony was conducted smoothly and Jane and Jennifer were soon walking back down the aisle together arm in arm, a married couple. Photos were taken in the rear courtyard under a large pagoda garlanded with more flowers before everyone was ushered inside an even larger room for the reception, keen to escape the cold.

'What do you think?' Rose anxiously asked the couple.

'It's absolutely beautiful,' murmured Jane, gazing at all the flowers and lights. 'And everything went off perfectly. You've done an amazing job.'

'I agree,' smiled Jennifer. 'It couldn't have been better.'

Rose breathed a sigh of relief as months of tension flowed out of her. Finally, she could relax and have fun.

Everyone enjoyed a delicious sit-down meal, after which the elaborate five-tiered cake was cut, then the dancing began. Some guests elected to prop up the bar while the remainder mingled and chatted. Jane asked Harry and Eddie to invite the Blood Brothers inside for a drink. They left and returned a couple of minutes later with the three men, who were grateful to be in the warmth. They offered their congratulations to the couple before Gary and Digger ordered a pint of lager each.

'I'll have a coffee,' said Logan.

'Ya big jessie,' commented Gary.

'I'm bloody freezing. I cannae stand the thought of a cold drink, and just one pint each, okay? We're still on duty.'

'Fine by me. I'll keep an eye out on all these fit birds,' Gary said, his gaze eagerly wandering over The Bitches as well as the two unwed Savage Sisters.

'I'm Rose,' she said, hurrying to introduce herself. 'Carly and Jane's younger sister. I've always wanted to meet the Blood Brothers.'

Her initial interest was in Logan but when she realised he was discreetly watching Carly, who was chatting with Derek and Brenda, she began flirting with both Gary and Digger instead.

Carly felt eyes on her. Glancing across the room, she saw Logan was watching her. When he realised he'd been caught out, he hastily looked down at his cappuccino. She considered approaching him to thank him for helping out with the wedding, until she recalled her sister telling her he fancied her, so she changed her mind. The last thing she wanted to do was give him any encouragement, even though he looked very handsome in his suit. He had that intensity she liked in a man.

'Why don't you go and talk to him?' said a voice.

Carly shook herself out of it. 'Sorry?'

'You've been staring at him for a while now,' replied Brenda kindly.

'I have? I didnae realise. I just happened to be looking in his direction.'

'Aye, course ya did,' Brenda replied sceptically. 'And I don't blame you, he's a good-looking boy. Why don't you ask him to dance?'

'No, thanks.'

'There's no harm in a wee dance,' prompted Derek. 'You might even have some fun.'

'I'm fine,' Carly said, turning her back on Logan and taking a sip of white wine. Because this was her sister's wedding day, she was allowing herself two glasses but no more.

Eddie came up to Brenda and wrapped an arm around her waist. 'Fancy a dance, doll?'

'I thought you'd never ask,' she smiled, taking his hand.

'What happened between you and Brenda?' Carly asked Derek. 'You were getting close at one point.'

'Aye but it fizzled oot,' he replied. 'I was a wee bit relieved, to be honest. She is a handful.'

They looked across the room to where Brenda was flinging a startled Eddie around the dance floor.

'You're no' wrong there,' said Carly. 'Maybe we can find you a lady?' she added, looking around the room.

'Naw. Most of them are too young for me.'

'Jennifer's aunt's really pretty and she's about your age.'

'Have you seen the eyebrows on her? I mean, they're huge. It looks like a wean's been doodling on her face in marker pen. I've never understood why women shave them off then draw them back on.'

'You fussy sod,' Carly smiled.

'I'm no' fussy, I just have standards. And what about you, doll? Are you no' ready to move on?'

She shook her head. 'I don't think I ever will be.'

'Course you will. You'll find the right man and he'll knock you off your feet. It'll be hard finding one worthy of you though.'

'You're so sweet, Derek,' Carly smiled, kissing his cheek. 'Uh-oh, it looks like Rose has got competition,' she continued, keen to change the subject.

Several of The Bitches had surrounded the Blood Brothers, eager to meet them. Rose stood among their number looking put out that she no longer had Gary and Digger's undivided attention. Digger had removed his suit jacket and was flexing his biceps, the shirt tightening around his enormous muscles, making the women giggle and coo.

'He should be careful,' commented Derek. 'They'll have him stripped off in seconds.'

'I think he'd enjoy it,' replied Carly.

'Logan's chatting to a couple of the lassies too.'

'Good for him.'

Derek decided not to push it.

Carly spotted two waiters slowly ambling around the room in their uniform of white shirt, black waistcoat, black trousers and long white apron. This was nothing unusual in itself, there was a team of half a dozen of them clearing plates and fetching drinks, but these two seemed to be paying more attention to the guests than their duties, especially the two brides.

'I don't like the look of those two waiters,' she told Derek.

He followed the direction in which she nodded. 'Aye, it's weird the way they're staring at Jane and Jen. Do you think it's anything to worry about?'

'Aye, I do.'

Carly looked around for her uncle and cousin. Eddie was still tangled up with Brenda, his face red and sweaty as he tried to keep up with her moves. Harry was dancing with two attractive female cousins of Jennifer's and Peanut had no less than four women dancing around him, throwing him flirtatious glances.

Rather than fight her way across the dance floor to try and extricate them from their partners, Carly hurried over to Logan with Derek following.

'I need your help,' she began.

'Is it about those two waiters walking around not doing any work?' he replied.

'Aye,' she said, surprised by his astuteness.

'I've already clocked them. I thought they were acting weird, so I asked the barman if he knew them. He said he's never seen them before. I've sent a couple of pals to sort them out. They should make their move any minute. Don't worry, they'll be discreet.'

Carly, Derek and The Bitches who'd been chatting to Logan turned to watch a short, scrawny ginger man the same age as the Blood Brothers make his way across the room towards one of the waiters. He was remarkable for the fact that he wore tracksuit bottoms, trainers and a puffer jacket, standing out amongst the smartly dressed guests.

'Excuse me, pal,' he said to one of the waiters. 'Where's the cludgy?'

As the waiter turned to point in the direction of the toilets, the taller man standing behind him whacked him across the back of the head, knocking him out. As the waiter fell, the taller man caught him and began hauling him towards the door that led into the courtyard where the photos had been taken earlier.

'Don't worry,' called the ginger man when several heads turned their way. 'He's just fainted, probably been on his feet too long. We'll take him outside for some fresh air.'

While this was going on and everyone was distracted, the second suspicious waiter was grabbed by two men and dragged backwards through a fire exit. No one even noticed.

Logan got to his feet. 'I'll go and deal with them.'

'I'm coming with you,' said Carly. 'I want a word with those wallopers.'

'As you like.'

'I'll come too,' said Derek. 'I won't let anyone spoil Jane and Jen's big day.'

The brides in question had noticed nothing unusual, too wrapped up in each other on the dance floor.

Carly turned to The Bitches gathered around them. 'I know you're guests here, girls, but could you keep an eye out in case anyone else tries something?'

'Of course, Carly,' replied Donna.

Carly headed outside to the courtyard with Derek and Logan where the two waiters had been taken. Logan's people had dragged them around the back of a storage shed, out of sight of the main building. The man who'd been hit across the head was slumped on the ground, dazed. His friend had been pushed back against the wall and glared at them defiantly.

Logan opened his mouth to question him, but Carly got there first.

'Right, you prick,' she began. 'What were you gonnae do in there?'

'What do you think, you stupid coo? We were gonnae serve drinks.'

Carly glanced around, ensuring no one was watching before driving her fist into his gut. The man gasped and collapsed to the ground.

'We already know Cole sent you,' she said, staring down at him pitilessly. 'What did he tell you to do?'

'Fuck off, slag.'

'Don't talk to the lady like that,' retorted Logan, drawing back his fist.

'Wait,' she told him. 'I've got a better idea.'

She stomped on the man's hand, grinding her high heel against it. When he squealed in pain, one of the men guarding him covered his mouth with his hand. Carly removed the fascinator from her hair, knelt down beside the man and inserted the pin of the fascinator under the fingernail of his left index finger. His eyes bulged and he screamed into the hand over his mouth.

'I repeat,' said Carly. 'What were you gonnae do?'

The hand was removed from his mouth so he could speak.

'We were supposed to throw fake blood all over the brides,' he rasped.

'What else?'

'Nothing.'

She retracted the pin and stuck it under the nail of his middle finger.

'What else?'

'While everyone was distracted, two other men were to abduct you.'

'Holy shit,' exclaimed Derek.

'And do what with me?' replied Carly steadily.

'Take you to Cole. After that, I've nae idea, I swear.' Despite the cold, sweat had popped out on his forehead.

'Where is Cole?'

'We don't know. The men were to call you when they'd got you and he'd gi'e them the address then.'

'Clever Cole.'

'Who are these other men?' Logan asked him.

'They snuck in as guests.'

'What do they look like?'

'One's big, over six feet tall in a grey suit. The other's big and tall too but he's got a thick red beard. He's wearing a light blue suit.' He groaned with relief when Carly retracted the pin from under his nail.

'We need to find those men,' said Logan. 'Wee Ginge, stay here and watch this pair.'

The scrawny ginger man nodded and produced a baton from his pocket, which he brandished with glee as he stood over his captives.

Carly, Derek and Logan rushed back inside the venue along with two of Logan's men. They frantically scanned the large room.

'Derek, tell Harry and Eddie what's happening,' said Carly.

'I'm no' leaving your side,' he replied. 'There are creeps here who want to kidnap you.'

'I promise I won't let anything happen to her,' Logan told him.

Derek didn't care that the Blood Brothers were supposed to be working with the Savage family. He refused to leave Carly with a man they'd known five minutes. 'You tell them,' he retorted.

Sensing his doubt, Logan nodded and rushed across the room to the dance floor.

'Don't leave my side, hen,' said Derek, wrapping an arm around Carly while Logan's men went off on the hunt.

'I don't see those two men,' said Carly. 'What if that prick gave us fake descriptions?'

'I doubt it. He was in too much pain to come up with a decent lie.'

'Maybe they saw their friends being dragged out and knew the game was up?'

'Hopefully.'

Derek's eyes widened and he groaned before collapsing to the floor.

'Derek,' she cried.

Carly turned to be confronted by the two men the fake waiter had described. Immediately she knew they would be a much tougher prospect than their friends. She jumped backwards when one of them tried to grab her, yanked the fascinator from her hair and stabbed him in the hand with the pin. He yelped and retracted his hand.

Carly gasped with surprise when arms wrapped around her from behind and lifted her up, her feet dangling a few inches from the floor, the fascinator falling from her hand. There was a third man she'd known nothing about.

'Get her out of here, quickly,' said the man with the red beard.

Carly frantically struggled as she was carried towards the fire exit. The panic started to rise inside her. These three men were a lot tougher and more professional than the usual neds Cole hung around with and she wasn't sure she'd be able to escape them. When she opened her mouth to call for help, a big hand smothered her cry. She drove the heel of her shoe into the shin of the man holding her. He grunted with pain but didn't release her. The door was shoved open, the guests continuing to drink and dance, oblivious as she was dragged outside.

20

The man holding Carly yelped and she was dropped onto the cobbles of the courtyard. She shot to her feet and turned. Wee Ginge was darting around all three men with what appeared to be a small blade in his hand, his mocking laughter high pitched and nasal.

'Come on, ya bunch of pricks,' he sneered, slashing at them when they got too close.

Carly took the opportunity to kick the man who'd grabbed her as hard as she could between the legs. As he dropped to his knees, she punched him in the face and he collapsed sideways.

The bearded man hit Wee Ginge in the jaw. His eyes widened and he dropped the knife.

'You're deid, ya wee shite,' growled the man.

Carly snatched up a chair that sat at one of the outdoor tables and smashed it across his back. The man cried out and staggered forward before falling to the ground.

Wee Ginge snatched up his knife and loomed over him. 'You're gonnae pay for hitting me, ya tadger.'

As Carly turned to face the man in the grey suit, the door burst open and Logan charged out. He took in the scene in an instant, not slowing his pace as he ran at the man. Carly gasped with surprise when Logan launched into a flying kick that would have made Harry proud, his foot connecting with the man's face, which was snapped sideways, blood bursting from his mouth. Logan landed in an elegant, cat-like crouch before jumping up and delivering an uppercut to the man's jaw that sent him sailing backwards.

Logan turned to Carly. 'Are you okay?'

She stared back at him, still astonished by the amazing kick. She was very aware that her heart was pounding and it was nothing to do with the fact that she'd almost been kidnapped.

'Err, yeah, fine,' she replied, shaking herself out of it. 'Your friend stopped them from taking me.'

'Good job, Wee Ginge,' said Logan.

'Nae bother,' he replied in his thin, reedy voice. 'It was fun.'

'These three are a different breed to the two waiters,' said Carly. 'They're professionals.'

'Really?' said Wee Ginge, raising an eyebrow. 'They seem like a bag of fannies to me.'

The door opened and Peanut, Harry and Eddie ran out.

'Carly, hen, are you all right?' exclaimed her uncle.

'Aye, fine,' she replied. 'Thanks to Logan and Wee Ginge.'

'You gave as good as you got, doll,' replied Wee Ginge. 'You should have seen the way she smashed the chair off that walloper's back,' he told the others. 'Bang. It was awesome.'

'Thanks,' she smiled.

'There were another two inside who tried to take Rose,' said Eddie. 'But The Bitches, along with Digger and Gary, caught them before they got anywhere near her and turfed them out.'

In response to his words, Rose charged out of the back of the building.

'Carly,' she cried, racing up to her.

The two sisters hugged.

'Are you okay?' Carly asked her anxiously. 'Someone tried to abduct you?'

'Aye, course. They didnae get anywhere near. The girls dragged them into the toilets and gave them a kicking.'

'Thank God. Wee Ginge and Logan saved me.'

Rose immediately noticed the new way Carly looked at Logan and guessed his performance had been impressive. 'Thanks for saving my sister, boys,' she told them.

'Nae bother, cutie,' smiled Wee Ginge. 'She didnae need much saving though.'

'This is our chance to catch Cole,' Carly told them.

She kicked the bearded man in the ribs.

'Fuck off, bitch,' he grunted.

'Call Cole and tell him you've got me.'

'Away and raffle yerself.'

'If you don't do it then my sister will twist your baws so hard you'll be singing soprano for the rest of your life,' she replied, pointing to Rose.

His mean, light grey eyes settled on Rose. 'Go ahead, sweetheart. Touch my baws and find out what a real man's like.'

Rose shrugged. 'Well, you cannae say you weren't warned.'

As she knelt beside the man, Harry clamped his hand down over his mouth, knowing what was coming. Rose grabbed their captive's crotch, twisted and squeezed as hard as she could, making him scream into Harry's hand. The other men winced, including the bearded man's friends.

'Aww, look, man, he's crying,' laughed Wee Ginge when tears filled the man's eyes.

'That's enough,' Carly told her sister.

Rose appeared disappointed but she released him and the man groaned and curled up into a ball, shaking.

'You two will get the same if you don't call Cole,' Carly snapped at the man's friends.

'I'll do it,' said the man in the grey suit.

'Finally, someone with a brain,' she sighed.

He took out his phone and dialled. 'Aye, Cole, we've got her. Where shall we bring her? I'm no' lying. But...' The man hung up, looking nervous. 'He doesnae believe me.'

'I bet he sent in a spy who told him his plan went tits up,' said Eddie.

'The two waiters probably told him,' said Wee Ginge. 'I had to stop guarding them when I saw these pricks dragging out Carly and they ran off.'

'Shit,' sighed Logan. 'I should have left more of my people out here but I wanted to catch these wallopers before they could take Carly.'

'It's all right. You weren't to know,' replied Eddie, patting his shoulder.

'If I'd made the right call we could have gone after Cole and ended this today.'

'Hey, don't blame yourself. You did your best and it's thanks to one of your people that Carly wasnae taken.'

This made Logan feel better and he nodded.

Carly snatched the phone from the man in the grey suit and dialled the last number he'd called.

'Cole,' she said when he answered, putting the call on speakerphone so the others could hear.

'I knew they'd failed,' he replied. 'Mind you, it was a gamble.'

'You didnae need to send these idiots to abduct me. I'll happily come to you. Tell me where you are,' she said darkly.

'I take it you don't want to talk?'

'No. I want to kill you for what happened to Jack.'

'I didnae kill him.'

'You spotted Dean's weakness. I bet you played on it, wound him up, persuaded him Jack had to be got out of the way.'

'He didnae need much persuading. Dean hated Jack because you loved him. Your love was his death sentence, no' me, and that's what you cannae stand, isn't it? I know you, Carly, I understand how you think. You half-killed Karen because you're angry at yourself. Jack would still be alive if you hadnae fallen for him. You condemned me and Dean too. You're a fucking Jonah when it comes to men.'

'This isnae my fault, you wanker, it's yours and I'm gonnae kill you for it.'

'No, you won't because I'll get to you first.'

'If you want me then come after me yourself, or are you too afraid to face me?'

'Fine, if that's what you want I will and I'll fuck up your face like you fucked up mine.'

With that, Cole hung up, Carly annoyed that he'd had the last word.

'We won't get hold of him today,' she said miserably.

'Never mind,' said Eddie. 'Today isnae about that walloper, it's about Jane and Jennifer.'

'Do they know about any of this?'

'Naw and I want to keep it that way. I don't want to spoil their big day. We can tell them tomorrow.'

Carly looked back at the man in the grey suit. 'How do you know Cole?'

'His da' was a pal of mine. He came to the pub where I work to hire me and my pals.'

'What pub?'

He gave them the address of one in the east side of the city.

'Is he paying you?'

'Aye, two grand each.'

When the man couldn't give them any more information, Logan gathered his people together and told them to kick out the three men. Digger and Gary had to haul the bearded man away because he couldn't stand up straight.

'Thanks, by the way,' Carly told Logan.

'I didnae do very much,' he replied, watching the men leave.

'Your intervention meant I didn't have to fight that third man.'

'You looked like you had the situation under control.'

'That kick was very impressive.' Carly was annoyed that he was looking at the departing men rather than at her, which she considered a little rude.

'Thanks,' he said, finally turning his attention to her.

'I didn't know you had skills like that.'

'I've Jamie to thank,' he said with a sad smile. 'I wouldnae have bothered learning any martial art but he told us we had to, he wanted us to be able to tackle the toughest situations. He had amazing skills, he even fought in some underground fights and he won them all. He was the hardest bastard I ever knew.'

'So I heard. His weapon of choice was a bike chain, wasn't it?'

Logan nodded and produced a bike chain from his pocket. 'This one to be precise. I use it now in his honour.'

'That's nice,' she smiled.

Logan replaced the chain in his pocket. 'I'll take a look inside, make sure everything's okay.'

Carly watched him go, surprised to realise she felt irritated that he'd dismissed her so easily. She saw Rose grinning at her and frowned. 'What?'

'You looked like you were enjoying that conversation.'

'He's an interesting man.'

'Oh, aye?' Rose said, arching a perfectly plucked eyebrow.

'Aye and that's all there is to it.'

'He did something to impress you. What was it?'

'An amazing flying kick,' said Carly eagerly. 'It was incredible.' Carly wiped the smile off her face when she realised how soppy she sounded. 'I just respect the man, that's all.'

'You should go for it, he obviously fancies you.'

'He does not. He hardly looked at me when I was talking to him. Well, I don't know about you, but I could use a glass of wine. Don't worry, I've only had one so far.'

'In that case, I'll join you, or would you rather have a drink with Logan?'

'Stop it.'

Rose smiled knowingly at her sister, her sharp brain ticking over the ways she could bring the two of them together.

* * *

After Jane and Jennifer had been safely dropped off at the luxury hotel where they would spend the night, completely unaware of what had happened at the wedding reception, Carly and Rose were escorted back to their flat by Eddie, Peanut, Harry and the Blood Brothers.

'I don't think Cole will try anything else today,' said Eddie as they all gathered around the kitchen table to enjoy a cup of tea together. 'But it's better to be safe than sorry. Me and Harry will spend the night here.'

'I will too,' said Peanut.

'Cheers, pal.'

'We have to end this quickly,' said Carly. 'Me and Rose cannae be constantly worrying about being abducted. He threatened Jane and Jennifer too. What I don't get is why he's threatening my sisters and sister-in-law?'

'He's targeting them because you love them. I daresay me and Harry are on his list too.'

'He must have been quite close to us today. He wouldnae want his people driving too far with two kidnap victims in their car.'

'The prick stands out a mile with his messed-up face,' said Digger. 'Someone will spot him and tell us.'

'That's what I don't understand,' replied Rose. 'We've all got lots of contacts and Toni has more than all of us put together, so why has no one seen him? The one time he was spotted was because he visited someone he knew would tell Toni. Where is he hiding, underground?'

'The lassie makes a very good point,' said Gary. 'He must be hiding somewhere we have no eyes and ears. Most importantly, it's somewhere Toni has no access to. Now where the hell in this city can you hide from Toni McVay?'

'He must be living off grid,' said Logan. 'Maybe a wee caravan somewhere.' He noticed Carly wince at the mention of a caravan, Jack having been murdered in one.

'That would make sense,' said Eddie. 'Somewhere just outside the city probably.'

'Even in a quiet place like that he'd still stand out because of his scars,' said Rose. 'But he's no' standing out.'

'He could be living in some twee wee place that has nothing to do with the local underworld,' said Harry. 'Somewhere no one's ever heard of Toni McVay.'

'Even people in the Outer Hebrides have heard of Toni,' replied Logan. 'She's always in the newspapers.'

'No, he's close,' said Carly. 'The shifty bastard's been working with some of the local families. He'll want to be near to keep an eye on them.'

'They don't know where he's staying either. Toni's tortured enough of them but the torture doesnae seem to scare people like it used to. They're just getting pissed off that she thinks she can keep throwing her weight about. Cole's managed to spread rebellion, which is a lot more dangerous than Toni's weapon of fear.'

'Because he's a sly, manipulative twat,' hissed Carly. 'We won't find him, so we have to figure out a way to draw him to us.'

There was silence as they all considered their dilemma.

'I cannae think, I'm too tired,' yawned Digger.

'Aye, me too,' said Gary. 'I'm done in.'

'We'll head back to the Gallowburn,' said Logan. 'Hopefully we'll come up with something tomorrow when we're all fresh.' He got to his feet and his friends followed suit.

'I'll see you out,' said Carly, ignoring Rose's smile.

She escorted the men to the door and opened it for them. Digger and Gary left but Logan hung back.

'Be careful, won't you?' he told Carly. 'Cole's clever and he might get someone you trust to help him.'

'I cannae imagine anyone I know doing that.'

'You never can tell. Don't trust anyone outside your family.'

'That's good advice, thanks.'

'Take care,' he said before leaving.

Carly watched him go thoughtfully, considering what he'd said.

'I knew it, you do fancy him,' said a voice behind her.

'Jesus,' said Carly, jumping. She closed and locked the door and turned to face Rose. 'Did you have to sneak up on me?'

Rose ignored the question. 'Why did you escort them to the door?'

'I was just being a good hostess.'

'Aye, right.'

'Don't start, please. I'm way too tired.'

'Okay,' Rose said sweetly. 'Cole was wrong when he said your love killed Jack. It didn't. Your love made Jack.'

A lump formed in Carly's throat. 'Thanks, sweetheart,' she said, patting her sister's arm. 'That means a lot to me.'

21

'Why didn't you tell me?' exclaimed Jane.

'No way were we gonnae let Cole ruin your big day,' retorted Rose. 'That was what the arsehole wanted and he is no' gonnae win.'

'We should still have been told. Me and Jen could have been targeted at the hotel.'

Jane and Jennifer had returned to the flat the following afternoon and were shocked to hear what had happened at their wedding reception.

'It was my call no' to tell you,' said Eddie.

'And mine,' added Carly. 'Besides, Elijah and David sent some of their men to watch over you.'

'Are you seriously telling me strangers were hanging around outside our hotel room on our wedding night?'

'No' right outside it, doll,' replied Eddie. 'They just stationed themselves so they could see anyone coming and going. They were very discreet.'

'They'd have better been,' she scowled.

'Did you have a nice night?' Carly asked them.

'It was lovely,' smiled Jennifer. 'We had a fantastic meal and the suite was gorgeous. The only downside was that they'd sprinkled the bed with rose petals, so we had to spend some time picking them out but other than that, it was wonderful.'

'Good.'

'And I've got a week off work to enjoy too,' she said, wrapping an arm around Jane. 'Cheer up,' she told her wife.

'Sorry,' replied Jane with a reluctant smile. 'I'm just pissed off about being kept out of the loop. My sisters could have been kidnapped.'

'But they weren't. Cole lost again and now the wedding's done and dusted we can give this situation our full attention.'

'I suppose,' Jane sighed. 'Well, what are we doing?'

'Trying to find Cole,' replied Eddie.

'How? You've no idea, do you?' she added when no one replied.

'We're still working on it.'

'That's just great,' she said, rolling her eyes.

'I still say we should use me as bait,' said Carly.

'Forget it,' Jane told her.

'By the way,' said Rose. 'I've got a date with Fergus tomorrow morning. I'm so excited.'

'You can't go out on a date,' said Jane.

'And why not?' her younger sister demanded, eyes flashing.

'Because someone tried to kidnap you yesterday. What if they try again when you've only got that big stupid lump to protect you?'

'For God's sake, I don't need protecting and Fergus is no' a big stupid lump.'

'You have to admit that he is a bit,' said Harry.

'Shut it, you,' she told him before turning back to her sister.

'I've waited for this date for a long time and Cole bloody Alexander is no' spoiling it for me.'

'It's too dangerous,' countered Jane.

'I'm still going and you cannae stop me. I'm nineteen now, a woman.'

'What would Fergus say if he knew you were flirting with Digger and Gary yesterday at the reception?'

'You wouldn't.'

'Try me.'

The sisters glared at each other with equal determination in their eyes.

'Calm down,' said Eddie. 'You both make a good point. Yes, Rose, you're an adult now and we cannae tell you what to do but Jane is right, it is dangerous, so I propose a compromise. Where are you going on your date?'

'Just into the city to grab a coffee,' she replied.

'Fine. Then we'll come too.'

'I am no' having my family chaperoning me. What is this, 1897?'

'We'll be discreet, Fergus won't even know we're there.'

'But I will. It would be too embarrassing.'

'Just think what Cole would do if he got hold of you. He'd probably slash your face to ribbons like he threatened to do to me,' Carly told her reasonably.

Rose was a brave girl and only the thought of her looks being ruined caused her to think twice, as Carly knew it would.

'You're right,' gasped Rose, pressing a hand to her cheek as though to reassure herself the skin was still smooth and intact. 'How about this then – one of you follows us at a distance just to keep a lookout? We'll only go to busy public places, I promise.'

'That's a great idea,' said Eddie. 'There, all sorted.'

'Cole will probably be too busy lurking around here to bother following you about the city,' Harry told Rose.

Carly's eyes widened. 'That's it.'

'What is?'

'He's staying right here in Haghill. That's why he cannae be found anywhere else.'

'That's no' possible, hen,' said Eddie. 'This scheme's small, we would have found him by now.'

'No' if he found the right place to hide.'

'And what would be the right place, his maw's?'

'He wouldnae go to that old cow.'

'No one else around here would dare shelter him.' Eddie broke off when his phone rang. 'It's Peanut, he's at the front door. He didnae want to knock in case it worried us.'

Eddie and Harry went to let him in and Peanut followed them into the kitchen, rubbing his hands together to warm them.

'Christ, it's freezing out there,' he said. A smile lit up his face. 'It's lovely and toasty in here.'

'Do you want a coffee to warm you up?' Rose asked him.

'That would be smashing, doll. I've found out something very interesting from a lady friend of mine.'

'Oh, aye,' said Harry. 'Who have you been shagging now?'

'Well, you know Mrs West, the old blind lady who has the flat under where Jack used to live?'

Harry's upper lip curled. 'You dirty bastard.'

'I'm no' shagging her, ya tube. I'm shagging her granddaughter, a gorgeous wee piece called Lily with big blue eyes, pale skin and blonde hair. Anyway, she told me her gran said someone moved into Jack's old flat a few days ago. Lily stays at her gran's a few nights a week to make sure she's okay and to do some cleaning. She's so caring and kind. She says whoever lives in the flat only comes out at night, a tall, slender man who always has his hood up when he goes out. Her gran doesnae sleep very much, so she's seen him coming back at four, five o'clock in the morning. He's never with anyone else and he never goes out during the day. I reckon it's Cole.'

'This is great information,' said Carly. 'Do you think Lily will let a couple of us into the flat one night so we can see for ourselves?'

His smile returned. 'Aye, I dae. She's a sweet lassie.'

'Are you sure she's no' just using you?' Harry asked him.

'What the hell's that supposed to mean?' demanded Peanut.

'It's a bit weird that you start seeing a woman whose gran lives in the flat under Jack's old flat.'

'Good point, son,' said Eddie.

'I'm no' making it up,' exclaimed Peanut.

'We don't think you are, pal, no' for a minute,' replied Eddie, patting his shoulder. 'If anything, we're suspicious of Lily.'

'You think she could be using me?' he replied, looking crestfallen.

'Cole's a crafty bastard, so it's possible.'

'I hope not, I really like her, but then I did wonder why that lovely lassie was interested in me. I mean, she's twenty years younger than me.'

'Don't sell yourself short,' Jane told him. 'You're handsome and charming, a catch for any woman.'

'I second that,' replied Carly.

'Me too,' chimed in Rose.

'Thanks, girls, that makes me feel better,' said Peanut, his smile returning. 'And I can ask her if she'll let us into her gran's flat. I can do it right now, actually,' he added, taking out his phone.

They all listened as Peanut made his call, cooing down the line at Lily in his deep, velvety tones. 'We're on,' he announced after he'd hung up. 'She's going round there tonight. We can turn up any time from eight o'clock.'

'Did she ask any questions?' said Harry.

'Naw, she just accepted it.'

'I don't like it.'

'God, I hope this isnae a trap,' said Peanut. 'I really like her.'

'Hopefully it won't be,' replied Eddie. 'Sometimes information just falls into your lap.'

'Or it's thrown there on purpose,' commented Harry cynically.

Rather than all of them pile into Mrs West's small flat, it was decided that only Carly, Eddie, Jane and Peanut would go. Harry would remain behind with Jennifer and Rose in case anything went wrong and they needed help. The four of them left the flat at ten o'clock that night. Fortunately, the snow held off, although Haghill was coated in a thick blanket of frost that twinkled beneath the streetlights.

Eddie called Logan on the way to ask for the Blood Brothers' back-up, giving him the address of Jack's old flat. Logan agreed and said they were on their way.

'Wow, this place actually looks pretty,' commented Eddie as Peanut drove them to Mrs West's flat. 'It's all sparkly in the moonlight.'

'You have the soul of a poet, Uncle Eddie,' smiled Jane.

'The road's slippery as hell even though it's been gritted,' replied Peanut, gripping the steering wheel tightly.

'Aye, it's shite,' said Eddie. 'Want me to drive?'

'I can handle it,' snapped Peanut indignantly.

'Park at the bottom of the street. We don't want Cole spotting us.'

Peanut did as he was asked and the two men, along with Carly and Jane, cautiously made their way up the road, taking their time on the slippery path. A mournful wind howled down the street, blasting them in the face, scattering dead leaves and litter.

'God, this sucks,' muttered Jane, shoving her hands deeper into her coat pockets, thinking at that moment she could be tucked up warm and cosy at home with her new wife.

So they wouldn't have to knock and attract the attention of whoever was in the flat above Mrs West's, Peanut had called Lily to let them know they were on their way. She was already looking out for them and she opened the front door as soon as they appeared. Carly glanced up at Jack's old flat and saw the curtains were closed but there was a glow behind them suggesting someone was inside.

Lily was as lovely as Peanut had said with her big soulful eyes, elegant swan neck and thick blonde hair.

'Hello, beautiful,' smiled Peanut, wrapping his hands around her small waist.

'Hi, sexy,' she beamed before kissing him.

'Let me introduce you,' said Peanut once she let him come up for air. 'This is my pal, Eddie, and his nieces Jane and Carly.'

'Nice to meet you,' smiled Lily.

Peanut had informed them that she was twenty-eight, but there was an impish playfulness about her that made her seem younger.

'It looks like someone's in upstairs,' said Carly.

'Aye,' replied Lily. 'I've heard them moving about. They usually go out at about midnight, one o'clock.'

'We've got a bit of a wait then,' said Eddie.

'Where's your gran?' Carly asked Lily.

'In bed, tucked up under the electric blanket. This weather's playing merry hell with her arthritis.'

'Does she know we're coming?'

'Aye, I told her, but she wanted to be out of the way. She doesnae like visitors.'

'I hope she doesn't mind us being here?'

'Naw. I just said you were friends of mine and she's fine with that.'

Lily led them into a small but cosy front room.

'So, you've no' had any interactions with whoever's in the flat above?' said Carly.

'Nope,' replied Lily. 'Like I told Peanut, I've just heard them moving about and seen a figure leaving at night.'

Carly didn't like this. She couldn't say what was making her uncomfortable, she just had a funny feeling. She glanced at her sister and could tell she felt the same.

'Can I use your loo?' Carly asked Lily.

'Do you really have to? Only I don't want Gran to be disturbed. She doesnae get enough sleep as it is.'

'I'll be really quiet. Sorry, it's the cold weather. It always goes straight to my bladder.'

'Well, okay,' Lily said reluctantly. 'It's down the hall second on the right but don't flush it.'

As Carly headed down the hall, she glanced back over her shoulder. All she could see were Peanut's and Eddie's backs sitting on the couch, unintentionally blocking Lily's view down the hall.

Ignoring the door Lily had indicated, Carly pushed open the door to the right of it, which was just a sparsely furnished spare room. Next, she pushed open the door opposite it and was shocked to find Mrs West gagged and tied to the bed, the room illuminated by the weak light of a lamp. Her sightless blue eyes were wide and frantic and she'd obviously heard the movement because her eyes filled with fear. Carly hastened to her side and gently clasped her hand.

'It's okay, it's me, Carly Savage,' she whispered in the old woman's ear. 'I'm here to help you. You're safe, don't worry. I'll be back in a minute.'

Mrs West rested a little easier but Carly didn't think she'd ever forget the terror in those unseeing eyes.

Carly turned and immediately brought up her arms to block a punch. The blow still found its target and Carly was knocked back onto the bed. Mrs West couldn't see what had happened, but she could feel the movement and she whimpered into the gag.

To Carly's astonishment, Lily's sweet, pretty face was twisted with rage. Before she could rise, Peanut's sweetheart had punched her in the stomach, driving all the air out of her lungs. When Lily tried to strike her again, Carly kicked her in the chest, flinging her backwards. Carly opened her mouth to call for help but all she could emit was a small gasp as she was still trying to catch her breath.

Lily came at her again with the alarm clock that she'd snatched off Mrs West's bedside cabinet and tried to bash her head in with it, but Carly rolled sideways and Lily toppled forward onto the bed. Carly leapt onto her back before she could recover, tore the clock from her hand, tossed it aside and twisted her arms up her back.

'Everyone, come here, quick,' she called.

22

There was the thunder of footsteps and Eddie, Peanut and Jane raced into the room.

'What the bloody hell is going on?' exclaimed Eddie.

'Peanut, help me,' cried Lily. 'She's gone mad.'

'Err...' he began.

'I'm mad?' exclaimed Carly. 'You're the one who tied up poor Mrs West.'

'It's okay, Mrs West,' said Jane, rushing to the old woman's side. 'My name's Jane, I'm Carly's sister. You're safe now. I'm going to untie you.'

Mrs West's light blue eyes filled with tears of gratitude, which spilled down her wrinkled cheeks.

Jane untied the gag while Eddie cut the cord binding her hands to the bedframe.

'Are you okay, Mrs West?' Jane asked her.

'Water, please,' the old woman rasped.

'I'll get it,' Jane said before hurrying from the room.

'All right, hen, you can let her go now,' Eddie told Carly.

'Are you sure? She tried to batter my heid in with an alarm clock.'

'Aye, I'm sure.'

Carly climbed off Lily and they all scowled down at her.

'Why did you do it?' demanded Peanut.

'I didn't,' cried Lily, slowly sitting up. 'She made me,' she added, pointing an accusing finger at Carly. 'She told me to tell Mrs West I was her home help so I could gain her trust. She tied up the old woman, no' me.'

Lily was knocked across the bed by Carly backhanding her across the face.

'You lying bitch,' yelled Carly.

'Take it easy,' Eddie urged her, gesturing to Mrs West, who was shaking.

'Don't apologise on my account,' replied the elderly woman. 'I hope that slap was that wee coo getting what she deserves.'

'It was,' replied Carly.

'Good.'

Jane returned. 'Here's some water, Mrs West.'

'Oh, thank you,' she said, holding her trembling hands out for it.

Jane placed it in her hands and Mrs West gulped down the cool liquid.

'No one believes your lies,' Eddie told Lily. 'So just gi'e us the truth.'

Lily turned her baby blues on Peanut, her lower lip wobbling. 'You believe me, don't you, babe? You know who I really am. I would never do anything so terrible to such a frail old lady.'

Peanut scowled. 'Show her what I think of her, Carly.'

Carly swung her fist into Lily's face, catapulting her back onto the bed.

'Tell us what you're up to or I'll batter the living shite out of you,' Carly snarled at the woman, being careful not to shout in case it warned whoever was in the flat above.

Lily's eyes turned up to the ceiling. When she opened her mouth to yell a warning, Carly clamped her hands down over her face, muffling her cries.

'Did she tell you why she's doing this, Mrs West?' Jane gently asked her.

'N... no,' the old lady replied, stammering slightly, although the trembling was subsiding now she knew she was safe. 'She just told me that if I kept quiet then I wouldn't get hurt. I heard her on the phone though. She was talking to a man, I think. Billing and cooing over him, she was. She said the Savages would soon be here.'

Jane looked to Eddie. 'What do we do now?'

'We need to find out who's up there,' he said, hard gaze turning on Lily.

'I'll make the bitch talk,' replied Carly before backhanding Lily twice across the face, knocking her head from side to side.

'Peanut, help me,' gasped Lily, blood trickling from one nostril.

'I cannae believe you did that to an auld yin,' he retorted. 'You deserve everything you get.'

'Tell us who's in the flat above and I won't rearrange your face,' Carly told her.

'Aye, you're good at that, aren't you?' Lily sneered back.

'I am and I won't think twice about doing the same to you.'

When Lily remained defiant, Carly punched her so hard Lily's jaw went slack, eyes staring out of her head.

'Jeezo, doll, be careful,' said Eddie. 'You could have broken her jaw.'

'I fucking will if she doesn't start talking,' Carly snapped back.

'A... Alexander,' murmured Lily, recovering the power of speech.

'Cole,' replied Carly. 'Is it Cole hiding upstairs?'

'No... brothers.'

'Dominic and Ross?'

'Aye.'

'Why the hell would they be up there?' said Eddie. 'They're moving to Dundee.'

'Lie... staying here... to help their brother.'

'I don't believe you,' said Carly.

'No,' breathed Lily, holding out her hands weakly when Carly drew back her fist again. 'Truth... swear to God.'

'Where's Cole?'

'Don't know... Won't tell anyone, no' even his brothers.'

'How are you involved in this?'

'I'm Ross's girlfriend.'

'How did you meet?'

'Bishopbriggs. I'm not known around here... It's why they sent me.'

'The sly twats,' said Jane. 'Let's go up there and kick their teeth in.'

'Hold your horses, doll,' replied Eddie. He looked back at Lily. 'What are they up to exactly?'

'Answer, bitch, before you get another smack,' Carly told the young woman when she remained silent, absolutely no pity in her voice.

'They want their brother on top,' said Lily. 'They want to topple Toni McVay.'

'The stupid bastards should have gone to Dundee. They'll lose and Toni will take your eyes right out of your heid when she hears you were involved,' snarled Jane.

'You're no' gonnae tell her about me, are you?' said Lily, looking truly afraid for the first time.

'Give us one reason why we shouldn't.'

'I'll tell you everything I know,' she said, looking more alert as she began to recover from the blow, although a large bruise was rapidly spreading across the left side of her face.

'Get on with it then,' said Eddie impatiently.

'I was to get close to Peanut so he'd slip you the information about Jack's old flat. They want you to go up there.'

'Why?'

'They said I don't need to know and that's the truth,' she replied, glancing nervously at Carly and her clenched fists. 'But it was clear they've set up some sort of trap for you.'

'What were they gonnae do to us when they got us?'

'I don't know about the rest of you. I just know Cole wants Carly so he can do to her face what she did to his before killing her. He wants to torture her.'

This statement didn't surprise any of them. The Alexanders had already captured Carly once and tortured her before she was rescued by her family.

'Do they know we're here right now?' said Eddie.

'Aye, they do.' A smile lifted the uninjured side of her mouth. 'They're probably watching through the camera.'

'Where?'

Lily nodded at the corner of the room to the left of the door. They all turned and saw the small spy camera sitting there.

'We're here, you fucking cowards,' Eddie growled up at it. 'Come down and get us or we'll come up there and get you.'

There was the sound of yells and thumps from above.

'You're in for it now,' said Lily, eyes lighting up with malicious glee.

'I don't think so,' replied Eddie. 'That's our pals going after them.'

Lily's jaw went slack again but this time with astonishment.

'Watch her,' Eddie told his nieces. 'And look after Mrs West. We'll be back in a minute.'

'Is there anyone we can call for you?' Jane asked Mrs West as Peanut and Eddie left.

'I don't know, I cannae think,' she croaked. 'I'm desperate for the toilet. I don't know how much longer I can hold it.'

'I'll help you,' said Jane. 'Carly, watch that bitch,' she added, nodding at Lily.

Jane assisted Mrs West up off the bed. She found it hard to move as her legs and arms were so stiff after being tethered. The old woman hobbled out of the room on Jane's arm.

Carly regarded Lily so coldly a chill ran down Lily's spine, but she made no move against her as Carly loomed over her like a prison guard.

At the soft pad of approaching footsteps, Carly assumed it was Jane returning. She got the shock of her life when a hooded figure entered the room.

'You're for it now, bitch,' Lily told her in a low, satisfied tone.

The figure threw back the hood and for the first time, Carly got a clear view of the terrible damage she'd done to Cole's face, the scars cutting through his once perfect skin standing out even more starkly in the lamplight. There was absolutely nothing left of the handsome man he'd once been.

One thing she hadn't noticed before was the upper lip on the left side had been pulled up slightly thanks to the scar transecting both lips, making it appear as though he were permanently snarling. There was no physical damage to his beautiful green eyes but the look in them had changed forever. Before he'd been sent to prison they'd sparkled with good humour and intelligence. When he'd been released, they'd been filled with nothing but coldness. Now all that was in them was rage. That anger was even more disturbing than the gun he held, a suppressor on the end to mask the sound of the shot.

'Don't shout,' he whispered, the barrel of the pistol trained on Carly. 'I would hate to shoot you, especially when I have something much better in mind.' He gestured to the door with the weapon. 'Now move, unless you want me to go down the hall and shoot your sister in the head.'

Once Carly would have called his bluff but the look in his eyes convinced her he would have absolutely no qualms about killing Jane.

'All right, I'll come quietly,' she whispered back.

The twisted side of his mouth lifted. 'Still sentimental.' His gaze slipped to Lily, who was drawing back her fist to hit Carly. 'No,' he told her. 'She isnae yours to hurt.'

Lily lowered her fist, not daring to argue.

'Carly, let's move.'

With a resigned sigh, she walked across the room towards him.

'What should I do?' said Lily.

'I don't gi'e a shite,' Cole retorted.

Cole nudged Carly in the back with the gun, urging her towards the rear of the flat. She could hear Jane talking kindly to Mrs West in the bathroom. Carly swallowed down the lump in her throat, wondering if that was the last she would ever hear of her beloved older sister.

Carly moved as quietly as she could, not wanting to draw Jane out of the bathroom and in front of Cole's gun but the thuds and bangs from the flat above drowned out any sound.

'Open the door,' whispered Cole, prodding her in the back of the right shoulder with the pistol.

Carly quietly pulled it open and stepped outside, the cold hitting her immediately, breath streaming out before her. They were in a small back yard that was bare apart from a shed and a few pots containing dead plants.

Carly glanced up at the window at the rear of what had once been Jack's flat, warmth filling her at the memories of the time she'd spent in there with her lover.

'Don't even think it,' growled Cole, misconstruing her thoughts, assuming she was considering calling out to her friends.

'I won't,' she replied. 'I'd never put them at risk.'

'Which makes you weak.'

'No. It means I have a heart.'

'Just fucking move.'

He marched her across the yard and indicated for her to pull open the gate, which she did to reveal three more men and a transit van.

'You came prepared,' she commented.

'I know how slippery you are.'

Cole nodded at one of the men, who grabbed Carly's right arm and pulled her towards the van. His feet went out from under him on the icy pavement and he fell to the ground, landing heavily on his back.

'Looks like I'm no' the only slippery one,' she smiled.

'Get up, you fucking dick,' Cole told him. 'It's your own fault for wearing trainers in this weather.'

Another of the men had to help him up, both of them slipping and sliding on the pavement. Carly had elected to wear her hiking boots, which gripped the ground much more firmly. The third man, who'd managed to remain on his feet, took her arm instead and escorted her to the back of the van, Cole following, keeping the gun trained on her.

The man pulled open one of the rear doors. 'Get in,' he told Carly.

With a sigh, she climbed inside, taking her time while desperately trying to come up with a way to escape.

Once she was inside, the man began to climb in after her but his foot slipped so Carly kicked out, hitting him in the face. She yanked the door closed, scrambled into the front of the van and climbed into the driver's seat. Desperately, she hunted around for the key but it wasn't there.

'Bollocks,' she sighed.

There was a knock on the driver's window and she turned to see Cole standing there, holding up the key.

'Nice try,' he called to her through the glass. 'Now get in the back.'

Carly obeyed, clambering back over the seats into the rear of the van. She scrabbled about on the floor of the vehicle with her hands as it was so dark, hunting for something she could use as a weapon, but she found nothing.

The rear door was pulled open, the streetlight illuminating the interior. This time the man managed to climb inside without falling. He looked angry, blood trickling from his nose where Carly's foot had struck him. He paused to assess whether she was going to attack him again. The way she remained in a crouch, as though ready to spring, didn't make him feel any easier.

'You look nervous,' she told him with a predatory smile.

'As if a wee bird like you could make me nervous,' he replied.

'But I think I do and you should be worried.'

'Shut your face, ya daft coo.'

He appeared alarmed at the sound of shouts and yells from outside. There was an enormous clang on the driver's side of the van, as though something heavy had been thrown against it, so forceful the vehicle rocked.

Carly took advantage of the man's surprise to spring at him, landing on top of him and knocking him onto his back. She slammed her fists into his face twice before he punched her in the stomach and kicked her off. Carly landed on her side with a bang, grimacing at the pain in her belly. The bastard was tougher than she'd thought.

'Cole said only he's allowed to hurt you,' growled the man, pushing himself upright. 'But fuck that.' He cracked his knuckles. 'I'm gonnae enjoy—'

She punched him hard in the groin. His eyes bulged before he collapsed to his knees.

Carly rose to her feet and kicked him in the face. As he fell backwards, he banged his head off the side of the van and dropped, out cold.

'If you're gonnae hurt someone then do it, don't talk about it,' she told his prone form.

She paused to listen. There was definitely a fight going on outside. She was alarmed to hear a few dull thuds, the sound that bullets would make when fired from a silenced gun. Carly rushed back to the driver's seat and used the wing mirrors to see what was going on. Through the right mirror she saw two figures locked in a desperate fight, throwing impressive punches and kicks. One of them was definitely Cole. Where the hell had he learned martial arts? She couldn't make out who the second figure was. Checking the left mirror, she saw the two idiots who'd been unable to stand upright sprawled on the ground, two other figures looming over them.

Shoving open the driver's door, she jumped out and ran up to Cole, who had his back turned to her. Hearing her approach, he glanced over his shoulder. She glimpsed his eyes, which flashed with rage, reflecting the frost all around them before he turned and sprinted off into the night.

'Logan,' she cried when Cole's opponent was revealed.

He staggered forward, a hand clamped to his left upper arm.

'Are you okay?' she said, hurrying to his side.

'The bastard grazed me with a bullet.'

'Oh my God, we need to get you to hospital.'

'It's no' that bad. It just needs stitching up.'

'My uncle can do that for you. Does Cole still have his gun?'

'Naw, I knocked it out of his hand and kicked it down a drain. Are you okay?'

'Fine.'

She prepared to fight when two more figures appeared from the other side of the van, but she relaxed when she saw it was Peanut and Digger.

'Carly, are you all right?' cried Peanut, embracing her.

'Aye. I got a punch to the gut but he came off a lot worse,' she said, flinging open the van door to reveal the unconscious man.

'Nice one,' Peanut grinned.

'How did you know what was happening?'

'We saw you getting put into the van from the upstairs window.'

'Did you get Ross and Dominic?'

'Naw, they escaped. There wasnae just the two of them. Four more men were waiting in that flat.'

'Is everyone okay?'

'Aye, our people are anyway. It was all a distraction so Cole could abduct you.'

'So it seems. Logan needs help, he's injured.'

'What's up, pal?' said Digger, clapping his friend on the back.

Logan grimaced. 'I got shot in the arm.'

Eddie and Gary emerged from the backyard.

'Uncle Eddie,' said Carly. 'Logan's shoulder got nicked by a bullet.'

'Bullet?' he exclaimed. 'Where the fuck did that come from?'

'Cole. He took me out of Mrs West's flat. He was gonnae abduct me. Logan, Peanut and Digger saved me.'

'Jeezo, hen,' said Eddie, pulling her into a hug. 'Come back with us and I'll sort out your shoulder,' he said to Logan.

'What about him?' said Carly, gesturing to the unconscious man.

'Leave him,' replied Eddie. 'We already know Cole tells his people nothing.'

Jane, who was still with Mrs West, had been completely unaware that anything had happened and was appalled to learn the truth. She'd phoned Mrs West's daughter for her and insisted on staying with the traumatised old lady until she arrived. Peanut and Digger said they'd wait with her, Peanut giving Eddie his car keys so he could drive Carly, Gary and Logan back to the flat. Carly wanted to remain with her sister, but her uncle insisted she return with them, as she was Cole's main target. They doubted Cole would be back that night, but they were taking no chances.

23

'Christ, what happened?' demanded Jennifer when they entered the flat with an injured Logan in tow. 'And where's Jane?'

'She's fine,' replied Eddie. 'Poor Mrs West had been tied up and traumatised by Peanut's girlfriend, so she's waiting with her until her daughter turns up to take her away. Don't worry, Peanut and Digger are with her.'

'Thank God,' Jennifer breathed, anxiously twiddling her wedding ring.

Carly explained what had happened while Eddie seated Logan at the table. Her eyes darted to Logan as her uncle helped him remove his coat and jumper. The memory returned of Dean being similarly treated by Eddie after his arm had been slashed with a knife. Logan was even on the same chair at the kitchen table. Back then Carly hadn't known Dean was a psycho who would betray her in the worst way possible. In fact, she'd thought she'd been in love with him. That was just a few short months ago. It was frightening how quickly things could change.

'Poor Peanut,' said Rose once her sister had finished explaining. 'He seemed really keen on Lily.'

'He was,' replied Eddie as he examined Logan's injury. 'This will hit him like a ten-tonne truck. He has the habit of falling for women fast and hard. Right, Logan,' he said. 'It's quite a deep nick. You're lucky though. It didnae hit the bone.'

'I'm just glad it didn't hit my heid because that's where the bastard was aiming,' Logan replied.

'Harry, get me my special first-aid kit,' said Eddie. 'Carly, you know the routine.'

She nodded and fetched him some hot water.

Everyone watched in silence as Eddie tended to Logan's wound.

'Excuse me,' said Carly, leaving the room.

Rose noted Logan's eyes followed her and he appeared disappointed that she'd gone. After giving it a couple of minutes, Rose left the room and knocked on her sister's bedroom door.

'Can I come in?'

'Aye,' called back Carly.

Rose pushed open the door to find Carly slumped on the edge of her bed, head bowed.

'What's wrong?' said Rose, sitting beside her.

'Seeing Logan like that reminded me of the time Dean's arm got injured and Uncle Eddie stitched it up. I cannae help but wish I'd stuck something nasty in the bastard's wound. Dean's I mean, no' Logan's. How different life would be now,' Carly said wistfully.

'And here's me thinking you were eyeing up Logan's fit body. You have to admit it's pretty impressive,' Rose added when Carly failed to respond.

'It's very nice,' Carly said distractedly.

'With his clothes on he looks a little skinny but he's actually pretty toned.'

'Aye.'

'He saved your life tonight.'

'I know.' Carly shook herself out of it. 'I really need to thank him properly. He could have been killed.'

'Oh, aye, and how will you thank him?' said Rose with a suggestive wiggle of the eyebrows.

'Verbally.'

'Haven't you already done that?'

'No. What?' she added when Rose sighed.

'It's frustrating because I think you'd make a good couple.'

'Forget it. I suppose I'm just feeling a bit miserable. Seeing Cole like that was pretty depressing too. He's so full of anger.'

'Don't feel sorry for him, he's a psycho. Come on, let's go and see how the hero of the hour is.'

'Aye, okay,' said Carly, dragging herself after her sister.

Eddie was still stitching up Logan's wound. Logan gripped on to the table hard with his free hand, jaw gritted. Jennifer stood by Eddie's side to assist.

'He's taking it like a man,' Harry told the sisters.

Carly noted how pale Logan's skin was and it wasn't because of blood loss or pain. It was all over. His skin was like marble and his body was long and lithe. Her sister had been right, every muscle was defined. She spotted Rose giving her a knowing smile and hastily averted her eyes.

Once Eddie had finished and had covered the wound with a dressing, he and Gary helped Logan to the couch, which he sank into gratefully.

'You can have some painkillers now,' said Eddie, handing him a couple of paracetamol and a glass of water.

'Haven't you got anything stronger?' he replied.

'Sorry, I'm no' a doctor and you cannae have a drink because it'll raise your blood pressure and you might start bleeding again.'

Logan nodded resignedly, tossed the tablets into his mouth and washed them down with the water. He glanced Carly's way, but she looked away from him. Disappointment once again filled his eyes.

'The snow's really started coming down again,' commented Gary, glancing out of the window just as Jane and Digger returned.

'You okay, pal?' Digger asked Logan.

'I'll live,' he mumbled back, looking tired and sore.

'How's Mrs West?' Carly asked her sister.

'Her daughter took her home with her. She said she can never go back to that flat. It's a shame because she's lived there for seventeen years with no problems. Her daughter's divorced and said she can move in with her, so that's one problem solved.'

'Where's Peanut?' Harry asked her.

'Gone to his pal's club to drown his sorrows. He's a wee bit depressed about Lily. He really liked her.'

'That bitch has a lot to answer for. At least Carly gave her a few good whacks.'

Jane turned to Logan. 'I want to say thanks for saving Carly. If it wasn't for you, Cole would have her by now.'

'No problem,' Logan mumbled. It was clear he didn't enjoy being the centre of attention.

'The snow's really bad out there,' said Jane. 'Digger's car was slipping and sliding down the street. They cannae go back to Gallowburn tonight.'

'They should stay here,' said Rose brightly, smiling when Carly narrowed her eyes.

'Aye, course they should,' said Eddie. 'No way are we throwing them out in this weather after they helped us so much. Me and Harry will stay over again tonight too in light of what's happened.'

'We'll be struggling for room,' said Carly.

'No, we won't,' said Rose. 'I can share with you, you've got a double bed. Uncle Eddie and Harry can take my room and Digger and Gary can have Da's old room. That leaves Logan on the couch.' She looked down at Logan, who had already nodded off.

'Good thinking, hen,' said Eddie. 'Well, I don't know about anyone else, but I could use a drink.' He opened the fridge and took out a bottle of lager. 'Anyone else want one?'

Harry, Digger and Gary accepted while the women opted for tea.

'Carly,' said Rose. 'Why don't you get the spare duvet for Logan before he gets cold?'

'Fine,' she sighed. It would be no use telling her sister to back off. When Rose got an idea in her head it was impossible to get it out.

Carly took the duvet out of the cupboard in the hallway and carried it into the living room. Logan had slumped sideways onto the couch, lying on his uninjured side, his head resting on the cushions. She covered him with the duvet and began tucking it in around him. Some of his curls had sprung loose and the corner of Carly's mouth lifted as she thought how peaceful he looked, sweet even. It was hard to believe that only recently he'd been fighting an armed psychopath. He was definitely a man of many layers.

Realising she was staring at him, she took a seat at the table, avoiding Rose's smiling gaze.

'Cole's trained in martial arts,' Carly told the others. 'He certainly couldnae fight like he did today just a few months ago.'

'It could be useful finding out who's his teacher,' said Eddie.

'We can ask around,' said Gary, pointing from himself to Digger. 'We know quite a few people in that world.'

'Cheers. You boys really came through for us today. I don't know what we would have done without you. We owe you big time.'

'Naw,' said Digger. 'You'd have done the same for us. Like Toni said, we're working together now.'

Eddie smiled and raised his bottle of lager in a toast. 'Aye, we are. To the Blood Brothers and the Savages. Long live our alliance.'

'You're so cheesy, Da',' grimaced Harry.

'Did you get any information out of the men in the flat?' Carly asked her uncle.

'I cornered Dominic in the kitchen. He admitted he and Ross did intend to move to Dundee, until Cole made them an offer they couldnae refuse.'

'He thinks he's the bloody Godfather now,' she muttered.

'He paid them two grand each to stay and help him set up that trap to take you. They don't know where he's hiding out, he's no' telling anyone that. Then Ross burst in and I had to fight him and they both got away.'

'Bugger.'

'It was bloody chaos, no' the right time for an interrogation.'

'I still say Cole is staying close.'

'Well, it's gonnae have to wait until tomorrow. I'm dead on my feet. I'll finish this beer then I'm off to bed and I suggest you all do the same because Cole will attack us again soon.'

* * *

Carly was woken at seven o'clock the next morning by Rose talking in her sleep, mumbling something about gerbils. Knowing she wouldn't be able to get back off, Carly pulled on her dressing gown and slippers and ambled into the kitchen, yawning. It was only when she walked through the door that she remembered Logan was on the couch. He was awake, lying on his back, tucked up under the duvet, playing a game on his phone.

'Sorry,' she cringed. 'I didnae mean to disturb you.'

Slowly he pushed himself upright. 'You didn't, I'm wide awake anyway.'

'Okay.' She wanted to leave him to it. Logan was still bare-chested and his curls were even more unruly and adorable, but the thought of going back to bed to listen to Rose mumbling was not appealing.

'Do you want a cup of tea?' she said, closing the kitchen door so as not to disturb the others before padding over to the kettle.

Logan smiled, pleased that he finally got to be alone with Carly Savage. 'Aye, that would be great.'

'How do you take it?'

'Milk, no sugar.'

'Coming right up.'

Logan watched her switch on the kettle and prepare the mugs. 'How are you feeling after last night?' he asked her.

'Oh, fine.'

'Your ex-boyfriend trying to abduct you must have come as a shock.'

She shrugged. 'It's no' the first time. Once he and his brothers kidnapped and tortured me.'

'What?' he said with surprise.

'My family got me out. Back then I knew he didn't want to kill me. Things have changed now. It's amazing how love can turn to hate,' she said thoughtfully. Carly turned to face Logan. 'I never thanked you properly for saving me last night. If it wasn't for you, I'd probably be dead by now.'

'You're very welcome but it wasn't just me. It was Peanut and Digger too.'

'Cole was the only one carrying a gun and you took him on. You're a very brave man.'

'I wouldnae go that far,' Logan said modestly.

'Well, I would. I owe you one.'

'You really don't. I was happy to help.'

Carly smiled. The man might be a feared gang leader, but he did seem rather shy. He possessed the intensity that Jack, Dean and Cole had all shared and which she found very attractive, but Logan's was tempered by an endearing sweetness. Once again, she got the feeling there were many hidden depths to this man, depths it would probably be fascinating to explore...

Carly turned around and began fussing with the mugs. These thoughts were unwanted and dangerous.

'How's the shoulder?' she said without looking at him.

'Stiff and sore,' he replied. 'Your uncle did a great job stitching me up.'

'He's had a lot of practice.'

There was a beat of silence before Logan said, 'Can I ask you something?'

She turned back to face him. 'How could I say no after what you did for me?'

'I seem to make you nervous. I hope I've no' done anything to offend you?'

Carly took a moment to consider her response. 'No, you haven't. It's just that...' She trailed off. Christ, how could she explain it? The man had saved her life, so he deserved an explanation, and an honest one at that. 'I was devastated when Jack was murdered and I couldnae go through that pain again. I never thought I'd ever meet another man I could like but I have and it scares me.'

Logan's eyes widened with surprise. 'You mean me?' he said, pointing at himself.

Carly nodded, blushing.

'Oh, err...'

He ran a hand through his hair, Carly enjoying the way his curls sprang off his head.

'Well,' he said, after pausing to consider his reply. 'I totally get where you're coming from. I cannae even imagine what you've been through, but you should know that I really like you, Carly. I never thought I could like a woman so much.'

It was Carly's turn to be lost for words and she blushed deeper, especially as the duvet had slipped down, revealing his chest and stomach. His ivory skin was beautiful.

Carly was relieved when the kettle boiled so she could turn her attention to pouring the tea. She heard the rustle of the duvet and soft footsteps padding across the floor towards her. As she replaced the kettle on its stand, a hand gently touched her shoulder.

'I would never pressure you into anything,' Logan said, his voice a gentle caress. 'But I do think it would be a shame if we never got to find out how we'd get on together. Regrets can be as bad as the pain of making a mistake.'

Carly turned to face him. He stood before her in all his pale, toned glory, eyes wide and soft.

'You're very wise,' she said.

'People are always telling me that. Personally, I cannae see it,' he added with a self-deprecating smile.

'But they're right. No wonder you're leader of the Blood Brothers.'

'I'm no' as good a leader as Jamie was.'

'Well, I don't know about that. Gallowburn is very lucky to have you.'

'I appreciate that,' he smiled. 'I really like you, Carly. You're very special and I'm willing to give you all the time you need, if you think there could be a chance for us in the future?'

'I...' She really didn't know the answer to that. She did like Logan but she also felt guilty, as though she were betraying Jack. Her hand went to Jack's necklace. 'I'll think about it.'

'Thank you. Shall I take my cup of tea?'

'Eh? Oh,' she added, having completely forgotten about the drinks. 'Aye, I'll just add the milk.'

Feeling flustered, she produced the carton of milk from the fridge and topped up both mugs. 'Bugger, I didnae take out the teabags.'

'Allow me,' he said before fishing them out with a teaspoon. 'Which is mine?'

Still blushing, she pointed to the mug on the left.

'Thanks,' he said, picking it up before retreating back to the couch, Carly admiring his bare back as he went. Jack's image popped into her mind and she hastily turned away, feeling disloyal.

Carly had never been more grateful to see her uncle. Eddie shuffled in, scratching his big belly, face coated in stubble, thinning hair stuck up at the back, yawning.

'All right, Carly, doll?' he said. 'Is there a brew for me?'

'Have this one,' she said, handing him her mug. 'I'll make myself another.'

'You're an angel, do you know that?' He smiled at their guest. 'How are you feeling, Logan?'

'No' so bad,' he replied. 'Just a wee bit sore.'

'Aye, well, that's what happens when you get shot. You'll be as right as rain in a few days.' Finally, he caught the atmosphere in the room and raised his eyebrows. 'Oh, aye? Am I interrupting anything?'

'No,' said Carly, turning away so he wouldn't see her blush.

Eddie looked at Logan, who similarly avoided his gaze. He smiled, pleased his niece was showing an interest in another man. It was about time she had some happiness in her life.

24

Once everyone was up and had eaten breakfast, the Savages and Blood Brothers put their heads together to discuss their next move.

'I've got a visit booked with Craig Lawson today in Barlinnie,' opened Logan. 'I didnae think he'd see me, he hates us, but I reckon he's curious. And bored.'

'That's great but are you up to it?' Eddie asked him.

'I'll be fine. Digger's gonnae drive me there.'

'Good because from what I've heard of Craig Lawson he's a predator and predators can smell a wounded gazelle.'

'Jeezo, Da', don't call him a gazelle,' sighed an embarrassed Harry.

'I wasnae. It was an analogy.' Eddie looked back at Logan. 'Is Craig likely to gi'e you any information?'

'He will if he thinks it will benefit him,' Logan replied.

'It's worth a try. I thought I recognised one of the men in Jack's old flat yesterday but I couldnae place him at the time. It came to me in the early hours of this morning. His name's Gideon Bell.'

'From the Bell family in Springboig?'

'Aye.'

'Another neighbourhood between here and Gallowburn,' said Jane.

'Exactly, doll.'

'Cole's recruited more people to his side,' said Jennifer.

'I thought while the Blood Brothers tackle Craig Lawson, we can speak to the Bells.'

'You sure you don't want our back-up?' Logan asked him.

'Aye. I've known Amos, the head of the family, for years. He'll parley with me.'

'He might no' if he's teamed up with Cole.'

'Then we'll make him,' said Eddie, his expression pitiless.

* * *

Amos Bell's house was tucked down a quiet street facing a grim grey block of flats three storeys high that seemed to absorb all the natural light. The Bell home was surprisingly pretty, the pebble dashing immaculate. Two bay trees stood sentinel either side of the front door and the garden was enclosed by a freshly painted white picket fence.

Everything seemed quiet, so Eddie, Harry, Carly, Jane and Jennifer confidently walked up the path together to the front door. Rose had gone on her date with Fergus that morning, so she hadn't nagged them to come. Peanut had agreed to keep a discreet eye on the pair, just in case Cole decided to target the youngest sister again.

A dour-looking young man answered the door. His heavy-lidded dark eyes showed no surprise when he saw so many people standing on his doorstep. He wore a pressed white shirt, black trousers and polished black brogues, looking more like a waiter than the son of a local thug.

'Yes?' he said politely.

'Hi, Isaiah. Do you remember me, Eddie Savage?'

'I do,' was his sombre reply.

'Is Amos in? We'd like a word.'

Isaiah nodded and stood aside, gesturing to the interior of the house with a sweep of his hand. They stepped into a hallway as immaculate as the exterior.

'If you would please remove your shoes,' Isaiah told them in his deep, slow voice. 'My maw does hate dirt.'

'Aye, okay,' said Eddie while the others glanced at each other uncertainly.

'Make sure you place them in a neat line,' continued Isaiah. 'My maw hates things untidy.'

They obeyed and finally they were escorted into the lounge. A short, thin man sat in an armchair with his legs crossed, wearing the same outfit as his son, reading the newspaper.

'Father,' said Isaiah. 'You have guests.'

Amos Bell lowered the newspaper and smiled, the gesture lacking warmth. He was in his late fifties but his dark hair still retained a lot of its natural colour. His facial features were as neat as the house, his small eyes, pursed mouth and button nose working together in perfect symmetry.

'Eddie Savage,' he said in a quiet, polite voice. He got to his feet and extended his hand. 'It's been a while.'

'Aye, it has, Amos,' Eddie replied, shaking his hand. 'Two, maybe three years?'

'Two years, nine months, seventeen days.'

'Precise as ever. I dinnae ken how you do it.'

'I have been blessed with a logical, orderly brain, something so many people today lack. And to what do we owe the honour of this visit?'

There was no sarcasm in his tone. His demeanour was respectful and gracious.

'Cole Alexander.'

'I see. Please, take a seat.'

The Savages occupied the two couches while Amos retook the armchair.

'Isaiah,' said Amos. 'Fetch our guests some tea.'

'Yes, Father,' he replied with a respectful bow before leaving.

Jane and Jennifer glanced at each other with raised eyebrows, thinking this family was very creepy.

'I believe my nephew, Gideon, was involved in some sort of skirmish last night in Haghill,' said Amos.

'Aye, he was,' replied Eddie. 'He helped Cole set a trap to kidnap my niece, Carly,' he said, gesturing to her.

'I'm very sorry to hear that. Gideon has always been a wild boy. I've tried disciplining him, but I fear it's too late. My sister, Clara, was an indulgent mother. She spoiled him rotten.'

'Did you know about the plan?'

'No' until he came to me in the early hours of the morning whining about his broken nose. Who did that, by the way?'

'A pal of ours,' said Eddie. Gary had in fact been the one responsible.

'I suppose he deserved it,' shrugged Amos.

'Cole's been causing havoc. He hates Carly for messing up his face when in truth she was only defending herself.'

'Come now, Eddie. There's far more to Cole's activities than that. Everyone knows he's after ousting Toni and he might just be capable of doing it.'

'The wee toerag's nowhere near strong enough.'

'Toni's a clever woman but she's grown lazy. She spends far

too much time revelling in luxury and having sex,' Amos said with distaste. 'She's become complacent, too confident in the fear she inspires. But people are quick to scent weakness and they've scented it in her.'

'Toni's no' weak. She's stronger than ever.'

'You would say that seeing how she's your employer.'

'I say it because it's true.'

'You're loyal to her and that's to be admired, especially as she'd drop you like a hot brick the moment you stopped being useful to her.'

'Perhaps but she still has our loyalty.'

'Which says a lot about your characters. Not enough people have that trait these days. I'm trying to give you some good advice here. Are you sure you're on the winning side?'

'Without a doubt.'

Amos sighed and leaned back in his chair. 'You're a stubborn man, Eddie, you always have been, but violent takeovers are the nature of this business. Toni's brother Frankie only became king around here by murdering his predecessor and Toni herself claimed her current position by killing her uncle. Why is it such an alien concept to you that someone could do the same to her?'

'I see what you mean but I absolutely believe that she will take out anyone who comes after her.'

'I do hope that belief of yours won't be your undoing.' Amos looked to Harry when he got to his feet. 'May I enquire where you're going?'

'Your son's been a long time getting the tea,' he replied.

'I wouldnae say that. It takes a while to boil the kettle and prepare the mugs and biscuits for so many unexpected guests.' His eyes narrowed at these last two words.

'How could we be unexpected?' chimed in Carly. 'You must have known we'd stop by after what your nephew did.'

Amos didn't reply, he just stared back at her with those strange dark eyes of his.

'Harry, Jane, go check on Isaiah,' said Eddie, his gaze never leaving Amos.

They left the room, everyone waiting in silence until they returned.

'He's gone,' said Jane. 'The back door was open.'

Carly shot to her feet and loomed over Amos. 'Where's Cole hiding?'

'As if he'd tell me,' the man replied coolly.

'So, you have been in contact with him?'

'Of course. No' even a wild card like Gideon would dare make a move like that without my permission.'

'Your family's joined the other gangs rebelling between Gallowburn and Haghill?' said Eddie.

'Separating Toni's territories is a clever move. It will cut right into her powerbase. My family is in the middle of that divide. It was either join or be conquered.'

'I thought you were smarter than that, Amos. Cole cannae win this battle.'

'What makes you so confident? We all know that without Toni her family will fall and that is her biggest weakness. So afraid has she been of a member of her own clan toppling her just as she did her own uncle that she's ensured not one of her relatives is strong enough to lead in the event of her death. Caesar would be but he's not a McVay and he would be taken out at the same time as his mistress. No one is invincible, Eddie. You should remember that. No' even yourselves, despite how quickly your family's risen in our world.'

'Err, Uncle Eddie,' said Carly. 'A load of people are piling out of the flats opposite.'

They all rushed to the window, shocked to see twenty people storming across the road, Isaiah at their head.

'Lock the doors,' Eddie yelled.

Harry rushed to lock the back door while Jennifer hurried to secure the front.

Half the group outside headed down the side of the house to the back and started banging on both doors.

'It's like being in the middle of a zombie movie,' exclaimed Harry, returning to the living room with Jennifer.

'What do we do now?' said Jane.

'I'll tell you what we do,' replied Eddie.

He grabbed Amos by the front of his shirt, yanked him out of his chair and threw him at the bay window. Amos hit the glass hard and slid down it with a groan.

Eddie opened one of the windows so he could yell out.

'Come any nearer and this walloper will suffer for it,' he told them, holding a stunned Amos by his shirt and shaking him about.

Instantly the people outside stopped, ten pairs of beady eyes glaring back at Eddie.

'And tell that lot at the back to stop it too,' he added.

One of the men ran down the side of the house and a few seconds later the banging at the back door also ceased.

'You were stupid to remain behind with us,' Eddie told Amos.

'Change demands a sacrifice,' he murmured.

'And you're that sacrifice, are you, ya fanny?' Eddie growled. 'What makes you think Cole will be any better than Toni?'

'He's young, he can be shaped.'

'He's no' a puppet you can control, you prick,' Carly told Amos. 'He'd be a lot worse than Toni. It would be like sending Glasgow back to the days of the mad Roman emperors.'

'Harry, take this fud,' said Eddie, practically slinging Amos at his son.

Amos fell onto his hands and knees and Harry dragged him up by the back of his shirt.

'Don't you fucking dare,' Harry yelled when two men ran at the door. To emphasise his words, he banged Amos's forehead off the window, causing his knees to buckle.

'They've backed off, for now,' said Jane. 'But that won't last long. They'll soon start trying to break in again.'

'Shall I call Peanut?' said Jennifer.

'Naw,' replied Eddie. 'I want him watching over Rose.'

'The Blood Brothers?'

'Logan's having his meeting with Craig Lawson. We need whatever information he has.'

'Then there's only one thing for it,' said Jane, taking out her phone. 'I'll have to call The Bitches.'

'But it's ten o'clock in the morning,' said Jennifer. 'Most of them will be at work.'

'What about Elijah or David?' offered Harry, who still had hold of Amos.

'Aye, good idea, son,' replied Eddie.

'Wait,' said Jennifer. 'Maybe we can use this as an opportunity to get to Cole.'

'How?' replied Jane.

'Amos must be in contact with him somehow.'

Eddie stared down at Amos severely. 'How have you been contacting Cole? Speak,' he barked. 'Before I ram your heid clean through your own window.'

'I have a phone number for him,' Amos replied.

'Call him and tell him you've got our family trapped here.'

'Well, it wouldnae be a lie,' commented Harry.

'And he'll turn up mobhanded meaning we won't stand a chance,' said Jennifer.

'Cole's playing us,' said Carly. 'He planted Gideon in Jack's flat last night in case his plan went wrong. He wanted to know where we'd go to next. He's probably already on his way here. It's the only explanation for why that lot were waiting in those flats for us to turn up,' she added, gesturing to the crowd outside.

'Holy shit, you're right,' said Jennifer.

'Aye, she is,' replied a troubled Eddie. 'Jeezo, the wee dick's craftier than I thought.'

'Cole's here somewhere, right now,' pressed Carly. 'If we play it right, we could turn his own trap against him.'

Her uncle smiled proudly. 'What the walloper doesnae realise is that you're just as crafty as he is, hen.'

'I have an idea,' Carly said before running upstairs.

She flung open the door of a bedroom that looked out over the front street, this room as freakishly neat as the rest of the house. To her surprise, she encountered a middle-aged woman kneeling before a cabinet with a large wooden cross on it, her hands clasped together. She wore a white blouse and a floor-length black skirt that had pooled around her. Her dark hair had been pulled back into a tight bun.

'Oh, sorry,' said Carly.

The woman didn't react, her eyes remaining closed, lips murmuring a prayer.

Carly shrugged, rushed over to the window and flung it open, drawing the attention of everyone below.

'Cole,' she called out. 'I'm right here. Why don't you come and get me?'

There was no response as the gathered crowd continued to gaze up at her.

'Just as I thought,' she said. 'You're a coward, Cole. You keep sending other people to do your dirty work because you're afraid of me.' Carly looked down at the assembled people. 'Is this who you want to support, a man who's too afraid to face a woman on his own?'

Just by scanning the people below, Carly could tell many of them were members of the Bell family. From this height, she also had a good view of her uncle's car and she saw that all the tyres had been slashed.

'Great,' she sighed. How would they get away now? 'Cole's so weak he daren't face me,' she continued, addressing the mob. 'How can such a coward ever hope to stand up against Toni McVay?'

The people began muttering amongst themselves as they considered her words.

'Here I am,' called a voice.

A hooded figure was making their way across the street, having exited the flats opposite. The person wandered down the garden path as the gathered group stood aside, forming a channel through their ranks for him to walk through. Cole threw back his hood, revealing his scarred face, and glared up at her with eyes that were still so full of rage and hate.

'So, you've decided to come out of hiding?' Carly said disdainfully.

'I wasnae hiding,' Cole replied. 'I was overseeing the operation.'

'What a load of bollocks. You're a coward, Cole, and everyone here has seen it.'

Rebellion was starting to filter through the ranks of the Bell family but they were all cowed by the power of Cole's furious gaze, as well as that horribly scarred face. The mutinous murmurings died down.

'Think you're brave enough to come in for a parley?' pressed Carly.

Cole looked back up at her and shrugged. 'Sure. I'm happy to prove I'm no' a coward.'

'Are you carrying a gun?'

'That's for you to find out.'

'You're no' coming in with it.'

'It's only fair. There's five of you against me.'

'You're no' bringing a gun in here.'

'Then we've reached an impasse. I think everyone here can see how unfair your terms are.'

In response, the Bells all nodded. Carly didn't like this family at all and not just because they'd got her own family trapped and cornered. They gave the impression of being a weird, backwards clan who committed incest and burnt people in wicker men.

There was a scream behind her and Carly turned to see the woman was on her feet, the face that had once been composed in peaceful prayer now wild, eyes bulging, lips drawn back over her teeth in a scream. In her right hand she held the heavy wooden cross, which she raised above her head ready to bring down on Carly.

25

'Kill the unbeliever,' shrieked the woman.

'Jesus,' cried Carly.

'Do not take our Saviour's name in vain,' she screamed.

Carly ducked as the woman swiped at her with the weapon, making her miss. As she drew back her arm for a second attempt, Carly grabbed her wrist and yanked her forward before punching her in the face. The woman collapsed to the floor with a groan and Carly tore the weapon from her hand.

'Stay down,' Carly told her.

Carly heard the thunder of footsteps on the stairs and Harry and Jane burst in.

'What the hell's going on?' demanded Harry.

'Do not utter that evil word in my house,' yelled the woman, blood trickling from the corner of her mouth.

'What, on?' he retorted sarcastically.

'She attacked me with a cross,' explained Carly.

'God, this lot are freaks,' said Jane.

'Irreverent unbelievers! You will all burn for eternity.'

'What a load of shite,' said Harry.

Carly's eyes widened. 'What's Cole doing?'

The three of them rushed to the window and Carly went cold when she saw Cole had vanished.

'Oh, Christ,' sighed Jane.

'Stop saying that,' cried the woman.

Harry grabbed her by the bun and yanked back her head. 'If you don't shut your hole, I'll ram that cross down your fucking throat.'

The woman glared back at him but wisely remained silent.

'We'd better get downstairs,' said Carly. 'Let's take her with us, we can use her as a hostage,' she added, gesturing to the woman.

Harry hauled their captive to her feet and escorted her out, with Jane and Carly following. They hastened downstairs and into the living room where Eddie still waited with Jennifer and Amos.

'First of all,' said Carly, 'your car's knackered, Uncle Eddie.'

'Aye, I thought so,' he replied.

'Did you see where Cole went?'

'He went down the side of the house,' replied Jennifer. 'I've looked out back but I cannae see him. All the people who were there have gone too.'

'Have you called anyone?' Carly asked her uncle.

'Aye, David,' he replied. 'The cavalry's on the way, we just need to hold on.'

'It's a siege,' announced Harry.

'It worries me how excited you sound about that,' Eddie frowned at his son.

'You've got to admit, it's a wee bit exciting.'

'No, it's bloody not. For the second time we've walked right into one of Cole's traps. He's making us look like dicks.'

'Your foul mouths will only incite divine retribution,' announced the woman.

'Well, well, well, Eliza Bell. Amos's wife,' Eddie added for the benefit of his family. 'And what's your role in all this?'

'To destroy anyone who will prevent our Saviour from returning in all his glory,' she announced fervently.

'Don't look at me,' muttered Amos when Eddie glanced his way. 'I've had to put up with that shite for twenty-four years.'

'Listen, Amos,' said Eddie, deciding to try to reason with the man. 'We've known each other a long time. We've helped each other out over the years. Have you already forgotten how my boys protected your Bart in Bar-L when he was given three years for assault?'

Amos sighed heavily. 'No.'

'So why would you turn on me and mine in favour of that wee upstart, Cole Alexander?'

'It's taking me a lot to admit this, you know how proud I am, but I'm into Toni for a lot of money.'

Eddie shook his head. 'It's all making sense now. You want rid of her so you don't have to pay her back. Why didnae you come to me for a loan?'

'Because I owe her a hundred and seventy grand.'

'Jesus Christ.'

'The disbelievers will be...' began Eliza.

'Shut your fucking heid, woman,' roared Amos. 'I'm sick of listening to your pish.'

Eliza went silent but her eyes glittered with anger.

'So much for that logical brain of yours, ya eejit,' Eddie told Amos. 'Fancy borrowing so much money off Toni McVay of all people.'

'I'm sorry, Eddie, but I've nae choice,' he replied. 'I cannae pay Toni back and she'll take my eyes for it.'

'I'm really sorry to hear that, pal, but no way is my family gonnae suffer for your mistake.' Eddie sighed and looked to the window. 'Jesus Christ,' he exclaimed when confronted with Cole's scarred face.

Amos narrowed his eyes at his wife when she opened her mouth. 'Don't even think about it,' he told her.

Eliza closed her mouth and sniffed haughtily.

'I thought we were gonnae parley,' Cole called through the glass.

'Don't, Uncle Eddie,' said Carly. 'He's got a gun.'

'That's right, I do,' said Cole, producing the weapon from inside his jacket.

Eddie grabbed Amos and hauled him in front of him. 'You come in here and I'll snap the bastard's neck.'

'Like I care.'

'You might no' but I'm guessing his family will.'

Cole hesitated and glanced back over his shoulder at Isaiah and Amos's relatives, who were all scowling at Cole. He turned back to face the window.

'I'll leave the gun if I can talk to Carly alone.'

'No fucking way,' replied Eddie.

'Then we're coming in.'

'And poor old Amos will get his neck broken.'

'You won't do that, he's an old pal of yours.'

'A pal who set us up. Like I told Amos, if it's a choice between him and us, I'll choose us every time. The reinforcements are also on the way, so you'd better do one, unless you want to be dragged in front of Toni McVay.'

'It's pathetic how you try to use her to scare people. She's lost her grip on this city. Her name no longer inspires the fear it once did. I've got a proposal for your family. Despite what Carly did to me...'

'What I did to you?' she exclaimed.

'...I know how good you are at what you do. Join me.'

'Never,' retorted Carly.

'Then you're dead meat. But it seems that won't be today.' He looked to the Bells. 'Let them go. Now's no' the time.' Cole turned back to the window. 'It's safe for you to come out.'

'No' until you lot have buggered off,' replied Eddie.

The crowd outside turned when there was an enormous bang.

'What's that?' demanded Jane as the Savages rushed to the window.

'Wait a minute,' said Harry. 'Jennifer's gone.'

'What?' cried Jane, whirling round. 'Where is she?'

'I get the feeling she's the source of that noise,' replied Carly.

'Go upstairs, see what it was, hen,' Eddie told her.

Carly nodded and raced upstairs. She pushed open one of the windows and leaned out to see the Bells racing down the street towards a van that had crashed into a parked car.

Carly ran back down to relate what she'd learnt just as Jane's phone rang.

'It's Jennifer,' she said, the handset pressed to her ear. 'She said to go out the back way.'

Cole was still standing at the window, staring in at them balefully, but he made no move to enter when they all rushed into the hallway to pull their shoes back on. They raced to the rear of the house, Eddie pulling Amos along with him. Eliza didn't even attempt to interfere.

They exited by the back door and hurried through the garden which was occupied by a gnome army. The back gate was pushed open by Jennifer.

'This way,' she told them.

Instead of heading down the street, Jennifer ran at a neighbour's fence and scrambled over it, dropping down into the back garden.

'Oh, shite,' sighed Eddie, staring at it despairingly. He was not the most athletic of men.

Carly looked up the street. 'It's Cole.'

'Look at him marching along like the fucking Terminator,' said Harry.

'Go, go,' Eddie urged them, noting the gun Cole held.

'You first,' said Jane, pushing Carly towards the fence.

Carly scrambled over it, followed by Jane and then Harry.

'Where's Uncle Eddie?' cried Carly while Jane and Jennifer embraced.

'He cannae get over the fence,' exclaimed Harry. 'Da',' he cried.

There was a bang and the fence panel collapsed forward, Eddie falling and landing on top of it.

Seeing Cole raising his gun, Harry kicked Amos in the back, knocking him towards him, blocking Cole's shot.

'Get up, Da',' yelled Harry, grabbing his dad's arm and hauling him to his feet.

'Run, don't wait for me,' Eddie told them.

The five of them rushed down the side of the house and into the front garden, dodging around the owner of the house who was just entering by the gate.

'Hey,' the man called lamely, making no effort to pursue them.

'Call... David,' panted Eddie as they ran.

Harry took out his phone to make the call, talking as he ran. 'Where are you? Moredun Street. Where the hell's that?' There was the honk of a horn and they turned to see David's car speeding towards them. 'Oh, we're on it.'

Carly looked back over her shoulder to see Cole was rapidly

gaining on them while her exhausted uncle lagged behind. She needn't have worried because David had spotted Cole and drove up on the pavement at him. Cole threw himself sideways into a hedge.

David brought the car to a screeching halt.

'Get in,' he yelled through the open driver's window.

Carly, Jennifer and Jane got into the back while Eddie jumped into the passenger seat.

'There's no room for me,' exclaimed Harry.

'Lie on top of us,' cried Carly when she saw Cole picking himself up.

'That's the best offer I've had all week,' he said, flinging himself across the three women's laps.

David sped off before Jane had even managed to yank the back door closed. He glanced in the rearview mirror.

'Get down.'

They all ducked as David's rear window exploded. He whipped the steering wheel to the right, speeding around a corner, and Cole vanished from view.

'All right, it's safe,' he told them.

They all breathed a sigh of relief and sat up, except for Harry, who had to remain lying down.

'I think that's my debt paid to you, Carly,' David told her.

'I agree,' she replied, brushing tiny shards of glass off the back of her neck.

26

Logan faced Craig Lawson across the table in the visits room. Craig's time in prison had only made him even more smug and arrogant, mainly because he was top dog, a position he'd achieved by brutally murdering Cameron Abernethy, father of Allegra, girlfriend of the previous leader of the Blood Brothers. Logan knew Craig of old. He'd been an enemy of him and his friends since they were children, although Craig was a few years older than them.

'Well, if it isn't the leader of the Blood Brothers in the flesh,' said Craig, leaning back in his chair to appraise Logan. He was a strong, handsome man with the same startling green eyes as his Alexander relatives. His looks were marred by the impression that there was something reptilian about the man, something that could never be trusted, not even by those closest to him. 'What have I done to be graced by your presence?'

'You know exactly what you've done,' replied Logan. 'You've been plotting with your cousin, Cole Alexander.'

Craig merely smiled as he appraised Logan. The lad he'd known had gone, replaced by a man completely at ease with his own power, a clever man who was not an opponent to take lightly. Craig was arrogant but he wasn't a fool.

'Of course I have. Why should I deny it? If you've come here thinking I'll tell you all about it then you're gonnae be disappointed.' Craig leaned on the table, those snake-like eyes assessing him carefully. 'I hear you're working with the Savage family. Tell me, are the Savage Sisters as hot as everyone says?'

'It's true that I'm working with the Savages,' was all Logan was willing to reply.

'You giving it to one of them?'

Logan regarded him disdainfully. 'I understand you've been stuck in prison with a bunch of men for a few years, but if that's what you're gonnae reduce the conversation to then I'm off.'

'Stay right where you are,' said Craig when Logan got to his feet.

'You don't gi'e the orders any more. Certainly no' outside this toilet. I know I'm the first visitor you've had in months. Even your own family's sick of your shite. If I stay, we talk like grown men.'

Craig's eyes glittered with malice but he nodded.

Logan retook his seat. 'I wouldnae expect you to tell me anything, which is why I made sure to come here with some information you really want to hear.'

'What can you possibly know that I don't? I'm king snake in this prison.'

'I know that one of your own crew has been feeding information about your activities to the governor.'

Craig's eyes widened and he stared back at Logan, unblinking, cheeks appearing to sink in as all the colour drained from his sharp, angular face. 'You fucking what?'

'Did you really think I havenae been keeping an eye on you all this time? I cultivated a relationship with no' just a couple of guards but several inmates too who give me all the information I need. I know how you're smuggling in the drugs you deal to the other prisoners. A guard brings them in and hides them in the exercise equipment in the gym.'

'Keep your fucking voice down,' hissed Craig, looking around anxiously.

'The prison's made it very hard for visitors to smuggle anything in. Letters laced with drugs were sent into inmates which could be smoked, but now prisoners only get photocopies of the letters. Then there's the body scanner that checks all visitors before they get into this room, plus the sniffer dog. You had to find a new route in and there was only one – the staff. The doctor's another of your smugglers. You go to him regularly for foot trouble, which is probably imaginary, and he slips you the drugs. Unfortunately, you told some of your crew the details of your operation and one of them is grassing on you in order to get themselves out of some hot water.'

'Give me their name.'

'No' until you give me something useful about Cole Alexander.'

Craig leaned back in his chair, studying him. 'You're making it up just to get me to talk.'

'Fine, if you want to play it that way but don't blame me when you get put in segregation and your wee operation collapses. I bet there'd be a lot of pissed-off prisoners who'd give you a good kicking for allowing their supply to be cut off.'

Craig drummed the fingers of his right hand on the table as he thought. 'All right, I'll gi'e you some information. Fuck Cole, it's no' like he can get me out of this place anyway. You probably already know he's after bringing down the bitch with the black eyes?'

Logan nodded.

'If you ask me, he's got ideas above his station,' continued Craig. 'But you never know. Everyone has to fall one day.'

'What's your role in his big scheme?'

'To target Toni's people in here. I've already put two of her men who were serving a stretch for armed robbery in intensive care. No one knows it was me though.'

'Just you or you and your crew?'

'Me and three others carefully chosen for their aggression and discretion.' Craig smiled, liking the way that sounded.

'If Toni found out she'd have you killed.'

'I don't think Toni cares. Everyone says she's getting complacent. All she wants to do these days is go to the opera and have lots of sex. She's middle-aged now and she's starting to let things slip.'

'That's totally different to the woman I know. Cole's exaggerating to get you onboard. And what did he pay you? Like you said, it's no' like he can get you released.'

'More product for me to distribute. Business is booming.'

'Oh, aye, and what are you gonnae do with all your hard-earned cash? Buy a yacht? Take a trip to the Seychelles?'

Craig scowled back at him.

'If I managed to find out about that prisoner grassing on you then Cole must know too,' continued Logan. 'I wonder why he hasnae told you?'

'That thought has already occurred to me,' Craig spat back, furious that Logan thought he might be stupid. 'And if he does, I'll get him back for it. I don't know how, but I'll find a way.'

Logan absolutely believed Craig. The man might be stuck in a high-security prison, but he was very wily.

'How are you communicating with Cole?'

'Burner phone,' was all Craig was willing to say.

'Has he ever mentioned the Savage family to you?'

'Aye. He really hates his ex-girlfriend for fucking up his face. I've never seen it, but I've heard it's bad.'

'It is.'

'I admit, I'm surprised that he's become the man he has. When he was younger, I thought he was a daft, soppy sod who'd never amount to much. Then he was flung in here and it changed him, hardened him into stone. Prison can do that to people. I was willing to bet he'd end up topping himself. I never thought this would happen. It's funny to think that he's pretty much head of our family now and that he could end up running Glasgow.'

'That will never happen. Toni will win.'

'She's ageing, getting slow. Cole's young and bursting with fire. Anyone who gets in his way will get burnt.'

'Has he asked you to do anything other than target Toni's people in here?'

'Naw. There's nothing much I can do. Toni prides herself on her name protecting all her people. Their being attacked makes it look like she's losing her grip. I'm no' the only one he's asked to do it because another of her men got shanked in the shower and that was nothing to do with me.'

'How does the Savage family fit into Cole's plan?'

'They're becoming a major force and it would be a big coup for him if he took them down and seized Haghill from Toni.' Craig's eyes glittered. 'The same applies to Gallowburn and you lot. He's recruiting the local families around your two schemes to divide your forces. When Haghill and the Gallowburn fall, Toni's reputation will be destroyed and she'll fall too. It didnae help her cause that she couldn't catch Cole's partner who killed Jack Alexander. That made her look weak. I heard his da' sent him away so he couldnae be found. Usually, Toni would have killed the da' and kept his eyeballs as a trophy but she needs him to help hold Haghill.' He chuckled. 'God help you all if Cole pulls it off because he'll make Mussolini look reasonable.'

'Where's he hiding out?'

Both corners of Craig's mouth lifted, only intensifying the reptilian look. 'Like he'd tell me that. He doesnae trust me any more than I trust him.'

'Do you think he'd stay close to Haghill?'

'Aye, probably. He knows that area like the back of his hand, so it makes sense. Right, I think I've shared more than enough with you. I want that name.'

At that point, the guard announced that visiting time was over and Logan got to his feet.

'Hey,' hissed Craig. 'We had a deal.'

'And you're keeping something back. Tell me what it is and I'll gi'e you that name.'

Craig grunted and shifted uneasily in his seat, rubbing one hand across the back of his neck.

'Who's more important to you, Cole or yourself?' pressed Logan.

Just as he'd known it would, this statement played on Craig's very strong sense of self-preservation.

'I don't know where he's hiding but whenever I've spoken to him on the phone, I've heard trains in the background. I don't know for sure, but I'm pretty certain he's hiding out near a train station. Once I heard a weird clanking sound. It reminded me of the time I spent at my aunty's caravan at Wemyss Bay when they changed the gas bottles on the vans. Now it's your turn,' he growled.

Logan glanced around the room. All the visitors were being ushered to the door. Hellish fury was in Craig's eyes as he thought Logan was going to renege on their agreement.

After tormenting his old adversary for a few more seconds, Logan leaned over to whisper. 'Wayne Aikenhead.'

Craig nodded and ground his palms together. He glared at the prisoner seated at the next table, who gave him a nervous, sideways look.

Logan got the feeling Wayne wouldn't be running to the governor with any more stories.

* * *

The Savages, along with David, slunk into the sisters' flat, looking tired and disappointed.

'I'm gonnae have to get my rear window fixed now,' muttered David. 'I've only had that car three months.'

'Better the window than our heids,' replied Harry. 'Isn't it?' he added when David frowned at him.

'Oh, God, what now?' said Eddie when there was a knock at the door.

'I wouldnae be surprised if it was an army of the undead,' commented Harry.

They went to the door en masse to answer it, relieved to see it was the Blood Brothers.

'I take it something's happened?' commented Logan.

'It's been an eventful morning,' said Eddie. 'Come away in.'

'I got some useful information out of Craig,' said Logan as he, Gary and Digger followed them through to the kitchen.

'We're glad to hear it because Cole's taking the piss out of us big style,' said Eddie.

'Craig didnae tell me anything we didn't already know apart from two things – he and his crew have battered two of Toni's people inside and they're no' the only ones. Cole got someone else to shiv another of her men in the shower. Craig also thinks wherever Cole's hiding is close to Haghill and he's staying near a train station. Every time he's spoken to him on a smuggled burner phone, Craig's heard trains in the background.'

'Toni already knows who's been attacking her people in Bar-L,' commented David. 'And she's planning a gruesome revenge on them, including Craig. She was waiting until you'd spoken to him first before making her move.'

'That's great info, pal,' Eddie told Logan. 'Have we got a map of the local area?'

'I can bring one up on my laptop,' replied Jane.

'Do it, hen.'

Jane placed the computer on the dining table, switched it on and brought up a map. Everyone gathered around to look, Digger apologising when he stood on Harry's foot.

'There's two train stations close by,' said Jane. 'Duke Street and Alexandra Parade. Carntyne and Bellgrove are a bit further out.'

'If he was staying close to any of them surely we would have heard by now?' said Jennifer. 'I mean, he does stand out.'

'Alexandra Parade is right next to the park,' said Digger. 'Could he be staying in there?'

'No' in this weather,' said David. 'He would have frozen to death by now.'

'Is there anyone in those areas who'd hide him from you?' Logan asked the Savages.

'Possibly,' said Eddie. 'There are people around here who resent our position.'

'Craig told me something else,' continued Logan. 'He said during one call he also heard a clanking sound, like gas bottles being knocked together.'

A memory hit Carly hard. It was of her and Cole fighting at the caravan park the night Jack was murdered. She could still recall the pain as her body had tumbled into a stack of empty gas bottles like a bowling ball into skittles, and the sound they'd made as they'd clanked together.

'Son of a bitch,' she exclaimed. 'He's done it again.'

'Done what, doll?' replied Eddie.

'I know where he's hiding – at the caravan site where Jack was murdered. It's next to the train track that runs between Bellgrove and Carntyne. You can hear the trains as they go by.' She regarded them all with sad eyes. 'It would be just like Cole to hide out there, another taunt to me.'

'Have you been there since you came back to Haghill?' David asked her.

'No. I havenae been there since that horrible night.' She shivered. 'Cole would know I wouldn't be in a rush to go back.'

'Sounds like you could be on to something. We have to check it out.'

'It could be another trap, like at Jack's flat,' replied Jennifer. 'And the Bells' house.'

'It's a chance we have to take. This time we'll be better prepared. We'll split up and approach it from different directions, hopefully taking anyone there by surprise.'

'Some of the other caravans could be occupied by innocent people nothing to do with Cole,' said Carly.

'We need to bear that in mind. How many entrances are there to the caravan park?'

'There's just one road in,' Carly replied. 'But there is some waste ground on the left side. It's separated from the caravan park by a fence but the fence can be easily scaled. To the right of the caravan park is a large industrial unit with security, so that's out. There's also a tall metal fence dividing the unit from the caravan park.'

'Okay. You, me, Logan, Jane and Eddie will approach it by the road. The rest of you take the route through the waste ground.'

'May I suggest another idea?'

'Go ahead.'

'I go in alone.' Carly sighed when everyone began objecting at once. 'Let me finish,' she cried over the din.

They all quietened down.

'I'll make it look like I'm visiting the spot where Jack died. You lot will be close. Cole doesnae know Logan spoke to Craig, so he'll think all his Christmases have come at once when he sees me there. It'll lure him out of hiding and you lot can grab him.'

'I don't know,' said David. 'There's a lot that could go wrong. For all we know, he might just shoot you.'

'He wants to make me suffer. A quick bullet to the heid won't be enough for him.'

Jane shuddered at her words and Jennifer wrapped a comforting arm around her wife.

'There'll be a fence to scale at the side of the waste ground,' continued Carly. 'Just so you're aware.'

'Where's Peanut?' David asked Eddie. 'We could really use him on this.'

'He messaged me half an hour ago to say Rose and Fergus had gone on to a pub.'

'Tell him we need him back here no later than eight.'

'Nae bother,' he replied, taking out his phone and calling his friend.

David nodded Carly to one side. 'Are you sure you're up to this?'

'Too right I am,' she replied determinedly.

'It could be upsetting being back there.'

'I know but I have to do this. We're all fighting for our lives and I cannae let sentiment get in the way.'

He smiled and patted her arm. 'You're still the same brave lassie.'

As David wandered off to talk to Eddie, Carly turned her back on everyone, steeling herself for what was to come. She'd sworn she'd never go back to that caravan park. Had Cole realised that and thought it would make it a safe place for him to hide and if she ever did find him there then she'd be at a psychological disadvantage? She hoped she'd dealt with her grief enough for it not to overwhelm her. Maybe finally facing the past would help her resolve her trauma once and for all.

27

Three cars pulled up at the kerb on Duke Street. One of these was the hire car Eddie was using, his old one having been towed away from Springboig to be fixed at a garage. The Savages and their associates piled out of the vehicles and, without a word, they split into two groups, walking off in different directions. It had been decided that Jane would go with the group who would approach through the woods as she would have a much better chance of scaling the fence than Peanut, so Carly was the only female in their group. Rose had wanted to come along but David had vetoed that. As he was their boss, she'd been unable to argue with him and she'd been dropped off at Tamara's for the night.

Carly fell to the back of her group, steeling herself to face the scene of Jack's murder. She knew the caravan in which he'd been killed was long gone; Toni's people had burnt it out to erase all evidence. But it would still be difficult being back there.

Logan fell into step beside her. 'You okay?' he said.

'Aye,' she replied.

'If you feel you cannae handle it, just let me know. There's no shame if it's too much for you.'

'You're a good man, Logan.'

'And you're a good woman.'

'I wouldn't go that far,' she said wryly.

'But I would. Cole's doing this to screw with your heid. You cannae let him win.'

Determination filled her eyes. 'I won't. Anyway,' she said, wanting to change the subject, 'it must have been difficult for you seeing the man who tried to kill your best pal.'

'Aye,' Logan slowly replied. 'The bastard's as vicious as ever. He's where he belongs and he's never getting out.'

'That's good to know. We've got enough enemies as it is.'

Sensing she was psyching herself up for this mission, Logan went silent, walking beside her in support.

Their group came to a halt as they reached the turning up to the caravan park.

'Are you really sure about this, hen?' Eddie asked Carly.

'I am.'

'The lassie can handle it,' David told him. He turned to Carly. 'You remember the plan?'

She nodded.

'Okay. Do your thing, sweetheart.'

Carly began the walk down the road that led to the caravan park. The road itself wasn't lit but the moon was bright, the sky clear and dotted with stars. The lights from the main road cast their glow, enabling her to see. It was still very cold, the branches of the trees either side of her coated in frost, but there was no sign of snow. Her pace was steady as she followed the curve of the road to the right and through the gates of the caravan park.

'Jesus,' she exclaimed when her right foot went out from under her.

Both feet slipped and slid before she managed to correct herself. Looking down, she saw she was standing on a puddle that had frozen over. She cringed as she recalled the way she'd shouted. Had she just lost the element of surprise? As she continued on her way, not only did she have to look out for any possible attack, but for more icy patches too. Despite her caution, she slipped on another one but this time she managed not to shout out loud with surprise.

'You could break your bloody neck around here,' she said when she spied the gleam of more of the icy traps. She didn't think Cole had placed these here on purpose. Rather the puddles had formed from the rain that had come down in the early hours of the morning then frozen in the rapidly falling temperature.

As the caravan park was revealed to her, Carly stopped to get her bearings. Everything was as it had been the night Jack had died – several static caravans huddled together in a little cul-de-sac, still sporting their patio furniture and garden ornaments.

The caravan Jack had died in hadn't been the one they'd stayed in together. That still stood to her left, looking exactly as it had the last time she'd seen it. She smiled as she recalled the small amount of time they'd shared in there, both so optimistic about their future.

'Stop it,' she whispered when tears filled her eyes.

Tearing her gaze off that van, she headed to the spot where Jack had been murdered. She had expected to see a large, empty space where the caravan had been but instead a brand new one stood in its place. This seemed irreverent to Carly, as though the world was moving on and forgetting all about him.

Despite these thoughts, she'd remained alert, so she was ready when she heard soft footsteps approaching on the pothole-ridden road. Carly turned, pulling the stun gun from her pocket and jamming it into the arm of the man standing behind her. The crackle of the electrodes lit up the darkened scene. She saw a mouth open wide in a scream and bulging eyes before the man dropped, twitching.

A dozen more figures rushed out of the surrounding caravans and formed a circle around her, their hoods up, masks obscuring the lower halves of their faces. Carly held the stun gun ready while drawing the baton from inside her jacket with the other.

'Who's next?' she snarled.

One man lunged at her, but his foot hit an icy puddle and he fell heavily on his back. While he was down, Carly jabbed him with the stun gun, the light from the weapon illuminating her malicious smile.

The assailants all jumped and whirled round when there was a loud bellow and Peanut, Logan, Eddie and David ran up the road towards them.

'Watch out for the ice,' called Carly.

Her warning came too late as Eddie slipped and went down with a startled cry.

As the attackers turned to face these new intruders, Carly took down another man with her stun gun.

'Cole, where are you?' she yelled.

Carly leapt back when a figure swiped at her with a hammer and she knocked the weapon from his hand with the baton.

'Where's Cole?' she demanded.

The man just groaned in pain, clutching his hand. Rolling her eyes, she shocked him with the stun gun and he fell.

More attackers emerged from the caravans and advanced on them, herding them into a tight circle. Carly frantically scanned their number but any one of them could have been Cole. All had their hoods up, obscuring their faces. One man sped towards them, slipped on an icy patch and kept on going, skidding past them all with a shocked look on his face before crashing into the side of a caravan, making Peanut double over with laughter.

'Cole, where are you?' yelled Carly.

One of the figures gestured to the caravan occupying the site where Jack had died.

'He's in there?'

The man nodded.

'He's lying,' said Eddie. 'He just wants you to go quietly.'

'No, don't,' said Logan, taking Carly's hand when she moved towards the van. 'It's a trap.'

'He's right, doll,' said Peanut, glaring at the men surrounding them. 'You go in there and we'll never see you again.'

'This could be our chance to end all this,' she retorted.

'Look around you, Carly,' David told her. 'They were waiting. It's another trap.'

'Fucking Craig Lawson,' growled Logan. 'He's gonnae pay for this.'

The attackers closed in on them, brandishing weapons, outnumbering them. What their assailants hadn't noticed were more shadowy figures approaching them from behind, keeping low, moving stealthily. This stealthiness was ruined by Harry slipping on some ice. As he fell, he accidentally kicked the legs out from under one of them, who toppled backwards, landing on him. This caused the man's friends to whip round with surprise.

'Aww, get off me, ya fat bastard,' groaned Harry, shoving the man off him.

Jane and Jennifer together grabbed one very large male and dragged him to the ground. Jane pressed down on his shoulders while Jennifer punched him repeatedly in the face. Digger and Gary managed to take down two men before their presences were even registered.

'Batter them,' roared Eddie, smacking one man in the face with the length of pipe he'd brought.

Logan whipped out the bike chain that had belonged to

Jamie and spun it, the vicious piece of metal biting through the air before whacking one man across the face with such force he was spun around a hundred and eighty degrees.

Carly saw someone watching from a window in the new caravan and ran towards it.

'Carly, wait,' she heard a voice call, but the noise of the battle was such she couldn't tell who it was.

She leapt back when one of the hooded men skidded past her on the ice, arms pinwheeling, shrieking with surprise before crashing into a wheelie bin.

Carly yanked open the door of the caravan and immediately threw herself aside when arms shot out to grab her. The moonlight reflected off fierce green eyes.

'Cole,' she snarled. 'Still hiding in the shadows, ya fucking jessie.'

He stepped out of the caravan, reaching inside his jacket for a weapon. Fearing it was a gun, she hit him in the hand with the baton and he cried out in pain.

'Try and hold a gun now, bitch,' she told him before swiping at him with the weapon again.

Cole reeled backwards. Carly attempted to shock him with the stun gun but missed.

'Another trap of yours has failed,' she told him. 'And now I'm gonnae kill you.'

She lunged at him again and again with the baton, rage and the desire for revenge making her movements wild and frantic, but she moved so quickly her opponent couldn't get a hit in and had to concentrate on defending himself.

When Cole attempted to retreat back into the caravan, his foot slipped on the icy step and his leg went out from under him. Carly kicked him in the chest and he fell backwards, his upper body landing in the caravan, legs on the steps. With a cry, she hit him with the stun gun. When his body relaxed from the shock, she pressed the button again, causing him to jump and jerk a second time while she laughed with wild glee. She repeated the process a third time, failing to realise the sounds of battle had stopped.

Her family and friends rushed around the side of the van.

'You've got the wee worm,' exclaimed Harry. 'Well done.'

Digger and Gary dragged him to his knees and yanked back his hood.

'That's no' Cole,' said Jane.

'It's John Lawson, Craig's younger brother,' said Logan.

'Why are you mixed up in all this, ya wee fanny?' Digger demanded of John, grabbing his face in one big hand and squeezing.

'Let's take him back with us,' said David. 'We cannae question him here.'

Digger and Gary hauled John off, the others following.

Logan noticed Carly hang back, staring at the caravan.

'You okay?' he asked her.

She nodded, tears glistening in her eyes. 'I wish I could forget the details of that night, but they're still as clear as day. It's just another torment.'

'One day they will fade,' he said, wrapping an arm around her.

'I want the horror to fade but no' his face,' she said, her voice barely a breath on the air. 'I never want to lose that.'

Logan glanced around, well aware their fallen foes could start picking themselves up at any moment. 'We'd better go.'

Carly nodded and allowed him to lead her away. Jane was waiting for them around the side of the caravan.

'What the hell's going on?' she demanded.

'Nothing's going on,' replied a puzzled Carly as Logan released her.

'I looked back and you weren't there. I was worried,' she said, glancing at Logan.

'I was just saying goodbye to the past.'

Jane's expression softened and she took her sister's hand. 'Come on, you're shaking with cold.'

'No, I'm not,' she frowned.

'Let's go,' said Jane firmly, leading her away, leaving Logan to bring up the rear.

As he passed one man who was trying to push himself upright, Logan kicked him in the ribs, taking out some of his frustration on him, knocking him back to the ground.

28

'What the hell are you doing?' Logan demanded of John Lawson. 'You were keeping your heid down after the chaos your older brother caused. Now you're joining in.'

They'd elected to take him to Gallowburn to be questioned and were gathered together in Logan's flat. John had been seated on a chair, looking very sorry for himself.

'What choice did I have?' he replied. 'I was told if I didnae help then I'd get my face smashed in. Cole's family and we're standing by him. So Craig says anyway.'

'That information he gave me was all part of the trap, wasn't it?'

'I dunno. I was just told to be at the caravan park.'

'Son of a bitch. And the information I gave him was solid. He's used it too. Wayne Aikenhead is in intensive care with lacerated kidneys.'

'You should know what my brother's like by now.'

'Aye. A two-faced fucking snake,' barked Logan, eyes flashing.

'Where's Cole hiding?' David asked John.

'Fuck knows. He tells no one that.'

'You must have some idea. Someone's got to be sheltering him.'

'If they are I don't know about it. God, I'm pissed off. I never wanted to be at the caravan park in the first place.'

'What was Cole's intention for tonight?'

'To take her,' he said, nodding at Carly. 'And put out of action as many of you as we could.'

'You failed miserably,' said Eddie.

'Aye, I suppose we did. I blame all that fucking ice.'

'I'm sick of being lured into traps and fighting our way out only to be lured into another one,' snapped Harry.

'I'm with you there, son,' replied Eddie.

Logan knelt before John. 'If you're family then you'll have a good idea which family members are hiding him.'

'Well, I don't,' he retorted. 'Cole probably wouldnae even stay with family. He'd be too worried about them turning him in.'

'You've got a point there. You fucking Lawsons are only ever out for yourselves. You've nae idea what loyalty is.'

'Maybe we've been wrong all this time,' said Jane. 'Maybe Cole's no' at Haghill but here in Gallowburn.'

'We would know if he was,' said Gary.

'That's no slight on your abilities. This scheme's a lot bigger than Haghill. I've always doubted he was at Haghill, there's no' many places to hide there.'

Logan straightened up and turned to his two friends. 'What do you think?'

Digger shrugged. 'It's possible.'

'I agree,' said Gary.

Logan's phone rang and he took it out of his pocket. 'What?' he said irritably. 'Great, that's all we need. Aye, thanks for the info, I appreciate it.' He hung up, looking grim. 'Cole's managed to recruit the Bloody MacGregors in Garthamlock.'

'Who?' replied Eddie.

'I'm no' surprised you've no' heard of them because they don't usually get involved in gangland shite. They're violent and aggressive but they spend their time intimidating their local community. This is a step up for them. Seven brothers, all shit-hot fighters. Their da' was obsessed with the Wild West. He used to go around in a Stetson. He even named his sons after the Earp brothers.'

'Seriously?' laughed Harry.

'Aye. Don't ever laugh at their names, they don't like it. The da' died a few months ago and the second oldest brother, Virgil, got sick of all their shite and went to live out in the sticks somewhere. Another brother was sent to Barlinnie for assault. That leaves five of them.'

'Is that all? We can take them.'

'This lot aren't like the arseholes we just fought at the caravan park. They're perfectly capable of hammering every single one of us. I cannae understand why they've sided with Cole. They normally don't gi'e a shite about this gang stuff.'

'He must have offered them something they want,' said Eddie. 'What could that be?'

'Money, probably,' replied David. 'I've known the MacGregors a long time and they're terminally short of cash. They'll be struggling even more now Jimmy MacGregor's died.'

'Was he killed?' Carly asked him.

'Naw, heart attack. He lived off fried food and lager. I can pay them a visit. I get the feeling offering them more cash than Cole could easily change their allegiance. The problem is, Jimmy and Virgil were the only reasonable members of the family. There is the mother though, Maria. She's a nice lady. It's a wonder she raised such a pack of animals.'

'Do you think Maria would listen to reason and convince her sons to back off?' Eddie asked David.

'It's worth a try. I'll speak to Toni, see if she's willing to pay them to stay out of it, but I doubt it. She'll think they should just automatically be loyal to her.'

While David called their boss, Carly noticed Logan slip out of the room, a hand pressed to his left upper arm. She followed and found him in the bathroom, gingerly removing his jacket.

'Are you okay?' she asked him.

'I think my wound might be bleeding again after the fight.'

'Why didn't you say something? Let me take a look.'

'You really don't need to.'

'Aye, I do. Now don't be stubborn. Get 'em off.'

Logan's smile was wry. 'How could I refuse an offer like that?'

After she'd helped him slide off his jacket and remove his left arm from his jumper, Carly rolled up the sleeve of his t-shirt.

'It is bleeding a wee bit,' she said. 'Luckily the stitches havenae burst. I can patch it up for you.'

'Thanks. There's a first-aid kit in the cupboard under the sink.'

Carly produced the kit and Logan closed the toilet seat lid so he could sit on it as she worked.

'Are you okay after what just happened?' he asked her.

'I'm fine. I just want this over with.'

'So do I, although I admit I'm enjoying working with your family. And you,' he added, colouring.

'Me too,' she smiled as she cleaned up the blood. 'I'm worried about these MacGregors though.'

'Aye, they are not people I want to fight.'

'That bad, are they?'

'I heard a story that the brothers got into a fight in a pub. It was the seven of them against twenty-two people. The brothers won.'

'In my experience, these tales are usually exaggerated.'

'Maybe, it was my da' who told me and he does exaggerate everything, but they've got a reputation for winning against all the odds. The rumour is there's a fire in all their veins that takes them over and makes them invincible. Their da' had it and their grandda' too. All the brothers have fought in illegal underground fights but they had to stop because people started refusing to take them on as they nearly killed everyone they went up against.'

'Sounds to me like they'd make good allies. This could be a blessing in disguise for us.'

'We'll see.'

'There, the bleeding's stopped,' said Carly. 'I'll put on a fresh bandage.'

'Something wrong?' said Logan when her eyes widened and her hand trembled.

'Nothing,' she replied before turning her back on him.

It had just occurred to her that the same thing had happened to Dean's wound. It had bled and she'd sorted it out for him. Was this something warning her that Logan was as bad as him? Was he also a lunatic who might turn on her and take from her someone she loved?

'I don't think it's nothing,' Logan said, getting to his feet and resting his hands on her shoulders. 'Please tell me what's wrong.'

'You'll think I'm mad.'

'No, I won't.'

There was something soft and reassuring in his tone that convinced her to come clean. She turned to face him, eyes full of unshed tears. 'History's repeating itself. No' long before he killed Jack, Dean got a wound in pretty much the same place as you.

His started bleeding and I patched it up for him, just like I'm patching up yours, and I'm terrified it's a sign that you're just like him.'

Carly didn't know what to expect; after all, she barely knew the man. Would he be angry, insulted? Or would his gaze fill with that frightening mania she'd seen in Dean?

What she wasn't expecting was the understanding that appeared in his eyes.

'All I can do is tell you that I'm nothing like him, but I know that's no' enough. Hopefully one day, I'll prove myself to you. I can understand why it's hard for you to trust a man again after what Cole and Dean did to you.'

'Jack betrayed me too once. He slept with Toni McVay to seal his deal with her. I loved him so much I forgave him. All three men I've had feelings for have deceived me and I'm so scared it will happen again.'

A tear slipped from the corner of her left eye and Logan brushed it away with his thumb. 'I would never do that to you, Carly. Loyalty is everything to me, just as it is to you. You cannae be a member of the Blood Brothers without it. I dumped my girlfriend Keira a few months ago because she slept with someone else, so I know what you mean about betrayal. I never want to feel pain like that again, but I think you're worth the risk.'

Logan's voice was soft and warm, a balm to her taut nerves. It was also infinitely seductive, as was the look in his kind but fierce eyes. As he leaned in to kiss her, she didn't back away, anticipating the touch of his lips against her own. The expected guilt didn't take hold of her. Instead, she kissed him back. Tenderly, he cupped the back of her head and she took the opportunity to finally run her fingers through those curls. They were soft and silky and she enjoyed the way they sprang through her fingers. As his hands slid down her waist and pulled her closer, she stroked the muscles of his back, liking his wiry strength. There was so much power in this man mentally as well as physically. One day he would make big waves in their world.

Lust drowned all other thoughts and they gripped onto each other tightly as the kiss deepened, Carly's heartbeat quickening as he moaned into her mouth, sensing his longing for her.

The door opened and they jumped apart, breathing furiously. Jane stood framed in the doorway, disapproval written all over her face.

'I was just sorting out Logan's wound,' said Carly, hating how breathless she sounded. 'It had started bleeding.'

'I see,' said Jane, eyes narrowing. 'We need you both. We've got a plan. Come on, Carly. Let Logan put his clothes back on.'

Carly glanced at Logan before slinking out of the bathroom sheepishly. Jane gave him a hard look before slamming the bathroom door shut.

'What's going on?' said Carly as she entered the living room.

'I've spoken to Toni,' replied David. 'As I suspected, she refused to pay the MacGregors any money. She says they owe her after Virgil MacGregor put one of her best fighters in a coma during an underground match. James MacGregor also battered another of her fighters senseless. She lost a lot of money betting on both fights but she does understand the wisdom of getting them on our side. She wants us to parley with them and to take you, Jane and Rose with us. Apparently, the Savage Sisters fascinate the brothers and they like a pretty face.'

'Rose isnae part of this life,' frowned Carly.

'She's nae choice.'

'What if it turns violent?'

'Then she'll rip the brothers' baws off.'

Carly turned to Jane. 'Are you in agreement with this?'

'David's right, there's no choice,' she replied. 'The MacGregors' support could finally turn this war in our favour.'

'Okay, I suppose and it's no' like she'll be going in alone. Who else will go?'

'Me, Eddie and Logan,' replied David. 'Peanut, you can come too. The brothers respect a boxer. Harry, Jen, Digger and Gary will be close by in case we need any back-up.'

'When?'

'I need to speak to the MacGregors to arrange it. I'll call a pal of mine. He lives in Garthamlock.'

Everyone waited in silence while David called his friend and got the phone number of Newton MacGregor, the oldest of the brothers.

'He's willing to talk so I'm taking that as a good sign,' said David once he'd hung up. 'I think saying the Savage Sisters would be accompanying me swung it. He and his brothers are eager to meet you. We've to be at their place at ten o'clock tomorrow morning. We'll all meet up here at half nine.' David glanced at his watch. 'Now I'm going home for some kip, I'm knackered. Oh, before I go, I have a couple of warnings. If Wyatt MacGregor's there then for God's sake don't stare. The man has plenty of issues. Being named after such a famous man has put enormous pressure on him since he was a wean and it's sort of cracked his mind. He's full of tics and twitches. Just don't stare and you'll be fine. They also have an Italian grandmother who lives with them called Ludovica who loves to curse people.'

'You what?' spluttered Harry and Digger in unison.

'Don't piss her off and you won't get cursed.'

'I'm glad I'm no' going in that house,' commented Gary.

'This sounds like it's gonnae be fun,' sighed Carly.

The Savage family and Peanut stayed over at the sisters' flat while the Blood Brothers remained behind in Gallowburn.

Jane managed to corner Carly for a private chat in her bedroom later that night.

'I was surprised to see you kissing Logan,' she opened.

'You're no' the only one,' replied Carly. 'I never thought I'd be interested in a man again.'

'I admit, I was angry at first. I warned him to back off because you're still vulnerable.'

'You did what?'

'Aye, I know I was wrong. You're an adult and I'd no right to interfere but I don't want anyone taking advantage of you while you're still grieving.'

'To be honest, I got over the grief while I was away. I realised that when I was at the caravan park today. The memory of the night Jack died will always be horribly painful, but I've moved through it now. I'm ready to start thinking about the future again.'

'With Logan?'

'I don't know about that; I've only known him five minutes but I do like him. He's a good starting point. Let's get through this mess and then we'll see.'

'Okay, it sounds like you're being sensible about it. I'm glad you're finally thinking about moving on.'

'It makes it easier knowing Jack would have liked Logan. The one thing that worries me is my track record with men – two psychos and then the love of my life is murdered.'

'Maybe Jack wasn't the love of your life? Maybe he was your first true love?'

'Listen to you sounding all soppy now you're married.'

Jane smiled. 'Jen has changed me for the better.' Jane's smile dropped. 'But I'll still fucking kill Logan if he hurts you.'

'You won't need to because I'll do it first. I'm taking no shite off any man again.'

29

The MacGregor family occupied not one but three terraced houses in a row in Garthamlock. The hedges and fences dividing the properties had been removed, creating one long expanse of grass. The Garthamlock and Craigend Water Towers sat just up the street, looking like two gigantic UFOs on stilts, their looming presence dominating the area.

Despite the cold weather, four of the brothers were already waiting for the Savages and their friends outside. They were ranged around the long garden, casually chatting.

'They're so tough they don't even need coats,' commented Jane.

The MacGregors watched the cars with interest as Eddie, Jane, Carly and Rose got out of one, Logan, Peanut and David the other. The rest of their group was waiting around the corner.

The brothers wolf-whistled when they saw the sisters.

'Well, if it isnae the Savage Sisters,' grinned one as the three of them confidently entered the communal garden.

The men's Italian heritage showed in their dark hair and liquid brown eyes. All were tall and strong, their powerful arms and shoulders a sign of their passion for boxing. Only one of the four didn't appear to be in the peak of health. Carly guessed this was Wyatt. He was tall but had a paunch and his left eye twitched intermittently as he regarded them with suspicion.

'Hello, pretty,' said one of the men, immediately homing in on Rose. 'I like them delicate-looking,' he said, fingers playing through the ends of her hair.

'Who the fuck are you calling delicate?' she retorted. 'And stop touching me,' she added, slapping his hand away. Her face scrunched up with anger when the brothers laughed.

'Feisty too,' added the man. 'I cannae stand weak wee saplings. I like 'em strong.'

'Touch me again and I'll twist your baws right off,' Rose snapped when he reached out a hand to her face.

'I wouldnae recommend laughing at her,' said Jane. 'She really will tear them off and turn them into earrings.'

Another of the MacGregors turned his attention to her. 'Tall and athletic, that's more my type. You look like Mackenzie Davis.'

'Who?'

'One of my favourite actresses. She kicked arse in *Terminator: Dark Fate*.'

'Good for her,' Jane replied flatly.

'Bugger, I can see I'm too late,' he said, taking her left hand, Jane's wedding band glittering in the weak winter sun. 'He's a lucky man.'

'You mean she's a lucky woman.'

His dark eyes twinkled. 'If you ever change your mind and decide a man—'

'I won't,' she said coldly, snatching her hand away.

A third brother had approached Carly and the two had stared at each other throughout these exchanges, the man smiling at her while Carly glared back at him. Only Wyatt hung back, content to watch the scene rather than to participate.

'She looks like she wants to kill me,' the brother told his siblings with a grin.

'No' yet,' she replied.

'So far you're more the Snippy Sisters than the Savage Sisters. You're no' getting into the house until you've proved you deserve your reputa—'

He didn't get to finish his sentence as Carly punched him hard in the mouth. He staggered back a few paces, spitting blood onto the ground while his brothers erupted into laughter, even Wyatt.

'Jeezo, the lassie can punch,' he said with surprise, wiping the blood from his mouth on the back of his hand.

The front door of the middle house was opened by a tall, stately woman with flawless olive skin. She wore a full-length black dress patterned with tiny red flowers and an elegant black cardigan with bell sleeves. Her long dark hair was streaked with silver and pulled back into a thick plait. It was clear her sons had inherited their chocolate-coloured eyes and long lashes from her.

Maria MacGregor stared at her bleeding son with pitiless eyes.

'Morgan,' she barked. 'What have you been saying to that lassie to get a smack in the mouth?'

Carly had expected her to talk with a beautiful, rolling Italian accent, which would have matched her looks, so the strong Glaswegian accent came as a surprise.

'I just asked her to prove that she and her sisters deserve their reputation,' he replied.

'Judging by the way your bottom lip's swelling, they do. Serves you bloody right.' Maria looked at their visitors. 'I do apologise for my sons. They never know when to shut their big fat geggies,' she barked, glaring at her boys. 'Come away in, it's freezing out here. My boys are like furnaces, they never feel the cold, just like their da', God rest his twisted soul.'

The sisters entered Maria's home along with Eddie, Peanut, Logan and David.

'Hey, I know you,' Morgan told Peanut as he passed him by. 'You're Boris the Battleaxe. I saw you fight a few times. You were amazing.'

'Thanks,' Peanut replied with a modest smile. 'I hate that nickname. Made me sound like an angry auld biddy. I wanted to be called Boris the Bulldozer but there were already two men known as The Bulldozer, so my manager vetoed it.'

Morgan laughed and clapped him on the shoulder. 'You'll have to tell me about how you beat The Widow Maker. He was at the top of his game, but you took him down like he was nothing.'

'You can save that sort of talk until later,' Maria told her son harshly. 'They're here to discuss business.'

'All right, Maw,' he sighed.

The house was larger inside than it looked from the outside. It was also ruthlessly clean, not a speck of dust permitted to land anywhere. The scent of furniture polish hung heavy in the air. All the pictures on the walls were prints of various black and white scenes from the old West – one was definitely Tombstone as there was a sign in the picture announcing the fact. The rest were all of similar towns made up of wooden buildings, people in period dress and horses and carts in the middle of the dusty streets, snapshots of a hundred and fifty years ago.

A man who appeared slightly older than the brothers with the same dark looks stood by the window, looking hostile.

'This is Newton, my eldest,' said Maria. 'I apologise for Virgil and Nick's absence. Nick's serving three months inside and

Virgil's still away finding himself,' she added with disdain. 'You all know Morgan, he has the unfortunate habit of making his presence felt. This is Warren,' she added, pointing to the one who'd called Rose pretty. Her finger swung round to the one who'd fancied Jane. 'And James. That's Wyatt,' she added, gesturing to the twitchy one who stood in the corner, regarding them all sullenly. 'As you've probably guessed, my husband was obsessed with the Wild West, especially the Earp family.'

'Well, obviously you already know me,' said David with a self-deprecating smile. 'And these are the Savage Sisters – Jane, Carly and Rose.'

'Rose,' said Warren. 'That's the perfect name because you look like a beautiful flower,' he told her.

Rose's answering smile told him he was forgiven.

'Shut your heid,' his mother told him fiercely.

If Warren had heard Maria, he made no response and continued to smile at Rose, who smiled back at him.

'This is the sisters' uncle, Eddie,' continued David.

'It's obvious you don't get your looks from him,' Morgan told the sisters.

Eddie appeared outraged but had the sense to remain silent.

'This is Peanut, an old friend of the Savage family,' said David. 'And Logan, leader of the Blood Brothers.'

The MacGregor brothers nodded in acknowledgement at the men but it was clear they were far more interested in the women. Even twitchy Wyatt sat smiling at them creepily.

'Can I get anyone a coffee?' said Maria. 'We have some beautiful espresso and my mother's just made a panforte, a fruit and nut cake with chocolate and cinnamon.'

'Do you mind if we skip the cake, doll?' said Peanut. 'I'm very allergic to nuts, which is how I got my nickname.'

'Oh, sorry, I didnae know. How about ciambella? Completely nut-free.'

'Aye, sounds smashing. Thanks, doll.'

'You're very welcome. Maw,' Maria called before launching into a stream of Italian. A powerful female voice replied in the same language from the depths of the house.

'The Widow Maker will be kicking himself for no' throwing a hazelnut at you,' Morgan told Peanut with a cheeky grin. 'He might have won then.'

'Naw, it still wouldnae have been enough,' he replied, broadening Morgan's grin.

'Now,' said Maria, taking the armchair by the window. 'You're here to discuss Cole Alexander's proposition to us?'

'Aye, we are,' replied David.

He sat on a couch with Peanut and Eddie while the sisters sat together on the other sofa. Logan occupied the only remaining chair at the back of the room, not liking the way Morgan kept looking at Carly. At least she was pointedly ignoring him. The MacGregor brothers elected to range around the room, leaning against the walls.

'And we want your family on our side,' added David.

'There's the problem,' said Maria. 'My family don't normally take sides. In fact, we couldnae care less if you lot tear each other apart. Garthamlock is what matters to us and here we rule absolutely. No' even Toni McVay's managed to get a foothold here and she has tried.'

'So why have you sided with Cole?'

'Simple. He promised to let my boys back into the underground fights if he took over. Toni's still in charge of those and she says my boys are never getting back in. Have you any idea what it's been like raising seven males packed full of energy and aggression? Those fights let them release that energy, making my life a hell of a lot easier. They're all men now but that's no' made it any better. If they don't have an outlet then they cause absolute havoc. It's why my Nick's in prison for assault. If that bitch had let my boys carry on fighting, he'd be free now.'

'Your boys have a rare talent,' said David. 'And there's very few people who can match them. They were obliterating all their opponents, destroying the betting odds. It was bad for business.'

'I cannae deny that,' Maria sighed. 'But they need an outlet and if this Cole can give it to them then he's got my support.'

'Cole's got nothing. He hasn't successfully taken any territory from Toni. All he's done is recruit a few dregs to his side. He's targeting this area to try and take the east side of the city from Toni but so far he's failed. The Savages and Blood Brothers have proved to be far too strong. You'd be better off negotiating with Toni to let your boys back into the fights.'

'She won't negotiate. The problem with Toni is she thinks she's above everyone else, that we should all bow down to her. Well, MacGregors bow down to no one.'

An elderly woman entered the room carrying a tray loaded with small coffee cups and cake. She was in her late seventies but very stout and strong, her forearms thick and wide, hips square. She too wore a dress with a cardigan, although her dress ended at her knees, woolly tights encasing her calves, which were like tree trunks. Her hair was a radiant silver, the style old-fashioned. It fell in waves about her ears, the remainder held back in a thick bun at the nape of her neck. Her face was as square as her hips, the skin heavily lined across the forehead and down both cheeks. Her lips curved down at the sides, indicating she spent most of her time scowling. Although her eyes were dark, they weren't beautiful like her daughter's and grandsons'. They were small and mean and as black as coal, but they were also incredibly sharp and regarded the visitors with suspicion. When Eddie rose and held out his hands to take the heavy tray from her, she glowered at him so furiously he hastily retook his seat.

'This is my maw, Ludovica,' announced Maria proudly.

'Beautiful name for a beautiful lady,' said Peanut.

Ludovica stared at him with such disdain he was forced to look down at the floor.

'This house is full of beautiful ladies today,' said Warren, winking at Rose, who beamed back at him.

Ludovica dumped the tray on the coffee table and spoke to Maria in Italian.

'English, Maw,' she replied. 'Don't be rude.'

'Fine,' said Ludovica in a thick Italian accent. 'Then I will say this one looks like the missing link,' she continued, patting Eddie so hard on the cheek he winced. She turned to Logan. 'I like this one. His curls remind me of your father's,' she added, rubbing her hand vigorously in Logan's hair, making him grimace. She turned to Peanut, who regarded her warily. Ludovica kneaded his upper arms with her meaty, sausage-like fingers. 'Strong, very strong.' She slapped him hard on the right shoulder. 'A fine specimen.'

'That actually hurt,' Peanut whispered to Eddie.

'At least she said you were a fine specimen,' he whispered back. 'She called me the missing link.'

'Pretty girls,' announced Ludovica, looking to the sisters. 'Are these new mates for the boys?'

Morgan squeezed himself between Carly and Jane and turned to Carly, resting his hand on her knee, which she batted away. 'I'm game if she is,' he said. Morgan noticed Logan staring at him jealously and gave him a provoking smile.

'No, we are not their mates,' Jane told Ludovica.

'If Morgan makes a nuisance of himself feel free to hit him

again,' Maria told Carly. She looked back at her mother. 'We're in a meeting here, Maw.'

'If they don't do what you want, I will curse them,' she announced, accompanying this statement with a wicked laugh.

Newton, who was sitting by the window, caught sight of movement outside and got to his feet. 'Who the hell's that come onto our turf?'

Everyone looked round. A large group of people was assembling outside the house twenty strong, their number including Ross, Dominic and Isaiah. A figure stood at their head, face obscured by a hood. The man threw back the hood.

'It's Cole.'

30

'I don't fucking believe it,' exclaimed Eddie. 'Cole's done it again. I bet he made sure someone called you to let you know the MacGregors had sided with him,' he told David.

'You mean it's *another* trap?' exclaimed Peanut. 'The wee bastard.'

'Just how many traps have you walked into?' said James with an amused smile.

The Savages and their companions chose not to answer that.

Wyatt's eyes, mouth and hands began twitching. 'They weren't supposed to come onto our territory,' he snarled. 'Everyone in Garthamlock will think we've lost our touch.'

'In that case, you'd better get out there and make an example of them,' Carly said slyly.

The MacGregor brothers rushed towards the door.

'Wait,' said Maria so forcefully they all stopped. 'Are you forgetting your deal with Cole to take part again in the underground fights?'

'Surely that's no' as important as your reputation?' said Carly. 'After all, you're nothing without that.'

'She's right,' exclaimed Newton.

Maria narrowed her eyes at Carly. 'You're a clever one, aren't you? Back off, madam.'

Carly smiled and shrugged.

Maria turned her attention back to her sons. 'This isnae our fight. Let them battle it out.'

'And what if Toni wins?' said David. 'Did you ever think of that?'

'No' even Toni would make war with our family.'

'You're just gonnae sit here and make peace with the winner, aren't you?'

'Aye because it's the smart move, unless you can convince Toni to let my boys back into the fights.'

'Carly,' yelled Cole. 'I'll leave the rest of your family alone if you come out.'

'Why does he want you?' Newton asked Carly.

'I'm the one who did that to his face.'

'You just get better and better, beautiful,' Morgan told her.

'Logan, what are you doing?' exclaimed Carly, hurrying after him as he stormed out of the living room and down the hallway.

'I'm gonnae tear his ugly head off his shoulders,' he growled, flinging open the front door.

'Jeezo, get after them,' exclaimed Eddie as Logan and Carly stomped down the garden path together.

'Stay here, boys,' Maria told her sons when they moved to follow. 'They all know where we stand. Let's see what happens.'

'If a fight starts on our patch and we do nothing, we'll look like a bunch of wallopers,' retorted Morgan.

'I said wait,' she yelled.

His eyes filled with rebellion but when his gran glared at him, Morgan decided to take his mother's advice and the brothers gathered at the window to watch.

'Someone looks jealous,' smirked Cole as Logan stormed onto the street. 'It seems Carly's cast her spell on another man. You should watch yourself, Logan. You could end up with a faceful of scars or your guts spilled out all over the floor.'

'You bastard,' yelled Carly, Jane and Rose grabbing her when she tried to rush at him. 'It's only right your face is like that because it shows who you truly are inside – twisted and ugly.'

'You've still got your big gob,' commented Ross in a bored tone.

'Shut your face, you,' Rose yelled at him. 'Unless you want me to twist your baws a third time?'

Ross didn't reply, looking much less smug as he recalled the agonising pain he'd already endured twice at the hands of the youngest Savage Sister.

'Come with us, Carly, and I'll leave your family alone,' said Cole.

'She's going nowhere with you,' Logan told him. 'Me and you will fight this out right now, just the two of us. No one else will interfere. If you lose, then you drop this mad plan, leave Scotland and never come back.'

'And if I win?'

'You won't,' glowered Logan.

Carly smiled at him, a thrill running through her.

'If I win, I get Carly,' countered Cole.

'No deal.'

'Then it looks like your people are gonnae be torn apart.'

'I cannae get hold of Harry,' Eddie told Peanut.

'I'll try Jen,' replied Jane, who'd overheard this comment.

'If you're trying to get hold of your friends, you should know they're a bit busy,' called back Cole.

'What the fuck have you done to them, you freak?' yelled Jane.

'Just ensured they're kept occupied.'

The Savages, David and Peanut grew nervous when another ten men marched up the street in a line from the direction of the water towers, blocking the road.

'Oh, shite,' sighed Eddie. 'There's too many of them.'

David took out his phone before turning to face the MacGregor home. Maria stood in the doorway, watching proceedings, her sons gathered behind her. 'I'm calling Toni,' he yelled to them. 'I'll ask her right now.'

'Ask her what?' said Cole.

'If she'll let the MacGregor boys back into the underground fights,' said a smug Eddie. 'If she agrees then they'll switch sides.'

'Do not let him make that call,' yelled Cole, pointing at David.

Immediately the Savages, Peanut and Logan formed a circle around David, protecting him as he attempted to negotiate with the notoriously stubborn Queen of Glasgow.

Cole's men charged at their circle while the ones further down the street broke into a run to meet them.

All three sisters tore stun guns from their pockets and jammed them into the chests of the men running at them, knocking them off their feet. They produced batons and slammed them into the faces of the men immediately behind them, causing the MacGregor brothers to cheer from the doorway, all except for the sombre Newton. Peanut knocked one man out with an uppercut, his eyes wild and hair standing on air with the frenzy of battle. He snatched up the next man as though he weighed nothing and hurled him into two more men, knocking them all off their feet, eliciting more cheers from the MacGregors. Logan kept a couple of assailants at bay with his high kicks while Eddie swung his meaty fist. But every time they knocked someone down, another man just replaced them.

'We're badly outnumbered,' David told Toni. 'And the MacGregors will only help us if you let them back in on the fights.' He winced at her response. 'Aye, I get that they were ruining your system but we're much better having them onside. Sorry, what was that?' he said, sticking a finger in his ear when Rose grabbed one man by the crotch and twisted, making him scream. 'I've figured out how it could work but if we don't get them onside right now then we're gonnae be ripped apart.'

Logan was knocked back into him and David was sent lurching forward, the phone falling from his hand.

'Oh, Christ, where is it?' he exclaimed, scrabbling about in the grass. 'Toni, I'm still here if you can hear me. Don't hang up.'

'Get the phone off him,' David heard Cole bellow over the din.

'Argh,' cried David when Peanut fell onto him.

The sisters used the stun guns to repel three more men when they tried to break through their line to David. Another man backhanded Carly across the face.

'You fucker,' snarled Logan, attempting to go to her aid, but Eddie grabbed him by the back of the coat and held him firm.

'Do not break the circle,' he told him, releasing Logan when he was punched in the side of the face by one of Cole's men. Eddie's head sang but he remained upright and punched the man back. He creased in half when someone else hit him in the stomach.

'Hurry, David,' cried Jane, driving her elbow into one man's face. 'We cannae hold them off for much longer.'

David gasped with relief when Peanut clambered off him and threw himself at the man who'd knocked him over. 'I cannae find my phone,' he cried.

Eddie looked down when there was a crack and saw he'd

stepped on David's phone and broken the screen. 'Oh, shite,' he said, scooping it up.

When one of Cole's men attempted to snatch it off him, Peanut grabbed the man by the throat and shoved him away.

'Toni, hello?' said Eddie, sticking his finger in his ear. 'It's deid,' he added before tossing it to David, who stared at his ruined phone in outrage. 'I'll call her,' continued Eddie, producing his own handset. 'Toni,' he said when she answered. 'We need the MacGregors onside right now and they'll only help us if you let them back into the underground fights. If they don't help us, we're gonnae be torn apart because we're badly outnumbered. If that happens, you'll lose Haghill and Gallowburn. Let the brothers back in and we can work out the details later.' He sagged with relief. 'Thank you.' He turned to the MacGregors. 'Toni says you're back in.'

Maria smiled with satisfaction. 'Off you go, boys.'

She stood to one side so her sons could rush out of the house, whooping jubilantly.

Cole saw the force of nature coming at them, grabbed his brothers by the backs of their jackets and hauled them away, Isaiah following, his nose bleeding from Logan's fist, a few more men who knew of the MacGregors' reputation hastening after them.

Carly drew back the baton with a war cry but the man she had intended to hit suddenly vanished, knocked to the ground by Morgan, who had punched him in the face and run at his next target before she'd even realised what had happened. The man lay on the ground, looking up at the turbulent sky with wide, staring eyes. Carly watched in astonishment as the five MacGregor brothers ripped a hole through the ranks of Cole's men, punching so rapidly not one of their opponents had the time to land a blow. Even Wyatt, who was flabbier than his leaner brothers, moved with cat-like speed. Warren flung one man over his shoulder as though he were simply pulling on a backpack. The MacGregors tossed more men about, seemingly for fun, laughing and joking as they moved.

'Jesus, they're so fast,' exclaimed Peanut.

Those who hadn't already been attacked bolted down the street in terror.

'Get 'em,' roared Newton before he and his brothers charged after the men, easily overtaking them and making mincemeat of them too.

'Wow,' said Rose. 'They're amazing.'

'That's my boys for you,' commented Maria, who had joined them outside. 'And they don't even have Virgil with them. He's the best fighter of the lot.' Her lip curled with disgust. 'Such a shame he now spends his time meditating and doing yoga.' Maria turned her attention to David. 'So, my boys are back in?'

'Aye, they are,' he replied.

'Excellent.' She tilted back her head. 'Tell Toni no' to forget what our family's capable of again.'

David nodded, even though he had no intention of telling Toni McVay any such thing.

The MacGregors made short work of the fleeing men, leaving them lying bleeding in the street.

Carly looked down at the blood pouring from the mouth of one man, who was struggling to push himself up on all fours and failing. 'No wonder they call them the Bloody MacGregors,' she commented.

The brothers came strutting back down the street looking very pleased with themselves.

'Nice baw twisting, Princess,' Warren called to Rose.

'You're no' so bad yourself,' she called back.

The MacGregors stood ready to fight when Jennifer, Harry, Gary and Digger charged up the road.

'Rip them apart,' roared Newton.

'No, wait,' cried Eddie. 'They're with us.'

The brothers relaxed, grumbling with disappointment.

'Jane, are you okay?' exclaimed Jennifer, running up to her.

When the two women kissed, the MacGregor boys cheered and whistled.

'I was so worried when we couldn't get hold of you,' Jane told her wife.

'Some of Cole's men attacked us but we fought them off.'

'What the bloody hell happened here?' demanded Harry, noting all the injured men lying on the ground.

'They happened,' replied Rose, pointing at the MacGregors. 'They're very impressive.'

The brothers preened at this, except for Wyatt, who twitched and glowered.

Harry looked to the MacGregors and his face twisted with anger. 'You.'

Morgan MacGregor's triumphant smile fell. 'What are you doing here, ya' prick?'

'I take it you two know each other?' said Eddie.

'He stole Jenny from me,' retorted Morgan, pointing at Harry.

'No, I didnae,' he replied. 'She dumped you a couple of hours before she got with me.'

'Hours?' chuckled Peanut. 'She doesnae hang about.'

'I'm gonnae fucking kill you,' Morgan roared at Harry.

'Stop him, boys,' called Maria.

James, Warren and Newton grabbed hold of him while the Blood Brothers restrained Harry. Wyatt just stood there, the tic in his left eye going into overdrive. Harry and Morgan were so furious they still fought to get at each other.

The front door of one of the neighbouring houses on the MacGregors' side of the street opened and a tall man with a red beard stepped out.

'What are you MacGregors up to now?' he demanded. 'Look at the state of the street,' he added, indicating all the injured men sprawled in the road. 'It looks fucking untidy. You're always causing trouble around here and I'm sick of it.'

'You don't like it then fucking move,' retorted Newton.

'Why should I? I've done nothing wrong. You're the ones who should leave.'

'You wantin' a battering?'

'Go on, do your worst. I'll have you prosecuted and thrown into Bar-L with your brother.'

A furious Ludovica, who'd been watching from the doorway, stepped outside and stomped through the garden towards him in her furry bootie slippers. The man appeared much more afraid of her than Newton and he retreated to the safety of his doorway, regarding her warily. Ludovica waved her hands in the air dramatically while speaking Italian in a strong, clear voice that carried down the street. She rounded off this speech by lowering her arms and pressing the thumb of her right hand to the ring finger, causing the index and middle fingers to curve, which she used to point at him while hissing like a snake. The man squeaked with fear, raced into his house and slammed the door shut. Ludovica threw back her large head and cackled.

Eddie grabbed his son, who was still fighting to get at Morgan, by the shoulders and forced him to look into his eyes.

'They just saved our arses, so instead of arguing over some wee bird, why don't you try saying thank you?'

Harry went still and sighed. 'All right, Da'. I'll call a truce if he will.'

Morgan glanced over at his mother, who threw him a warning look. 'Okay,' he said, and his brothers released him.

'Now shake hands,' Maria told the two men.

They obeyed grudgingly.

She turned to the Savages and their friends. 'It's time for you to leave Garthamlock.'

'Aye, all right,' said David. 'We appreciate your assistance,' he added respectfully.

'Get back to the car,' Eddie growled at his son, shoving him in the shoulder.

'Better obey your daddy,' Morgan called to Harry in a taunting sing-song voice. 'Or he'll spank your wee arse.'

'Oh, Christ,' sighed Eddie when Harry charged at him.

To everyone's astonishment, Morgan grabbed Harry around the waist and flipped him as though he weighed nothing. Harry, however, wasn't so easily beaten. He hit the ground, rolled and was back on his feet in an instant. He launched into a kick at Morgan, his foot catching him in the shoulder.

'Stop it, Harry,' yelled Carly. 'We don't have time for this shite. Cole's getting away.'

Harry stopped and looked at her before turning back to Morgan, who stood with his fists clenched, ready to fight.

'Fine,' he sighed.

'You running away like a wee lassie?' Morgan goaded him.

'I don't need to fight you. I'm the one who shagged Jenny in the back of her car when she wouldnae let you touch her.'

'Bastard.'

Morgan's brothers rushed to intercept him when he attempted to run at Harry, who laughed mockingly as he left with his family.

'Did you have to wind him up?' Jane demanded of Harry as they left.

'He's a walloper.'

'That walloper just saved our skins. And he flipped you like a pancake.'

'Let's just find Cole,' Harry grunted.

31

The Savages and Blood Brothers drove around Garthamlock but there was no sign of Cole, so they reconvened back at Logan's flat to discuss their options.

'Well, that trap backfired on Cole,' said Digger heartily. 'The Bloody MacGregors are on our side now.'

'They're no' on our side,' replied Gary. 'They just wanted to prove that they were in control of the situation.'

'Gary's right,' David told them all. 'They're no gonnae help us.'

'At least we don't have to fight them,' said Logan. 'I wouldnae want to have them as enemies.'

'Don't tell me you're scared of them?' demanded Harry.

'You didnae see them fight.'

'Forget the MacGregors,' said David impatiently. 'They're out of it now. I'm sick of falling for Cole's traps. We're looking like morons,' he yelled, bouncing his fist off Logan's sideboard. 'Which in turn hurts Toni's reputation and believe me, she is no' appreciating that.'

'But he's tried the same thing each time,' said Carly. 'Surely that proves he's got no imagination?'

'The lassie's right,' said Eddie. 'He keeps setting the same trap.'

'Which makes us look like even bigger wallopers because we repeatedly fall into them,' exclaimed David. 'Well, I've had enough. I want this wee shite deid.'

'What do you suggest?' said Eddie.

David pursed his lips when he couldn't reply.

'I'm still up for being used as bait,' said Carly.

'No way,' replied Eddie when David appeared thoughtful.

'We're running out of options and the more Cole makes us look like fools the stronger he gets.'

'We've asked around and we cannae find who's trained him to fight,' said Gary. 'Or if they have they're no' admitting it to us.'

'Cole's looking as big an idiot as we are,' said Harry. 'He failed to beat us or capture you, Carly, every single time.'

'But he's showing everyone he can get us dancing to his tune,' replied Logan.

'And we've still no idea where he's hiding out,' said Jane.

'Instead of him luring us to places, we need to lure him somewhere,' said Carly. 'Let's do to him what he's been doing to us. We just need to get word to him by the right person, someone he trusts.'

'I don't think he trusts anyone,' said Jane.

'What about Lonny at The Wheatsheaf?' said Jennifer, referring to The Horseshoe Bar's closest rival.

They all turned to look at her.

'I bet we could get word to Cole through him,' she added.

'It's possible,' said Eddie slowly as he mulled it over.

'Has anyone checked The Wheatsheaf?' said Carly.

'The Bitches searched it but there was no sign of Cole,' replied Jane.

'How long ago was that?'

'The day before the wedding.'

'Cole's probably moving around. He could have gone there after The Bitches searched it and even if he isnae there, I bet Lonny will know how to contact him. That wee weasel's at the centre of everything dodgy that goes on around here.'

'Perhaps.'

'I've got an idea and I want you to hear me out before you start objecting. I'll go into The Wheatsheaf alone and tell Lonny I want to speak to Cole. The worm will pretend he's no idea where he is but he will contact him.'

'And when Cole turns up with a big gang of his thugs?' said Jane, expression doubtful.

'I'll say we want to ditch Toni and switch to his side.'

'He won't believe that,' said Harry.

'He won't be able to take the chance of not believing me. By now everyone will have heard that the MacGregors sided with us over him and with their reputations that will have put the wind up quite a few people. He'll also be worried that his other allies will ditch him just as easily. Getting us and the Blood Brothers onside would make him a hell of a lot stronger.'

'You think he'd be willing to give up his revenge on you in order to win?' said Logan.

'Aye because he'll know it'll only be temporary. He could take me out at his leisure once he's secure in his new position. I think his ambition is big enough to encourage him to delay his revenge for a while.'

'Supposing Lonny does know how to contact Cole and by some miracle he turns up at The Wheatsheaf,' said Jane. 'What then? We turn up too, batter his men and grab the wee bastard?'

'Of course not because Cole will take precautions against that. He'll tell us we've to kill Toni ourselves to prove we really want to switch to his side, just like Neil Tallan wanted us to kill his brother, and we've to agree.'

'You cannae say that, even if you don't mean it,' replied Eddie. 'Toni's like royalty that way. She considers any threat to herself as treason and the only punishment is death.'

'Even if she's in on the plan and knows it's only a set-up?'

'If you tell Cole you're willing to kill Toni for him, even only to take him out, you sign your own death warrant because Toni will always be wondering if you meant it. She'll never be able to trust you again.'

Carly sighed with frustration. 'Then there's only one way – I'll have to kill Cole myself in The Wheatsheaf.'

'Have you gone aff your bloody heid?' exclaimed Harry. 'You cannae do that in a public place.'

'If we don't end this soon then Toni will probably kill us for being incompetent.' She turned to David. 'Where's Elijah anyway? Why's he no' helping us?'

'He's busy,' he replied.

'Doing what? We're the ones running around taking all the risks.'

'Fine. Elijah, our men and the rest of Toni's people have been putting down rebellions all over the city and they've been successful too. They've all done such a good job those areas have gone quiet again.'

'They're probably waiting to see if Cole wins first,' said Logan.

'Which means we can't fail. The consequences of him triumphing would be too massive for us all.'

'So that's why only you came to help us when we were

cornered by the Bell family,' said Jane. 'I wondered why you didnae bring anyone else with you.'

'I was holding the fort at the office. Elijah had taken the rest of our men to put down a rebellion in Govan. Right now, they're in Bishopbriggs ensuring no one gets out of line there because there have been rumours that a couple of local families who've been loyal to the McVays for decades are turning against them. It's clear you havenae understood yet how big this insurrection is.'

'So basically, we're on our own?' said Gary.

'Aye, that's about the long and short of it.'

'Ah-ha,' yelled Harry, slapping his palm off the sideboard.

'Jeezo, are you trying to gi'e me a heart attack?' cried Eddie, putting a hand to his chest.

'I've had an idea.'

'Aye, right,' said Eddie cynically.

'Don't say it like I've never had a good idea in my life. This one's a cracker.'

'Go on,' David told him.

'Carly can tell Cole that Jack knew the location of all his grandda's cash and that she has it.'

'Oh my God, that's brilliant,' beamed Carly. 'Harry, you're a genius.'

'How can we be sure he hasnae got hold of it yet?' said Logan. 'After all, he's been bribing people to work for him.'

'He's no' found it,' said Peanut. 'If he had he would have paid a plastic surgeon to fix his face.'

'So I can tell Cole I have his grandda's money,' said Carly.

'That would be a much better lie than you're ditching Toni,' replied David. 'And I bet the greedy bastard won't be able to resist it. But what will you tell him you want in return?'

'I'll say I think Toni will lose and I want him to leave my

family alone. He can have me if he wants, as long as he leaves the others be.'

'He won't fall for that.'

'It doesnae matter. All we need him to do is want the money. And he will.'

'Saying he does turn up at the pub,' said Jennifer. 'What then?'

'We use the money as a lure to take him away somewhere we can control, although I'm no' sure where that will be yet.'

'And the small army he'll bring with him?' said Jane with a raised eyebrow.

'You lot will have to take care of them. I'll handle Cole.'

'Goddammit, Carly, I don't want you killing him,' Jane exclaimed. 'You used to love the man, for God's sake.'

'That man is deid and I hate the one he's become.'

'You're no' killing anyone and no arguments,' Eddie barked.

'They're right,' Rose told her reasonably. 'You don't want Cole's death on your conscience.'

'It wouldnae bother me,' Carly replied icily.

'Well, I think it would. Don't do it to our family.'

Carly shrugged. 'If you insist.'

An awkward silence filled the room.

'I've had an idea,' said Logan, breaking the uncomfortable moment. 'Jamie was shit hot at urban guerilla warfare. We learnt a lot from him,' he added, gesturing from himself to Gary and Digger. 'We can employ similar tactics against Cole. They worked a treat before.'

'We're listening,' said David.

As Logan continued to talk, Carly was filled with admiration for the man. He was clever and brave and she found herself wondering what it would be like to be with him.

After they'd agreed on their plan, Carly managed to get Logan alone as he was coming out of the bathroom.

'We have to stop meeting here,' he smiled.

'I need to talk to you,' she replied, ushering him back inside and locking the door. 'Do you know how to use a gun?'

'Aye. How?'

'I want you to show me. Cole always carries one now and it would help if I knew how to use one too.'

'I don't think your family—'

'It's no' their call. I'll be the one going into The Wheatsheaf alone and Cole will have a pistol on him.'

'I get where you're coming from but if your family found out...'

'They won't.'

'They won't want you going anywhere alone.'

'I'll tell them I've got a doctor's appointment. Harry will cover for me.'

'Well, if you think you can work it, I'm happy to show you. There's a piece of farmland I go to to practise. I know the farmer, so he won't mind. You and Harry come here tomorrow morning around ten and I'll drive you there.'

'Great. Thanks, Logan. I really appreciate it.'

'Anytime. I'll do whatever I can to help you.'

He cupped her face in one hand and they leaned in to kiss. Jack's image flickered through Carly's mind, but she felt less guilty this time. She knew he wouldn't object to her finding someone else.

Her body responded passionately to Logan's touch, as though it was waking up after a long sleep. Her stomach twisted with desire and Logan must have sensed this because he pulled her tighter against him, his hands running down her sides, just brushing her breasts. She moaned as she realised how long it had been since she'd been touched by a man, the sound inflaming Logan even more, his hands holding her backside. Carly's thigh slid up his leg, wrapping around his waist as he kissed her neck.

'Hurry up in there,' called a voice, accompanied by banging on the door. 'I need a dump.'

'Urgh,' grimaced Carly.

'Is that you, Digger?' called back a breathless Logan.

'Aye, it's me. Be quick, the turtle's head is showing.'

This instantly killed the passion and Carly and Logan released each other.

'For fuck's sake,' muttered Logan, unlocking the door and flinging it open.

'What's taking you so long in there?' demanded Digger. 'You're no' tarting about with your hair, are you?' His eyebrows shot up when he spotted Carly. 'Oh. Am I interrupting something?'

Carly just smiled coyly and hurried out of the bathroom before scurrying down the hallway.

'You've got terrible timing,' Logan told his friend.

'Sorry, pal,' Digger replied. 'If I'd known I would have gone next door. Still, Carly Savage, you lucky bastard. I wonder if she's savage in bed too.'

* * *

'Squeeze the trigger,' Logan's voice murmured in Carly's ear. 'You're pulling it. You need to squeeze it.'

There was so much suggestion in his tone she blushed, the Glock pistol she held out in front of her almost forgotten.

'Shall I leave you to it?' called Harry, who was perched on a tree stump several feet behind them. They were out in the middle of nowhere, protected from view of the narrow rough track they'd used to get up here in Logan's car by a small copse of trees.

Carly focused her mind on the task at hand. This was a skill she really needed to learn.

'Take the shot again,' said Logan. 'And remember – just squeeze.'

Carly obeyed his instruction and fired. A small piece of bark flew up in the air as she nicked the side of the tree the target was pinned to.

'Bugger, missed,' she said.

'You were closer that time. Remember to keep your supporting arm bent.' He was teaching her the standard Isosceles Stance where the shooter clasps the gun with both hands, forming a triangle with the arms while leaning forward slightly.

'I will.'

With each shot she got closer to the target until finally she hit the bullseye.

'That was awesome,' exclaimed Logan. 'And you've only been practising for half an hour. You're a natural.'

'Thanks,' she beamed.

When they gazed at each other, Harry rolled his eyes. 'Seriously,' he said. 'I'm happy to go for a wee stroll if you two want to go off into the woods together.'

'Shut it, you,' Carly barked at him.

'I'll show you how to change the magazine now,' said Logan, taking the gun from her. 'You eject it by pushing the release. Keep the gun straight up and let gravity help it fall out.' He demonstrated and the magazine fell onto the grass. 'Tilt the gun to the right, exposing the bottom of the mag well. Make sure you've got the magazine the right way up and slide it in, then slap it with your palm to make sure it goes all the way in.'

'I had a date like that once,' said Harry, making Carly roll her eyes.

'And you're good to go,' added Logan. He handed her the weapon. 'Now you try. It's best to practise this over and over so it's in your muscle memory.'

Carly practised the manoeuvre repeatedly until she had it down to a fine art.

'Perfect,' smiled Logan. 'You're a quick learner.'

'You mean you're a good teacher.'

It was Harry's turn to roll his eyes when they stared at each other again. 'Can I have a go now?'

'Oh, aye,' said Logan, who had almost forgotten Harry was there.

Harry picked it up quickly too and an hour later Logan was driving them back down the track, the heating cranked up full as they were all feeling the cold after standing in a bleak field.

They drove back to Logan's flat where Harry had left his car.

'I need to speak to Logan in private,' said Carly, turning in the passenger seat to face her cousin.

'Oh, I get it,' he winked. 'Far be it from me to play gooseberry. I'll wait in my car.'

Harry got out and Carly didn't speak until her cousin was settled in the driver's seat of his own car.

'I need to ask you another favour,' she told Logan. 'A big one.'

'As I said before, you can ask me anything,' he replied.

'I need you to bring me a gun to the trap we're setting for Cole and I don't want you to tell anyone else about it, no' even Digger and Gary.'

'You're really determined to kill Cole, aren't you?'

She nodded.

'And can you live with it?'

'He's no' the man I once loved. He's already taken so much from me but that's no' enough. He wants to kill me too. He's leaving me no choice.'

'You could turn him over to Toni to be dealt with.'

'Maybe I won't be able to go through with it when the moment comes. Who knows?'

'Carly, if you're bringing a gun to a fight then you have to be prepared to use it.'

'And I will, even if I just incapacitate him. Please, Logan. I need you to do this for me.'

'I will, if it's what you really want. It feels like we could be at the beginning of something really great between us and I want you to get through this in one piece. I know that sounds selfish but I cannae help it.'

'I think it could be too, and don't worry. Cole Alexander is no' gonnae win.'

'Okay. I'll bring the gun you've been practising with as you're familiar with how it feels. It'll be loaded and I'll bring a couple of spare clips too.'

'Thank you,' she said, clasping his hand. 'I really appreciate everything you're doing for me.'

'I'll do anything for you, Carly.'

His eyes filled with a delicious intensity and they leaned in to kiss.

'I wish Harry wasn't here,' murmured Logan, stroking her face with the back of his hand.

'Me too,' she said, wrapping her arms around his neck and kissing him harder. 'I never thought I'd want another man again, but I want you, Logan.'

'I want you too,' he said as she fell back into her seat, pulling him down with her.

At the sound of voices outside, they hastily sat up. A gaggle of teenage girls was walking down the street, looking at their phones and laughing. They only spotted the occupants of the car once they were level with it.

'Hi, Logan,' they chimed in unison in flirtatious voices, accompanied by coy giggles before continuing on their way.

'Someone's popular around here,' commented Carly.

'It's only because I'm leader of the Blood Brothers. Personally, I find it embarrassing. Jamie did too.'

'Some men would revel in it.'

'No' me. I like to be left alone.'

'Then you're in the wrong business.' Recognising the romantic moment was over, she added, 'I'd better get home before the family starts asking questions. Speaking of which, it's Jane,' she said when her phone rang. 'Aye, we're fine,' said Carly as she answered the call. 'We're on our way back, we won't be long.' She hung up and smiled at Logan. 'Got to go.'

'I won't see you before we confront Cole, so be careful, okay?'

'I will.'

She pecked him on the lips before getting out of the car and climbing into Harry's vehicle.

'You were steaming up the windows there,' he commented.

'I hope you weren't watching.'

'Course no', I'm a gentleman.'

'No, you're not, Harry.'

'Aye, all right, but I did avert my eyes. I'm glad you're finally moving on, Carly. You deserve to be happy.'

'Don't get carried away, we've only shared a few kisses. We'd better get back, Jane called to see where we are. God, I hate lying to her but I've no choice. I needed to learn how to use a gun.'

32

It was early evening and The Wheatsheaf was already busy. The atmosphere was convivial, the interior warm and bright against the cold dark night outside. The door opened, letting in a blast of chilly air, causing those sitting closest to it to grimace and bark at the newcomer to shut the door.

Their protests were soon silenced when they saw who the newcomer was. All they could do was gawp as Carly Savage made her way towards the bar.

'Evening, Lonny,' she smiled at the landlord. 'A glass of dry white wine, please.'

He stared at her like she was an apparition that had been conjured out of thin air. 'But...' he began.

Her smile dropped. 'If you don't pour it, I'll come round there and get it myself.'

Lonny turned to one of his regulars propping up the bar, who shrugged. 'Right, okay,' he said slowly before producing a bottle of white wine from the fridge.

As Lonny poured, Carly casually glanced around the room. Every single customer was staring at her, but this was only to be expected. This pub was an Alexander stronghold and that had continued even after Ross and Dominic had left Haghill and Cole had gone into hiding.

When her gaze settled on Jessica, Carly's amused smile fell. Jessica sat with her single remaining friend, both women nursing gin and tonics. The convivial atmosphere had gone, replaced with hostility.

Jessica got to her feet and scuttled over to Carly.

'What are you doing here?' she asked the younger woman, keeping her voice low. 'They'll tear you apart.'

'No, they won't,' Carly whispered back. 'They all know Cole's after me, so they'll contact him.'

'So that's your plan, is it? My God, Carly, you've got to leave. He wants to kill you.'

'I know.'

'So why are you here?'

'This needs to end. I have to talk to Cole.'

Jessica took her by the elbow and ushered her to a quiet corner. 'He won't listen. You don't know what he's become.'

'I think I've got a pretty good idea.'

'Please listen to me, Carly. If you don't leave right now, you won't see the morning. My son is disturbed and violent. He's no' interested in having a parley with anyone. He just wants you and Toni McVay dead. The boy you knew is long gone. I know you loved him once but if you're trying to save him for the sake of sentiment then you're on a fool's errand. Go now, please, while you still have time.'

Carly was startled by the anguish in Jessica's eyes. The woman really seemed to be worried for her, but Carly wasn't about to believe she'd changed. She could still be part of Cole's plot.

'Carly,' called Lonny from the bar.

'What?' she replied while keeping her gaze on Jessica.

'Cole wants to talk to you,' he said, holding out the bar phone.

'Don't do it,' Jessica told her. 'Go back to your family where it's safe.' She sighed when Carly gave her a haughty look, strode over to the bar and snatched the phone from Lonny's hand.

'Hello, Cole,' she said icily.

'I've been told you're in The Wheatsheaf,' he replied.

'Your wee spies have been talking already.'

'Which is exactly what you wanted them to do. What do you want?'

'To talk.'

'I think you want me to walk into a trap. Let me guess – your family and the Blood Brothers are hiding outside the pub, waiting for me to turn up?'

'No. I'm the only one here.'

'Liar.'

'I want to talk, that's all. This has to end.'

'Because you're losing.'

'The way I see it neither side is winning. We're stuck in stalemate. I know you want this over as much as I do. Besides, I've got something you want.'

'I seriously doubt that.'

'Your grandda's money.'

There was a hesitation on the other end of the line before he said, 'I don't believe you.'

'How do you think I managed to travel around the world for a year?'

'How did you get hold of it?' demanded Cole.

'Ted left it to Jack as compensation for what he suffered.'

There was another thoughtful pause.

'All right,' he said. 'We can talk but I'm no' coming to the pub. Ross and Isaiah will be there soon to collect you.'

With that he hung up.

'Are you meeting him?' demanded Jessica.

'Aye. He's sending two of his men to pick me up.'

'Run, now, while you still can. Don't you understand that he's going to kill you?'

'You mean he's going to try,' countered Carly.

'And what if he succeeds? How will your sisters feel then?'

'Listen, lady,' said Carly impatiently. 'Your son's gonnae lose. You should be more worried about him.'

'I am. In fact, I'm terrified for him, but I'm also terrified *of* him. If you're hoping to use your past relationship to get through to him then you'll be disappointed. He doesn't care about you, he doesn't care about me or his brothers. We're all expendable in his eyes.'

'Did you see what I did to his face?'

'I don't know what that's got to do with it.'

'Did you see?' pressed Carly.

'Yes, I saw.'

'Why are you trying to help me when you know what damage I did to him?'

'You didn't do the damage, Carly, I did three and a half years ago when I called the polis on him and he was sent to Barlinnie. You were right. This is all my fault.'

Carly grabbed Jessica by the front of her cashmere jumper and yanked her towards her. 'I don't know whether this is really the new you or just another trick but I'm no' interested. Leave me alone.'

Carly shoved Jessica away and she staggered backwards on her high heels, banging her back painfully against a vacant table. It showed how much she'd fallen in the world when no one moved to help her, although her one remaining friend did appear to be pained on her behalf. Only recently, pushing Jessica Alexander in this pub would have led to the customers attacking the culprit. Now it seemed absolutely no one held her in any sort of regard. In fact, contempt shone in all their eyes and she returned to her table, hanging her head in shame.

Five minutes later, the door opened and Ross and Isaiah strode in, Ross looking smug, Isaiah dour.

'Time to go, Mouth Almighty,' Ross told Carly.

'Ever the charmer,' she replied. 'What happened to Dundee?'

'I got a better offer. Now move.'

'Wait,' said Isaiah. 'We've got to search her first.'

'Oh, aye. You do it. The bitch has probably got a mouse trap hidden in her pocket.'

Isaiah regarded him with his usual flat expression before turning back to Carly. 'Turn around, hands on the bar.'

'You sound like a polis,' she told him before obeying.

The way he patted her down indicated he'd done it many times before. Isaiah quickly located her phone, which he placed on the bar. From his own pocket he produced a device that looked like a walkie talkie with a big red button.

'What's that?' she said, watching him from over her shoulder.

'It looks for any bugs,' replied Isaiah.

'I've no' got a cold,' she told him with a sardonic smile.

'Jesus, your gob's getting on my nerves already,' growled Ross.

Isaiah frowned at him. 'Don't blaspheme.'

'Just get on with it.'

Isaiah waved the device up and down Carly, eyes narrowing when it beeped.

'Take off your left trainer,' he said.

'Why?' she replied innocently.

'Do it.'

With a sigh, Carly pushed off her trainer with the toe of her right shoe. Isaiah picked it up and stuck his hand inside. He removed a small black object the size of a sim card.

'A tracking device,' he said.

'Nice try, Gobby,' said Ross. 'Now your family won't be able to find you. Give me that,' he told Isaiah, indicating the tracking device.

He handed it to him and Ross waved over a man who'd always been loyal to the Alexanders.

'Take this and drive into the city,' Ross told the man. 'Send her family on a wild goose chase.'

The man smiled with approval at the plan, took the device from him and left.

'Put it back on,' Isaiah told Carly, dumping her shoe on the floor by her left foot.

Carly pushed her foot back into the trainer before shoving Isaiah in the chest, knocking him into Ross. As Isaiah fell, she punched him in the stomach too.

She bolted to the door and burst through it. The moment she hit the pavement her arms were grabbed and pulled behind her back, wrists cable-tied before she'd even realised Dominic and another five men were waiting for her.

Ross and Isaiah followed her out.

'We were taking no chances this time,' said Ross. 'You have a habit of escaping. Get her in the van before her family turn up,' he told the men.

While Carly was dragged kicking and fighting into the back of a waiting transit van, Jessica burst out of the front of the pub.

'Ross,' she cried, rushing up to her oldest son. 'You've got to let her go.'

'You must be joking,' he replied. 'The mouthy bitch is finally gonnae get what's coming to her.'

'Carly is not your enemy.'

'Course she is. She has been for years.'

Jessica grasped him by the shoulders. 'Cole doesn't care about you. He doesn't care about any of us. Whatever reward he's promised you will never materialise. Don't you see that he's just using you?'

'Oh, shut it, ya daft tart,' he retorted, pushing her away.

His mother hit the pavement hard, painfully banging her knee.

'This won't end well for you or Dominic,' she told him while grimacing at the pain in her leg. 'And I don't want to lose all my sons.'

'I hate to break this to you, but you lost us years ago,' Ross said with his usual belligerence. He turned to his men. 'Let's move.'

Ross, Dominic, Isaiah and two big men jumped into the back of the van with Carly and her captors while the other men got into the cab.

Jessica dragged herself to her feet, watching the van speed off down the street until its rear lights vanished into the darkness.

Ignoring the throbbing in her knee, she hobbled off in the direction of the Savage Sisters' flat.

* * *

Carly was pinned down to the dirty floor of the van and her ankles tied together. She writhed about but her attempts to free herself were futile. The only illumination was from two small lights mounted to both walls in the interior of the van. There were no windows and a wall divided the rear of the van from the front cab. The men occupied benches either side of the van, staring down at her coldly, their faces nightmarish in the minimal light.

Ross laughed. 'You're no' getting out of this one. Your family cannae follow you now because you've lost your tracking device. It's gonnae be just you and Cole. Say goodbye to your face, Gobby. With any luck my brother will take your flapping tongue out too.'

When she began to yell back at him, Ross slapped some tape over her mouth.

'Silenced at last,' he gloated.

Carly was forced to content herself with glaring at him, infuriated when he chuckled.

She attempted to keep track of where they were going, noting each turn, but she quickly found the task impossible. Adding to the sense of disorientation was the fact that she kept sliding about on the floor, her momentum only stopped by one of her captors putting out his foot to arrest her movement.

'Careful,' Dominic told the man who'd planted his foot hard in Carly's stomach, making her groan. 'Cole doesnae want her damaging.'

The man just shrugged, looking pleased with himself.

Carly spotted the knife tucked into the man's boot, the glint of its blade in the limited light tempting her to take it. He spotted the direction of her gaze, grinned and produced the blade.

'You want it, sweetheart?' he said, waving it before her face. 'Take it then.' He guffawed when she just stared back at him. 'You can't, can you?'

'Well, of course she can't,' said Isaiah dourly, who was sitting beside him. 'Her hands are tied behind her back, or are you simple?'

The man rounded on him, still clutching the knife. 'What did you say?'

'You heard,' replied Isaiah coolly. 'Or are you deif as well as stupid?'

'I'm gonnae stick this right up your arse,' snarled the man, waving the knife around.

'Stop it, ya prick,' Ross told him. 'You're gonnae have someone's eye out.'

'It'll be his eye,' he replied, nodding at Isaiah.

'Take it easy and put that thing away.'

There was a startled cry from the front of the cab and the brakes were suddenly slammed on, causing Carly to slide to the back of the van, hitting the dividing wall painfully. This was followed by a loud crunch that shook them all. The men fell off the benches and landed in a heap in the middle of the floor.

33

There was a moment of absolute silence, Carly frantically blinking to clear her vision. Then there was a loud hiss and the van listed to the left. Someone was bursting the tyres. Hope soared inside her. Her family were here.

Not wanting to just lie there waiting to be rescued, she looked over at the heavy who'd been holding the knife. He'd not had time to put the weapon away before the van had crashed. He was stuck in the pile of men, blood trickling from a cut to his forehead, his eyes closed. Following the direction of his limp right hand, she saw the knife had fallen to the floor, sitting invitingly between her and the pile of injured morons.

Frantically, she sat up and began to shuffle on her bottom towards it. Ross, who had landed on his front, trapped beneath the bulk of the biggest man in their group, saw what she was attempting to do and began trying to disentangle himself from the pile.

'Wake up, you stupid bastards,' he snarled.

There were a few groans and Dominic, who'd landed on the

floor behind the rest of the men, tried to push himself upright but flopped back down again.

Ross attempted to slide out from under the dead weight of the man on top of him, who was out cold, as Carly reached the knife.

'Rick, wake up,' he yelled at the unconscious man as Carly turned, her back to the knife, and managed to pick it up with her fingertips.

Tugging one arm free, Ross planted his hand on the floor of the van and pushed with all his considerable strength, but it still wasn't enough to shake off the man lying on top of him.

'Someone stop her,' he cried.

Another loud hiss and the list of the van was corrected as the tyres on the right side were taken out too.

There were a few more groans and the men started to shift. The one at the bottom of the pile wheezed that he was being suffocated.

Carly managed to manoeuvre the knife into an upright position, the sharp edge facing her back, and slowly moved the knife back and forth, cutting through the cable tie biting into her wrists.

Ross succeeded in tugging his left arm free and planted that on the floor of the van too. With a determined grunt, he pushed up. The big man's body started to slide off him.

Carly gasped with relief when the cable tie around her wrists snapped. She scooted back against the wall while tearing the tape from her mouth.

'Help, I'm in here,' Carly yelled before determinedly attacking the cable tie around her ankles with the blade.

Tendons popping out of his neck, Ross managed to push himself up even further and the big man's limp form finally slid off him entirely, enabling Ross to tear himself free of the pile.

This release of pressure caused the man at the bottom to gasp with relief and drag in a lungful of air.

Ross dragged himself across the van floor towards her, body still recovering from the shock of the accident and then being squashed, rage lighting up his eyes. Carly sawed faster at the cable tie around her ankles, which gave way just as Ross reached out for her. Her feet free, Carly kicked him in the face twice, snapping back his head, and he collapsed forward, unconscious, this blow too much for his body on top of the crash.

Before the men could get to their feet, Carly had dragged herself up and staggered towards the doors, stomping on the men to keep them down. She pushed at the door but nothing happened, then she realised she had to turn a handle first. Before she could turn it, however, the door was pulled open. As she still had hold of the handle, she was yanked out of the van and fell into the person who'd opened it, both of them tumbling to the ground.

Carly landed on top of her saviour. Their hood fell back and she was astonished to find herself staring into a twisted, scarred face.

'Got you at last,' said Cole.

With a cry of shock, she leapt up but he kicked her legs out from under her and she crashed back against the van. Carly groaned with pain and her knees crumpled. Cole was on her before she could recover, whipping her round and forcing her forward, yanking her arms painfully up her back, making her cry out a second time. Cole had never been able to pull off moves like this before.

'Who trained you?' she grimaced.

'Dean,' he retorted.

'I might have known. You'll never get your grandda's money like this.'

'I already know you don't have it. It was just a lie to draw me out of hiding but I was willing to risk it to finally get hold of you.'

Carly's blood turned cold. 'Who betrayed us?' Pain lanced through her chest as she considered whether it could have been Logan. God, she hoped not.

'Like I'm gonnae tell you. Now, move,' he said, dragging her down the side of the van.

The hold he had her in forced her to walk almost doubled over, meaning she couldn't escape. It was taking her everything she had just to keep up with him. It was difficult for her to look around in this position, but she could see the street was deserted, her family and friends nowhere in sight. Neither were any of her surroundings familiar. Carly's heart sank when she realised she was no longer in Haghill. But where was she? It was hard to tell in the darkness but at least they were still in civilisation, shops that were closed for the night lining either side of the street.

As they passed the van, Carly saw the front end had struck a car that had been parked across the road.

'You did that, didn't you?' she demanded. 'You sabotaged your own people.'

'I wanted it to be just you and me,' he replied.

'What about your brothers? Do you care that they're injured?'

'No. They're fucking useless.'

'You're a monster, do you know that?'

'You made me into one.'

Eerie music filled the air, a chime similar to a musical jewellery box only this sound was creepier, the sort you'd get at the start of a horror film. Carly half expected a girl in a white dress with long black hair covering her face to appear. What appeared instead was an ice cream van. It slowly rolled down the street, coming to a halt just a few feet from them.

They stared at it, puzzled, as it just sat there.

'Come on,' muttered Cole, hauling Carly forward.

The hatch at the side of the van was flipped up, the interior illuminated. A man with a jet-black mullet and a craggy face scowled out at them.

'You wantin' an icy?' he called.

'It's ten o'clock at night in December,' replied Cole.

'It's never too late for an icy. I've got them all – vanilla, mint choc chip, strawberry, chocolate, pistachio, rum and raisin.' The man held up a baseball bat with nails sticking out of it. 'Blood with shattered teeth.'

As the insane ice cream man leapt out of the hatch and landed on the road, gripping the bat, Cole whistled through his teeth and his own men emerged from the alleyways, pouring onto the street. The ice cream man regarded them with quiet fury which glittered in his eyes.

'I thought you wanted me all to yourself?' Carly told Cole.

'Call this lot a little insurance policy in case things went wrong,' he replied.

'Let the lassie go,' the ice cream man told Cole. 'Or you'll be eating bat and nails.'

'What's it to you, ya mad bastard?' Cole retorted.

'I said let her go, ya cowardly wee shite.'

'Deal with this walloper,' Cole told his men.

The ice cream man drew back the bat, ready to strike the first person who got near.

'Bring it on, ya bastards,' he roared.

His wild eyes, the way his hair stood on end as well as his utter fearlessness caused Cole's men to hesitate and look at each other.

'He's only one man, for Christ's sake,' exclaimed Cole impatiently. 'Get him.'

Carly, who was still doubled forward, had to strain her neck to see what was going on and she was full of admiration for the mad ice cream man but she was also afraid for him. She struggled against Cole, but he only tightened his grip, pushing her arms even further up her back, making her groan with pain.

'Oy,' yelled a voice.

'What now?' sighed Cole.

Carly turned her head in the direction he was looking.

'Logan,' she breathed.

Logan marched up the street determinedly, Digger and Gary either side of him. Out of the darkness emerged more figures, numbering twenty in total, all brandishing weapons. Cole's men turned their attention from the ice cream man to them. Without a word, Logan slowly raised his arms before pointing his index fingers at the enemy. Digger, Gary and his men charged down the street, bellowing, and Cole's men ran to meet them. Logan's gesture was so assured and commanding Carly couldn't help but smile, her stomach fluttering with butterflies.

From the opposite end of the street appeared The Bitches, penning in Cole's men.

'Hey,' yelled the ice cream man when it seemed he'd been forgotten. 'Face me, ya cowards,' he shouted before whacking one of them in the side with the bat. The man screamed and fell.

Carly's own car, driven by Jennifer, screeched to a halt and the back door was flung open.

'Let go of my sister, you freak,' screamed a voice.

Rose leapt out of the vehicle, Jane and Jennifer rushing after her. Rose raised the taser she held, aimed it at Cole and fired. He was forced to release Carly to jump out of the way to avoid being struck by the barbs.

'How did they find us?' he demanded.

'Your people took the tracking device off me,' said Carly,

gratefully straightening up. 'But I stuck one on Isaiah when I knocked him over.'

'Fucking idiots,' he grunted before running off.

'Don't let him get away,' she cried.

Cole tried to run down a back street but a car tore up it, Peanut behind the wheel. He stopped the car at the end of the street, blocking it, and leapt out along with Harry and Eddie, forcing Cole to detour into the centre of the road where the battle was taking place. Carly was determinedly making chase, her sisters rushing to catch up.

Lily appeared in front of her like a wild banshee, screaming as she raised a golf club over her head.

Carly watched with a raised eyebrow as Jennifer appeared behind her, yanked the club from her hands and smacked her in the back of the legs with it, causing her to drop to her knees.

'Thanks,' Carly told her sister-in-law.

Jennifer nodded in acknowledgement before whacking Lily in the ribs with the club.

Logan had joined in the fight and Carly was alarmed to see a man sneaking up on him from behind, clutching a large knife. Horrifying memories of what had happened to Jack almost overwhelmed her and she screamed out Logan's name in warning while rushing to intercept the man with the knife, knowing she wouldn't reach him in time.

There was a loud clang; a frying pan connected with the back of the man's head and he dropped. Wielding the pan was an attractive middle-aged woman with blonde hair.

'Thank God,' breathed Carly.

She ran to Logan, who embraced her, lifting her off her feet.

'I was so afraid you'd get stabbed,' she said.

'But I didnae,' he replied, putting her back down. 'Are you okay?'

'Aye, fine. Cole ran off.'

Logan's eyes widened and he pulled her behind him. There was a second clang and another man dropped beside them.

'Thanks, Jackie,' said Logan. 'This is Jamie's maw,' he told Carly.

'Jamie's maw?' repeated Carly. 'This is Gallowburn, isn't it?'

Logan nodded.

'Explanations later,' called a tall, striking-looking man as he delivered a karate kick to his opponent's chest. 'Fight now.'

Carly and Logan threw themselves into the fight. The Bitches tore up the street, dragging men to the ground, kicking and punching them and tearing off their clothes while shrieking wildly.

Ross staggered out of the damaged van to this scene of carnage.

'What the bloody hell?' he murmured.

There was a blood-curdling shriek off to his left and he looked to see Isaiah was on the ground, screaming in agony while some wild creature twisted his genitals. The creature looked up, eyes narrowing when they settled on him.

'No, please, no' again,' cried Ross, stumbling backwards. Tears filled his eyes as Rose ran at him. 'They'll probably come right off this time.'

He tried to run but he was still dazed from the crash and he tripped and fell on his backside, knocked flat onto his back when Rose jumped on him, his screams drowning out the sounds of battle as she viciously twisted his crotch.

The ice cream man was fighting with glee, a woman beside him wielding nunchucks. To Carly's astonishment, she sported a white collar. The woman was a vicar but she was also a vicious streetfighter.

It was then she spotted Cole. He'd got caught up fighting her uncle, who was fending off all his fancy kicks with the cricket bat he held.

'Logan,' she said. 'Have you brought what I asked?'

'Aye,' he replied, punching the man he was fighting. 'But I wish you wouldnae do it.'

'I have to.'

He nodded and headbutted the man when he came at him again, knocking him to the ground. From his pocket Logan produced the Glock and two clips.

'It's already loaded, as promised,' he told her.

She smiled and nodded. No way was this man a traitor. It had to be someone else. 'What if someone hears the shots?'

'Don't worry. No one calls the polis in Gallowburn.'

'Uncle Eddie,' she heard Jane yell.

Carly whipped round to see her older sister, Rose and Jennifer racing to the spot where Eddie was fighting Cole.

'No,' cried Carly when she saw her uncle stumble backwards, a knife sticking out of his stomach. Cole stood over him triumphantly.

'You bastard,' Carly screamed, raising the gun.

Cole's eyes widened and he darted off, weaving in and out of the fighting groups.

'No, Uncle Eddie,' yelled Jane as the big man who'd been in the van loomed over him, ready to bring a crowbar down on his head.

Jessica Alexander appeared out of nowhere, snatched up the cricket bat Eddie had been using and walloped the man around the back of the head with it before he could strike. He dropped, out cold.

Carly ran to her fallen uncle and reached him at the same time as her sisters and sister-in-law.

'We need to stop the bleeding,' said Jessica, pulling off her expensive designer scarf and pressing it to the side of the wound from which blood leaked. 'Someone elevate his legs. We need to keep his feet higher than his heart.'

Lacking an object with which they could prop up his feet, Jennifer knelt before Eddie and placed his feet on her lap. Carly stared at Jessica in astonishment. It was the first time she'd known her do something completely selfless.

'Da',' roared Harry, charging towards his father with Peanut. When someone tried to intercept them, Peanut punched the man so hard he was lifted off his feet and he sailed backwards before landing in a crumpled heap on the pavement.

'I… I'll be okay,' rasped Eddie.

'You've got a knife sticking out of your belly,' exclaimed Harry.

'Luckily for me I've got plenty of padding.'

The memory of Jack being stabbed returned to Carly. Her head snapped up to stare in the direction Cole had gone, eyes narrowing to slits, lips drawing back over her teeth.

'Fucker,' she hissed before tearing off after him.

'Stop her,' murmured Eddie, growing weaker.

'We'll go,' said Jane, gesturing from herself to Rose. 'You lot get him to a hospital.'

34

Carly raced down a back street, gripped by blind rage. Cole had helped take Jack from her and now he might have taken her uncle too. She slipped on an icy puddle but managed to stay on her feet. Cole was up ahead. He'd been slowed down by slipping on the same icy patch, only he'd fallen, which had delayed his escape.

They exited the alley and an enormous but deformed shape loomed before them. It was a church, but it was in a ruinous state, the old building missing its entire roof, creating a jagged, uneven gothic silhouette that clawed at the sky. A metal fence surrounded the site, signs warning people to keep out of the unsafe building stuck to it. Clearly this warning had been ignored as a panel in the fence had been prised open, as had the metal door that had replaced the original wooden one when it had been burnt away.

'You murdering bastard,' yelled Carly, drawing the gun and firing in Cole's direction.

The shots forced him towards the ruined church and his slim form slipped through the gap in the fence and he vanished inside. Carly raced after him, ducking through the fence. She wasn't so enraged that she didn't have the presence of mind to pause at the door. Straining to listen, she heard movement inside, footsteps pounding off the stone floor of the church.

'Carly, don't.'

She whipped round and through the fence she saw Rose and Jane racing towards her.

'I'm sorry,' she told them before stepping inside the building and pushing the door shut. There was a discarded crowbar on the floor which she slid through the handle so the door couldn't be pulled open.

Banging started up on the other side, her sisters pleading to be let in, but Carly ignored them. She turned to face the interior. There were no pews, although there were a few charred remains indicating where they had once stood. Chunks of fallen masonry lay on the floor. At the opposite side of the building was an enormous gaping gothic arch that had probably once contained a stunning piece of stained glass that had been shattered by the heat of the fire.

Looking up, she could see the sky through the broken vaulted roof, the crescent moon casting its silvery light into the interior. A few dark clouds scudded overhead, blown by the breeze, and Carly feared if they covered the moon then they would be plunged entirely into darkness. There was a rattle at the back of the room, as though someone was trying to open a door that refused to yield. Carly hurried to stand behind the one remaining supporting stone pillar.

'It's just me and you, Cole,' she called. 'You've got what you wanted.'

She ducked when there was the sound of a gunshot, which chipped off some of the stone close to her head. Spying the outline of his figure, she shot back and Cole threw himself sideways. More shots were exchanged, the sound of her sisters' desperate cries to be let in growing in volume. One of Cole's bullets hit the metal door, ricocheted and went pinging around the room, making them both duck. Carly lay flat on her belly and took aim at Cole, who she could see crouched behind the remnants of a pew. She fired and was horrified when nothing happened.

'Shit,' she hissed.

Cole tried to shoot back but his gun was also empty and he slid the useless weapon into the back of his jeans.

For a moment, everything Logan had taught Carly vanished from her mind. She drew a complete blank as she desperately tried to recollect how to change the magazine. Then she recalled his smile, the touch of his hand on her arm, and she remembered what she had to do.

Carly pressed the button to release the magazine, which clattered to the stone floor.

Cole took advantage of this delay to rush her. As Carly drew the fresh clip from the back of her jeans, he kicked out, knocking both gun and magazine from her hands, pain shooting up her wrists. As she was in a crouch, Carly found herself in the weaker position and she was knocked over by the blow. She rolled when he tried to stamp on her face and kicked him in the knee, making his leg crumple, giving her the precious few seconds she needed to scramble to her feet. Carly had the second magazine in the back of her jeans but she couldn't see where the gun had fallen in the gloom. Cole swung his fists at her and she wove and dodged but he was so fast she couldn't find an opportunity to strike him back. Bringing up her left arm, she blocked a punch from his right fist but he struck her in the jaw with his left. The blow stunned Carly, blood filling her mouth and spilling down her chin, her eyes widening as she staggered back, desperately trying to stay on her feet. She tripped over a chunk of fallen stone and fell, landing on her bottom and jarring her lower back.

The banging at the main door had stopped and Carly wondered if her sisters had found another entrance. She prayed they hadn't because not even together could they stand up to Cole. He'd learnt far too much from Dean. Anger filled her. Her bastard of a cousin was thousands of miles away and he was still hurting them. She regarded Cole with fury. Now she didn't just see one man. She saw Dean too.

Cole produced a knife as he loomed over her. 'You know you can't beat me, Carly. Now it's time to do to you what you did to me.'

As she pushed herself to her feet, he lashed out with the weapon with such speed she gasped. The blade sliced through her left cheek and she recoiled in shock, hand pressed to the wound, blood trickling through her fingers.

'That's just the first,' he told her, advancing on her coldly as she stumbled backwards away from him. 'I'm gonnae cut you to fucking ribbons.'

Rage lighting up his green eyes, he drew back the weapon again. Carly reached around for the second spare magazine and tore it free as she raised her left arm while jerking back her head. The knife sliced through her forearm instead of her face. The pain felt like fire but she kept her arm raised, pushing away his hand holding the knife while raising the magazine, which she gripped in her right hand. She plunged the base of it into his left eye. Cole screamed with pain and horror as the brilliant green orb burst, the knife falling from his hand. Carly wrapped both her arms around his waist like a lover.

'You should have run,' she told him.

Carly pulled the gun from the back of his jeans and took two steps backwards while ejecting the spent magazine, blood trickling from her face and left arm. Slamming the spare mag into the weapon, she gripped the gun in both hands and aimed it at Cole. Her finger squeezed the trigger, but she found she couldn't pull it as he staggered about blindly, wailing in pain.

Closing her eyes, she recalled the memory of Jack's insides spilling out, the horrifying moment all the life had died in his eyes, as well as the knife sticking out of her uncle's belly.

Deep breath.

When Carly opened her eyes, they were filled with determination.

She squeezed the trigger, the sound of the shot shockingly loud. The first bullet struck him in the chest, immediately silencing his pained wail. He stared down at the wound in surprise with his one good eye. With a grunt, Carly pulled the trigger again and again, emptying the clip into him, walking forwards while his body was knocked back a step with each shot, jumping and jerking like a puppet. When the gun clicked empty, Cole's jaw fell open, blood pouring from his mouth before that single orb rolled back in his head and he toppled to the ground.

Carly stood over him, feeling nothing for the man he'd once been. She'd already mourned and buried her first love. The monster was dead and the real man had been set free. The rays of moonlight slanting through the broken roof caressed his body, as though death had redeemed him of his sins.

Soft white flakes eddied through the air and Carly looked up to see it was snowing through the shattered roof. Closing her eyes, she enjoyed the cool soothing touch of the snow.

At the sound of movement, she whipped round, raising the gun, even though it was empty.

'It's just us,' said Jane, holding up her hands.

Carly rushed to place herself before the body. 'Don't look,' she told them. 'He gave me no choice,' she added sadly.

Her sisters' eyes widened when they settled on her face, so Carly knew the wound to her cheek was bad.

'So we see,' replied Jane.

'Oh my God, your face,' cried Rose. 'And your arm's bleeding.'

Carly's knees went weak with the shock of what had just happened as well as blood loss, the gun falling from her hand. Jane wrapped her arms around her, keeping her upright.

'Uncle Eddie?' murmured Carly.

'He'll be fine, they were taking him to hospital. We need to get out of here,' said Jane as the snow increased. It coated their hair and clothes, draping itself over the remains of the pews, the charred stone and Cole's dead body.

'We need to stop her bleeding first,' said Rose.

Determinedly not looking at Cole, Rose tore a strip off her jumper and wrapped it tightly around Carly's injured arm, making her cry out.

'I'm sorry,' rasped Rose before pulling it even tighter until the blood stopped. She then tied it around Carly's arm as a makeshift bandage. She and Jane between them helped her hobble to the back door they'd entered by, Carly scooping up Cole's dropped knife on the way, her own blood staining the blade.

They exited the church to find snow had powdered the road and pavement. As they came down the side of the church and onto the main street, they found a group of men ten strong were waiting for them, among their number Isaiah Bell and several of his cousins. At their head was, to the sisters' astonishment, David.

'What the fuck are you doing with that lot?' Jane demanded of him.

'Did you really think Cole was responsible for all this?' he replied. 'Where is he by the way?'

'Dead.'

He shrugged. 'That's a shame but I'll easily find someone to replace him. Do you think he had the money to bribe all those people and to incite the local families against Toni?'

'It was you all the time,' she murmured in astonishment. 'You were working with Cole and Dean even when Jack was alive.'

'You always were a smart lassie.'

'Why did you save us from the Bells then?'

'Because you'd already got away. It was better to make you think I was on your side so I could manipulate you later.'

'So you could lure us to Garthamlock?'

'Aye. I didnae think the MacGregors would turn so quickly but they always were fickle twats.'

'And that's why those men were waiting for us at the caravan park, because you told Cole about our plan.'

'Of course.'

'You never phoned Toni when we were at the MacGregors, you just pretended you did. If Uncle Eddie hadnae called her, we would have been ripped apart.'

'Aye. If only I hadnae dropped my bloody phone, we wouldn't be here now and Cole would still be alive. Oh well, never mind. There's plenty more where he came from.'

'Why? We've always worked so well with you.'

'Rod Tallan was my best pal from childhood. We grew up together. Did you really think I'd take his murder lying down?'

'Aye, after what he tried to do to Carly.'

'That was Rod, he'd attacked loads of women over the years, but I always stood by him. Toni signed her own death warrant when she killed him. More families have rebelled against her. Tonight, Gallowburn and Haghill will fall and the east side of the city will belong to me.'

'Is Elijah in on it too?'

'You must be joking. He's got his tongue wedged so far up Toni's arse he could lick her tonsils.'

'Because he's smart.'

'Enough talk. Sorry, ladies. I like you three but you have to go. It's a shame because I want you on my side but there's too much water under the bridge.'

With a groan, Carly slid from her sisters' grasp to the pavement.

'What's up with her?' said David.

'She's lost blood, she needs a hospital,' said Jane.

'Well, if she dies that saves us a job.'

'You cold bastard,' yelled Rose. 'I'm gonnae rip your baws off.'

David produced a gun and took aim. 'Sorry, pretty. I would have left you alone, but you would insist on involving yourself in all this.'

'Do you think that scares me, you dickless bastard?'

When Rose tried to advance on David, Jane grabbed her arm and yanked her back, putting herself between her younger sister and the barrel of the gun.

'Such a pity,' said David. 'Brave and beautiful.'

Suddenly, David's eyes bulged and he started to choke, the gun wavering in his hand. Jane pulled Rose down as his finger involuntarily squeezed the trigger and the weapon discharged, the bullet slamming into the front of the church. Everyone regarded David curiously, wondering if he was having some sort of fit, until the tip of a knife erupted through the front of his neck. Toni's face appeared over his shoulder, her lips curled back with pleasure.

'I knew you'd turn traitor one day,' she hissed before licking his cheek.

Toni tore the blade from his neck and David dropped. The remaining men whipped round and saw she was flanked by

Caesar and Elijah. Without giving David's men time to recover, Toni hurled her knife with deadly precision and struck another man in the chest. Immediately, she drew a second knife and hurled that at another man while Elijah and Caesar tore into another two.

'Stay with Carly,' Jane told Rose before rushing to help them.

Rose knelt beside her sister, who appeared to be lapsing in and out of consciousness. Her left arm had started bleeding again, so Rose clamped her hand down on it. One of David's men ran up to them but Rose determinedly kept the pressure on her sister's arm, refusing to allow her to lose any more blood. She faced the man unflinchingly as he drew back a baseball bat.

A woman wearing a white collar appeared behind him, and Rose blinked up at her in astonishment. The vicar hit the man in the back of the head with a pair of nunchucks and he fell.

'Awesome,' grinned Rose.

The woman winked at her and turned to face another man. The ice cream man ran into the street, a machete raised above his head, a roar flying from his lips. Another of David's men squeaked with fear at the sight and turned tail and fled.

'Leave me,' Carly weakly told Rose. 'Protect yourself.'

'Fuck that. Anyway, the bleeding's finally stopping.'

Carly's eyes widened and she pushed her sister aside, drawing Cole's knife from her jeans and slashing at Isaiah, who was standing behind her. As he screamed, Rose tore the crowbar from his hand and whacked him in the face with it before driving the end into his crotch. Carly sighed with relief when he fell back onto the pavement.

The Blood Brothers ran onto the street and paused to take in the scene.

'Carly?' yelled Logan.

'Here,' called back Rose.

While Digger and Gary joined in the fight, he raced over to the sisters and threw himself down by Carly's side.

'Jesus, she's covered in blood,' Logan cried.

'It was Cole,' said Rose. 'He cut her face and arm.'

'Where is he?' he demanded.

'Dead.'

'Good. Carly, can you hear me? Christ, we need to get her some help,' he added when she didn't respond.

'Are the others okay?' said Rose.

'Aye. The fight's over back there. Toni and Elijah's men are mopping up the leftovers.'

'What about Uncle Eddie?'

'On his way to hospital, which is where Carly should be too. My car's just around the corner, I can take her.'

Logan scooped her up in his arms, as Rose hurried to follow.

'Jane,' she called.

Her sister kicked the man she was fighting in the chest while the vicar hit him in the face with the nunchucks. He was the last man to fall, the fight won.

'Where do you think you're going?' Toni called to Logan and Rose, a bloodied knife clutched in one hand.

'Taking Carly to hospital,' Logan called back. 'She's lost a lot of blood.'

Toni strode over to them and peered down at Carly. 'Someone made a mess of her face.'

'It was Cole,' replied Rose.

Toni's eyes narrowed at the mention of his name. 'Where is the wee shite?'

'In there,' said Rose, pointing to the church. 'Dead.'

'Shame. I was looking forward to that pleasure myself. I don't want any mention at the hospital of this. It's going to take a lot of covering up, but it won't be the first time.'

'I know what to do,' Logan told her coldly.

Toni's black eyes narrowed. 'A Blood Brother and a Savage Sister. How interesting.'

'Antoinette,' called the vicar, who jogged up to them with Jane. 'Let them go. That lassie needs a hospital.'

'I'm just making sure they know what to do, Valerie,' Toni sniffed back.

'Of course they do.' The vicar looked to Logan. 'Go and get her help, quick.'

Logan nodded back at her in gratitude and raced off with Carly in his arms, Rose and Jane following.

'Who is that woman?' Jane asked him as they went.

'Gallowburn's local vicar and Toni's cousin. The ice cream man is her boyfriend, Ephraim.'

'Wow, this place is mental,' commented Rose.

'You have no idea.'

35

Cole's single undamaged eye widened as the bullets ploughed into his body. Carly's own body jumped in response and she awoke to bright lights and the soft murmur of voices.

Rose appeared, standing on one side of her hospital bed while Jane and Jennifer stood on the other. It appeared she was in a private room.

'Carly, can you hear me?' said Rose as though she were deaf.

'Aye,' she mumbled back.

'How are you feeling?'

'Worse than when I had alcohol poisoning.' Carly forced her eyes open fully and realised Logan was there too, making her feel a little better. 'Hi,' she said, smiling and then wincing at the pain in the left side of her face.

'Hi,' he smiled back.

'Uncle Eddie?'

'He's okay,' said Jane. 'He's on the next ward. They operated on him and he should recover well. We owe Jessica Alexander. The surgeon said the first aid she gave him saved his life.'

Carly inwardly grimaced, hating the thought of owing that cow anything, but she was always one to pay her debts.

'We told the polis you were both attacked by unknown assailants when taking a walk,' continued Jane.

'Understood.' Tentatively, Carly reached up to touch the left side of her face and felt the gauze covering it. 'How bad is it? The truth,' she pressed when Rose and Jane glanced at each other.

'It's a long cut,' said Jennifer, glancing at Jane uncertainly.

'Deep?'

'Aye. They did a neat job stitching it up though, so that's something.'

'Am I gonnae be scarred?'

'That doesnae matter now,' said Jane. 'You can think about it later.'

'Am I gonnae be scarred?' pressed Carly.

Jane bit her lip and nodded.

Carly inhaled sharply. 'Cole did get his revenge then.'

'It's nothing compared to his scars.'

'And the doctor said a good plastic surgeon should be able to help,' said Rose earnestly. 'He said you can never get rid of a scar entirely, but it can be minimised. Toni's already said she'll pay for it as a thank you for... doing what you did,' she ended tactfully.

'And my arm?'

'That will be scarred too but there's no damage. It won't restrict your use of it.'

'I want a mirror.'

'You should let it heal a bit first. Besides, you cannae see much.'

'Mirror,' Carly said firmly.

Rose sighed and produced a compact from her jacket pocket. She opened it and held it before her sister.

Carly was shocked by the woman who stared back at her. Her skin was ashen, her left eye bloodshot and a nasty thick gauze covered the entire left side of her face. The track of the wound was visible beneath, the wound running from her left jaw to an inch below her left eye. It was large and vicious and her face was changed forever.

'Oh, God,' she breathed.

Rose hurriedly closed the compact and replaced it in her pocket.

'Don't let the scar worry you,' said Logan. 'You're still beautiful.'

'That's sweet of you to say,' replied Carly miserably.

'I mean it. It doesnae matter.'

'Let's give them some space,' said Jane, realising Logan was probably the one to cheer her sister up.

Jane left with Jennifer and Rose. When they'd gone, Logan perched on the edge of Carly's bed and took her hand.

'I don't care if you do have a scar,' he told her. 'I still want to be with you.'

'I'm such a mess,' she breathed, a tear slipping from the corner of her eye.

'No, you're not. It's come as a shock and you're still no' feeling well.'

'You should find someone else.'

'I'm going nowhere. I'm crazy about you, Carly.'

'I just killed one of my ex-boyfriends and now I'm a scarred mess. Run, Logan, while you still can. I'd rather you went now than later down the line when you realise you're only with me out of pity.'

'You're no' getting rid of me that easily.'

'Why do you want to be with someone with a fucked-up face?

You're leader of the Blood Brothers, you could have anyone you wanted.'

'But I don't want anyone else, I want you. I don't just want you for your face, I want you for who you are and believe me, Carly, you are completely unique.' He cupped her face in his hands, being mindful of her injury. 'I'll prove I want to be with you.'

He leaned in to kiss her and Carly felt his passion for her hadn't diminished.

'You might change your mind when you see the wound properly,' she said.

'I've already seen it. I brought you here with your sisters. That gauze isnae hiding any surprises from me. Nothing's changed for me. The question is, do you still want me? I'm in this for the long haul,' he said. 'If that's no' what you want then please tell me now but if it is, then I'm going nowhere. I'll be with you every step of the way while you recover.'

'It's what I want too,' Carly said, another tear sliding down her cheek, only this one was born of happiness.

36

TWO AND A HALF YEARS LATER

Carly smiled as she rested her head on Logan's chest, his arms sliding around her. She sighed with contentment and gazed up at the blue sky, the Spanish sun beating down on them as they enjoyed the outdoor pool of their honeymoon villa. He'd proposed eighteen months into their relationship and she'd eagerly said yes. When they'd started seeing each other, Carly had stopped wearing Jack's ring on the chain around her neck. It now lived in her jewellery box and always would. She realised Jane had been right. Jack hadn't been the love of her life. Had he lived, undoubtedly he would have been, but Logan was now the love of her life and Jack was her first true love. He would always live on in her heart, but she'd managed to put their relationship in the past, where it belonged. The facial scar Cole had left her with had been thick and ugly but it hadn't bothered Logan at all. Toni McVay had been true to her word and had paid for plastic surgery and now there was just a faint white line which would never fade but could at least be hidden by make-up.

Eddie had recovered with no ill effects from being stabbed and had proudly walked Carly down the aisle as he'd done for

Jane. Carly's sisters and Jennifer had been her bridesmaids while Gary and Digger had acted as joint best men for Logan. Unlike Jane and Jennifer's wedding reception, there had been no violence or attempted abductions. Rose was dating Warren, one of the MacGregor brothers, and the two families were now good friends. They'd even attended the wedding.

Even though Carly had been the one to take Cole's life, she'd grown quite close to Jessica Alexander. Without Jessica, she knew her uncle wouldn't be alive now, so she'd finally been able to forgive her for the affair she'd had with her father. Jessica had even been invited to the wedding. The assistance she'd provided the Savage family had raised Jessica's standing in Haghill once again, thankfully the arrogant bitch she'd once been completely eradicated. Her two surviving sons had fled to Dundee and sworn never to return to Glasgow, but Jessica no longer felt lonely as she now had people who genuinely cared about her.

Carly was surprised that she felt no guilt over killing Cole. If she hadn't done it, he would have killed her. It had been a matter of survival. Occasionally she did have nightmares, but Logan was always there to soothe her when she woke up bathed in sweat and shaking.

In the wake of David's shocking betrayal, Eddie had been promoted into his position and was now Elijah's partner. Jane was directly below them, taking up Eddie's previous position. Harry and Carly ran the crew together. Harry had been more than happy not to climb the ladder. After seeing what ambition had done to others, he had no desire to go the same way. Toni had given all four members of the Savage family as well as the three Blood Brothers generous pay rises.

'Who's that?' sighed Carly when her new husband's phone beeped.

Logan stretched to reach his phone, which sat on the edge of the pool, picked it up and glanced at the screen. 'You know my friends who were stopping by later?'

'Aye.'

'They're early. They'll be here in ten minutes.'

'Oh, crap.' She turned in his arms to face him and straddled his lap, running her fingers through his curls. 'I was hoping for a little something else first.'

'Don't tempt me,' he breathed, running his hands up and down her bikini-clad body.

They were staying in a holiday villa for a couple of weeks in Gran Canaria. Logan had told her he had some friends in the area who he rarely got to see, so Carly had agreed to book here so he could meet up with them again, Logan promising his friends wouldn't intrude on their time together.

'We'd better get dressed then,' she said, grinding herself against him.

'Well, we could be quick.'

'What every bride wants to hear from her new husband,' she said before kissing him. 'Come on then, let's go and put some clothes on.'

'You're a tease, Carly.'

'Aye, I am. I'll make it up to you later,' she winked.

The two of them got out of the pool and padded through the large luxury villa to get changed. Carly pulled on a light blue backless summer dress and matching sandals while Logan wore a white shirt and cargo shorts.

'I'm nervous,' said Carly as they waited in the plush lounge for Logan's friends to arrive.

'Don't be, they're really nice.'

'What are their names again?' she said, pacing anxiously.

'Josh and Alice.' He smiled and took her hands. 'After everything you've been through, how can meeting them make you so nervous?'

'Because they mean a lot to you and I want them to like me.'

Logan smiled and kissed her. 'They're gonnae love you as much as I do.'

'Oh, God,' Carly said when there was a knock at the door.

'Relax, it'll be fine,' Logan said before walking over to the front door and pulling it open.

'Logan,' squealed a woman with short chocolate-brown hair, flinging her arms around him.

The woman was beautiful and glamorous in her designer white dress, matching sandals and expensive sunglasses. The man by her side was tall and muscular with a shaved head and thick black beard. He looked like someone you didn't want to mess with. When the woman released Logan, the two men embraced, the love and close friendship between them clear to see.

'God, it's good to see you again, pal,' said the man in a thick Glaswegian accent.

'You too, mate,' replied Logan. 'Come on in.'

They stepped inside and the woman smiled at Carly. 'So, this is your new wife, is it?' She was also Scottish but she sounded much posher than her husband.

'Aye, this is Carly,' replied Logan, standing by her side and taking her hand.

'Aww, she's gorgeous. Come here, you,' Alice said, finally addressing Carly directly.

Logan was forced to release his wife's hand when the woman swept Carly into a hug, grinning at her startled expression.

The woman released her and beamed. 'It's so nice to finally meet you. Logan's told us so much about you.'

The man then hugged Carly and kissed her cheek. He was

friendly and amiable, but Carly could see in his jet-black eyes that he was dangerous.

'Josh, Alice,' said Logan. 'This is Carly McVitie née Savage.'

'It's a shame,' said Alice. 'You had such an awesome last name. Now you just sound like a biscuit.'

Whilst Logan chuckled, Josh rolled his eyes. 'Excuse her, sweetheart,' he told Carly. 'She has absolutely no filter.'

'I speak as I find,' said Alice. 'And no offence,' she told Carly.

'None taken,' Carly smiled back. 'Would you like something to drink?'

'Aye, that would be great,' said Josh.

They both declined anything alcoholic, settling for orange juices, and the four of them sat down to talk. Carly liked them both immediately. Alice was funny, saying whatever came into her head but somehow she was never insulting, while Josh, although quite intense like Logan, was very amiable and clearly enjoyed being in the company of his friend again. Carly's nerves soon evaporated as she found she got on very well with them both. She ordered some food from a local restaurant and day turned into night.

'Why don't you stay over?' said Logan. 'Then you can have a drink and relax.'

'Fine by me,' replied Josh. 'As long as Carly doesnae mind. We don't want to intrude on your honeymoon.'

'I don't mind at all,' she smiled.

'Then it's agreed,' Alice smiled back.

'Great,' said Carly, getting to her feet. 'How about I make us some margaritas?'

'That sounds lovely but before that, I think it's time.' Alice looked to her husband, who nodded in agreement.

'Time for what?' frowned Carly.

Logan took her hand. 'Sit back down a minute, hen.'

'Okay,' she slowly replied, retaking her seat.

'We've got something to tell you,' Logan told her. 'It's a wee bit shocking but I want you to know. I don't like keeping secrets from you.'

'Secrets?' Carly said, stomach plummeting. She'd had her fill of bloody secrets.

'Don't look so worried, it's okay. I wanted Josh and Alice to meet you first before agreeing to tell you. The secret's really theirs, no' mine.'

'Okay,' she said, turning back to face their guests, wondering what sort of secret they were harbouring. Were they international arms dealers? Escaped prisoners? Just what the hell was going on?

'You tell her, Logan,' said Alice. 'I think it would be better coming from you.'

'Aye, okay. Carly, this isnae Josh and Alice. This is Jamie and Allegra Gray née Abernethy.'

'Stop saying née,' Jamie told his friend with an amused smile.

Carly stared at them both in shock. 'But... they're deid.'

'That's what we wanted everyone to think,' said Allegra. 'It was the only way to escape from my father. He was an evil bastard who killed my mother and he was never punished for it because he was rich and connected. I knew the only way to get justice was to frame him for killing me. He did actually try and he drove me out to Cathkin Braes to dump my body, thinking I was dead, but I escaped and set him up for my murder. He also tried to kill Jamie. If he hadn't been put in prison he would never have stopped coming after us. Toni McVay helped us. She set it up it so it looked like my father had arranged Jamie's murder, meaning he would never get out of prison. Fleeing abroad and changing our identities was the only way to have a future. Then he was killed in prison, meaning we were safe from him, but we'll forever be exiles from home.'

Carly leaned back in her seat, jaw hanging open as she attempted to process this information. She recalled the images she'd seen in the newspaper and these two looked nothing like Jamie and Allegra. Jamie had short black hair and had been clean-shaven whereas Allegra had long blonde hair and blue eyes. The fact that her eyes were now brown told Carly she was wearing coloured contact lenses.

'What do you think, babe?' said Logan when she'd been silent for a while.

'Who else knows?' she said.

'Just Gary, Digger, Jamie's maw, his stepda' and Toni McVay. Jamie has a wee brother but they're no' telling him until he's older.'

'I... I'm stunned. The secret's been kept very well,' she told Jamie and Allegra. 'No one has any idea you're still alive.'

'Good,' said Jamie. 'That's the way we want it.'

'I want you to know that I'll never tell another living soul, no' even my sisters.'

'We know you won't,' said Allegra with a kind smile. 'That's why we're trusting you. Besides, the secret is also Toni McVay's and that's enough insurance in itself.'

Carly knew what Allegra was saying. If she ever did reveal the secret, then Toni would kill her. 'You're both so brave.'

'I don't know about that,' said Allegra modestly. 'And we have a great life, travelling wherever we want. We've opened a few businesses in various places – restaurants, hair salons...'

'She runs the hair salons, no' me,' smiled Jamie.

'Aye, I think they know that, baldy,' laughed Allegra, running her hand over his stubbly head. 'We don't like to linger in one place for too long, so when we've built up the business, we sell it for a profit and move on to the next place. We're doing pretty well too.'

'That sounds great,' said Carly. 'You're so free.'

'We are, but we're always looking over our shoulders, wondering if someone will recognise us.'

'I doubt that will happen, you look totally different. I saw your photos in the papers and on the news loads of times and I had no clue. Do you think you'd ever be able to return to Scotland?'

'If we did, we could never return to Glasgow,' said Jamie. 'It would be too risky. We'd have to go way up north but it would be nice being back in the motherland,' he added with a wistful smile. 'We both miss it.'

Carly couldn't imagine what they'd been through. She'd hate to be exiled from her home and everyone she loved, no matter how well she might be living abroad.

'I'm just so glad you're both here now,' Logan told his friends. 'Christ, we really miss you in Gallowburn.'

'We miss you too,' said Allegra, lovely eyes filling with emotion. 'And one day we will figure out a way to come home.'

'Maybe we can help?' said Carly, eager to help these people, not just for her husband's sake but because she was quickly becoming very fond of them. 'There must be something that can be done.'

'Time is our best ally. We just need to wait for the world to forget about us.'

This sad statement took the edge off the happy mood, but Carly mixed them margaritas as promised, which got the party going again. To give the two men a chance to catch up, Allegra and Carly went out on the balcony together to talk.

'I'm so glad you're here,' said Carly, gazing out at the mountains, which were nothing but dark silhouettes against the starry sky. 'It means so much to Logan.' She turned to face Allegra. 'It also means a lot to me that you've entrusted me with your secret, especially when you don't even know me.'

'Logan vouched for you, which is all the guarantee we need. He hated keeping something so big from you. He loves you so much.'

'I love him too. I don't know what I'd do without him. I suppose he's told you all about my disastrous history with my exes?'

'He has.'

'I never thought I'd find a man like him or share something so special with him. It amazes me every day.'

Allegra smiled at the happiness in Carly's eyes. 'So, what's next, children?'

'One day but no' yet. We want it to be just the two of us for a while. We also want to travel. What about you and Jamie?'

'We'd like children but it would be unfair of us to drag them into our situation. Every year we have to move again. That's no life for a wee one.'

'It won't always be like that, I just know it.'

Allegra smiled. 'You're probably right. Besides, we have good people on our side.'

'Too right you do.'

'I can't tell you what a breath of fresh air tonight has been. It's hard not being allowed to be yourself.'

'We can come out to you each year for a holiday, make meeting up a regular thing.'

Allegra's eyes filled with tears. 'I'd really like that. Logan couldn't have chosen a better wife.'

37

‘That was a wonderful evening,’ smiled Carly, nuzzling up to Logan in bed. The villa was all on one floor and their room looked out over the pool. They’d left the curtains open so they could see it through the patio door.

‘It really was,’ he smiled, wrapping his arms around her. ‘And you got on well with Jamie and Allegra.’

‘They’re brilliant and so brave. I don’t know how they cope.’

‘They cope because they’ve got each other,’ he said, squeezing her tighter.

Carly smiled. ‘Is this the feared leader of the Blood Brothers I hear?’

‘I only talk like this around you.’ Logan rolled her onto her back and kissed her, hand sliding up her bare thigh. ‘There’s only one thing that can make this night even more perfect.’

Carly moaned as they kissed. She smiled with pleasure as his lips moved to her neck then further down her body, enjoying caressing his curls with her fingers. Her eyes slowly rolled open and widened. A black-clad figure stood over them, a balaclava concealing their face. Eyes bulged out of the mask as they drew back a knife.

'Logan,' Carly screamed.

As her husband sat up, Carly kicked him off her and the blade the intruder wielded missed him by inches. She snatched up the bottle of water sitting on the bedside cabinet and hurled it at the intruder. It hit his shoulder and he grunted with pain.

A half-naked Logan threw himself at the man and the two of them tumbled to the floor. Logan landed on top of him, but the intruder threw him off, leapt to his feet and swiped at Logan with the blade. He jumped backwards, the tip of the weapon just missing his bare stomach.

Carly scrambled out of bed and charged at the attacker. She managed to punch him in the side before he shoulder-barged her, knocking her back against the wall. His eyes locked with hers and she gasped.

'It's Dean,' she cried.

Snatching up the clock off the bedside cabinet, she hurled it and he dodged. The clock struck the glass of the patio door, cracking it.

The door burst open and Jamie and Allegra ran in.

'Stay here, babe,' Jamie told his wife before rushing to help his friends.

Dean fought furiously but both men were just as well trained as he was, especially Jamie, who delivered a scissor kick that sent Dean reeling. Logan followed this up with a punch to the jaw and Jamie ended it with a roundhouse kick to the stomach. Dean was flung backwards through the patio door, the already cracked glass shattering beneath his weight. Such was the force of Jamie's kick that Dean skidded on his back across the patio, coming to a halt by the edge of the pool.

'You bastard,' screamed Carly, stuffing her feet into her sandals so she wouldn't cut her feet on the glass and leaping through the shattered door. 'You took Jack from me and now you're trying to take Logan too. I'll kill you before you hurt a hair on his heid.'

She grabbed a handful of Dean's hair and yanked him backwards, so his head went under the water, and she pressed down in an attempt to drown him, his arms frantically flailing.

Logan grabbed her around the waist and pulled her back while Jamie dragged Dean out of the water.

Jamie pulled the balaclava from the intruder's head, revealing Dean's wet face.

'Is this walloper her mad cousin?' he asked Logan.

'Aye.'

'How the hell did you find us?' Carly demanded of Dean.

'Talk, ya fanny,' said Jamie, kicking him in the ribs.

Dean grunted with pain. 'Lonny.'

'The landlord of The Wheatsheaf? But he doesnae know we're staying here.'

'It's all around the scheme that you were staying just outside Maspalomas. I've been here for days, looking for you. I saw you both in the town this morning and followed you back here.'

'Why?' cried Carly.

'Because you belong with me, no' him,' Dean snarled back, gesturing at Logan.

'Have you still no' got over this weird obsession, you freak? Why can't you just leave me alone?'

'We're meant to be together, Carly, I know it.'

'For God's sake, what do I have to do to convince you that I don't want you?' she exclaimed. 'And have you forgotten what I said I'd do if I ever saw you again?'

'You said you'd kill me, but I was willing to take the chance. I thought if you saw me again, that if we were together...'

'That I'd leave my husband for you, ya stupid bastard.'

She snatched up the knife Dean had dropped and ran at him. He remained where he was, making no move to defend himself. It was Jamie who intercepted her this time, grabbing her arm and pulling it behind her back before taking the weapon from her.

'That's no' gonnae make you feel better,' he told her.

'Aye, it will,' Carly snapped back, struggling to free herself.

'And how will you face Harry and your uncle again?' Logan asked her.

Carly stopped struggling. 'I couldn't.'

'Exactly. This prick's no' ruining anything else for you.'

'Okay. So what do we do with him?'

Jamie kicked Dean in the side of the head, knocking him out.

'I've got a smuggler friend who could dump him far away from here,' Jamie told them.

'How far can this smuggler take him?' said Carly.

'That depends. I'll gi'e him a call.'

At three o'clock that morning, Jamie brought his car to a halt at the Las Palmas Port, a forty-minute drive north of Maspalomas. Carly and Allegra had remained behind at the villa. He drove to a shady part of the dock and parked beside a large fishing vessel. He and Logan climbed out of the car and a bearded man in a thick jumper and jeans walked off the boat to greet them. His face was sharp, eyes vulture-like, a cigarette clamped between his lips.

'All right, Nils,' said Jamie, shaking his hand.

'It's good to see you again, Jamie,' the man replied in a strong Dutch accent.

'I'm glad you were in the area.'

'Not a problem. What's my cargo?'

Logan opened the boot and Nils walked around the car to

peer in at a bound and unconscious Dean. The smuggler didn't even react. This wasn't a first for him. 'Is he likely to give me any trouble?'

'Aye,' replied Jamie. 'So don't untie him until you're ready to kick him off the boat.'

'Understood.'

'How far are you going?'

'Namibia, southwest Africa.'

'Perfect,' said Logan. 'The further the better.'

'You got my money?'

Logan handed him a wad of cash.

'No offence,' said Nils as he started to count it.

'None taken,' replied Logan.

Nils nodded with satisfaction and pocketed the money. 'Willem, Pieter,' he called. 'Take the cargo on board.'

Two enormous men with bald heads and stubbly faces walked off the gangplank, pulled Dean from the boot and carried him onto the boat.

'How long will it take you to get there?' Jamie asked Nils.

The smuggler shrugged. 'We have a few stops to make on the way, so about two weeks.'

'We don't want him hurt. We just need him far away,' said Logan.

'I understand. He will have my best cabin. It is the one that stinks of fish the least,' he chuckled.

'Sounds perfect,' smiled Logan.

Nils climbed back onto the boat and Jamie and Logan watched from the dock as it set sail.

'It's a relief that walloper's finally gone,' said Logan as the fishing vessel chugged off into the distance. 'I'm just grateful he decided to attack when you were at the villa.'

'The prick's as mad as a box of frogs. Hopefully it's the last you see of him.'

'We can only hope.'

'Would Carly really have killed him?'

'Aye, if she'd got the chance.'

'She's a cracker.'

'I wish I could see Dean's face when he realises he's in Africa,' grinned Logan.

The two men looked at each other and laughed.

* * *

Allegra handed Carly a mug of tea and sat on the couch beside her.

'It's a while since I've had a proper cup of tea,' smiled Allegra after taking a sip.

'Logan brought some bags out with him,' replied Carly in a faraway voice. 'He cannae do without a brew for long.'

'How are you feeling?'

'Shocked. Being in exile has sent Dean off his heid even more. He almost stabbed Logan like he did Jack,' she croaked, a tear sliding down her cheek.

'But he didn't. That's the important thing.'

'Thank God you and Jamie were here.'

'Well, I didn't do very much.'

'You make a mean cup of tea,' said Carly, forcing a smile. She scrambled to answer her phone when it rang. 'It's Logan,' she told Allegra. 'Hi, babe. Is everything okay?' She sagged with relief. 'That's brilliant. You'll be back soon, won't you?' she said anxiously. 'Great, see you soon. Love you.'

'Well?' said Allegra when she'd hung up.

'They're fine and they're on their way back. Dean's currently on a fishing boat to Namibia.'

Allegra sniggered. 'Namibia?'

'Aye,' Carly grinned back in response.

'Hopefully this will teach Dean to leave you alone.'

'Or his boat might sink,' replied Carly with a hopeful smile.

'You never know your luck. Are you going to tell the rest of your family about this?'

'I suppose I'll have to. Dean's in regular contact with my uncle.'

Tiredness overtook the two women and they began to nod off. When Carly realised her eyes were closing, she got to her feet and paced back and forth while Allegra dozed on the couch, determined to stay awake until Logan returned.

At the sound of the front door opening, she raced into the hall and threw herself at her husband, who embraced her with a smile.

'Thank you,' she told him.

'Any time,' he replied, kissing her.

'And thank you too, Jamie.'

'Nae bother.' He caught the sound of snoring emanating from the lounge. 'I take it I'm no' gonnae be greeted with a kiss.'

Logan planted one on his cheek. 'There you go, pal.'

'Silly bastard,' grinned Jamie. 'I'd better get Allegra back in bed. Her snoring can get epic. Once we were staying in Sierra de la Culebra and she set off the local wolves. They all started howling along with her.'

As he headed into the lounge to his wife, Carly turned back to Logan.

'I hope you're no' regretting marrying me now,' she said.

'I always knew I wouldnae have a quiet life marrying a Savage Sister.'

Carly smiled. 'And I knew marrying a Blood Brother would be the best thing I ever did.'

MORE FROM HEATHER ATKINSON

In case you missed it, the previous book in The Savage Sisters series from Heather Atkinson, *A Savage Inheritance*, is available to order now here:

www.mybook.to/SavageInheritance

ABOUT THE AUTHOR

Heather Atkinson is the author of over fifty books - predominantly in the crime fiction genre. Although Lancashire born and bred she now lives with her family, including twin teenage daughters, on the beautiful west coast of Scotland.

Sign up to Heather Atkinson's mailing list here for news, competitions and updates on future books.

Visit Heather's website: www.thebooksofheatheratkinson.godaddysites.com

Follow Heather on social media:

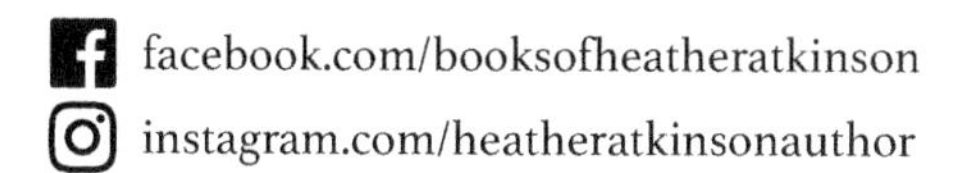

ALSO BY HEATHER ATKINSON

Wicked Girls

The Savage Sisters Series

Savage Sisters

A Savage Feud

A Savage Betrayal

A Savage Inheritance

Savage Blood

The Gallowburn Series

Blood Brothers

Bad Blood

Blood Ties

Blood Pact

The Alardyce Series

The Missing Girls of Alardyce House

The Cursed Heir

His Fatal Legacy

Evil at Alardyce House

Printed in Great Britain
by Amazon

62362053R00208